YESTERDAY

SHEILA NORTON

'Mods and rockers!' Andy shouts at me down the phone, so enthusiastically that I blink in surprise. 'Rampaging idiots on bikes and scooters, terrorising quiet seaside resorts, beating the shit out of each other, scaring old ladies and little kids. That's what I need, OK?'

'Right.' I blink again. 'I'll see if I can ...'

'Find someone who lived through it, yeah? Someone who was there – actually there, taking part. I don't care which side they were on. I just want a good story. Right?'

'Andy. *I* lived through it. You seem to forget I'm approaching my dotage.'

'You were ... actually around in the sixties? Christ, Cath – yes, I s'pose you must have been. You're wearing well!' he jokes.

He doesn't mean to be offensive. He's only about thirty. I've got children almost as old as him. Come to think of it, I've probably got knickers almost as old as him, although they sure as hell don't fit me anymore. Andy's the editor of one of the magazines I write for as a freelance – one of the best, in fact, with one of the biggest circulations: *Xtra*, the supplement to one of the tabloid Sunday newspapers – you know the one. Sensationalist, but somehow managing to style itself as a middle-class, middle-of-the-road, man-of-the-people publication. I haven't done anything for them for months, and I just decided, today, to give him a call to see if I could write anything topical – I don't know, perhaps interviewing some local Essex environmentalists who are protesting about the plans for the new runway at Stansted – when he sprung this Sixties thing on me. You could call it serendipity. Or you could call it a dilemma.

'Well,' he's saying now, sounding like an excited schoolboy at Christmas, 'that's even better! You've got the background already – if you can remember that far back!'

'Very funny. I remember it all too well, thanks, Andy.' I hesitate. 'How soon do you need this story? Only ... I'm not sure ...'

'I'm thinking Easter – to coincide with the fortieth anniversary, get it? It was Easter 1964, apparently, when it all kicked off.'

'I know,' I say, wearily. 'I was there.'

'You were actually *there*?' he says in a squawk. 'What – at, where was it? Brighton?'

'Clacton.'

'At Clacton on a seaside day out with your parents? An innocent bystander, caught up in all the riots, forced off the beach by the rampaging ...'

'Who's writing this, you or me?'

'So you'll do it? I mean – Christ, you've got the story there already, in your head, by the sound of it. It'll be a piece of cake. I shouldn't even have to pay you.'

I ignore this. He'll pay me, and well, and we both know it.

'Look, I'll have to think about it,' I tell him with a sigh. 'It's ... kind of difficult.'

'Come off it, Cath – it'll be a piece of ...' He stops, and then goes on more quietly, sounding slightly aggrieved, 'Is there a problem? I mean – sorry, but *you* phoned *me* looking for work. I don't need Stansted protestors – you're way too late, it's been done to death already. I need *this* piece done, and it looks like you're the right person for the job, but if you're not up for it, tell me and I'll give it to Juliana.'

Juliana Baxter-Smythe. Fresh out of uni, the new big thing. As posh as her name, all long hair, long legs and *OK, yah*. Even her *parents* probably weren't alive in the sixties – and if they were, they'd have been immune from the whole scene – at some expensive boarding school or doing the *Grand Tour* of Europe. She wouldn't recognise a rocker if one jumped up in front of her with *Greaser* tattooed on his forehead.

'No you *won't* give it to bloody Juliana,' I tell Andy with feeling. 'I'll do it – OK? I'll do it, but ... you'll have to give me time.'

'I told you: it's going out at Easter – April, right? You've got forever. Jesus, how long can it take, to write a piece about your own bloody childhood memories? What's the problem?'

'I've got ... some issues, that's all. Personal issues, from that time. It might be ...'. I stop, give myself a shake. What's wrong with me? I pride myself on my professionalism. Since when did I get offered a great piece of work, and start whingeing to the editor about my personal issues with it? If Andy does decide to give it to bloody Juliana I'll only have myself to blame.

'If it's going to be difficult ...' he says, beginning to sound impatient.

'No. It's not. I'll do it. You won't find anyone better qualified to write this, Andy – but I want a good fee. I'll give you the best fucking story you've ever published, but I'm going to need to speak to people I haven't seen for nearly forty years.'

I can almost hear his eyebrows going up. 'If it's that good, I'll double your normal fee. But you'd better not be messing with me.'

'You know me better than that.'

I snap my phone shut and spend about five minutes just staring out of my window. I need this job: the money's too good to turn down. I'm fifty-four, on my own, with a mortgage that brings tears to my eyes. Every day, more new young *Julianas* are bursting onto the scene, producing sharp, *cutting-edge* copy about celebrities, sex, marriage and divorce that gets snapped up as if it's actually original. I haven't been competing. My income's in retreat, my lifestyle's pathetic. I live in a one-bedroom cottage with two cats and a computer that hums with dangerous rage every time I turn it on, threatening to wipe its memory out faster than my own is deteriorating. I need a new laptop. I need a new *coat*, damn it. I need to get my name out there again. I have to write this story, and it has to be more than just a piece of history. It's got to be *my* story. It's time it was told; but more to the point, it's time I faced up to it myself.

Forty years is a long time to bury your past. I've got to start digging.

March 1963

I was just coming up to fourteen when I met Janice Baker. We were at the same school – St Margaret's Grammar School for Girls in Romford – but she was two years older than me, a fifth-former. Given the age difference, it would've been inconceivable that we'd become friends, if it wasn't for the fact that we travelled to school and back on the same bus, and we were among the few from our school who lived right at the end of the route. Both our homes were in the furthest reaches of the Harold Hill estate, where most of the kids went to one of the local schools, but (as it was constantly drummed into me by my mother) we were *privileged* to have passed the Eleven-Plus exam, and (as far as I was concerned) unfortunate to have been given a place at St Margaret's rather than the much closer, and much more interesting, modern co-ed grammar school on the estate.

The first time I actually remember talking to Janice, I'd been sitting behind her on the journey home. I'd been watching her, with a certain amount of admiration. She'd taken off her school hat, and pulled her long blonde hair out of its ponytail so that it hung loosely around her shoulders. Even more daring, when she turned to look out of the window I could see she was wearing mascara. She'd get a detention, for sure, if there'd been any prefects on the bus who felt like reporting her. She was thumbing through a copy of *Pop Weekly*, and I was squirming in my seat, trying to see, over her shoulder, whether the pictures were of Cliff Richard or Adam Faith. Or maybe Billy Fury. To tell the truth, I wasn't particularly fussed about any of them, although obviously I'd never admitted that to any of the girls in my class. Nothing worse than being considered *square*.

Suddenly, Janice turned round and gave me a look. It wasn't unfriendly, but I immediately dropped my eyes, embarrassed that I'd been caught out being nosy.

'Watcha,' she said, displaying a mouthful of chewing-gum. 'You all right?'

'Yeah.' I tried desperately to appear cool. 'You?'

'Want to sit next to me and look at the mag with me?' she said. 'As you're obviously trying to see it.'

'Sorry. I was just trying to see who …'

''s all right,' she said, laughing. 'I don't mind. Come on.' She patted the seat next to her. There were only two stops to go till we got off, but I moved eagerly, flattered at being invited.

'Who's in the mag this week?' I asked, a bit shyly.

'Beatles. D'you like 'em?' Janice held up the magazine to show me the page she'd been staring at.

'Yeah, course I like them.' Although most of the girls in my class were still swooning over Cliff, the Beatles were becoming the new big thing. Their second record, *Please Please Me,* had just come out, and for the first time, I could really see what all the fuss was about, with pop music. And with pop stars.

'Which one d'you like best?' Janice said, turning a bit further round in her seat so that she could watch my reaction to the picture. It was a glossy black-and-white full-page photo of the four boys, their mop-cut heads close together, their collars and ties almost hidden by the exciting new fashion of their round-neck jackets.

'Paul, of course.' I stared at the picture, transfixed by Paul's face – his smile, his beautiful, beautiful eyes. 'I love him.'

'Another Paul fan. Boring, boring, boring,' Janice sighed. 'I know he's got a pretty face, pretty eyes, pretty voice, but come on! *Every*body likes Paul. I prefer John. He's more interesting.' She went to close the magazine, and then stopped and looked at me again.

'D'you want it? Here y'are, then.'

She tore the picture roughly out of the magazine and handed it to me.

'You sure?' I couldn't believe her generosity. 'It's a fab pic, you sure you don't mind?'

'I've got loads of pics of 'em indoors. Running out of space on my wall!' She picked up her school bag and got to her feet as the bus lurched to a stop at its final destination. 'Anyway, we'll be able to see them on the telly soon, won't we.'

'On the telly?' I followed Janice off the bus, the picture in one hand, trying desperately not to spoil it by creasing it as I struggled to slide it into my school bag, between two books.

'Yeah. They're gonna be on *Six-Five Special* in a few weeks. Don't you watch it? Crikey, I wouldn't miss it for anything.' She gave me an off-hand kind of wave as she crossed the road. 'See ya later.'

I ran the rest of the way home. It was nice to be running, anyway, now I'd finally been able to leave off my heavy boots and go back into the regulation brown school shoes. It'd been the worst winter anyone could remember (apart from old people like my mum, who kept saying it wasn't as bad as some ancient year back before I was born) – it had started snowing just after Christmas and it was only now, early in March, that the freeze had finally come to an end. I could almost smell spring in the air and with my Beatles picture safely stowed in my bag I felt happy and excited, like everything ahead of me was good. Or at least, it *could* be. If only ...

'Mum!' I yelled as I walked into the house, slamming the front door behind me. 'Mum, we *need* a *telly*!'

My mother's head, wrapped in a nylon floral scarf from which curlers and pins were jutting at all angles, appeared over the upstairs banister.

'What?' she yelled. 'You're not on about that again, are you, Cathy? I've told you – we can't afford it. Stop going on about it. Be grateful you've got the wireless.'

'I can't watch the wireless! *Everybody*'s got a telly now, Mum – I'm the only person in the whole school who hasn't got one!'

'Cathy, I'm not having this conversation with you. Stop acting like a spoilt brat, and get the potatoes peeled for dinner. I've got to be back at work in an hour.'

I dumped my bag and coat in the hall and stomped into the kitchen, where I threw potatoes sulkily into the sink and pulled up my sleeves to start peeling them. By the time I'd finished, Mum had joined me and was starting to fry sausages and onions.

'What's brought all this on again, then?' she asked after I'd kept up my silence throughout the slicing of a cabbage.

'I told you. I want to be like everyone else. *Everyone* watches telly! They all talk about it at school, and I feel left out and stupid.'

'Well, I'm sorry about that. I'm sorry you feel left out and stupid.' Her voice was heavy with sarcasm. 'Maybe when we win the pools …'

'You don't even *do* the pools! You always say you're not wasting your money on it! Well, I'm *sick* of never having anything!'

The silence this time, broken only by the sizzling of sausages and the bubbling of the water as the potatoes came to the boil on the gas stove, went on for far longer.

'Well,' Mum said eventually, her voice tight with offence, 'I'm sorry if you think you have nothing. I suppose your expensive school uniform is nothing? And your nice shoes, and coat, and all the extras I've had to fork out for, the past three years – hockey stick, tennis racquet, running shoes?'

'I know, Mum. But …'

'To say nothing of *having your own room*!' She threw down the fork she'd been turning the sausages with and confronted me, her hands on her hips. 'You have no idea how lucky you are to *have your own room*!'

Having my own room was always Mum's trump card. The next thing, unless I could pre-empt it, would be a long, guilt-inducing account of her own childhood, spent in a damp, overcrowded tenement in Hackney with an orange box for a table, four children sleeping in one bug-infested bed and an outside toilet. Why this always succeeded in making me feel guilty, I couldn't quite fathom, as it certainly wasn't my fault Mum had grown up in such poverty, or that I'd inherited the benefit of living in a nice three-bedroom council house. My parents had moved to the new Harold Hill housing estate soon after it was built as an 'overflow' estate for London County Council. I could quite well imagine how they'd viewed it as paradise, compared with what they'd left behind. But things changed, didn't they – times had moved on, and as far as I was concerned, Mum hadn't moved with them!

'The sausages are burning,' I said. 'And I know, about having my own room. But I still need a telly.'

'How can you possibly expect me to believe you *need* television? It's a luxury, girl – the height of luxury. When I was a child …'

'I need it for school work!' I interrupted quickly.

'School work?' My grammar school education was like a religion to my mum. Apart from having our own rooms, it was the greatest privilege she could imagine having provided for her children. It was almost, I thought resentfully, as if Mum had actually sat the eleven-plus exam herself, the way she showed off about my brother and me 'getting a scholarship' to grammar schools. 'What do you mean? How can you need a television for school work?'

'For projects,' I said vaguely. 'For geography, and history, and stuff. There are educational programmes on the telly, Mum. All the others learn a lot more than me because they watch the programmes.' I paused there, aware that Mum was actually looking worried. 'They'll get better marks than me,' I added.

I couldn't actually meet her eyes as I said this bit. I knew how important it was to Mum that I got good marks. My brother Derek had already disappointed her by leaving school after the fifth form, with mediocre O-levels, instead of going on to the sixth form and university as she'd always hoped. Now, it was up to me to make up for his under-achievement – and although in a way I did think it might be quite nice to go to university instead of having to get a job as soon as I finished school, in another way I resented Derek for passing this responsibility on to me. He was eighteen now and since he'd left school and started working at Ford's in Dagenham, he spent most of his free time out with his mates. In some ways, though, that was better than when he *was* at home, playing rock music at such a volume that Mum yelled up the stairs at him, and I kept moaning at him because I couldn't concentrate on my homework.

'Have your teachers actually *said* you need to watch these television programmes?' Mum was asking me now. 'You haven't brought home a note about it.'

'Why would they send a note? They just assume everyone's watching the programmes. They assume everyone's got a telly.'

There was silence again as she dished up the dinner, plonking sausages on each plate, dolloping great helpings of mash and cabbage and covering the lot with a thick onion gravy. I waited, not wanting to push my luck. But I'd already gone too far.

'It's not for them to *assume*,' she said eventually. There was an icy tone to her voice. She was obviously offended now – not just by me, but by the whole teaching profession and their sheer effrontery at making assumptions about what she could, or couldn't, afford. 'Your teachers need to come down a peg or two, if you ask me. We haven't all had their education. We don't all earn their kind of wages.'

'They're not saying that, exactly.'

'They can say what they like.' She put Derek's heaped-up dinner plate on top of a saucepan of water, to re-heat when he got home from work, and dropped the lid on top with a determined clank. 'They're not telling *me* what to spend my money on. I work long and hard to keep a roof over our heads, and food on our plates, and ...'

I closed my eyes and switched off. I knew it was true. I knew how hard Mum had to work at the pub, but it was annoying to be constantly reminded about it, constantly asked to be grateful and to appreciate what I had. I knew what I had, but it wasn't enough! It wasn't as much as everyone else had! And now, I just *had* to have a telly! It was so unfair. I stared at my plate, picking at the food as Mum sat opposite me at the kitchen table, eating fast and looking at her watch.

'I've got to go,' she said, getting to her feet and putting her plate in the sink. 'Wash up, please, Cathy, before you start your homework.' She paused. 'And don't sulk. Nobody likes a sulker.'

'I'm not sulking,' I muttered. 'It's just not fair, that's all.'

'Life's not fair, girl. Get used to it.'

As soon as I heard the front door shut, I went to my school bag and got out the picture of the Beatles. I sat at the kitchen table again, smoothed the photo out and stared at Paul until my eyes started to go funny.

'I *will* see you on *Six-Five Special*,' I said out loud to the picture. 'I'm not going to miss that, like I miss everything else that's on the telly!'

And I knew exactly what I was going to do about it.

My best friend in my class was Linda. We'd been friends since primary school, but to be honest, I was beginning to find her a bit of a drag recently. She lived a couple of bus stops away, and had got off the bus that afternoon just before the whole thing with Janice, so I was bursting to tell her about it the next day at school. I wanted her to be impressed about Janice talking to me, and giving me a picture of the Beatles, but as always she just raised her eyebrows and looked bored.

'What did she talk to you about?'

'Pop music, mostly. We were looking at her mag. She's been to see Cliff. Twice.'

'So what?' said Linda. She might have been my best mate, but she could be very annoying. She didn't care about the sort of stuff everyone else cared about – trying to look right, dress right, have your hair right. Liking the right film stars and pop stars. It irritated me, in a way I didn't quite understand.

'*So*, she's actually seen him! In the flesh. Twice!' I shook my head and sighed. Janice Baker was known as one of the most with-it girls in the fifth form, if not in the whole school, and the fact that she was troubling herself to speak to me should have merited more respect. 'We talked about sex, as well,' I added for effect. It wasn't strictly true. Janice had only said that she was meeting her boyfriend that evening and was hoping for a good snog. I hadn't even known how to respond, and had just had to concentrate on not going bright red with embarrassment.

'Sex?' Linda retorted, laughing in my face. 'What do you think *you* know about it, Cathy Ferguson?'

'More than you, probably!' I shot back.

'If you say so,' Linda said calmly, with a shrug and another one of her raised-eyes looks.

Like I say, her friendship was beginning to feel like a drag. And not only that – she was the only other girl in the class who didn't have a telly. She was no better off than me. And – to put it bluntly – it didn't look like she was going to be any use to me now, did it? I was going to have to look elsewhere.

April 1963

'Don't sit so close. It'll ruin your eyes.'

'I don't care.' I was sitting cross-legged on the floor in front of the TV set, and now I shuffled even closer and reached out a hand to touch the grainy black and white image of Paul's face.

'Hey, you're not going to start snogging with the telly, are you?' Janice said, giggling.

I didn't answer. I couldn't tear my eyes away from Paul, and anyway I was too busy singing along to the words of their new song, *From Me To You.*

It was the second time I'd seen the Beatles on TV at Janice's house. I'd been round there a lot of other times, too, to watch a whole load of other programmes that Mum probably wouldn't have approved of. I wasn't exactly deceiving her: I just said I was going to a friend's house to watch the things I needed to see for school. It was true in a sort of way. I *did* need to see what everyone else was seeing – I wasn't going to be the boring square of the class who didn't even watch television. It wasn't my fault that Mum had just presumed the friend in question to be Linda. It was a natural thing to presume, as Linda was the only friend I'd taken home much.

Still, it hadn't been easy, asking Janice. I'd spent almost a week trying to pluck up courage. She'd been really friendly to me on the bus every day, ever since that first time, and I didn't want her to think I had a flipping cheek, and never speak to me again. In the end, though, with only a day to spare before the appearance of the Beatles on *625 Special*, I blurted it out in a squeak just as we were getting off the bus and parting company:

'Could I come round yours to watch the Beatles?'

Janice looked at me curiously for a moment before shrugging.

'Yeah, why not. What's up? Won't your mum let you watch it? What's on the other side?'

'We haven't even got a telly,' I admitted, sighing.

'Oh, right. Well, don't look so sorry about it. Not your fault, is it!' She laughed. 'Course you can come round. See you tomorrow.'

And that was how it had started. That was how she came to be my new best friend.

Janice's house was, from the outside at least, much the same as ours, and much the same as every other terraced, three-bed house on the estate. Once through the door, though, the similarity ended. Where my mum's main preoccupation in life seemed to be keeping everything *spick and span*, Janice's parents had apparently either given up trying, or had never bothered. But I loved Janice's battered, scruffy home and her easy-going parents – whose attitude to everything seemed to be that as long as nobody hurt anybody else, it was all right. It would've been quite all right with them if I went round there every night of the week. All right if Janice, their only child, went out every night and showed no evidence of doing any homework. All right if she wore short skirts, high heeled boots, make-up and got into trouble at school. As long as she wasn't hurting anyone.

'Good, weren't they?' Janice said now, when the show finished. 'I still say John's the best.'

'No. Paul,' I said, smiling at her dreamily. I sighed and hugged myself. 'Ooh, he's *fab.*'

'Want to see them for real?'

'Cor, who wouldn't! If only!'

'Well, you can. June the sixteenth. You're not doing anything, are you?'

I looked at Janice suspiciously. Was she teasing me?

'Don't be daft. See the Beatles, for real? Oh, sure!'

'Yes, sure. They're gonna be at Romford Odeon. Come with me?'

I sighed and shook my head. 'I'd never be allowed to go. And I'd never be able to afford a ticket.'

'You don't have to. I've got two.'

'Oh, sure!' I said again, laughing out loud this time. Impossible!

'Cath, I'm not kidding. Mum and Dad queued up and got them for me. They said I could take whoever I like.'

I stared at her now, beginning to realise it could actually be true. Janice's parents were nice enough, and unusual enough, to do such a strange thing, even if no other parents I'd ever met would ever dream of it.

'But you'll want to take one of your friends from your class,' I said in a whisper, 'won't you?'

'Nah. Some of them are already going. And if I gave the ticket to one person, all the others would get the hump. So I haven't told any of them.' She grinned at me. 'D'you wanna come or not?'

'*Yeah* – course!' I said. I could feel my voice beginning to quiver with excitement. 'But it'll take me ages to pay you back for the ticket.'

'Don't be stupid – I told you, Mum and Dad paid for them. And I wouldn't want to go on my own, would I. Will your mum be OK about it though?'

'She'll have to be,' I said. 'I'll think of something. At least I've got till June.'

Derek was in his bedroom when I got home, playing Elvis records at the usual excruciating volume.

'Can't you turn it down?' I yelled, looking round his door. He was lying on his bed, nodding to the beat of the music.

'Bloomin' 'eck – you sound just like Mum – moan, moan, moan.' But he got off the bed and lowered the volume anyway. 'I suppose you'd rather listen to that Beatles rubbish.'

'It's not rubbish. And as for listening to them, *I* haven't got a record-player, anyway. I can only listen to the radio downstairs, and Mum's usually got it on the Home Service. It takes forever to tune it to Luxembourg when she goes out, and it's always all crackly.'

'You can still swoon over their photo, though, can't you,' he teased. 'Which one is it you like? Paul? All the girls like Paul.'

'So? So what if I do?'

'*Ooh, Paul, I love you, Paul, you're so sexy, Paul ...*'

'Shut up!' I started to flounce out of the room, fed up with his teasing, but he caught hold of my arm.

'Sorry,' he said. 'Didn't realise you were taking it so seriously.'

'Well, I am. Very seriously,' I told him, trying to maintain some dignity. 'In fact, I've just been watching them on the telly. *And* I'm going to see them at the Odeon in June.'

Of course, as soon as the words were out of my mouth, I wished I hadn't spoken them. What an idiot! Now Derek would probably tell Mum, and that'd be the end of that.

Derek whistled. 'Blimey. My little sister *is* growing up. I presume Mum doesn't know about any of this?'

'No, and if you tell ...'

'Relax, I'm the last one to tell her anything she doesn't need to know. What makes you think she's going to let you go to the concert?'

'She won't, obviously. I'll have to think of something.'

He nodded, slowly, still looking at me thoughtfully. 'Well, if you like, I could always say I was going with you. If you think that'd help.'

'It might, I suppose.' I grinned at him. 'It's worth a try. Thanks, Del.'

''s OK. I don't s'pose it's much fun, being the youngest. And a girl. I don't think it's very fair on you, the way Mum expects you to help with everything.'

'I don't mind all that much, really.' I shrugged and sat down on the bed. I didn't often get the chance to talk to my brother properly. He was normally either at work or out with his mates on their motorbikes, and I didn't really think he bothered to take much notice of me, so this sudden show of sympathy came as a complete surprise. 'I know Mum has to work hard, being you know, on her own. I don't mind helping out with things. But I wish we could afford more stuff. Like a telly.' I glanced enviously at Derek's Dansette record-player. 'And one of those.'

'I've told you before, you can come in here and use mine, when I'm out. If you're careful.'

'Yeah, thanks. I'm *not* listening to your Elvis collection, though.'

'I thought you bought yourself the Beatles' record – what's it called? *Please Me Do*?'

'*Please Please Me*!' I said, laughing at him. '*Love Me Do* was their first one, and I haven't even got that. *And* they've got a new one out now – *From Me To You*. I'm trying to save up my pocket money for it but I've only got four shillings so far. I wish I could afford to get them all!'

'Here!' He pulled a battered wallet out of his pocket and handed me a one pound note. 'Will that help?'

I stared at the money, hardly daring to touch it. 'Del! You can't afford to give me all that!'

'Course I can!' He laughed and pushed the note into my hand. 'I give Mum my pay packet, but I'm getting overtime now, and it comes separately. I save it up.'

'What?' I tried to push the pound back at him. 'You mean to say you *keep* it, and don't tell Mum? I can't believe you'd do that! She struggles to make ends meet, and you keep money back?'

'For Christmas,' he went on calmly. 'I'm saving it up for Christmas, so I can surprise her, buy us a turkey and sweets and nuts and stuff, and presents for everybody. Don't tell her. Don't spoil it.'

'Oh. Sorry. Course I won't. But I can't spend this pound on myself, can I, now you've told me that.'

'Yeah, course you can. You deserve a treat now and then.' He smiled. 'Have the Beatles got an LP out yet?'

I nodded. I didn't know anyone who'd actually bought it, though. LPs were just too expensive for most people's pocket money.

'I'll get you that for your birthday. As long as I don't have to listen to it!' Derek said, pulling a face.

'Oh! *Thanks!* That'd be fab!' I felt like kissing him, but that wasn't really something we'd ever done. 'Anyway *you* can talk, with your Elvis blaring right through the house!' I said quickly to get past the moment. I got up and stretched. 'Better go and do my homework. Mum thinks I've been at Linda's, watching something educational about the Civil War.'

'Go on, then. She won't be in from work for ages.' He watched me heading for the room. 'Don't neglect your school work, will you, with all this?'

I pulled a face. 'It's getting boring.'

'Don't let Mum down, Cathy. I've already done that. She's counting on you now.'

'Now who's being unfair? Why do *I* have to make up for you dropping out of school? You're right – sometimes I do hate being the youngest.'

'What, even though you've got a big brother who buys you records?' he teased. He turned *Return To Sender* back up to its previous volume and I closed the door on him, going into my own room and closing that door too so that I had half a chance of concentrating on my maths homework. I didn't want to shout at him again, not after he'd given me a whole pound! Although if he carried on like this perhaps I'd be better off spending it on ear plugs.

Even on Sundays, Mum always got up early. I used to lie in bed, listening to her moving around downstairs, boiling the kettle, making breakfast. I knew it was only a matter of time before she hollered up the stairs to me and Derek, telling us we were lazy layabouts, wasting the day God had given. Mum wasn't in the least religious, but that didn't make any difference to the reverence she gave to Sundays. It seemed to be a matter of pride to her, for a start, that we should all eat a heaped-up plate of eggs and bacon for Sunday breakfast – and that having it any later than nine o'clock was bad for the digestion, given that the Sunday roast would follow at one o'clock on the dot.

'I might have been raised in an East End slum,' she was fond of saying, 'but I've still got my standards.'

Of all Mum's standards, those concerning Sunday were the most irritating. Some of the other girls at school talked about having long lie-ins on Sundays. Some stayed in bed until dinner-time, dispensing with breakfast altogether – a luxury I could only dream of. Then there was the thing about noise. Even when we were little children, Derek and I had to play indoors on Sundays no matter how warm the weather might have been, in case of disturbing the neighbours. It wasn't until Derek left school that he was allowed to go out with his friends on Sundays, but even now, there were regular Sunday arguments between him and Mum about the noise his mates made when they turned up on their motorbikes, and the volume of his rock music. As for me, I was still subject to the ban on going out on Sunday evenings at all. Which was going to be a problem. Because the Beatles' concert was on a Sunday – and by the time the day arrived I still hadn't even found a way to tell her about it.

'Breakfast is ready, you two!' The expected holler floated up the stairs at a quarter to nine. 'Get your lazy backsides out of bed! Wasting the God-given day … oh! You're early, miss!'

I'd got up just in time.

'Come on, Del,' I hissed as I passed his bedroom door. 'Please! Keep her happy, today. I've got to tell her ...'

'All right, all right,' Derek groaned sleepily.

Mum was standing at the bottom of the stairs, watching me come down.

'Dressed already, too? What's come over you?' she commented.

'Well, it's a nice day. You're always saying we should get up earlier on Sundays.'

'I see. Next thing I know, you'll tell me you're going out for a nice healthy walk in the sunshine instead of lying around all day listening to your Beatles' rubbish.'

'I am going out. But not till later.' I sat down at the kitchen table and waited while she slid two slices of toast, two eggs and two rashers onto the plate in front of me. 'Derek's taking me out.' I paused, and then added quickly, looking at my plate, 'Didn't he tell you?'

'Derek?' Mum echoed as if she'd never heard his name before. 'Taking you out?'

'Yes.' I looked up defiantly, holding my breath. 'This evening.'

She sat down opposite me and folded her arms. 'Taking you out on a Sunday evening? You'll be telling me next you're going to church.'

'We're going to a concert. We've got the tickets already.'

'I see.' Mum's voice had an edge to it now. 'And why didn't you think to tell me about this concert yourself?'

'I forgot.' I shrugged. 'Just remembered it today, when I woke up.'

'And I suppose it's some sort of classical music concert, is it, for your school work?'

'Yes. Yes, it's ...'

'You must think I was born yesterday,' she interrupted. 'Tell me the truth, Catherine.'

'All right – it's the Beatles,' I said, looking up at her with desperation. 'They're at Romford Odeon, Mum, and it's probably the only chance I'll ever get, *ever*, to see them, actually *see* them, and if you say I can't go, you'll ruin my whole life, and ...'

'How did you pay for the ticket?'

'I bought it for her!' Derek was pounding down the stairs, still in his dressing-gown, his hair standing up. 'She deserves a treat, Mum.

Lay off her. It's the early show, six o'clock, and I'm taking her. She'll be all right.'

'You've got more money than sense, if you ask me,' she grumbled, getting up to serve up his breakfast.

'Yes, well, as long as I'm handing over my pay packet every week and you're only giving me back what you want me to have, I don't think we need a conversation about that, do we, Mum.' Derek smiled at her and winked at me. 'So let's all calm down and have a nice day.'

'Have a nice day?' she repeated, looking at him in disgust. 'Yes, well, I suppose that's easy to say if you're spending the day mooning about listening to *pop* music. And taking your sister off out to a *pop concert* – on a *Sunday*. I don't call that very respectable. You should have asked me first, Derek, before you wasted your money on tickets. You know I don't approve of Cathy going out on Sundays.'

'Sorry, Mum.' Derek shrugged. 'But it's only this once. Just this once, a special occasion. A birthday treat.'

I grinned at him gratefully. My fourteenth birthday was the previous month, and his present to me (the *Please Please Me* LP) had been my best birthday present ever. But I knew Mum always felt upset that she couldn't afford to give us more expensive presents herself. Don't get me wrong, I'd been dead grateful for the dressing-table set she bought me – a pink hairbrush, comb and mirror. I knew Mum had to save up carefully, to afford such niceties, and I appreciated the trouble she must have gone to, to choose something I'd like – something grown-up and modern for my room. But I guess Derek bringing home much more money than she did herself was making her both proud and resentful in equal measures.

I got up and gave her a hug.

'I'll help you with the dinner when I've finished my homework.'

Mum grunted and turned back to the stove. Hugs weren't really her thing.

Derek and I walked to the bus-stop together to meet Janice.

'Thanks, Del. Mum would never have let me come if she hadn't seen us walk down the street together.'

'You're welcome.' He nodded at Janice. 'Watcha. You OK to look after Cathy if there's a crush outside?'

'I don't need looking after!' I said, annoyed. 'Thanks very much!'

I noticed him glancing again at Janice – who at sixteen was a good four or five inches taller than me, and what Mum would have described as *well developed* – and then back at me. I knew he was making the obvious comparisons, but he kept his mouth shut and just shrugged.

'She'll be OK,' Janice said. 'Thanks for covering for her.'

'Yeah, we'll be all right now, Del,' I said. 'See you later.'

'I'm getting the bus with you. Meeting someone in Romford.'

'Girlfriend?' Janice asked coyly. I looked at her in surprise. She was – definitely – fluttering her eyelashes. And giving him *a look*.

'Maybe.' Derek stuck his hands in his jeans pockets and turned away, whistling.

We both watched him. I supposed, for a brother, he was quite good-looking. Like me, he had hazel eyes and thick, wavy brown hair. But whereas I would get so frustrated, trying to grow my hair into the long, fringe-in-your-eyes style favoured by Janice and her friends, because I couldn't get it to go straight, Derek's slicked-back rocker style looked good on him. Like me, he wasn't very tall – but while I was slim and (as far as I was concerned) shapeless, he was wiry and muscular. I looked back at Janice again. *She* was everything I wanted to be myself: tall and blonde with a proper figure – to say nothing of having a wardrobe full of fab mod clothes and a drawer full of her own make-up!

'Here's the bus,' said Janice. She grabbed my arm excitedly. 'Ooh, Cathy – we'll be seeing them soon! Get ready to scream your head off!'

We sat behind Derek on the top deck, and talked, all the way into Romford, about which Beatles' numbers 'the boys' might perform that night. When we got off the bus, we parted company with Derek who said he was waiting for someone at the station.

'You be all right going home after the show?' he said, looking at me doubtfully.

'Course she will,' Janice said. 'She's with me! Thanks, Derek. Have a nice evening!' she added with a giggle.

'D'you fancy him?' I asked her as we walked away.

'Who – your brother?' Janice shrugged. 'Yeah, he's not bad.'

Not bad was a compliment. I raised my eyebrows. 'What – d'you want to go out with him?'

At that, Janice stopped dead and stared at me like I'd spoken in tongues. 'Are you crazy? He's a rocker. I might *fancy* him but I couldn't go *out* with him, could I! I mean, I know he's your brother, and he's a nice bloke and everything, and it's a shame because he's a bit of all right. But he's a rocker. We don't go *out* with rockers, Cathy!'

'No. Course not,' I said at once. Actually I couldn't see anything wrong with it myself, but I wasn't about to tell Janice that.

Until I'd started hanging around with Janice, I hadn't been too bothered about being a mod. It was only just catching on with the girls in my class, and I secretly thought some of them only said they were mods because it sounded good, like belonging to a club. For a start, I couldn't believe many of them could afford the fashions. But their perception of rockers was of greasy older blokes, somehow stuck in the 1950s, evolved from the Teddy Boys, so as far as the girls in my class were concerned, you were either a mod or you were square (like Linda).

But now I'd met Janice, and been introduced to some of Janice's friends – including some who had already left school – I'd started to admire the way they dressed, their hairstyles, their whole attitude to life. It was so glamorous, so grown-up, so *enviable* and unlike my own life! I really wanted, now, to be accepted as a real mod girl, even if I couldn't afford to dress like one. I looked down at my home-made cotton shift dress and ordinary brown school shoes and marveled again at my luck, that Janice was happy to be seen out with me.

'No offence to your brother,' Janice said now, linking arms with me as we approached the Odeon. She had to raise her voice to be heard over the excited chatter of crowds of girls hanging around outside. 'But honestly, I'd rather die than go out with a rocker. Wouldn't you?'

'Yeah,' I yelled back. Suddenly my excitement at the thought of seeing the Beatles – seeing Paul! – *live*, in the flesh, within *minutes* from now, swelled up inside me so that I couldn't even speak anymore, much less worry about mods or rockers.

'Come on!' Janice tugged me towards the entrance. 'This way – I've got the tickets! Seats near the front! Ooh, I can't *wait*! This is going to be *fabulous*!'

Afterwards, I wondered how I'd managed not to faint. We saw several other girls being carried out. The build-up of hysteria in the Odeon had been almost unbearable as Billy J Kramer and the Dakotas, and Gerry and the Pacemakers performed their hit numbers – and when the Beatles were announced, the whole place had erupted. I hadn't actually expected to scream. I didn't think I'd ever screamed before, at anything – not since I was a baby, anyway – and it had seemed slightly silly and embarrassing. But suddenly, there they were on the stage, just yards away from me! There was Paul – really, actually Paul! – *smiling* at *me*! And almost without realising it, I was yelling my head off along with all the other girls in the audience.

'Weren't they *fab*!' Janice sighed as we poured out of the cinema with the rest of the crowd, shoving our way through the throng already gathering for the second performance. 'Oh, blast – look at the queue at the bus-stop.'

'We won't get on the first bus along,' I said huskily. My throat was sore and my voice had almost gone. 'Oh, I wish we could stay, and see them all over again!'

Janice laughed. 'There'll be another time. I'm in the fan club – they'll let me know when they're going to be on tour again.'

By the time we'd managed to get on a bus, and by the time the bus crawled to a halt at Harold Hill, we were quite a bit later than we expected. I wasn't too worried, though, as Mum was doing a shift at the pub, and wouldn't be home for ages yet. Or at least, she shouldn't be. So what on earth …

'It's your mum,' Janice whispered, unnecessarily, as we got off the bus. She was walking towards us from the direction of the pub. It was close to midsummer's day, and still bright daylight. 'She's seen us.'

'Mum!' I croaked. For a moment, we all stood still in the street, staring at each other. 'I thought you were working.'

'I was. It was quiet. Got let off early.' She gave Janice a disapproving look and added immediately: 'Where's Derek?'

'He … um …'

'He had to go, Mrs Ferguson,' Janice spoke up at once. 'But he saw us onto the bus first, didn't he Cathy.'

'Yes,' I said, looking at the pavement. 'He had to go on somewhere after the concert. To, er … to meet a friend.'

'I see.' Mum stepped forward and took hold of my arm. 'Come along then, Cathy, it's getting late, and it's school tomorrow. Good night, Janice.'

'Night, Mrs Ferguson. Night, Cath. See you tomorrow.'

'I'll have a word with Derek about this,' she said as we walked the rest of the way home. 'He should have brought you all the way back. At least you had a friend with you, I suppose, if you can call her that.' She glanced at me suspiciously. 'What's the matter with your throat? Have you got a cold coming?'

'I think so,' I said, trying to sound sorry for myself. Trying not to giggle. Trying to keep the fabulous, fantastic excitement of the evening safe in my heart, to sigh and dream about, over and over. 'Maybe I'd better stay off school tomorrow.'

'Not a chance,' Mum said firmly. 'You can just go straight to bed with a hot drink and an aspirin.'

It didn't matter. I stayed awake until nearly midnight anyway, writing about the concert in my diary by the light of my torch under the bedclothes – so that I'd never forget a single minute of it, as long as I lived. And so I'd never forget what a great friend Janice was, either, and how lucky I was to have met her!

I definitely seemed to be getting more popular at school these days. It had started since I bought all the Beatles' records and got the *Please Please Me* LP for my birthday, and then of course, when I went to see the Beatles' concert I definitely went up in most people's estimation. Only two other girls in my class had been there, and they weren't sitting near the front, like me – so I'd been bombarded with questions the next day. *What did they sing first? What did they say? Did Paul say anything? What did John say? What did George look like in real life?* Everyone was particularly impressed by my sore throat and husky voice. (*Did you scream the whole time? Did you almost faint?*). Everyone, that is, apart from Linda, who raised her eyes to the ceiling and turned her back on us all.

Things had changed, anyway, since we'd gone up to the fourth year. Because of choosing different subjects, we weren't all in the same lessons all the time and I'd got new friends who were avid Beatles' fans like me. But I'd felt guilty about Linda for some time now. I knew I'd been neglecting her, and Linda didn't really have any other friends, because she was so quiet and, well, so square. She didn't talk about pop music or boys and to be honest, she was boring. But it was difficult to completely break off with her, we'd been friends for so long that it was a question of loyalty really.

On the twenty-second of November the new Beatles' LP, *With the Beatles,* was being released, and almost everyone was expecting to get it for Christmas, if they could bear to wait that long. There was a new single, *I Wanna Hold Your Hand,* coming out the following week, too. So there was even more excited talk about the Beatles going on than usual. As we packed up our books after an English class – one of the lessons we still all took together – I noticed Linda looking particularly left out.

'D'you want to come round this evening?' I offered on a sudden impulse.

Linda looked back at me impassively. 'Why? So you can show off some more about joining the Beatles' fan club and having all their records?'

'Don't be like that. I ...'

'Look, we're not really friends anymore, are we,' Linda said. Her voice was steady but she'd gone a bit pink. 'You prefer hanging around with sixth-formers. So don't worry about it. I'm not interested in the Beatles, or being a mod, or anything you seem to be interested in these days. And anyway, we've got a telly now. So I'd rather stay in, and watch it with my mum.'

Linda had a telly now? Linda who lived alone with her sickly mother in a one-bedroom flat, and slept on the sofa, and had even less fashionable clothes than me? How could they afford one? So now I was the *only* girl in the class with no TV at home! 'Suit yourself, then!' I said crossly, slamming my desk lid shut. I knew it wasn't fair to take my frustration out on Linda but I was too upset to help it. Stupid square! I'd only invited her round out of pity! Who cared if she didn't have any friends – what could she expect, if she didn't even like the Beatles?

I watched Linda put her books in her bag and walk off stiffly for her Latin lesson without another word.

'What's up with Prim Lin?' one of the other girls asked me loudly – loudly enough for Linda to hear as she left the classroom.

'Who knows?' I said, ignoring the little voice telling me I should be sticking up for her.

'Probably the time of the month,' said the other girl, nastily.

'Or probably not getting any You-Know-What,' joined in another, making everyone laugh and nudge each other.

I turned away, swallowing back the sick feeling of shame that had come over me. None of them knew what they were talking about anyway – they were all just pretending. Sometimes I really hated being fourteen, and having to pretend, like they all did, to know about things none of us had actually experienced. It was different with Janice. Janice knew what she was talking about – she'd really had boyfriends, lots of them, and didn't have to pretend or exaggerate – or expect me to try to prove myself. *Your turn will come, mate,* she'd said to me recently. *You'll meet a boy soon enough.* Not that I particularly wanted to meet a boy, to be honest. Not a real one, like the spotty, loud-mouthed lads from the boys' school who got on our bus. I was only really interested in Paul McCartney.

Annoyingly, I was still feeling guilty about Linda at the end of the day. I didn't even have Janice to talk to on the bus, as she'd been picked up by one of her boyfriends straight from school to go for a ride on his new Lambretta. Trying to stop myself from thinking about Linda's dignified departure from the classroom, with her head held high as if she couldn't hear the taunts, I spent the journey home fuming about the television situation instead. I'd have to talk Mum about it again. It just wasn't fair – I was going to be the laughing stock at school now – the *only one* who couldn't watch *Thank Your Lucky Stars* without going to someone else's house!

Mum was out when I got home. There was a note on the kitchen table, asking me to start the dinner. I prepared all the vegetables and put the mince and onions on a low gas, not knowing where Mum was or how long she was going to be. Then I took my homework books upstairs, put my LP on Derek's record-player and closed the door. These days I couldn't concentrate on my homework without a background of Beatles' music. About an hour later I heard the door slam and Mum calling up the stairs that she was home.

'I'll be down in a minute!' I yelled back. I was in the middle of an essay, and the music had calmed me down a bit, so I decided to wait till we were eating dinner to confront Mum again on the thorny subject of the TV. By the time I went downstairs, she was dishing up the dinner and listening to the radio.

'Can I help?' I said. I wanted her to be in a good mood for the planned discussion. I'd decided the best approach this time would be a reasoned argument rather than a tantrum. I could even offer to take a cut in my pocket money. I knew it wouldn't make a lot of difference towards the price of a TV, but at least Mum would know I was willing to make sacrifices. And maybe Derek would chip in, if only Mum would agree to it. I took a serving spoon off the hook on the wall and began to dish up the mash. 'Mum, I wanted to ask …'

'Shush!' she held up her hand. 'Wait a minute.' She turned up the wireless, which was crackling slightly as the news headlines were read out. 'Oh, no! Oh my gawd, no!'

'What? What's happened, Mum? – I didn't hear it. Mum?'

She'd sat down at the kitchen table, her legs buckling as if the shock had made them go weak.

'President Kennedy. Oh dear, oh dear! They've killed him. Someone's gone and murdered the American president!' She stared at me, wide-eyed. 'It's the Russians. None of us are safe in our beds. There'll be another war. Gawd help us, there'll be another war.'

'What! Mum, come on – they didn't say anything about a war, did they? What happened? Who's murdered him?'

She sat, shaking her head, staring straight in front of her.

'To think of what we went through!' she muttered. She looked close to crying. 'All our brave boys dying, shot down in the sky! All our homes bombed! It was supposed to be for peace – for *peace!*' She looked up at me again. 'And now it's come to this!'

'Mum!' I went over to her, anxiously. 'Don't! You're frightening me.'

'Turn the wireless up a bit more, Cathy.' She ran a hand across her eyes and sat up straighter. 'We must keep listening. This is terrible news – a terrible day.' She stared at the dinner in front of her. 'Eat yours if you can, love. I can't face anything now.'

I was badly shaken, both by the news and by Mum's reaction. I sat down and picked at my dinner, listening to the rest of the broadcast with an increasing feeling of horror. Was the world really heading towards another war? What had the Russians got to do with it? I didn't understand, but I couldn't ask Mum right now. And the subject of television quite obviously couldn't now be raised until another time. If ever.

But by the strangest twist of fate, when the news broadcast finished and was followed, frustratingly, by classical music, Mum stood up, looked out of the window, and announced whilst sighing and shaking her head:

'At times like this, I must admit I do wonder whether a television might actually be a good thing. I think perhaps we should get one after all.'

'Did you see it on the telly?'

'Did you see the bit where Jackie Kennedy threw herself across him?'

'Yeah! Oh, I was in *tears*. It was *so* sad.'

'I still can't believe it. It's the worst thing that's ever happened in our lifetime, isn't it?'

The whole class was abuzz with the Kennedy assassination that Monday morning. The teachers even discussed it in lesson times. The funeral was taking place that very day, in Washington, and I'd be watching it that evening with Mum on our own TV. To my complete amazement, without me having to say a word, she'd gone into Romford on the Saturday morning, chosen the set, and it was being delivered that morning.

'Are you buying it on HP?' I dared to ask her. Hire purchase had always been, in Mum's view, only marginally less corrupting than booze and gambling. All tools of the devil.

'No, I am not,' she replied shortly.

'Then how …? I mean, I thought we couldn't afford it? Is Del helping with it?'

'It's no concern of yours how I pay for it, Cathy.'

I could tell by the tone of her voice that the subject was closed. I just hoped the news about President Kennedy hadn't unhinged Mum's mind so badly that she'd gone and stolen the money from somewhere. I couldn't think how on earth she'd done it otherwise.

Janice had her own theories about the assassination, which she told me on the bus home that night.

'Probably just some drugged-up nutter wanting to make himself famous,' she declared of Lee Harvey Oswald, the suspected assassin.

'D'you think so? My mum's doing her nut, thinking the Russians are coming and we're all going to die.'

Janice nodded. 'My dad says lots of people think that – because of Cuba. He says Khrushchev might've been humiliated by Kennedy forcing his hand about getting their missiles out of Cuba – but that doesn't mean he was going to start a world war by having him assassinated.'

I listened, impressed as always by the way Janice and her parents seemed to be able to talk about anything – politics, religion, pop music – even sex! I couldn't imagine, in a million years, sitting down with my mum to have a mature conversation about whether or not I should wait until I was married before I lost my virginity, as Janice apparently did with her own mother when she was only about my age.

'Anyway, he's dead too now – Oswald,' Janice added. 'So we'll never know, will we.'

'But he got his wish, didn't he – if that's why he did it. He's famous.'

'*In*famous. If he *did* do it.'

We sat in silence for a while, looking out at the gloomy November afternoon.

'I asked Mum if I could come on Saturday, by the way,' I said eventually. Janice had invited me to go out with her and some friends to the coffee-bar in Romford.

'Oh, fab. Did she say yes?'

I pulled a face. 'She said she'd *think* about it. But now she won't even discuss it. She won't talk about anything except the Russians and nuclear war.'

'Ask her while she's watching the funeral. She'll be distracted. But promise to come home early, and all that stuff. Or you could always pretend your brother's coming with us, again!' she added, laughing.

'No chance! He got a telling-off from Mum last time, for not bringing us home!'

'Yeah. Anyway, he wouldn't be seen dead at the Zodiac. All the rockers go to the Cauldron in North Street, don't they.'

'Do they?' I'd never bothered to wonder where Derek and his mates hung out. I'd just assumed they rode around all night on their motorbikes. I also hadn't realised that mods and rockers frequented different coffee-bars, although now I came to think about it, it was kind of obvious. 'Do you still fancy Del?' I added, curiously. Janice had never mentioned it since the night of the Beatles' concert.

'Never really see him, do I,' she said with a shrug.

'I can always let you know when he's home, and you can come round,' I offered with a giggle.

'Nah. No point, really. He's off limits anyway, and I don't want to risk falling for someone I can't have.'

'But if you *really* liked each other,' I said, frowning. 'Surely …'

Janice looked at me sharply. 'Forget it, Cathy. He's a rocker. And anyway,' she added as if it was only a secondary consideration, 'I'm going out with Ian now, aren't I.'

Ian was the latest boyfriend, the one with the new Lambretta. It seemed to me that Janice was a lot more interested in the scooter than she was in Ian – but what would I know?

'Yeah, course,' I agreed quickly. 'Right. Well, I'd better get my homework done quick tonight – there's television to watch, now!'

'Yeah. And I s'pose I need to get mine done before Ian comes round for me.'

I looked out of the window again and wondered how it would feel to have a boyfriend who was coming to take me out on his scooter. I imagined how excited I'd feel; how I'd spend the whole day at school counting the hours, looking forward to seeing him, dreaming of him when I should be concentrating on my work. Like I felt whenever I was going to see the Beatles on TV ... but more *real*. Surely that was how anyone would feel – wouldn't they? I was sure, anyway, that I wouldn't feel bored and not-bothered, like Janice seemed to feel about going out with Ian!

But I kept my mouth shut, of course. Because, after all, I was only fourteen and knew nothing about anything.

March 1964

'Your hair's grown a lot now, hasn't it. It's looking good, really with-it,' Janice said, sipping her coffee and studying me through the steam.

'Thanks.' I tugged at the ends. 'Wish it was straight, like yours, though.'

'Told you before: iron it. It'll be easier now it's longer. Get your mum to do it for you next time you wash it.'

I laughed. 'My mum's not like yours, you know. She'd have a fit if I said I was going to iron my hair. She still won't let me wear make-up, not even lipstick. *When you're fifteen I'll think about it,* she keeps saying. When I'm fifteen she'll probably say *when you're sixteen ...*'

'Ah, never mind. At least she lets you come down here with me now.'

We were in the Zodiac coffee bar in Romford. It was Saturday lunchtime and it had become a regular thing recently.

'Yeah. But not in the evenings.'

'She's made a compromise, I suppose, letting you come during the day. If you keep coming home unscathed and in one piece, she'll probably relent soon.' She paused, and then added quietly. 'It's only cos she cares about you.'

'Your mum and dad care about *you*. But they treat you like an adult.'

'Well, that's just the way they are: different!' She laughed. 'Anyway, I'll be leaving school soon and getting a job. So I can do what I want, can't I.'

I stared at her. 'Leaving school? Not for another year, are you?'

'Yeah. I'm going at the end of the lower sixth. Had enough.' She shrugged. 'I'll get a job in London. Glad I did the typing course – plenty of work around.'

'But ...' I couldn't believe what I was hearing. 'But surely you want to carry on and get your A-levels? Now you've started, now you've done so much work for them?'

'What work?' Janice retorted. 'That's one of the reasons I'm going. Haven't been bothering much with the work – been getting Cs and Ds for everything. My report's going to be terrible.'

'What do your parents say? Are they upset?'

'Nah. Had a talk about it last weekend. Dad reckons there's never been a better time to get a job – first time in his lifetime there's hardly any unemployment, he says, so why not get out there and earn some money. They want me to enjoy myself while I'm young. You know, cos they couldn't. Cos of the war.'

'Lucky you.' I tried to force a smile on my face. I wanted to try to be pleased: she was my best friend and I was supposed to be happy for her. But the truth was, all I could think about was how awful it was going to be without Janice around.

'Yeah. I can't *wait*. I wanted to leave at Easter, but Dad said I need to give myself time to apply for jobs, and go for interviews. It'll be *fab* to work in London – can you imagine? All those swinging clothes shops and records shops! Hey!' She stopped and looked at me more carefully. 'What's up?'

'What do you think?' I stirred my milk-shake and added quietly. 'I'll miss you, won't I.'

'I'm only leaving school – not leaving the flippin' country, you daft moo! We'll still see each other all the time!'

'No we won't. You won't get home till late, and you won't be around in the school holidays anymore, and anyway, you'll make new friends at work. Why would you want to hang around with *kids*?'

'Don't talk stupid. Course I'll still want to hang around with you. We'll still come down here on Saturdays, for a start, won't we. And anyway, it isn't gonna happen for months yet. And it's nearly the Easter holiday, so cheer up.'

I shrugged and nodded. I supposed Janice was right – no point crying about it till it happened. But I couldn't help feeling jealous. How come everyone else's parents wanted their kids to enjoy their lives? Sometimes it felt like *my* mum did everything she could to prevent me having any fun!

Although … although … in some ways Mum *had* relaxed, recently. Like getting the TV, and then buying me a transistor radio for Christmas. I'd been absolutely flabbergasted when I unwrapped it.

It'd been a fab Christmas altogether – what with Derek giving Mum the money he'd been saving from his overtime; she'd been really chuffed and surprised. I half expected her to say it needed to go on something boring like the gas bill or the rent, but no – she went out and bought a big Christmas tree, and a set of electric fairy lights, and lots of new fancy paper garlands to replace the old torn and faded crepe paper streamers we'd been re-using for as long as I could remember. She got a turkey, a ham and a box of Christmas crackers, and not only that – a tin of biscuits, a big box of chocolates and even a bottle of sherry for herself – all things she would normally have said were luxuries and *not for the likes of us*. After Christmas dinner we watched the queen on TV, and it was so nice to see Mum smiling with pleasure as she sat with her feet up, in the new slippers Derek had given her, sipping a glass of sherry with such evident enjoyment.

And since then, it had carried on the same way. She'd been buying all sorts of new things for the house: new curtains for the kitchen, and then new nets for all the bedroom windows. A standard lamp for the sitting-room. Some saucepans – she'd burnt a hole in one of the old ones on the gas but instead of just replacing that one, she'd gone out and bought a whole set, and they were those new non-stick ones she'd seen advertised on the telly. And – even more surprising – she took me out during the January sales and bought me some new clothes from Marks & Spencer's in Romford. I was too grateful, not to say gobsmacked, to mention that the really with-it clothes came from shops like Martin Ford. Beggars can't be choosers, and at least Mum did agree to buy me a reasonably short skirt, a green suedette jacket and a pair of long boots, almost as groovy as Janice's. I wasn't going to push my luck! But I *was* puzzled about the money. Where was it coming from? What happened to all the worries and moans about making ends meet?

'If we're going to be blown up by the Russians any time now, we might as well spend it all,' was all she'd say when I asked her about it. 'You've complained often enough about not having anything. Nothing to do with you, if I get a little bit extra now and then.'

Derek didn't have any answers, either. 'I can't believe that tightwad at the pub's paying her any extra,' he said. 'Has she got another job she's keeping secret from us?'

'Why would she keep it secret, though? I don't get it.' I kept thinking about all the times recently, that I'd come home from school to find a note saying Mum had gone out. I'd just assumed she was out shopping. If she was working at another job, it wasn't exactly regular. And anyway – why wouldn't she want to tell us about it?

'Don't worry about it,' Janice said when I talked to her about it. 'Make the most of it, if she's suddenly buying you new clobber and stuff. P'raps she's won some money – you know, on the horses.'

'Mum doesn't bet. She's dead against it. She's always talking about doing the pools, but she never does. I think she's against that too, really.'

'Well, I hardly think she's going out robbing banks. She'll tell you in her own good time, I s'pose. I like your boots, by the way.'

'Thank you!' I was dead chuffed that Janice liked them. She was right. I was finally getting some with-it gear, so I shouldn't rock the boat by asking too many questions!

'Here's Ian,' Janice was saying now. 'And his mates.'

I watched the three boys parking their scooters outside the coffee-bar and heading for the door. I felt cheated and disappointed. Janice already spent most of her evenings with Ian; Saturday afternoons were supposed to be just for the two of us. Especially now I knew Janice wasn't going to be around so much, after the summer. The boys shrugged off their parkas and Ian came over to our table while his two mates headed straight for the juke-box in the corner.

'All right, Jan? All right, Cathy?' Ian sat down next to Janice at the table and put his arm round her. He gave me a look, eyebrows raised. 'You just off, are you?'

'Don't be mean, Ian,' Janice protested. 'She's not going anywhere.'

I didn't like Ian, and from the nasty comments he always seemed to be making to me, it was obvious it was mutual. I couldn't understand what Janice saw in him. He was rude and stupid and wasn't even good-looking. If she was only going out with him because of the scooter, I'd have thought either of his two mates, Dan and John, would have been better choices – they both had Lambrettas too, and at least they were a bit less surly. I got up and picked up my jacket. Janice and Ian looked like they were going to start snogging, and I didn't want to be sitting opposite them like a gooseberry, wondering where to look.

'Don't go,' Janice said, looking up at me from beneath Ian's face.

''s all right. Got homework to do anyway.'

I waited for the bus in South Street, watching all the Saturday shoppers rushing back from the market with their bags and baskets, the men on their way home from watching football, the young couples strolling along with their arms wrapped round each other. I thought about Janice, snogging in the coffee-bar with a boy she didn't even seem to be particularly mad about, and I thought about her leaving school and going to work in London. And I suddenly felt really lonely. For the first time, I wondered if it was sensible having a best friend who was two years older than me. I had a feeling she was going to leave me behind sooner or later.

'You shouldn't have run off like that on Saturday,' Janice said on the way to school on the Monday. 'You don't want to take any notice of Ian. He's an idiot.'

'What you going out with him for, then?'

'I know, I know I should've chucked him. But I can't now – not till after Easter.'

'Why? What's happening at Easter?' I looked at her suspiciously. 'You haven't promised to have sex with him or anything revolting like that?'

'No!' Janice laughed. 'I'm not doing it with him. Not quite, if you know what I mean.'

I didn't, not really, but I didn't even *want* to know. Not where Ian was concerned.

'No, listen,' she went on, dropping her voice. 'There's going to be stuff going on over Easter. At Clacton. Ian's taking me on his scooter. All the mods are going.' She stopped and looked at me, like she was weighing something up. 'Wanna come?' she said eventually.

'I don't know. What do you mean, *stuff going on?*'

'Like, a big gigantic outing. A *convention*. Loads of mods are going – from all over, not just from round here. Easter Monday. Go on – come with us. It'll be a rave.'

'I can't, can I. I can't come if you're going on Ian's scooter.'

'That's OK – you can come on the train. There's loads of girls from my class going. Bring some of your own friends. It's just a day out, Cathy!' she added, seeing the look on my face. 'That's all it is. Tell your mum it's just a day out at the seaside!'

I thought about it all day at school. Well – why not? After all, if I didn't want to be left behind by Janice, I'd have to start doing more of the things she was doing, whether Mum liked it or not. I was nearly fifteen now – not a kid anymore. I'd have to talk to Mum about it tonight. And if she agreed, I'd ask some of my friends from my class to go with me on the train. We could meet up with Janice and Idiot Ian when we got to Clacton. We could go on the beach, if it was nice weather, or maybe go on the pier. Get an ice-cream, play the slot-machines. I felt considerably cheered up at the thought of it. Even *my* mum wouldn't be able to complain about this. A day out at the seaside. Couldn't get much more harmless than that, could you?

Easter Monday: March 1964

It wasn't turning out to be quite how I expected it. For a start, the weather was horrible. And the two friends who'd come with me were already moaning that they were bored.

'Let's go down to the beach,' I said, trying to feign enthusiasm. I looked at my watch. Janice and the others should all be here by now. We'd seen loads of mods on scooters arriving already. 'We're meant to be meeting them under the pier.'

'Who cares?' said Heather, who was doing most of the complaining. 'I don't care about meeting them. Who wants to go on the beach in this weather?'

'We can have a closer look at the boat, too,' I said, pointing out to sea at the distant grey shape on the horizon. 'I *bet* that's the one.'

'Can hardly see it,' Heather carried on grumbling. 'And anyway, so what if it *is* Radio Caroline? We'll be able to listen to it on our trannies from home, won't we. Looking at the boat isn't going to make any difference to the music.'

'Well,' Susan admitted, 'It is quite exciting, isn't it, to think we're actually looking at the first pirate radio ship and they've only just started broadcasting. But now we've seen it, let's just find a coffee-bar and chat up the local boys,' she added, laughing.

Susan and Heather were the only two of my classmates whose parents had let them come today. Mind you, my mum hadn't agreed either – until I told her that little white lie about Susan's mum and dad coming with us.

'It's just a day out on the train,' I told her, fingers crossed behind my back. 'Susan's parents said she could bring a couple of friends along.'

'And you'll be staying with them all day? And they'll bring you back before dark?'

'Course.' I had to avoid her eyes, but I noticed Derek staring at me. 'What?' I asked him sharply.

'Nothing,' Derek said, getting up and putting his plate in the sink. 'Nothing at all.'

Later though, after Mum went to work, he cornered me.

'What's going on?' he said. 'Are you lying to Mum? Are you girls planning on going to Clacton on your own?'

'No! Mind your own business, Del!'

'Cathy,' he said more gently, 'I'm on your side, all right? I know Mum doesn't let you do a lot. But you *are* only fourteen ...'

'Nearly fifteen!'

'... and I don't know what your friends are expecting at Clacton, but I can tell you there's probably going to be trouble.'

'What d'you mean, trouble? Janice says it's just a kind-of outing, for all the mods.'

He shook his head at me. 'Think about it, will you? D'you really think it's only mods going down there? *We* had the idea before the mods even thought of it.'

'*We*? What, you mean the rockers?'

'Of course!' He laughed. 'You hang around with older girls, Cathy, but that doesn't make you streetwise, does it. Sometimes you're just so bloody naïve.'

'No I'm not! OK, so there'll be mods *and* rockers there. So what? I'll just stay with the mods.'

He sighed. 'Has Mum said you can go?'

'Yes, with a whole list of conditions, as usual. So don't you dare ...'

'OK, OK, I'm not going to say anything. But I don't like it. You could get mixed up in all sorts.'

'Do you really think I'm that stupid?'

'No, Cathy. But if it all kicks off down there, you could get separated from your mates, and ... well, don't say I haven't warned you.' He turned to walk away, then stopped and added: 'Look, I'll be at the Red Arrow coffee-bar in the High Street there, if you need me. OK?'

'*You're* going? I exclaimed. 'After you've told me how bad it's going to be!'

'There's a crowd of us going. But we're not looking for trouble. Just ... tell me you'll come and find me if you need me. All right?'

'All right,' I agreed grumpily. 'But I won't need you. I'll be fine.'

We were standing at the steps down to the beach now. Despite the cold, miserable weather it was packed down there – large groups of teenagers were gathering, huddled round trannies playing loudly enough to scare away anyone over the age of about twenty, or running around at the edge of the water – boys shouting to each other and girls shrieking and flirting with the boys. It was only a short way along the beach from here to the pier, but it was impossible to see that far, through the crowd.

'Let's go down,' I said after a moment's hesitation. 'We've got to meet up with the others.'

'Why?' Heather demanded. 'Why do we have to, Cathy? I'm not bothered about meeting Janice and her gang. I thought we were spending the day together, just us three.'

'Anyway, it's freezing,' Susan agreed. 'And I don't particularly want to be down on the beach with all that lot. Come on. Let's go and get some chips.'

I looked at my watch again. The thing was, I'd *promised* Janice I'd meet her under the pier at twelve o'clock, and it was already ten past.

'Well, I just want to find her, and let her know what we're doing,' I said. To be honest the attraction of the beach was wearing off for me too. 'So she doesn't hang around waiting for us.'

'I doubt she would anyway,' Heather muttered. 'You shouldn't bother, Cath, honest.'

There was a roaring noise behind us, and a huge fleet of motorbikes came thundering along the Esplanade, to shouts of *Greasers! Rockers out!* from the parka-wearing mob on the beach, some of whom started a futile chase after the bikes, jeering and waving their arms.

'Come on – let's go,' said Susan decisively.

'Yeah – I'm getting out of here,' agreed Heather.

It was all right for them. Janice wasn't their friend – it was me she'd invited to come here today, invited to meet her here. I really didn't want to fall out with Janice just because I couldn't even be bothered to have a quick look for her.

'OK – but just give me two minutes. I'll catch up with you,' I said – and I ran quickly down the steps onto the beach before I could change my mind. Immediately I was swallowed up by the jostling crowd, which seemed to be growing larger and louder all the time. Someone, not looking where he was going, ran into me and nearly knocked me over.

'Watch where you're going, stupid cow!' he snarled, and his friends all screamed with laughter.

Nearly at the pier, I looked back anxiously to make sure the girls were still waiting for me at the top of the steps – but it was impossible to see through the mob. I ploughed on, finally reaching the gloomy shelter of the damp sand directly under the pier. Here, couples were propped up against the slimy supports of the pier, snogging, and there were huddled shapes in parkas writhing on the beach together.

'What you looking at, bitch?' a girl screamed at me from underneath a skinny boy much smaller than herself. Her blouse was undone and her skirt was up round her waist. 'Piss off out of it!'

'Sorry! I'm … just looking for someone,' I mumbled, picking my way through other, oblivious couples.

Suddenly, a heavy hand fell on my shoulder and I wheeled round, my heart in my mouth. It was actually a relief to see it was Ian.

'What the bleedin' hell are *you* doing here?' he said in his usual unpleasant tone.

'Oh – I'm glad I've found *you*, at least. Where's Janice?' I asked him. I had to shout above the noise of the crowd and the radios blaring.

'What d'you want to know for?'

'I'm s' posed to be meeting her here. Didn't she say?'

'Nah. You must've got it wrong.'

'No, I didn't. It was definitely here – at twelve o'clock, and now it's quarter past, so …'

'So, looks like you've missed 'er, don't it.'

'Well, where is she, then? Why aren't you with her?'

He looked at me for a moment like he was trying to decide something. 'I'll take you to her,' he said. 'Come on.'

'Wait!' I stumbled after him. 'I need to let my friends know – they're waiting up the top.'

'Come on,' he said again, without pausing to wait for me. 'This way.'

I shrugged to myself and followed him. He was going back the way I'd come, anyway, so I'd be able to see Susan and Heather – and get them to come with me.

'You don't wanna be hanging around here,' Ian shouted back at me. There was a fight starting, down by the water's edge. Pushing, jeering, punching – crowds surging towards the centre of the fight, piling into it, falling into the sea as they joined in the melee. I shivered, beginning to feel really nervous now. Thank goodness, Ian was heading towards the steps, off the beach, and up to the prom again. Even up here it was more crowded now – with large groups of rockers hanging around, looking down at the mob on the beach, calling out insults. I stopped, looking around anxiously.

'I can't see my mates,' I shouted after him. 'They were supposed to wait for me here.'

'Probably gone home, if they've got any sense,' he said. 'Bloody stupid, kids like you coming down here today.'

'We're not kids,' I retorted. 'And they wouldn't go home without me. Oh!'

A leather-clad rocker just next to me had picked up a deckchair from the prom and lobbed it down onto the beach below, where it landed over the heads of a couple of mods. 'Oi! Dirty *greasers*!' yelled one of the boys who'd been hit – and immediately there was a stampede of mods up the steps, charging towards the rockers, fists raised, threatening, swearing, kicking.

Ian grabbed my arm and steered me in the opposite direction.

'Like I said,' he yelled, above the noise of police sirens heading our way, 'You don't wanna be hanging around here, do you.'

'N … no!' I stammered. 'But where's Janice? Are we going to find her?'

'Yeah. Come on. 's not far.'

He led me along the seafront, past more huge groups of mods and rockers, scooters and bikes, until we finally reached a quieter stretch where we turned down a side road.

'Why did Janice come all the way down here?' I asked him, feeling cross now – cross with Janice for not waiting for me, cross with him for not being with her. My voice sounded funny now I didn't have to shout anymore. 'Why isn't she with you? Is she with her mates?'

'Yeah. Didn't want her getting involved in all that stuff on the beach, did I.'

'But where is she? Did you leave them at a café, or what?'

'You ask too many bloody questions,' he growled, steering me round another corner and then into a narrow alleyway. 'You're worse than *her*.'

It was quiet down here – too quiet. Nobody about. I felt sure Janice wouldn't have come down here – would she?

'What do you mean, worse than … ouch! You're hurting me!' He'd swung me round roughly, suddenly gripping both my wrists.

'Shut up asking questions,' he said. 'Now, I'll show you what happens to stupid little girls who try to act like they're all grown-up, shall I?'

He pushed me against the wall and, so quickly that I didn't even have time to gasp, thrust his whole weight against me and pulled my skirt up.

'Skinny little thing, aren't you!' he laughed nastily. 'Bet you've never had anyone feel you up like this before, have you, eh?'

'Get off me!' I squealed. I pushed at him hard, trying to shove him away, but he just leant against me even harder. He'd undone the zip of his trousers and had his hand inside my knickers, pawing at me, and trying to tug them down. I felt sick with disgust, and scared out of my mind. He was huge compared with me: I'd never be able to get him off me. I knew what I needed to do – scream. Scream as loud as I could, right in his ear. But my throat seemed to have seized up. Why couldn't I scream now, when I really needed to, like I'd screamed at that Beatles' concert? The memory of it seemed to act like a trigger – I opened my mouth and let it rip – the loudest, highest scream I could muster. For just the split second I needed, he flinched and drew back from me, and then immediately tried to clamp a hand over my mouth. Instinct took over: I bit down hard on his finger and, as he swore and pulled back his hand, I managed to slip out of his grasp and run.

I ran and ran and ran, sobbing, gasping, not daring to look behind me, not daring to stop until I was back on the seafront, back amongst the crowds, where I found a public convenience and locked myself in a cubicle of the Ladies. I sat there, shivering and crying, for about fifteen minutes, trying to get my breath back, trying not to be sick.

Eventually, I took a deep breath and told myself sternly that I had to pull myself together. I'd done it – I'd got away from him. It could have been worse, much worse – I was all right, I'd live, but I couldn't stay in there all day. I got up, straightened up my clothes, and went to wash my face at the grubby sink. *Derek.* Thank God, Derek was here somewhere; he'd promised to look after me if I needed help. I tried frantically to remember the coffee-bar where he'd said I'd be able to find him. What was the name again? *Red* something. In the High Street, he said, didn't he? I'd walked down the High Street with the girls when we first got here this morning, looking in the shop windows. I could find my way back there, and walk up and down till I found the right place.

In fact it took me half an hour, struggling through the crowds, trying to avoid any of the gangs of boys still congregating on the seafront, before I finally found it: the Red *Arrow*. I breathed a sigh of relief as I pushed open the door and went inside. I was going to find my brother now, and then I'd be safe.

The coffee-bar was packed, full of smoke and throbbing with noise; the juke-box was pumping out an Elvis number, almost drowned by the raucous shouts and laughter of the crowd. As I walked up to the counter, everyone seemed to turn at once and stare at me. I looked around. They were all in denim and leather. They all had rockers' hairstyles. And I realised, too late, that there'd been about a dozen motorbikes parked outside. I'd been in such a hurry to get inside, to *safety*, that I hadn't taken the significance on board. This was a rockers' café – of course it was! Why else would Del be likely to come here? And where was he, anyway? Holding my breath, I looked round at the crowd, searching for him. No – he wasn't here. What the hell was I going to do now? The way they were all leering at me, I had a horrible feeling I might have jumped out of the frying pan straight into the fire.

The next day

'Where were you?' I demanded. I'd phoned Janice as soon as I could – as soon as Mum went to work the next morning.

'Oh – sorry, Cath. I did try and find you under the pier, but Ian was there so I didn't want to hang around.'

I know he was there. Unfortunately, I thought grimly.

'Why – I thought you went to Clacton *with* him? What happened?'

'I dumped him. I was going to do it anyway, afterwards. But he got on my nerves so much – as soon as we got to Clacton, he was on and on and on, as usual, about finding somewhere to get off together. I mean – it was cold and horrible, wasn't it: the last thing I fancied was snogging with him on the wet sand – and anyway, that wouldn't have been enough for him, you know? He was getting really demanding, wanting to go the whole way. And I didn't. So I told him to bugger off.'

I took a deep breath. I was just about to explode with my own story about Ian, when Janice added calmly:

'Anyway, you were all right, weren't you? I mean, I knew you were with your mates, so I didn't worry about you.'

'No!' I said crossly. 'I *wasn't* with my mates, because I insisted on coming to find *you*, and they wouldn't come with me. And then they came home without me, and flippin' well phoned my mum and now she knows I lied to her and I'm grounded!'

'Oh, crikey. Did you get home all right, though?'

'Yes, eventually. I went to meet Del at a coffee-bar, but it was full of rockers, and really scary …'

'Oh, no. How horrible for you. Your mates really should have waited for you.'

'But it was *you* that asked me to come to Clacton – I wouldn't have come otherwise! You *promised* to meet me, and because you didn't …' I broke off, embarrassed now because I was crying. 'Because of you, I got into trouble,' I finished abruptly, and hung up. I couldn't say it. I couldn't tell Janice what had happened with Ian. I was too upset with her at the moment, but more to the point, it was all too horrible, too dirty and disgusting and I didn't think I'd ever be able to tell anybody.

When I'd finally arrived home from Clacton, Mum had been waiting for me, arms folded, a grim expression on her face.

'Sorry I'm a bit late … we had to wait ages for a bus,' I started.

'That's enough of your lies. I know Susan's parents weren't with you. And I know you didn't even stay with your friends. Susan phoned here over an hour ago, to find out if you'd got home all right on your own.'

I just sighed and looked at the ground. I was tired, and still feeling shaky and upset. I really wished I had parents like Janice's. Janice would probably be able to confide in her mother about what had happened, whereas the very idea of sharing it with my mum was completely unthinkable. I knew I'd have got no sympathy – she'd probably have blamed me for wearing a short skirt, showing my legs and giving boys ideas.

'So what happened?' she demanded. 'Had an argument with your friends, did you, I suppose, and went off on your own?'

'Kind of,' I said. 'It was their fault. They were supposed to wait for me.'

'That's *exactly* why I wouldn't allow you to go there without an adult. I know what you girls are like – you get out somewhere, start eyeing up the boys …'

'We *weren't*!'

'Just think yourself lucky you didn't get into any sort of trouble, miss!'

I tried to suppress a shudder. 'I was OK, Mum,' I lied. 'I met up with Derek. He looked after me.'

'*Did* he? Well, you can't go through life depending on your brother. He's no better than you are, half the time. And as for your lies about Susan's parents taking you!' She shook her head, looking at me with disgust. 'I thought I'd brought you up better than that.'

'Well, what am I supposed to do? Susan and Heather were both *allowed* to go to Clacton without their parents. Maybe their parents trust them.'

'And now you can see why I *can't* trust *you*!' She turned away from me, throwing back over her shoulder: 'You're grounded for the rest of the holiday, miss. And don't let me find out you've disobeyed me.'

I didn't doubt for a minute that she'd find out, if I did. When I was little, I used to think Mum must have had a magic telescope. She always seemed to know what I was up to, even when she wasn't with me. Now, though, I knew the reality was much more powerful and dangerous – a network of nosy neighbours who took delight in reporting any misdemeanors of each others' children. I stomped up the stairs and changed out of the clothes that had felt uncomfortable ever since Ian's horrible fat hands had been pawing at them, and went back to the kitchen to make some tea and toast.

'Want a cup of tea?' I asked Mum, who was in the sitting-room with the TV on. I realised it'd only make matters worse if I sulked or showed any disrespect at this stage.

There was no reply. I put my head round the sitting-room door. Mum was sitting in her armchair, gripping the arms, staring at the TV screen with a look of horror on her face. The News was showing scenes of mayhem and violence on Clacton beach. She turned slowly to look at me.

'*That's* where you've been today – *that's* what was going on there, while you were wandering around on your own? *Mods* and *rockers*?' She spat out the words as if they were types of vermin. 'Clashes with the police? Bottles being thrown? Troublemakers arrested? What on *earth* are you getting yourself involved in, Cathy?'

'Nothing, Mum! Honestly, we had no idea it was going to be like that. We didn't get involved! We just … got split up, in the crowds.'

'And your brother's still down there! With those terrible motorbike friends of his, no doubt. Well, I just hope *he's* got enough sense to stay with his friends, and keep out of trouble.'

'I expect they're exaggerating, on the telly … it really wasn't that bad!'

'I can't believe a word you say anymore, can I,' Mum said quietly, and turned back to the TV, leaving me standing there, dismissed. She hardly spoke to me for the rest of the evening. I felt like I was being blamed for every scuffle between every mod and every rocker in Clacton. It was so unfair!

Janice came round a little while after I'd hung up on her. I held the door open without a word and let her walk in.

'Look, I'm *sorry*,' she said. 'Really. Don't be mad at me. I was a bit upset myself, you know – splitting up with Ian and everything.'

I raised my eyebrows and shook my head. Huh!

'Cath?' she persisted. 'I'm really sorry you got into trouble with your Mum. But let's not fall out over it. I'll come round and see you all the time while you're grounded.'

She put an arm round my shoulders. I closed my eyes and sighed. I didn't want to lose her friendship, and I supposed it hadn't all really been her fault.

'It wasn't just the trouble with Mum,' I said quietly. 'It was worse than that ...'

'Oh – the coffee-bar. Blimey, yeah, it sounds awful. You poor thing. Come on, let's sit down and you can tell me all about it.'

She led me into my own sitting-room and sat me down on my own sofa, patting my hand and putting a cushion behind me as if I was an invalid. It was nice to be fussed over, nice to have someone actually prepared to listen to me. So I started to tell her all about the Red Arrow coffee-bar, and she made the right sympathetic noises and gradually I suppose I just forgot I was annoyed with her.

I hadn't had too many choices in that coffee-bar. I knew I'd either have to wait there and hope Del turned up, or walk the rest of the way back to the station on my own – but the streets outside were even scarier than the people in there. With everyone still staring at me, I straightened my shoulders, got my purse out of my shoulder bag and asked the bored-looking woman behind the counter for a Coca-Cola. Trying to ignore the thumping of my heart, I found a seat near the window, sat down, and started to sip my drink.

'Lost your friends?' someone shouted above the din. I looked up warily. A tall, dark boy was leaning across from the next table, looking at me. 'Been stood up?' he added, and the rest of his group started laughing and nudging each other.

'No.' I felt the blood rush to my face. 'I'm waiting for someone.'

'Go and wait in the playground, kid,' one of the group said, with a nasty laugh. 'You don't wanna get hurt.' He was big, loud, older than all the others – probably the leader of their gang. He'd have been intimidating enough even without all the tattoos, and the studs and chains on his leather jacket.

'Yeah, your boyfriend's probably got hurt already!' another boy said, 'He's probably one of the mods I beat up on the beach earlier.'

'Or one of the ones we threw the deckchairs at!' said another, and they all laughed again and punched each other like it was a great joke. All except the first boy who'd spoken to me. I noticed he was still looking at me, and – although I was nervous of him – I also noticed that his eyes were just like Paul McCartney's. Big, brown and soulful.

'Leave her alone,' he said to the others without taking his eyes off me. 'She's only a kid.'

'I'm nearly fifteen,' I retorted, trying to make myself sound braver than I felt. 'And it's not my boyfriend I'm waiting for. It's my brother.'

'Looks like your brother's stood you up!' the gang leader laughed again. 'Bad luck, kid!'

'Are you on your own?' the first boy asked. He pushed past the others and leant against the wall next to my table. 'You shouldn't be hanging round here on your own. There's been trouble.'

'And there's gonna be more, if your brother walks in here and he's a mod!' shouted one of the others.

'Shut up, Max,' said the boy with the Beatle eyes, calmly. 'But he's right,' he told me quietly. 'You better get yourself home.'

I finished my drink and stood up. They all turned to look at me again. I could feel my knees trembling, beneath the hem of my short corduroy skirt. I pulled my jacket on and walked to the door, but when I opened it, I saw that the place was now surrounded by motorbikes – and by more boys in leather. Dozens of them, leaning against their bikes, talking, laughing, smoking. And girls, in leather jackets like the boys, twining themselves round the boys' necks, screeching, calling out to each other. Even as I watched, more bikes roared up outside, more leather-clad rockers dismounted, more shouts and laughter floated in the air. I was getting really worried now. I knew the talk about beatings and deckchair throwing wasn't just showing-off – I'd seen it myself, hadn't I. How could I walk outside, through that lot, on my own? Where was Derek? What was I going to do if he didn't show up?

'D'you live round here?'

I turned round, to see the boy with the Beatle eyes looking at me again. He'd followed me to the door, and was standing next to me, towering over me.

'No.' I looked back at the crowds outside again. Should I just make a dash for it?

'Where d'you live, then? How d'you get here? With your brother, or what?'

'Near Romford. I came on the train, with ...'. I scowled to myself. 'With some mates.'

'Got separated in the fighting?'

I nodded, and he looked at me for a minute, like he was debating something.

'Come on, then,' he said. 'I'll take you back to the station.'

Some of the boys standing nearest him started to laugh again. There were a few wolf-whistles and some crude comments.

'It's all right,' I said. I'd had enough trouble today already, without agreeing to go with a complete stranger. 'I'll find it on my own.'

'You don't even know the way? You can't go out there on your own. They'll eat you alive.' He nodded at the ever-increasing crowd outside. 'Come on.' He grinned at me. 'You been on a bike before?'

Been on a *bike*? I gulped, imagining what Janice and my other friends would say if they saw me on a motorbike, with a rocker. Just the thought of Janice made me feel cross again. And then I thought about Mum, who was already unhappy about Derek going on his friends' motorbikes, never mind what she'd say, or do, if she thought *I* was getting on one – with someone I didn't even know. At the thought of Mum, sitting at home imagining me safe with my friends, and supposedly with their parents, I gulped and blinked, trying to stay in control.

'Don't cry, kid,' said Beatle-eyes, looking worried. 'I ain't gonna hurt you.'

And just as the wolf-whistles started again, and the others began once more to berate him, with less humour in their voices this time, just as I was struggling to decide which might be the worst fate – going with one rocker or running the gauntlet of what now looked like hundreds of them – the café door was pushed open, nearly sending me flying, and there, with blood running down his cheek from a cut above his eye, was Derek.

The whole place seemed to erupt.

'What the hell happened to you?'

'Who hit you? Did you get 'em back?'

'How many of them? Which way did they go? Let's go after them!'

'Leave it!' Derek held up his hands and bellowed into the crowd. 'I'm all right, it's nothing. I just got in the way of a missile. Give it a rest. There's been enough.' Then he caught sight of me and his face melted into concern. 'Bloody hell, Cathy, I'm sorry. I didn't know you'd be here.'

'You *told* me to come here!' I was so relieved to see him, I felt like punching him. 'Did you forget, or what?'

'She your sister, Del?' said Beatle-eyes, and there was an echoing mutter around the café: *She's his sister ... the kid's Del's sister.*

'Yeah, she is, Jimmy. My kid sister. Sorry, Cath,' he said again. 'I know I *said* to come here, but I only meant, like, if there was an emergency, if you were in trouble, or ...' He stopped and widened his eyes at me. 'You're not hurt, or anything? I *told* you, you shouldn't come, didn't I. Mum'd do her nut if she knew you were on your own here.'

Irritated at being called a kid again, and at being lectured by him, in front of everyone (although in fact most of them had turned away again now they realised there wasn't another fight brewing), I decided straight away that I wasn't going to tell Derek about what had really happened.

'I just lost my mates. We got separated in the crowds,' I said. 'I'm all right, though,' I added with a lot more bravado than I felt.

'Right. Well, I think you'd better go straight home. I'll see you back to the station. You got your train ticket?'

'Yeah, course I have. Thanks.' I looked back at the boy with the nice eyes. The one Derek had called Jimmy. Now I knew he was a friend of Derek's, and not a complete stranger, he didn't seem so scary, even though he was a rocker. 'Thanks for offering to take me,' I said.

'That's OK.' Jimmy shrugged. 'I never knew you had a sister, Del.'

'I keep her away from you lot. She's not even fifteen yet and she hangs around with mods.'

'She'll learn,' Jimmy said. He grinned at me as Derek, tugging me behind him, opened the café door again and we got engulfed by the noise of roaring motorbike engines outside. 'See you later, Cathy,' he bellowed after us.

We walked quickly back to the station, through the littered streets of Clacton, now emptying of both mods and rockers as the police gradually regained control of the town.

'Sure you'll be all right on the train on your own?' Derek said. 'You're a bit quiet. You upset about your mates? They've probably gone home already if they've got any sense.'

'Yes. S'pose so. See you later, Del. Don't ... get into any more fights, will you.'

'No chance. Just hanging out with my mates. Be home late. See you.'

I was so exhausted, I almost fell asleep on the train back to Romford. But every time I closed my eyes, I saw Ian's horrible face leering at me. Instead, I pictured the boy with the nice Paul McCartney eyes: Jimmy. At least I had one good memory from the day.

'You poor thing,' Janice said again when I'd finished telling her. I'd actually missed a few details out. I'd told her about Jimmy, and how he was the only one who was nice to me – but I didn't tell her how much I'd actually fancied him. He was a rocker: it wasn't supposed to be allowed. And when she got up to leave I still hadn't managed to tell her what actually happened with Ian. It was still too raw, and I didn't want to say it. And anyway, really, what was the point? What could anyone possibly do about it, now?

By the week before the Whitsun half term, Mum had got over her shock and anger about Clacton, but that didn't stop her giving me the third degree about what I might be doing during the school holiday.

'Revision, mostly.' I had mock O-levels coming up. 'But I might go to the coffee-bar with Janice a couple of times. If that's OK.'

'All right.' Mum gave me a look. 'I know you think I'm hard on you, Cath. But now you're fifteen, I suppose I'd better let you have a bit more freedom. I'd rather that, than having you lie to me again.'

I nearly choked on my dinner – it was so unexpected, and so unlike Mum to say anything like this. In fact, everything she did these days seemed unlike her usual self. She was still buying new things for the house almost every week, and for my fifteenth birthday the previous week she'd given me enough money to buy new shoes and a new summer dress. I'd actually been allowed to choose it myself from the shops instead of having it made from a Butterick pattern on Mum's sewing machine. She'd even finally relented and got rid of the old gramophone we inherited from my granddad – which had only played old seventy-eights – replacing it with a Dansette record-player even more with-it than Derek's one. I'd been listening to my new Beatles' record over and over whenever Mum was at work – dreaming of Paul while I was supposed to be revising.

'Thanks, Mum!' I spluttered. 'So can I go ...'

'Not on school nights, mind,' she qualified. 'Or Sunday nights. And only if I know who you're with, where you'll be and what time you'll be home. And as long as your school work gets done!'

'So can I go ... '

'And if you let me down, that'll be *it*,' she added.

'But ... does that mean I can go to the coffee-bar in the evenings now?'

'Friday or Saturday evenings, and in the holidays. But not staying out late, mind!'

I couldn't wait to tell Janice I was finally being treated *almost* like a grown-up.

I'd kept my horrible secret about Ian to myself for the whole of the half term since Easter, and it was still giving me nightmares. I'd left it so long now, I didn't really see how I could suddenly come out and tell Janice about it, even though I knew that sharing it might help me to get over it. But that evening, she came round to listen to records with me. She'd got some groovy new ones by The Searchers and The Kinks.

'That's great!' she said when I told her about my Mum's latest concession. 'What time will you have to be home?'

'Ten o'clock.' I pulled a face. 'Sorry.'

'Never mind. Do what your mum says, and maybe she'll let you stay later after a while.'

'Yeah.' I glanced at her. 'It must be annoying for you, though, having to kind-of babysit me. Some of my mates at school think it's weird, us being friends. You know – cos you're older than me.'

'Take no notice what they say. We *are* friends, and who cares if I'm a bit older than you?' She lowered her voice and admitted with a shrug. 'Look, when I was a kid, I always used to pretend I had a little sister. I used to drive my mum mad, demanding she got me one for my birthday, for Christmas, whatever. I *like* having you around. Get it? I like you, you're different from my other mates. I like you coming out with me. And I wish I'd been with you at Clacton. I would've protected you from all those horrible rockers in that coffee-bar!' she added, with a grin. 'I'd have told them where to get off!'

'It wasn't the rockers I needed protecting from,' I admitted, suddenly encouraged by the idea of Janice being my big sister. If I couldn't confide in her now, I'd never confide in anybody. 'It was Ian.'

Janice, misunderstanding, nodded grimly. 'You were right about him. I should never have gone to Clacton with him – should have chucked him long ago. I had to get away from him, on the beach there, Cath. To be honest, he wasn't just being demanding. He was … getting a bit rough.'

I bit my lip. 'I … need to tell you something,' I tried again. 'I should have told you before, but … it was difficult to talk about.'

'Go on then. What?'

'When I went to look for you at Clacton – Ian was still there. Under the pier.'

Janice looked up in surprise. 'Was he? Still hanging around there after I'd finished with him? Ha! Did he see you?'

I nodded.

'What did he say? Did he tell you I'd chucked him?'

'No. He *said* he was going to take me to find you. But he didn't. He took me to … to an alleyway. And …' I started to tremble, like I did every time I remembered it.

'Cathy!' Janice's voice was full of alarm now. 'What did he do to you? He didn't …'

'He tried. You know. He … touched me, and … and he …' I started, embarrassingly, to cry. 'But I screamed, and bit his hand, and … I just ran.'

'Oh my *gawd,* Cathy – that's awful! Now I really *do* feel like it's all my fault. What did your mum say?'

'I didn't tell her. She'd have said it was my own fault. I haven't told anyone, till now.'

'But you should. He could get done for trying to rape you. It's serious.'

'No!' I felt a rush of panic. 'No, I don't want any of that. I just want to forget it. But I can't stop thinking about it. I wasn't going to tell you – I mean, he *was* your boyfriend.'

'Yeah, although I can't think what I ever saw in him. He's such a slimy pig!' She shook her head. 'He really needs to be taught a lesson, one way or another.'

'Yeah,' I agreed, 'He does.' Not that there was anything we could do about him now. I was just glad I'd finally got it off my chest. I smiled at Janice gratefully. 'Anyway, I'm glad you chucked him in the end. I hope I never have to see him again, as long as I live.'

There was something else playing on my mind as well, and I brought it up a bit later in the evening.

'Jan, do you think my mum might have *men friends*?'

I half expected her to laugh, but she just looked back at me thoughtfully.

'Why, because she's started being nicer to you?'

'Well – yes, that and the money thing. Buying all the stuff she always said she couldn't afford.'

'What?' Janice raised her eyebrows. 'Blimey, Cath – you don't mean ... you don't think she's like, *on the game*, do you?'

'Well, I can't help wondering, can I?' I flushed, feeling ashamed now for even thinking it. 'Whenever Del or I ask her about the money situation, she just tells us to mind our own business.'

'I'm sure it's not that. I mean – sorry, but flippin' heck, your mum's really old and not, you know, at all *sexy*, is she!'

'No!' I laughed, feeling immensely relieved. 'I suppose I should just be grateful she's changed, and not worry about it.'

'Yeah. Del doesn't seem to be worried, does he, so why should you?'

Janice hadn't said anything for ages now about fancying Derek. If he was at home when she came round they always chatted, and I saw Del giving her the eye sometimes, but it didn't seem to lead to anything.

But the very next night after this, I came back into the sitting-room from making a cup of tea, to find the pair of them deep in serious conversation, their voices very low. They stopped talking as soon as I came in.

'What're you two talking about?' I asked lightly, putting Janice's tea down in front of her.

'Oh, nothing!' Janice laughed. 'Just about what's on the News.'

But I thought Del looked a bit upset. In fact, he banged the front door when he went out later, without even saying goodbye.

'What's up with him?' I commented. I looked at Janice suspiciously. 'Did he ask you out, or something?'

'Nah – told you, we were watching the News. Talking about the abolition of the death penalty.'

This seemed so unlikely, I just laughed and waited for Janice to admit it was something more personal. I wouldn't have been surprised if Del *had* asked her out – she was very attractive and popular after all. She'd have turned him down, of course, because of him being a rocker. That'd definitely account for his bad mood.

'You do still fancy Derek, don't you?' I persisted when she didn't say anything else.

'No. I keep telling you – I like him, but he's a rocker.' She sounded grim. 'None of my friends would ever speak to me again if I went out with a rocker.'

'I would,' I protested.

Janice stared at me. '*What* – you'd go out with a rocker? You wouldn't, would you?'

'I mean, I would still speak to you,' I said, laughing. 'Anyway, nobody's ever asked me out, so I don't know what I'd do. But if I *liked* someone enough – I don't see why ...'

'*Cathy*!' Janice exclaimed in shocked tones. She looked at me in horror. 'You haven't met someone you fancy, have you? A *rocker*?'

'No,' I lied. 'Course not.'

I wasn't telling *anyone* about Jimmy. Not even Janice. Especially not after that conversation!

I'd seen Jimmy several times since Clacton. OK, I actually knew exactly how many times I'd seen him – five. I didn't know why he'd started turning up at the house to see Del, when I'd never noticed him before even though he didn't live far from us. I didn't even dare to hope it had anything to do with me – after all, I was just a kid, Derek's kid sister. But it was nice to dream – and I did – almost as much as I dreamed about Paul McCartney. Even if I was upstairs when he called round, or in the kitchen, or – as I was on one embarrassing occasion, lying on a blanket on the lawn on a sunny Saturday afternoon, sunbathing in my shorts while supposedly revising English Lit – Jimmy always made a point of finding me, just to say hello and ask how I was. I liked him so much, I found it almost impossible to talk to him properly. I told myself it was just because he'd been so kind to me at Clacton – but really I knew it was also because I fancied him desperately. Almost as much, although I could hardly admit this, even to myself, as I fancied Paul!

'There's stuff going on again this bank holiday,' Janice told me.

'What sort of stuff?'

'You know. Like Clacton. Everyone's heading down to Brighton this time.'

'You're not going, are you?'

'Nah.' Janice shook her head. 'Mum and Dad are going to see my grandparents in Cambridge and they're saying I ought to go with them cos I haven't seen them for ages. Anyway, it'll just be trouble again, I reckon. Not worth it.' She hesitated and then added, 'Are your brother and his mates going?'

'No idea. He hasn't mentioned it. Mum'll do her nut if he does. She nearly had a fit about him coming back from Clacton with that cut over his eye. He kept telling her he wasn't involved in any fighting, just got hit by a bottle someone chucked – but she was even more freaked out by the idea that someone could get hurt without even doing anything.'

'I don't s'pose he'll go, then. Not after getting hurt last time.'

'No.' I thought, suddenly, about Jimmy. I hoped Del and his friends *weren't* going to Brighton. I didn't want *him* getting hurt either!

I asked Del about it the next day when Mum was out.

'You're not going to Brighton, are you?'

He spun round, narrowing his eyes at me. 'Why? Why d'you want to know?'

'Only asking! Only thinking I didn't want you to get hurt again! Sorry for breathing!'

'No. I didn't mean to snap your head off. I just didn't realise you knew about it. *You're* not flippin' well going!'

'No, I know I'm not! Not that it's up to you whether I do or not!' I was irritated by his attitude. I was only trying to show some sisterly concern! 'Are any of your mates going?' I added as casually as possible.

'Probably not.' He shrugged. 'Probably be boring.'

'*Boring*?' I stared at him. Whatever else it was going to be like down there, I doubted whether *boring* would describe it.

'Well, you know. Not worth the aggro.'

'Right, OK. Well, I hope you *don't* go, Del. Or any of your mates.'

'All right, Mother Hen,' he said, lightly. 'If you say so.'

On Saturday, Jimmy turned up to borrow a record from Del.

'Hi, Cath,' he said, peeking round the sitting-room door. 'How're you?'

'Fine, thanks,' I said feeling my cheeks turning pink as soon as I looked at him. He was wearing jeans as usual, and a plain white T-shirt that showed off his tan and his muscles. He worked at Tilbury Docks and I could just imagine him hauling heavy crates and things around.

'What are you up to?' he asked.

'Oh, the usual.' I held up my history text book. 'Revision for boring exams.'

'Never mind,' he said, giving me a lovely smile. 'It'll be worth it if you pass all your exams and get a dead good job. I wish I'd tried harder at school. Have a nice weekend.'

'You too. What are *you* up to over the bank holiday?' I added quickly.

'Nothing much. Better spend a bit of time with my mum and dad before they forget what I look like,' he joked.

I breathed a sigh of relief. Surely he'd have said, if he was intending to go to Brighton, wouldn't he? I went back to revising the causes of the First World War.

Bank Holiday Monday was warm, and I took my books out into the garden again, spreading an old blanket on the grass and listening to Radio Caroline on my tranny at the same time as revising French verbs. Mum joined me in the afternoon, putting a deckchair up and taking off her stockings.

'This is nice,' she said contentedly, turning her face up to the sun. It was nice to see her relaxing for a change. 'I'll just sit for ten minutes and then I'll make a cup of tea.'

'No, Mum. Sit for the whole afternoon! Have a break, for once – you never stop! I'll make the tea.'

I jumped up and went into the kitchen to turn on the new electric kettle. As I waited for it to boil, I looked around at all the other new things we'd acquired in the past few months – an electric toaster, a complete new set of crockery and, most amazingly of all because it must have been so expensive, one of the new twin-tub washing machines. *That* had certainly made Mum's life easier – and mine, because I didn't have to turn the handle of the mangle now, if I was at home on washing days. But how *was* Mum paying for all this? Perhaps now she was in a relaxed mood, I might persuade her to talk to me about it. I warmed the teapot, and while I was waiting for the tea to brew I turned on the radio. Mum kept it tuned to the Home Service, and at three o'clock there was a news update. I poured milk into the cups, only half-listening, but suddenly stopped, almost spilling the milk as I lunged at the radio to turn the volume up. More fighting between mods and rockers – this time at several seaside resorts, including Hastings, Margate, Bournemouth ... and Brighton. More clashes with police, more arrests, more injuries. *Please God, don't let Del or Jimmy be there!*

I poured out the tea and turned the radio off before going back out to the garden. I couldn't concentrate on revision for the rest of the afternoon, and completely forgot about discussing Mum's spending.

The next day

I woke up late, and went downstairs in my dressing-gown. There was a note from Mum – she'd already gone out, shopping or wherever it was she kept going these days. I put bread in the toaster, turned on the kettle and sat down, yawning.

We'd had a late night. Derek had come in at half past ten, bringing a girlfriend with him. This, in itself, was unusual – Del had his share of girlfriends, but I could rarely, if ever, remember him bringing one home, especially at this time of night. Mum, who had by now seen extensive footage on the TV about the latest seaside riots, was in no frame of mind to be introduced to Pauline – an attractive brunette wearing a short skirt, leather jacket and too much make-up who was at least two inches taller than Derek. Mum had spent most of the evening telling me exactly what she thought of *so-called mods and rockers with nothing better to do than cause trouble and blight the lives of innocent families trying to enjoy their days out* – and how she rued the day National Service had been abolished and she, personally, could have told the government this would be the result.

'I was just off to bed – and so was Cathy,' she said, looking pointedly at the clock on the mantelpiece.

'Sorry, Mum. We've been out all day – haven't we, Pauline.'

'Yeah,' Pauline agreed, looking bored.

'Not at one of those *riots*, I hope!' Mum put in at once.

'Nah. Not after last time. Stayed away, didn't we, Pauline.' Pauline duly nodded. 'Been round Jimmy's house – he had a few mates round there.'

I had to stop myself from gasping out loud with relief. Jimmy wasn't at the coast.

'So why haven't you taken Pauline straight home? Not that it isn't very nice to meet you, Pauline,' Mum said, 'But I'm sure your mother will be wondering where you are.'

'Don't live with me mum anymore. Share a flat with me mate.'

I looked at her with a new respect. How fab it would be to *share a flat with a mate*. I wondered whether I'd ever be old enough for

Mum to allow such a thing. Probably not till I was ancient, at least twenty!

Mum pursed her lips with disapproval.

'I am taking Pauline home,' Derek said quickly. 'We're en route. Just popped in for ... you know, call of nature. Won't be a minute, Pauline.'

He bounded upstairs to the bathroom.

'I hope he's not been drinking beer,' Mum commented to Pauline. 'Riding around on that machine.' Derek had his own bike now – his pride and joy – and she was deeply unhappy about it. 'God knows it's dangerous enough without that, and I suppose you are aware that there's a law now against driving under the influence?'

'Yes, Mrs Ferguson, I do know that, and so does Derek,' Pauline said, still looking bored. 'He hasn't had any booze, but he has drunk a lot of Coca-Cola, so I s'pose that's had an effect on his bladder.'

Derek was coming back downstairs now, looking as surprised by the mention of his bladder as Mum was looking disgusted.

'Right – we'll be off again now, then,' he said cheerfully. 'Don't wait up, Mum. Won't be long, just got to drop Pauline back to Goodmayes and I'll be ...'

'Goodmayes!' Mum exclaimed as if it was the other side of the world instead of just the other side of Romford. 'At this time of night!'

'Doesn't take long on the bike!' Derek said with a grin as he led Pauline to the front door. 'See you later, Mum. See you later, Cath.'

'Nice to meet you, Pauline,' Mum said again, begrudgingly. 'But not at this unearthly hour,' she added under her breath as they went.

I went upstairs and got ready for bed, but lay awake for an hour, listening for his bike to come back. I didn't know why. It all just felt a bit strange.

When I'd finished breakfast I called Janice.

'Really glad you didn't go to Brighton. Did you see it on the TV?'

'Yeah.' Janice sounded sombre. 'Did you hear about the guy who got knifed?'

'*Knifed*?' I shuddered. 'No. That wasn't on the news.'

'It's only been reported this morning.'

'Oh my gawd – that's horrible. Did they say how bad he is?'

'No. Only that he's in hospital.'

'I'm so glad you didn't go,' I repeated. 'Or Del.' *Or Jimmy* I added mentally.

'Yeah. Sounds like it was really bad down there.' She sighed. 'It was good to see my Nan and Granddad anyway. What did you get up to?'

'Nothing much. Revision. And – Del brought a girlfriend round! Really late – they'd been out all day apparently, but Mum wasn't amused.'

'What's her name?'

'Pauline. She seemed all right – but he never stays with a girl for long anyway.'

'She's a rocker, I suppose?'

'I guess so.' I felt a brief flicker of irritation at her obsessive categorising of everyone she met. 'Does it really matter?'

'Of course it does! Can you imagine what his mates would say, if he went out with a mod?'

'Not really, no.' I changed the subject. 'What you doing today, anyway?'

'Got two interviews up in London. Got to go in a minute to get my train.' Janice had had lots of replies to her job applications and had booked all the interviews for the Whitsun holiday. 'The one this afternoon's the job I really want. It's with a firm of solicitors in the West End – wouldn't it be fab to work up there! You could come and meet me for lunch in your holidays,' she added. 'And we could go shopping in Carnaby Street.'

'Yeah.' I tried to sound enthusiastic. Where did Janice think I was going to get the money for Carnaby Street fashions? 'Well, good luck, then.'

Working in the West End, shopping in Carnaby Street – it all sounded completely unreal compared with the task of revising for mock O-levels.

I was helping Mum get dinner ready, late that afternoon, when Janice knocked on the front door.

'Come in. How did the interviews go?' I asked, but Janice waved this aside.

'Can we go upstairs?' she whispered. She looked shaken.

'OK. Won't be a minute, Mum!' I called, leading the way up to my room.

'Close the door,' Janice said, sitting down in a slump on the bed.

'What's going on? What's the matter?' I closed the door and came back to sit next to her.

'It's Ian.'

'What is? For Pete's sake Janice – just tell me. What's he done?'

'It's not what *he's* done – it's what someone's done to him. It's him that got knifed, at Brighton. He's in hospital, in a serious condition.'

I felt my mouth drop open with shock.

'*Flipping* heck,' I whispered. 'How did you find out? I haven't heard it on the radio or anything.'

'I called in at the Zodiac on my way home from the station. Everyone in there's talking about it. He's ...' She swallowed and blinked quickly. 'He's really popular with all the boys.'

I looked at Janice quickly. 'You *said* he needed to be taught a lesson! But ...'

'Yeah, I did – but not like this!' Janice shook her head. There were tears of fright in her eyes. 'What if he dies, Cathy! I mean, blimey – I know I said a lot of stuff about him, especially after you told me what he did to you. But even so!'

'Who ... ? Do the police know who did it? Have they got anyone?'

'No. He'd got separated from the mates he was with. They reckon there was a big fight going on, and the cops charged in to break it up, so everyone scarpered. And ... there was Ian, lying on the ground. The cops tried to chase after people but obviously all the rockers had gone off on bikes – doing the ton straight out of town, I bet. Ian's mates went to the police station to try and help but basically, nobody saw what happened. There were too many people involved.'

'Bloomin' hell.' I put my arms round Janice. 'Come on – I'm sure he won't *die*.'

'I know I said I hated him!' Janice was crying now. 'I know I said he ought to be taught a lesson, but I didn't want *this*!'

'Of course you didn't. Nobody would think you did.'

'Yes, they would!' She looked at me in anguish. 'They already do! Half the people in the coffee-bar were giving me filthy looks and saying stuff about how I chucked him.'

'Yeah, well. Chucking him was one thing, knifing him's another!'

'I know. But it's like ... now he's in hospital, hurt, he's suddenly everyone's hero and I'm the wicked witch!' She sniffed and started crying again. 'It wasn't *me* that knifed him! It was the bloody rockers!'

'Exactly. Everyone must realise he was just in the wrong place at the wrong time.' I sat there, hugging Janice until she'd calmed down a bit, not knowing what else to say.

'*Catherine!* Your dinner's ready!' Mum called up the stairs in a disapproving voice. She didn't like people turning up at dinnertime, especially when I was supposed to have been helping.

'I'd better go,' Janice said, fumbling for her hankie and blowing her nose.

'Will you tell me if you hear anything else?'

'Course I will. A couple of the boys are going to the hospital down in Brighton tonight to see if they can see him.' She got to her feet and I opened the bedroom door. 'I'll call you as soon as I know anything,' she whispered as we went downstairs.

'What's up?' Mum asked suspiciously as we sat down to dinner. 'You look like you've lost a pound and found a penny.'

'Nothing.' I couldn't face eating. I'd never known anyone who'd got seriously hurt before. I'd spent a lot of time hating Ian – probably more than Janice had – but the thought of him lying on the ground with knife wounds was almost impossible to take in. 'Just feel a bit sick.'

'Had an argument with your fine friend?' Mum said sarcastically.

'No. Leave it, Mum – I'm all right. Just not hungry.' I pushed my plate away and sat with my head resting on my arms. 'I'll wash up when you've finished.'

'By the way,' Mum went on conversationally, as she put a forkful of cabbage up to her lips, 'I heard on the news that one of those so-called mods got stabbed in the fighting down at Brighton yesterday. He's in hospital, in a bad way, they said. *Now* do you see why I'm not letting you ...'

'All right, Mum, all *right!*' I jumped up and ran straight back upstairs without even asking to be excused from the table. Mum didn't say a word.

I was waiting for Derek when he got home from work.

'Have you heard?' I demanded before he'd even taken his jacket off.

'Heard what? Calm down – what's the matter?'

'Ian – you know, Ian Vincent, that Janice used to go out with? He got stabbed in the fighting at Brighton. He's in hospital, Del!'

'Blimey!' He stood stock still, staring at me. '*Stabbed?*'

'Yes. Knifed. He's in Intensive Care, apparently.'

'*Stabbed?*' Derek repeated again.

'Yes, Derek – stabbed. The police found him after the fight broke up. Nobody saw who did it. Isn't it awful? I mean, I know I didn't like him, but ...'

'Flippin' hell.' Derek sat down on the stairs. He shook his head and repeated yet again, '*Stabbed* – I can't believe that.'

'It must have been really bad, down there. I'm so glad you didn't go, or ... any of your mates.'

'Yeah.' He looked shell-shocked. 'Yeah, so am I.' He glanced at the kitchen door and added, 'Mum at work?'

'Yes. Your dinner's on the stove, if you can face eating. I couldn't, after Janice came round and told me about it. She says everyone at the Zodiac thinks she's a bitch now because she chucked him.'

'That's got nothing to do with it!' He sighed. 'I suppose all the mods will assume he got stabbed by a rocker, and there'll be more trouble. I'm fed up with it all, to be honest. It was never meant to be like this – bleedin' warfare, for flip's sake.'

'I know. And the papers are full of it, aren't they – they just love it, making out every teenager in the country is some kind of yob.'

Derek got up and headed for the kitchen.

'Try not to worry,' he said quietly, giving me a fleeting smile. 'Nothing to do with you, is it.'

I knew it wasn't. But somehow it felt like it was.

The next day Jimmy turned up at the house before Derek had arrived home.

'Come in, if you want to wait for him,' I said, shyly. Mum was out yet again, and I was conscious that it was the first time I'd ever been on my own with Jimmy.

'I heard about that bloke – your friend's ex,' he said as we went into the sitting-room. 'Do you know how he is?'

We sat down opposite each other and I sighed.

'I don't think it looks very good. Janice phoned this morning and said the boys from the Zodiac who went down to Brighton to see him, got turned away. Nobody's allowed to see him apart from his family. His condition's too serious.'

'Poor bloke.' Jimmy whistled and shook his head. 'It's ridiculous, isn't it. I mean – this is supposed to be about the sort of music you like and what clothes you wear, and all that. Not about killing each other.'

'I know. I don't understand why they need to fight at all. Just because someone's wearing a parka instead of a leather, or whatever.'

Jimmy nodded. 'It's a free country, isn't it.' He paused, and then gave me a very deliberate look – a look that made my stomach feel fluttery, the way it did when I was going in for an exam. 'I don't care whether someone's a mod or a rocker. If I like them, I like them.'

'Me too,' I said. My voice came out a bit hoarse. I stared back at him. He was so gorgeous – I felt like I could've sat there looking into his eyes forever. Did he really mean what I thought he might mean? Was there a chance that he might actually ... *like* me? Finally I blinked and looked away, remembering:

'But most of my friends don't think like that. Some of them wouldn't even *talk* to a rocker.'

He smiled and shrugged. 'What would they say if you got asked out by a rocker, then?'

'They'd expect me to say no,' I said, my heart suddenly pounding.

'And would you?' He persisted gently, still smiling at me. 'Would you say no?'

There was a moment of silence. I felt almost giddy with hope.

'If it was someone I liked,' I said very quietly, 'then I'd say yes. Whatever my friends thought about it.'

Jimmy got to his feet, holding out his hands to me – looking, I thought afterwards, like he was about to ask me to dance. But just at that moment there was a knock on the door. He looked at me regretfully and sat back down while I went to answer it.

'Hello,' said Janice, stepping into the hall. She looked round the sitting-room door, and her face immediately changed. 'What's *he* doing here?'

'Jimmy's waiting for Derek!' I replied indignantly. 'What's the matter?'

'What's the matter? I'll tell you what – he's a flipping rocker, and as far as I'm concerned, from now on we don't talk to any of them, we don't go anywhere near them, we don't even *look* at them if we can help it. I don't care if Del's your brother – not *any* of them? All right?'

'What ... what's happened?' I said, seeing the tears in Janice's eyes. Behind her, Jimmy was muttering that he'd better go and wait outside for Del. 'No – don't go, Jimmy! You shouldn't have to ...'

'Yes, he should!' Janice spat at him. 'Although he might as well hear this first: Ian's in a coma. He lost so much blood, they think it's damaged his brain. He's in a coma, and he'll probably never come out of it. Satisfied now, *rocker*?'

'For Pete's sake, Jan – it was nothing to do with Jimmy! Or Del!' I said, feeling close to tears myself. 'Look, I'm sorry about Ian, but you didn't even *like* him anymore, and ...'

'He's a *mod*,' she said. 'And *rockers* have done this to him. Isn't that enough for you?'

'I'll go and wait outside,' Jimmy said again. His eyes met mine as he opened the front door. 'She's upset,' he said quietly. 'It's understandable.'

'Of course I'm bloody upset!' Janice raged as he walked out. 'It's nothing to do with what *I* thought of Ian, is it: he's as good as *dead* because some rocker decided to stick a knife in him!'

I put my arms round Janice, led her into the kitchen, and turned the kettle on.

'I know. It's awful.' I hesitated, and then decided to come out with what had been going through my mind: 'And you probably feel worse because you said all that stuff – you know, about him being a pig, and needing to be taught a lesson. But you shouldn't feel guilty.'

'*Guilty*? I *don't* feel guilty! Why should *I* feel guilty? It was the bloody rockers, not me!'

'I know. Sorry. Look, I only meant ...'

'Forget it!' Janice shouted. She turned and marched back out to the hall. I was following, trying frantically to appease her. 'Don't bother! Don't even try to understand, Cathy – you're obviously just too immature!'

She slammed the door behind her.

February 2004

I'm at my computer, working on the 1960s story, when Linda calls me. She's the only person from my schooldays I'm still in touch with. She lives in Berkshire now so we don't get together too often, but I've e-mailed her to tell her about the commission for *Xtra*.

'How's it going?' she asks me. 'Are you finding it difficult?'

'Not as difficult as I thought. So far.'

'So far? I thought you said it wouldn't take long?'

'Well, it might not. If I can't find out any more.'

She doesn't respond for a minute. Then: 'What are you up to, Cath?'

'I want to try and get to the bottom of it – what happened, back in sixty-four. Whether anyone actually knew who stabbed Ian Vincent.'

'But if they did, the police would have found out, wouldn't they,' she says. 'Don't you think?'

'I used to tell myself that. But you know, in the back of my mind I've always wondered.'

'You don't think it was just part of the whole thing – mods and rockers? Part of the violence that went on? That was what the police decided at the time.'

'I know. But – OK, I know there were loads of fights, a lot of aggression and punch-ups going on. But don't you think it was quite unusual, for those days, for someone to actually get *stabbed*, just as a random act of violence? I don't know; something about it always seemed odd, to me.'

'I'm surprised you bothered to think much about it. You hated the guy, didn't you. With good reason.'

'Yes. I did. But ...' I hesitate, unsure how to explain myself. 'Looking back now, I think the day Ian got stabbed, everything changed.'

'Everything got worse. More serious.'

'Exactly. And it *affected* me. Me and Jimmy. It was the catalyst for everything else that happened back then, really.'

'So what are you going to do? How can you try to find anything out now, after all this time?'

'I'm not sure. I ... think, for now, I'll just crack on and finish the story, and then I'll start trying to contact people. People from back then – see if I can trace anyone who might be able to help me get some answers.'

'And this is just for the story? For the magazine?' she asks gently.

'Kind of. Partly, yes, of course.'

'And partly for you.'

'A little late in the day, but yes, now I've started going back down memory lane, I want to find out more, if I can. Or at least satisfy myself that there's nothing *to* find out.'

'Well, let me know if I can help at all.'

'Sure.'

'Although – well, I wasn't particularly involved in the mods and rockers thing, was I.'

'No. But you knew everyone who was. If you think of anything ...'

'I'll try and dredge out the old memories. God, Cathy, it was so long ago! Is it making you feel nostalgic, going back over it all now?'

'Yes. And a bit sad.' I sigh. 'So much has happened since then.'

'Of course it has,' she says, laughing. 'Forty years! We'd be sad old gits if nothing had happened to us over the course of forty years!' Then she stops laughing and adds quietly, 'Ring me again, OK? Ring me if you want to ask anything.'

'I will. Thanks, love.'

'And don't let it all ... upset you, Cathy. Not all over again.'

'No. I'll try not to.' The first time round was bad enough.

July 1964

On the last day of term – the last day of being a fourth-year – the atmosphere in the class was rowdy with excitement. Formal lessons had been abandoned by the teachers in favour of games and quizzes. Annual reports had been handed out in their unfriendly brown envelopes addressed to parents, which some of my classmates had daringly opened in their impatient need to see how badly they'd been rated – and were now regretting it and trying to stick the flap of the envelope back down in a way that made it look un-tampered with.

During the whole of the half term following Whitsun, the only thing everyone was talking about was the mods and rockers situation. One of the most popular girls, Frances, who was captain of the netball team and the swimming squad, turned out also to be a distant cousin of Ian's, and everyone had rallied round her with fierce and indignant sympathy. The level of anger against rockers – all rockers everywhere – was such that even those quieter girls who'd previously had no interest or inclination one way or the other, suddenly became avowed supporters of the mods. *Mods for Ever, Rockers Never!* was inscribed on everyone's pencil-cases and rulers, alongside the name of their favourite Beatle and (in the case of those more politically aware, and those pretending to be), the *Ban the Bomb* symbol. Everyone seemed to be simmering with pent-up aggression, stewing with resentment over the sad fate of a boy most of them had never even met, and might not have liked if they had.

Needless to say, I was finding it difficult to listen to the baying for rocker blood. What would they all say if they knew I'd fallen in love with a rocker? They seemed prepared to forgive me for my brother – even now, they could understand I could hardly help that – but I could only imagine the outcry if they knew I'd started seeing Jimmy secretly – that he'd been coming round when Mum was out, and pretending when Del got home that he'd only just turned up. It hadn't taken Del long to guess that he was being used as an excuse.

To my mortal embarrassment, he proceeded to give Jimmy dire warnings about what he'd do to him if he hurt me – and then followed this up with a speech, horribly reminiscent of a father of the bride, saying that if I had to go out with anyone, he was glad it was Jimmy because he knew he'd look after me.

What would my friends say if they knew Jimmy had kissed me – lots of times – on the sofa while I neglected my homework and forgot about getting the dinner ready and, (although I hadn't quite admitted this to myself yet, as it seemed quite shocking), I'd even started to forget my adoration of Paul McCartney. I was crazy about Jimmy, but I couldn't tell *any*one. I couldn't write his name on my pencil case or the cover of my Rough Book, or giggle about him with the other girls like they all did about their boyfriends. And we hadn't, actually, even been *out* together yet. Even in the unlikely event that Mum would agree to that, I didn't even want to imagine what would happen if anyone saw us together in public. And more particularly, I didn't want to imagine what *Janice* would say if she found out.

Janice, to be fair, had quickly apologised about calling me immature and walking out on me – and I'd accepted it, knowing how upset she'd been. But it had hurt, at the time, and added to the fact that I was finding it more and more difficult sitting with her on the bus, listening to the same anti-rocker tirade day after day that I'd already heard from the girls in my class, I was beginning to feel less sorry that she was leaving school and going to work in London. After all, I had Jimmy now.

The only other girl in the class who kept right out of the anti-rocker frenzy was Linda, and I found myself being drawn back into her company purely to avoid having to join in with the others.

'I couldn't care less about it,' she told me one day with her usual shrug. 'I mean – I'm sorry for the boy who got stabbed. But I just don't see the point of it – being a mod or a rocker.'

Before, I would have dismissed her as a square, but now I was realising something about Linda. Ever since about the second year, when most of the girls started getting interested in pop music and clothes, she'd refused to follow any fashion or craze that she didn't see the point of. She liked some groups, she didn't like others. She liked some of their records and not others. She liked certain fashions, but she didn't pretend to like anything just to be one of the in-crowd. I'd ignored her for much of this time, wanting to be in with everyone else, but now I was starting to admire Linda's honesty. I'd been wrong about her: she wasn't a square. She was actually more mature than all the rest of us put together.

With the goodbye shouts echoing on the warm summer air that final afternoon of term, I found myself walking out of school with Linda. Although we lived within a mile or so of each other, we never saw each other outside of school these days. It was my fault, of course – I'd neglected her, and now I was regretting it.

'Can I sit with you today?' I asked her as we waited at the bus-stop.

'Your friend Janice not around?'

'No. She's left school today. The leavers had a special assembly this morning and finished at lunchtime. I think the teachers always want them out of the way early in case they chuck ink around or anything.'

'You don't seem to be quite so friendly with her now.' It was a statement, made without any particular emphasis.

'No – we are still friends,' I said quickly. 'But it's just ... a bit difficult, at the moment.' I hesitated, and then decided suddenly that, if I was ever going to confide in anyone, Linda was the perfect choice. I leant closer to her and whispered, 'Can you keep a secret?'

'Of course I can.'

'Well, I've got a boyfriend.' Saying it aloud, even in a whisper, felt unbelievably thrilling. 'And he's a rocker.'

'So what?' said Linda. 'I mean, sorry, I'm glad you've got a boyfriend. But so what if he's a rocker?'

'Well – you know. Most of the girls would go berserk. And as for Janice – well, she's so livid and upset about Ian ...'

'She doesn't even know who stabbed him. It might not even have been a rocker,' Linda said – so calmly that I wanted to laugh. Everything must be so simple to people like Linda, I thought. It was, after all, quite reasonable to say that nobody knew who stabbed Ian. But nobody else was being reasonable about it. Apart from Jimmy, of course.

'No, but let's face it, it was bound to be a rocker.'

Linda sighed. 'Cathy, Janice is just using Ian as an excuse for stirring things up – and so are all the nitwits in our class – none of *them* even know him, apart from Frances. It's just a pathetic tribal thing – he was a mod, so everyone else who calls themselves a mod has to pretend to care, and pretend to hate all rockers. You know that's how Hitler came to power – getting everyone to follow like sheep without thinking things through for themselves. Getting them to think they hated all Jews. Sometimes it seems like our generation haven't learnt anything!'

I sat in silence, taking this in for a moment. I had to admit, I was impressed.

'You're dead right,' I said eventually. 'But that doesn't make it any easier for me and Jimmy, does it.' I felt a little shiver, saying his name. *Jimmy*. Finally, I was telling someone about him. It felt nice.

'No.' Linda smiled at me. 'I can imagine. Maybe you'll have to keep it quiet until all the fuss dies down. If you're still together – then people might start to respect you for it.'

'I can't imagine that. But I hope you're right.' The bus was pulling into the stop, and we stood back to let a crowd of overexcited first-years get on first. 'Thanks, Lin. You will keep it secret, won't you,' I whispered.

'Course I will. I keep enough secrets of my own,' Linda said calmly as we got on the bus. But she wouldn't say any more on the subject, no matter how much I prodded on the way home.

Mum was in a chatty mood that evening. She'd been pleased with my report – which luckily from my point of view had been written before I'd started spending more time kissing Jimmy on the sofa than doing my homework. I'd passed all my mock O-levels and apparently I was expected to get good grades in the exams next year as long as I kept working hard. I'd always known I wasn't one of the cleverest girls in the class; I'd kept my head above water because I put in plenty of effort. Although I complained, like everyone, that it was boring, I didn't actually mind the slow drudgery of exam revision. Learning things off by heart – dates in history, quotations from Shakespeare, scientific and mathematical formulae – was easy enough as long as you slogged away at it. But now it was over, the thought of doing it all again next summer, and then going on to the sixth form and spending two years working for the much harder A-levels, was so appalling that I was trying to push it firmly out of my mind. Mum wasn't working that night, though, and she seemed determined to have a discussion about my future.

'You'll need to be thinking about your A-levels. What subjects you're going to choose,' she said cheerfully as we were washing up the dinner things.

'No, Mum! Not yet!'

'You've done well in history,' she went on regardless, nodding at the report still lying on its envelope on the table. 'Perhaps you should think about a degree in that.'

'Mum! I'm not even sure I want to go on to university! Give me a chance – I'm not even in the fifth year yet!'

'It doesn't hurt to make plans, Cathy. Give some thought to what you intend to do with your life. You don't want to end up like me.'

'What's that supposed to mean?' I protested. 'It's not like you've had a miserable life, is it?'

Mum put down the dishcloth and looked at me carefully.

'I left school at fourteen,' she said. 'With no exams, nothing.'

'I know. I know that. You had to go out to work, to help your family.'

'I had to work in a factory – it was the only job I could do; either that or go into service as a housemaid, a skivvy. It was the thirties – the great depression. Lots of men were out of work and their families starving. We were surviving, but only just.'

'I know, Mum,' I said again, gently. I'd heard the story many times, and I understood why Mum's experience had made her determined to make sure we got a good education. 'But things are different now. There are plenty of jobs around – good jobs. I could do the typing course, in the sixth form, and get a good secretarial job in London. That's what Janice is doing, and she hasn't even taken A-levels. She's going to be working in a solicitor's office and earning ten guineas a week!'

'Is she, now. As some kind of junior typist, I suppose.'

'Yes, but they'll train her up, and she thinks eventually she'll be a secretary to one of the solicitors.'

'If she doesn't get herself pregnant and have to get married before then,' Mum said dismissively, turning back to the washing-up.

'Janice doesn't sleep around, if that's what you're implying. She's not a slut.'

For a minute, while she emptied the washing-up bowl and wiped it out, rinsing away the suds, Mum didn't respond. Finally she turned to face me while she dried her hands.

'I'm not saying she sleeps around. I'm just trying to warn you – don't rush into anything. Once you go out to work, you'll never get another chance to get a better education. You'll meet someone, and before you know it, you'll be married with babies and you'll look back and wonder what happened. You'll be trapped, and you'll always wish you'd made something more of yourself.'

'Is that what you thought,' I asked her quietly, 'when you got married to Dad?'

'Not at first.' She sat down heavily at the kitchen table, shaking her head. 'No, at first it was exciting, of course. Like all the young girls back then in the wartime, I thought being courted by an American GI was the most romantic thing in the world. Getting nylon stockings and chocolate ...' She laughed ruefully. 'But I got more than I bargained for, didn't I. I hadn't planned on falling for a baby just as the war was ending. We'd all been fighting for freedom, but that wasn't what I ended up with!'

'At least he married you, though, didn't he. When he knew you were expecting Derek.'

'Yes, he did. And then buggered off five years later.' She sighed again and stared into the distance, as if she was reliving those dark days, struggling on her own with a four-year-old and a baby. I'd never known my father, and I wasn't sorry. Mum had no idea where he'd gone, and never heard a word from him. He obviously didn't even care enough about either me or Derek to keep in touch, all these years, with so much as a birthday card or letter. I knew it must hurt Del more than me – he had memories of Dad, although he never talked about him.

'You've done all right, though, Mum,' I said. Although I never said it, I was proud of her. 'You've made a good home for us all, and worked hard, and ...'

'I want more than that for you, Cathy,' she replied brusquely. 'More than working hard to keep a home together. Get a good education. That's all I'm saying. And stay away from the boys!'

I nodded briefly and turned back to the wiping-up. I wasn't ready to enter into *that* field of conversation with her!

August 1964

'Do you want to see *A Hard Day's Night*?' Jimmy asked. The Beatles' film was on general release now and coming to the cinema in Romford that week.

'Course I do!' I laughed.

'I meant, do you want to see it with me. Together.'

I looked at him in surprise. 'With you? But – I didn't think you liked the Beatles!'

'Yeah, I do. I'm just not madly in love with them, like you are,' he teased me, smiling.

'I'm not madly in love with them anymore!' I didn't quite dare tell him why – that these days, it was only Jimmy himself I was madly in love with. 'I do still want to see the film – but I don't see how we can go together.'

'Cathy.' He touched my face gently. We were sprawled on the sofa together, his arm around me, my head resting on his shoulder. I felt like I never wanted to be anywhere else. 'I've had enough of keeping this a secret. Why shouldn't we go out together?'

'You know why. We've both got friends who would never speak to us again if they knew about us.'

'Then they're not really friends, are they?'

I considered this for a minute. 'I s'pose you're right. But ...'. I sat up and looked at him, pushing my hair off my face. 'Since Ian got stabbed, it's so much more serious, Jimmy. I'm frightened you might get attacked, just for being seen out with me. Aren't you?'

'Frightened? No. I can look after myself. And I can look after you, too,' he added, pulling me closer. 'It doesn't make me feel much like a man, Cathy – hiding away indoors like this, like a big baby.'

'I just don't want any trouble, that's all. I don't care about mods and rockers anymore. It's got beyond a joke now – all that fighting all over again!' There'd been more trouble at some of the seaside towns over the bank holiday at the beginning of August, just like at Whitsun and Easter. 'You'd think everyone would have stopped all that, after what happened to Ian. My friend Linda says our generation should have learnt something from what happened with Hitler.'

'Your friend Linda's dead right,' Jimmy said, smiling again. 'And so are you. I'm not like that either – just cos I ride a bike and wear a leather jacket doesn't make me a thug.'

'Of course you're not!' I couldn't think of anyone less like a thug than Jimmy. He might have been big and strong but he was the sweetest, most gentle person I knew.

'And it doesn't make me hate mods, either. But I don't want to be skulking around, scared to be seen out with you. Come on – say you'll come to the flicks with me. Please?' He pulled me close again. 'We can snog in the back row,' he whispered.

I giggled. 'If I do come, it'll be to watch the film, Jimmy Kent! We can snog any time!'

'I'm glad you said that,' he muttered, tickling my ear gently until I couldn't bear it anymore and fell on top of him for another kissing session.

But I still hadn't said yes to his invitation. And I still didn't know whether I would.

It wasn't just because of the mods and rockers situation, either. I knew that if we started going out properly, I'd have to tell Mum about him. And Mum had made it pretty clear, on numerous occasions, that she thought fifteen was far too young to start going out with boys. As it was, she'd have had a fit if she found out what Jimmy and I got up to on the sofa whenever she went out. When he first started coming round, the secrecy was all part of the thrill; but the longer it went on, the greater the chance of Mum finding out.

'Tell her, then,' Jimmy said when I talked to him about it. He looked at me with his head on one side. 'D'you want me to talk to her? Promise to look after you, bring you home on time and behave like a gentleman? All that stuff?'

'No!' I shuddered. I couldn't even begin to imagine Mum's reaction to such a conversation.

'But you will tell her, won't you? I'd rather she knew, to be honest, Cath. So it's all above-board. It's not like we're doing anything wrong.' He grinned at her. 'Not *that* wrong, anyway.'

I shivered with excitement. We hadn't gone much further than kissing. I wanted to, but Jimmy said it wasn't going to happen because I was under-age and he cared too much about me to risk getting me into trouble.

'I've told *my* parents about *you*,' he added unexpectedly.

'Have you? What did you tell them?'

'That you're Del's sister, and you're a couple of years younger than me. And ... that you're kind of special,' he added, smiling a bit shyly.

'Oh.' I felt myself glow with pleasure. 'And what did they say?'

'That I should be careful and not get you up the duff!' he laughed. 'Honestly – parents, eh! One track minds!'

'Yeah.' I laughed too. 'Trouble is, that's what happened to my mum. She got pregnant with Del and my dad had to marry her – and then he walked out on her after I was born.'

'Oh. Del never said. I s'pose I just assumed your dad was dead.'

'I know – that's what most people think, so I just let them. He might as well be.' I shrugged. 'But you see? That's why my mum's got such a bee in her bonnet about me not having a boyfriend.'

'Well, that's why she needs to see I'm not just someone who's going to take advantage of you. That's why you need to tell her about me, Cath, before she finds out, and wants to know why we've kept it secret.'

'Mm. Maybe. But I'll have to find the right time.'

And somehow, of course, that time never seemed to come.

It was turning out to be a strange summer holiday. I was spending a lot more time than usual with Linda during the day, when Jimmy was at work – or on my own, just mooching about the house waiting for the evening when he'd be coming round. During the previous summer, I'd spent most of my time with Janice, but now she was working in the West End, and as I'd expected, she hadn't had a lot of time for me. In a way, it was a relief, because the fear of Janice turning up unexpectedly and finding me with Jimmy was even more scary than the thought of Mum finding out.

Coincidentally, the very next day after Jimmy asked me about going to see the Beatles' film, I had a call from Janice about the same thing. It was the first time I'd heard from her for ages. I'd tried calling her several times but she never seemed to be in.

'How ya doing, Cath?' she said now, as if we'd been in touch regularly every single day.

'Not bad. You?'

'Yeah, good, thanks. The job's going all right.'

'Good.'

There was a silence.

'Sorry I haven't called before.'

'Well, I suppose you're too busy to talk to me now, what with commuting to London and everything.'

'Yeah, but like I said, I'm sorry.' She paused. 'Sorry I've been a scabby cow and a lousy friend.'

I couldn't help laughing. Despite everything, I did miss her.

'Well, maybe I was expecting too much,' I conceded.

'No. My fault. Like you say, just been really busy. Anyway, what've you been doing with yourself in your hols?'

'Been going out with Linda.'

'Ooh. Prim Lin? You watch yourself!'

'What's that supposed to mean?'

'Nothing.' Silence again, then: 'Where you been going, then?'

'Nowhere much. We hang around the shops, go to the Zodiac ...'

'Linda, in the Zodiac? I can't imagine that.'

'Look, don't be like that – she's all right, as it happens. At least she's *loyal*.'

'Ouch.' Janice laughed lightly, and then added: 'Fair enough. Well, look – I'd better go. I'm calling from a phone box, in Oxford Street. In my lunch hour.'

'Right.' I refused to sound impressed.

'But I just wondered if you want to come out with me on Friday night? Make up for lost time?'

'OK, groovy.' Even as I spoke, I found myself wondering whether Janice had just split up with another boyfriend and found herself with no-one to go out with. But I didn't want to spoil the moment. 'So where d'you want to go? The Zodiac?'

'No – I thought I might treat you to the flicks. *A Hard Day's Night*'s gonna be on. I knew you'd be gagging to see it.'

'Oh. Oh, right.'

'Well, don't sound too flippin' excited, will you. I'm paying – I'm a working girl now, you know. Look, my money's running out. I'll see you at the bus-stop at seven on Friday. OK?'

The line went dead, and I stood for a minute, staring at the phone. Bother. Friday was the same evening that Jimmy wanted me to go to the flicks with *him*. And I hadn't given him my answer yet. Or spoken to Mum about him. What now?

'It's not that I'd rather go out with Janice,' I told Jimmy when we were together that evening. 'You know that.'

'Do I?' He sounded uncharacteristically moody about it.

'Jimmy, I'd rather be with you than anyone else in the world. Honestly.'

'As long as you can keep me hidden away from everyone. Like some dirty little secret?' He gave me a smile that didn't quite reach his eyes.

'Oh – please don't be like that!' I really didn't want him to be upset with me. 'Of course not – I *do* want to go out with you, but Friday is too soon – I still haven't had a chance to talk to my mum.'

'Will you ever have the chance? Or are you going to keep putting it off until we both get fed up with sitting on your sofa every night, and break up?'

'*Don't* say that! I don't ever want to break up with you, Jimmy! I couldn't bear it if you wanted to ... you don't want to break up, do you?'

'No, of course I don't.' He softened immediately, taking hold me tightly and kissing the top of my head. 'I'm sorry, baby. I'm just being grumpy because I was looking forward to taking you out. But of course, I understand you want to go with your friend. You haven't seen her for ages, have you.'

He was so sweet to me, so understanding and kind – at that moment I thought I must be the luckiest girl in the world. But he'd frightened me half to death with his talk about breaking up. I was suddenly aware that things definitely had to change, and quickly. He was seventeen, two years older than me, and I couldn't expect him to go on being happy with just sitting on my sofa every evening. He was going to get bored, and whatever he said now, in time he might really finish with me. Being seen together worried me much more than it seemed to bother him – but if I didn't want to lose him, I was going to have to face it. Compared with that, telling Mum about it didn't seem quite so scary. I'd get that over with first!

I picked my time carefully – when Derek was there to back me up, and when Mum was in a good mood, having come back from one of her shopping expeditions with a bag of new clothes.

'Mum, I've got a friend coming round later, for a little while,' I said. My voice shook slightly on the word *friend*.

'Who – Janice? All right. As long as it's not for too long, and you've done all your homework first.'

It was ironic. At one time, Mum didn't have a good word to say about Janice – but now she was hardly ever around, she seemed to be prepared to tolerate her.

'No – not Janice. It's ... a boy,' I said quietly. I watched her wheel round in surprise. 'We're just friends!' I added quickly, but I felt myself blush at the lie.

'Who? What boy?' she asked sharply. 'Do I know him?'

'Yes.' I glanced at Derek for support. 'Del's mate, Jimmy Kent. You've met him.'

'I see.' Mum looked from me to Derek and back again. Del was nodding.

'You know Jim. He's a nice bloke, Mum.'

'And what does he want to be friends with *you* for?' she demanded, fixing me with a glare. 'As if I didn't know?'

'We just get on well together. We chat sometimes, you know, when he comes round to see Del. We're going to listen to records together. That's all.'

'I see,' she said again. 'Listen to records, and have a fumble on the sofa, I suppose.'

'No, Mum, it's not ...'

'And how long has this been going on?' she carried on, ignoring my protests. 'How long has he been coming round for little chats and to *listen to records*, while I've been at work?'

I looked at Derek desperately. This wasn't going the way I'd hoped.

'Cath's doing the right thing, telling you about Jimmy,' Derek said calmly, 'She could've just carried on seeing him behind your back.'

Mum continued to stare at me as if she'd never seen me before.

'So *Jimmy* wants my permission, does he, to mess around with my under-age daughter? Is he too frightened to talk to me himself?'

'He's not *messing around* with me! But he did offer to talk to you, if that's what you really want.'

'What I *really* want is for you to finish your education without getting involved with boys. But I suppose that's too much to ask, of teenagers today. Too much freedom, in my opinion – everyone's gone sex-mad.' She shook her head. 'Well, I'm not happy about it, Cathy, but at least you've had the decency to tell me you're seeing him. I don't like the fact that he's older than you. You do realise he's probably had girlfriends already?'

'Yes, I know, but ...'

'He'll be expecting things from you. You understand me? Things you're not old enough for.'

'Mum!' I was mortified. 'I'm not *stupid*!'

'He's a decent bloke, Mum,' Derek repeated, looking at me and shrugging as if to say he was doing his best. 'He won't mess her around.'

'I'm just warning you, Cathy, that's all. I don't care how nice he might be, he's a young man – and young men only have one thing on their minds. Don't get carried away. You hear me? Nothing *below the waist.*'

'Oh, *Mum!*' I covered my face with embarrassment. 'For Pete's sake!'

'And don't go all coy on me, either, miss. If you're old enough to have a boyfriend, you're old enough to hear this, and remember it. If you let him have his way with you, you won't see him again for dust. He'll have had his bit of fun, and you could be left with a whole lot of trouble.'

'He's not *like* that, Mum! He's ...'

'Mr Wonderful, by the sound of it,' she said sarcastically, looking at her watch. 'I'm off to work. Just remember what I said.'

'That went all right, didn't it!' Derek said with a grin as the door shut behind them. Then he frowned. 'She's right, though. I'll flippin' well cut his nuts off myself if he gets you into trouble. You can tell him that from me!'

September 1964

Whenever Jimmy came round, Mum carried on embarrassing me with more dire warnings about keeping my knees together and both feet on the floor. But she did seem generally a bit more relaxed about me going out. She'd actually extended my permitted hours out on my occasional Friday or Saturday evenings with Janice so that I could now get the last bus home. I couldn't help thinking this was her way of saying she considered me to be safer on the streets of Romford with a girl friend, albeit one she didn't really trust, than on our own sofa supposedly fighting off the carnal intentions of the likes of Jimmy Kent. But it did mean that Janice could now introduce me to some alternatives to the Zodiac coffee-bar.

One of these was the regular Saturday night dance at the Windham Hall, where I usually found myself sitting on a row of chairs with all the girls on one side of the hall, facing a similar row of boys on the other side, until such time as the music from the local band of Beatles-imitators had warmed everyone up sufficiently to mingle uneasily on the dance-floor. I enjoyed the dancing, and I was quite surprised to discover I was pretty good at the twist, but if a boy happened to approach me, wanting to dance with me, I feigned exhaustion or a pain in my leg and went to sit back down again.

'What's up with you?' Janice asked me the first time this happened. 'Don't you fancy him? He only wanted to dance with you, not marry you!'

When I just shrugged and said I didn't like dancing with boys, Janice burst out laughing and said I'd never get a boyfriend if I wouldn't even dance with one. But apart from the occasional bit of teasing about it, Janice was mostly too busy organising her own love life to bother much about mine. Which was just as well, because I was finding it harder and harder to keep quiet about Jimmy. I really wanted to be dancing with *him* at the Windham Hall, instead of spending those evenings apart – but I knew Janice would start getting suspicious if I didn't spend some time with her, when she managed to fit me into her social calendar. Besides which, the dances weren't frequented by rockers. If he'd walked into the hall on a Saturday evening he'd have been jeered and chased out by the mods. And of course, the biggest issue for us was avoiding being seen together by people who knew us.

Jimmy's mates weren't a problem. He'd told his closest friends about me, and they seemed to have accepted me. He'd even taken me to the Cauldron coffee-bar where they all met – and because I was with him, wearing one of his old leather jackets which he'd lent me to ride behind him on the motorbike, nobody had turned a hair. The ride there had been scary but thrilling – holding onto Jimmy's waist and pressing my face against his back as he roared down the road – and although the first time we went into the coffee-bar full of loud rock music and smoke, I'd had a flashback to that horrible afternoon in Clacton, I soon got over it because there wasn't any atmosphere of threat or aggression there. And when Jimmy introduced me to his mates as his girlfriend, it felt really good.

But I couldn't reciprocate. I couldn't tell Janice about him, and I couldn't take him to any of the mods' haunts. As long as Ian was still in hospital in a coma, I couldn't see the anti-rocker fury getting any less. As it was, we got some funny looks occasionally from complete strangers when we walked down the streets or got on a bus together – even though neither of us were particularly extreme in the way we dressed. And I was aware that it was a miracle Janice had never turned up at our house when Jimmy was there, not since that very first time anyway. It'd be impossible to explain it away now!

Jimmy always phoned me every night if we weren't seeing each other. I loved hearing his voice, and if it was an evening when I was going out with Janice it always made me wish I was seeing him instead.

'Have a good time at the dance, then,' he said one Saturday evening after we'd talked for a while. 'Don't do anything I wouldn't do!'

'I'm just going to be chatting to Janice! And having a bit of a dance.'

'Hmm.' He laughed gently. 'You watch those boys, if they've had a few drinks, that's all.'

'I don't care how many drinks they've had. I'm not interested in any of them,' I retorted. 'Only you!'

'I'm pleased to hear it,' he said. 'Although I'd rather it was me dancing with you.'

'Me too.' I sighed. Would things ever change? Or was I going to spend the rest of my life hiding Jimmy from my friends?

I was pretty naive, wasn't I. And anyway – I soon had other things to worry about.

In October it was Janice's eighteenth birthday, and she announced that she was having a birthday party at her house the following Saturday evening.

'Mum and Dad are going out, so we've got an empty house,' she told me enthusiastically. 'Bring a bottle.'

'OK, but it'll only be Coke.' I laughed. 'I can't believe your parents are letting you have booze there!'

She shrugged. 'I've told them it's just a few friends from my class at school, so they're getting us some beers and cider in. But I'm hoping some of the older blokes are going to bring gin and vodka.'

'I don't know if I want to come, really,' I said doubtfully. 'I thought it *was* just girls from school. Where are the older blokes from? The coffee-bar?'

'Oh, come on, Cathy. Don't be a party pooper all your life! Yeah, the crowd from the Zodiac are coming, and a few people from my work. You'll like them. I've told them all about you.'

'Have you?' I didn't believe this for a minute. Why would any of the *older blokes* working at Janice's company be in the slightest bit interested in a fifteen-year-old girl she hung around with at home? But I'd already agreed to go early to the party to help Janice get everything ready. And Mum, probably thinking it was going to be a nice genteel birthday party with games and cake, had amazingly given me a midnight curfew, provided she herself, or Del, came to pick me up afterwards. It seemed a shame to look a gift horse in the mouth.

'All right,' I relented. 'I'll come, but only to please you, cos it's your birthday.'

Janice hugged me and grinned happily. 'It's gonna be a rave, honest. We'll have such a swinging time.' She looked at me thoughtfully for a minute. 'D'you want to ask whatsername? Linda?'

'What? No, not really. Why?'

'I dunno. In case you feel a bit out of it, you know, being the only one your age.'

'No. 's all right. Linda wouldn't want to come, anyway. She doesn't go out much in the evenings. Her mum's an invalid, and she stays in with her to watch telly.'

'Groovy,' Janice said sarcastically. 'All right, then. See you on Saturday. Be there or be square!'

I thought it was nice of her to suggest I might want to bring another friend. To be honest, in some ways I'd have liked to have Linda with me. We spent a lot more time together nowadays and I was enjoying her company again. I felt a bit guilty for not asking her – although I knew she probably wouldn't have wanted to come. She didn't really like Janice, and the feeling was mutual, and the truth was, I didn't think she'd fit in with Janice's friends. Anyway, I wasn't going to be on my own, was I – I'd be with Janice! I wasn't sure whether I was looking forward to it or not, but at least we'd be able to have a bit of a dance, without being lined up along the walls of a dance-hall and stared at, like the cattle in Romford market.

Janice seemed excited to the point of near hysteria.

'*Loads* of people from London are coming,' she squealed as I helped her push back the furniture in the sitting-room and roll up the carpets. I was privately wondering whether Janice's parents were completely mad, going away for the whole weekend and letting her do virtually whatever she wanted in the house. 'I can't wait for you to meet them all. Do you want me to do your hair for you and help you get ready?'

'I got ready at home!' I protested, offended. 'What's wrong with how I look?'

'Nothing.' Janice looked at me carefully. 'You could do with a bit of make-up, that's all. Don't you want to try wearing some?'

'Mum says not till I'm sixteen.'

'Yeah, but your mum's not here now, is she.' Janice laughed. 'Come on – I'll just put a bit of eye-shadow and lipstick on you. You'll look fab.'

I followed her upstairs to her bedroom.

'Actually, you can help me tidy up in here a bit, too, before everyone comes.' We both glanced round at the heaps of clothes on the bed, the shoes scattered across the floor. 'Just in case. You know.'

'In case what?'

'In case I get off with Phillip from my accounts department,' she said casually, picking a blue eye-shadow out of her drawer and smearing it carefully on my eyelids while I sat obediently at the dressing table.

'Is that what you're so excited about? You fancy this Phillip?'

'Mm, he's a bit of a hunk. Wait till you see him.' She stood back and surveyed her handiwork, nodding with satisfaction before going back to the drawer to choose a lipstick. 'Married, but – you know. His wife's frigid.'

'He's *married*? You're trying to get off with a married man? How old is he?'

'Oh, I don't know.' She waved the lipstick, airily. 'Maybe about thirty. It's irrelevant, really, isn't it.'

'Is it?' I was beginning to wish I hadn't come. I'd expected this to be a party for teenagers – not married men in their thirties looking for fun. But I didn't want to sound like a square. Janice was living a much more sophisticated life now she worked in London. I supposed this was how they all carried on, up there: fashionable people living in flat-shares, having all-night raves, taking drugs and swapping partners – according to the papers, anyway. I wondered why on earth a thirty-year-old *hunk* would want to come all the way to Harold Hill for a comparatively tame birthday party with a group of schoolgirls in a suburban house.

'Don't get me wrong,' Janice was giggling as she threw screwed-up clothes into her wardrobe, pulled out a new blue mini shift dress and started to change into it. 'I'm not saying I'm going to go all the way with him. But ...' She did a twirl in front of the mirror and smiled at her reflection. 'I might, if I feel like it.'

'But he's *married*.'

'That's his problem, isn't it. And his wife's problem, if she's frigid.'

I decided not to argue about something I didn't really understand, but it made me feel distinctly uncomfortable.

'Come on!' Janice was squealing now. 'They'll be here soon! Let's go down and get some music on, and have a *drink*!'

A couple of hours later, I was sitting in a corner of the sitting-room as a heaving, crushing, throng of bodies moved frantically together to Manfred Mann belting out *Do Wah Diddy Diddy*. At the beginning of the party, I'd joined in with the dancing, but as more and more people arrived – all of them strangers to me, and (it seemed) many of them strangers to Janice herself, I started to feel awkward and lonely. I'd expected Janice to stay with me, but she was here, there and everywhere, flitting about the house with a drink constantly in her hand, screeching with laughter and not really acting like Janice at all. Far from introducing me to all the colleagues she'd supposedly told about me, she was completely ignoring me. And there was nobody here from school – *nobody*, not from Janice's old class, not from any class. Not even anybody from the Zodiac! I really wished, now, that I'd asked Linda to come.

'Get yourself a *drink*!' Janice had shouted at me, the last time she passed my corner on the way to put a new record on the turntable. 'It'll help you relax!'

Feeling cross and fed up, I made my way through the crowd to the kitchen, rinsed out one of the dirty glasses already littering the worktop and poured myself another Coca-Cola. As I stood at the sink taking a sip, I noticed a half-empty bottle of vodka standing amongst the whiskeys and gins. Vodka and Coke – that was what Janice was drinking, wasn't it. Well, OK, I might as well try it. One wouldn't hurt, and I might as well at least get something out of this party – I hadn't enjoyed it one bit, up till now. I drank half the Coca-Cola in the glass and topped it up with vodka, sniffed it and shrugged with surprise. It still smelled pretty much just of Coca-Cola, so it couldn't be too strong. I took a mouthful, swirled it around my mouth and swallowed. Not bad. I couldn't see what all the fuss was about really.

By half past nine, I'd had a second glass of vodka and Coke and was getting a taste for it. But when I stood up, the room felt like it was swaying, and people's faces looked strange and distorted.

'Where's Janice?' I asked a woman who was leaning against the inside of the front door. I felt a bit sick, and suddenly just wanted to go home.

'Janice who?' the woman shouted back.

I looked around and realised again that I didn't know a single person there. I wasn't enjoying it, I wished I hadn't had the second drink, and I wanted to be at home, preferably in bed, asleep.

'Excuse me,' I said to the woman leaning on the door. 'I need to get out.'

I hurtled down the front path, through the huddles of people now crowding the front garden and even the pavement outside, smoking and drinking from bottles, and ran all the way home. I felt so peculiar, that I'd actually let myself into the house before I'd properly taken in the fact that there was a car – a new Ford Cortina – parked outside. Hardly anyone in our street had a car, and neither did anyone who might visit us. I was halfway up the stairs, stumbling, anxious to get into my bedroom without Mum finding out I'd been drinking, when I heard the voices coming from the sitting-room: Mum's voice – and a man's.

I hesitated on the stairs, holding the banister, listening – and then the sitting-room door opened and Mum was looking up at me, surprised.

'You're back early,' she said. She sounded flustered and was quite obviously trying to block my view of the man standing behind her.

'Yeah.' I stared over her shoulder. The vodka must have made me feel bolder than normal so that I came straight out with it: 'Who's he?'

There was a long silence, during which Mum exchanged a look with the man, and finally opened the sitting-room door fully so I could see him properly. He smiled at me, and although I still had no idea who he was, there was something I didn't like about the smile. After another moment of hesitation, Mum said with a sigh:

'All right, you might as well hear it now. I was going to tell you soon anyway. This is Fred, Cathy. He's going to be living with us.'

The next day

It wasn't until about two o'clock the next afternoon that Janice arrived at my front door, looking like she'd just got out of bed and demanding, as soon as I let her in:

'Why did you bugger off like that last night?'

'*Me*?' I could feel tears threatening again. I'd been crying on and off all day, after lying awake crying for most of the night – what was left of it, after all the rows had finished. 'That's great, coming from you. I hardly saw you at the party at all. I don't know why you bothered to invite me.'

'Look, I was the hostess. I had to circulate,' Janice said, following me into the sitting-room.

'Yeah, all right then.' I couldn't be bothered to argue. 'If you say so.'

'I was worried about you! I couldn't find you, nobody saw you go ...'

'You mean nobody *noticed* me go. That's cos there was nobody there who knew me.'

'Well, I'm sorry, Cath, but that's the way it goes, isn't it. I did invite people from school, but obviously they didn't turn up.' She was looking at me suspiciously now. 'You all right? What's happened?'

'Nothing.' I sat down and looked the other way, trying to swallow back the tears. I wanted to tell Janice about it really, but I felt so choked up I didn't know where to start. 'Look at the state of you,' I said instead, pretending to laugh. It came out as a shaky kind-of cry. 'You just got up?'

'Yeah. Bit hung-over,' Janice said, waving this aside. 'But it was worth it,' she added with a grin. She looked at me closely again. 'There *is* something wrong, isn't there. Are you really upset about last night? Look, I am sorry if you didn't enjoy it. And sorry I had a go at you – it's just that I was worried. You know – after what happened with Ian, at Clacton, I don't like to think of you wandering off on your tod.'

'It was only half past nine when I left.'

'Well, I did phone, late last night. Didn't Derek tell you? I must say, he was a bit off with me. Sounded like he was in a foul mood – and your mum was shouting in the background too, so I just checked you'd got home OK and hung up.' She paused. 'She wasn't shouting at *you*, was she?'

'Probably. We were all shouting at each other.' I took a deep breath and let it out again. Even thinking about it now was making me start to cry again – yet again. It had all been so horrible!

'Cath.' Janice put her arm round me. 'What's happened? Come on, you can tell me. Remember what I said before? You're like my little sister. I care about you. Sorry if sometimes I act like I don't – but I really do. I don't like to see you upset like this.'

'It's my mum,' I said finally, in a whisper. 'She's got a boyfriend. He was here. Last night, when I got home, he was here with Mum.'

'A boyfriend, really? Blimey. What's he like?'

'Horrible! His name's Fred and Mum says he's moving in with us! He expects me and Del to call him *Uncle* Fred – can you imagine? We're not going to! Mum's been meeting him, secretly, and taking *money* off him!'

'You're joking! That's where she's been getting all the dough from, for all these things?' Janice hugged me closer. 'D'you reckon he's been bribing her, to get his wicked way with her?'

'Yuck! Stop it, Jan – I can't bear to think of it! You don't think they're doing *that* together, do you? They're too old!'

'Who knows? Where'd she meet him, anyway?'

'Down the pub, apparently. He was in there one night when she was behind the bar, and he started talking to her, and then he kept on coming back in and begging her to go out with him. Apparently she said no at first.' I snorted. 'She says it was Kennedy being murdered that made her change her mind.'

'Kennedy being murdered? What's that got to do with anything?'

'You don't know my mum.'

'It was when I thought about the poor president, shot down like that.' Mum had shaken her head, looking like she still couldn't believe it had happened. Fred, standing behind her in the sitting-room, shook his head too. 'It was such a shock,' she went on. 'I thought to myself right then – if we're all going to die, if the world's going to be blown to smithereens by the Russians – well.' She turned and looked at Fred and gave him a sickly smile. He gave her an equally sickly smile back, and I just wanted to walk straight up to him and smack him. 'Well, I thought to myself, we should all snatch what happiness we can, while we're still alive.'

'He doesn't have to move in with us, though!' I said. 'You don't even really *know* him! I mean, who the hell is he – just someone you met in the pub?'

'Don't be rude, Cathy.' Mum glared at me and looked apologetically at Fred. 'Of course I know him. He wants to look after me. And you, too.'

He nodded, his face a picture of apparent sincerity. 'I love your mum, Cathy, and she's had a hard life since your dad walked out on her. I intend to make up for all that.'

'You can't! You can't *ever* make up for *all that*! How can you possibly understand what Mum's had to go through, all these years? You've only just met her! You can't just walk in here and decide you're going to live with us!'

'That's enough, Catherine,' Mum said warningly.

'No, it's not enough! Mum, you can't just spring this on us – you didn't even tell us you were going out with him! Why was it such a big secret? I've been *asking* you how you could afford all these new things. I wouldn't have touched them with a bargepole if I'd known it was some strange man buying them for you!'

'I'm not a stranger – your mother and I have been going out together now for nearly a year,' Fred told me in a cold, quiet voice. The creepy smile had vanished and was replaced by a look of dislike. I didn't know which was worse.

'Nearly a year without telling us! What about Del? Have you told him yet?'

'I haven't exactly had a chance, have I. You've just burst in on us like this – we were planning on giving it a little longer before we sat you down and told you ...'

'What – the day before you moved him in? Or the day after, when it was too late? I suppose that's what you were planning to do, were you – let him move in while I was at school one day, so I'd just come home and find him sitting at the table? Did you really think that was going to work?'

'I said, *that's enough, Cathy*.' Mum's tone was icy. 'I know this is a shock to you. We wanted to do it differently – tell you both at a better time. But whether you like it or not, Fred's moving in.'

I started crying then. It didn't help that I still wasn't feeling too good from the vodka. 'Mum, no ... please! Don't let him move in! Why would you do that? OK, if you want to go out with him – if you want a friend to go out with, that's one thing, but why ...?'

'I should have thought it was obvious why, Catherine,' Fred said. Every time he opened his mouth I liked him less. He was fat and bald and spoke like a headmaster, like he was used to being in charge. 'Your mother and I have fallen in love. She deserves a bit of happiness, doesn't she? Would you deny your mother that?'

'Of course I wouldn't!' I shouted at him. 'She's *been* happy with us – with me and Del! We don't need you moving in here! We're doing fine without you!'

'And I'm going to spend the rest of my life proving your mum will be even happier with *me* here.' He put his arm around Mum's shoulders so that I jumped up again and had a job to stop myself pushing him away from her. 'I love your mother, Catherine, and she loves me. In time I hope you'll look upon me as the father you never knew.'

'Bloomin' 'eck.' Janice stared at me in horror. 'What did you say to *that*?'

'What do you think? I said I'll never look on him as a father long as I live, and that if he moves in with us I'll move out as soon as I'm old enough.' I sniffed and blew my nose. 'I hate him – he's horrible! I went up to my room and slammed the door. What is my mum *thinking* of? It's like she's turned into a different person. She actually lectured me about it this morning, telling me off for being rude to him and saying I need to learn some respect! Can you believe that?' I closed my eyes and sighed. 'And of course, I'm in trouble with her for the drinking as well.'

'You were drinking? What – at my party?'

'Only a couple.' I forced a smile. 'Vodka and Coke, like you drink. I wanted to try it. It made me feel a bit funny.'

'Well, yeah – it would! I'm surprised you weren't sick, your first time. Did your mum smell it on your breath, then? Vodka doesn't smell that much.'

'I think I was kind of swaying a bit, and maybe my words were coming out wrong. And because I was shouting at Fred, Mum looked at me and said *Have you been drinking?* And I said *Yes, I have, what are you going to do about it?* Pretty stupid, really, but I was just so angry.'

'I don't blame you. Poor you.' She whistled. 'So where was Derek while all this was going on?'

'Out. But he came home a little while after I'd gone to bed. And then it *really* all kicked off. Fred was still here, of course, and they obviously told Del about him moving in. Del went absolutely mad. He's normally so easy-going; I've never known him lose his temper like that. He was screaming and shouting, saying stuff about how Fred must have *bought* Mum's affections by giving her money for all this stuff.' I waved my arm around the sitting-room at the TV, the record-player, the new furniture. 'And ... he said she was like a prostitute, going with him just for the money, for what she could get out of him. Mum was crying and screaming back at him. When I heard glass smashing, I came downstairs, begging him to stop. It was really scary: Del was crying himself, telling Fred to get out. He'd thrown a glass at him! Mum had hold of his arm, trying to stop him, but ... well, in the end, Fred went, saying stuff about leaving him to calm down and expecting an apology.'

'I can't see *that* happening!' Janice said, her eyes wide.

'No.' I started to cry again. My eyes were so sore from crying, my head was aching from it, but I couldn't help it. 'And now Del says he's moving out. He means it – he's actually going, straight away, moving in with his girlfriend. I don't think they're even that serious, but she's got a flat and he's just moving in with her to get away from home. I wish I could go with him!' I cried. 'I wish he'd take me! I don't want to stay here with *him* moving in!'

Janice looked at me solemnly. 'You could move in with me, if you like.'

'Oh, sure.' I almost laughed. 'Just like that!'

'My mum and dad wouldn't mind.'

'No, but my mum would. And I'm only fifteen-and-a-half, don't forget. I have to do what she says. If I left home against her wishes, she'd get me taken into Dr Barnardo's.'

'Ask her. See what she says. She might be glad to have you and Derek out of the way so she can concentrate on Fred.'

'Yuck. Don't. It makes me feel sick.'

'Ask her, yeah?' Janice said again. 'It'd be fab, wouldn't it – living together? I told you I always wanted a little sister!'

I smiled at her shakily. 'OK. Yeah, maybe I'll ask her.'

I wasn't going to, of course. Mum would never countenance me moving in with Janice anyway – she still suspected her of being a bad influence, and now I'd admitted drinking at her party, there'd be no doubt of it in her mind. But more to the point, of all the people in the world, I couldn't live with Janice. I'd never be able to see Jimmy! I was absolutely dreading the horrible Fred moving in – and absolutely livid that Mum was letting him. But I was just going to have to find a way of bearing it. At least I still had Jimmy. That was the only thing keeping me going.

October 1964

In fact, Fred moved in within a week or so of me and Derek finding out about him.

'No point wasting any more time,' Mum said with a shrug. 'Now you both know what's happening.'

'Knowing about it is one thing,' Del retorted. 'Liking it is another.'

'Yes, well, I'm afraid you'll just have to get used to it.'

'*I* won't. I've told you: I'm out of here. It's Cathy I feel sorry for.'

I couldn't even speak. The thought of being in the house with Fred, but without Derek, made me want to howl with grief.

'Please don't go,' I whispered to him. 'Please! I don't think I can stand it without you.'

'You're both overreacting, and being just plain childish,' Mum snapped. 'Anyone would think I was moving a complete *stranger* into the house.'

'You are,' Derek said flatly.

'He's a stranger to *us*,' I reminded her. 'And I wish it was going to stay that way.'

I helped Derek pack up his things, the evening before Fred was moving in. A friend with a car was coming to take all the boxes and bags over to Pauline's place in Goodmayes – Del would follow on his bike.

'You can come round whenever you like,' Derek said. He looked at me with sympathy. 'And I'll phone you. Every night – OK? To make sure you're all right.'

'But I won't be, will I,' I said in a small voice. 'It's all going to be different, and horrible.'

Derek clipped his suitcase shut and closed the last of the cardboard boxes.

'Thanks for helping, sis.' He kissed the top of my head. 'Nick'll be here in a minute with his motor. Listen: try not to let it get to you.

Keep out of that so-and-so's way as much as you can. Concentrate on your schoolwork, yeah? And good old Jimmy, of course!'

I smiled, despite myself, at the mention of Jimmy's name.

A car horn sounded outside. Derek ran downstairs to let his friend in. Between them, it only took a few minutes to load the car up with his stuff.

'I'm off now, Mum,' he called. Mum had stayed out of the way in the kitchen, and she looked round the door now and shook her head at him.

'Fine way to carry on,' she said defiantly, her words contradicting the pain in her eyes. 'Walking out on your family, going off to live with some *hussy* without even bothering to marry her.'

'Right. Well, if that's all you can say – I'll see you around,' he said. And with a last sad smile at me, he was gone. I was too miserable, at that point, to even think about the irony of Mum's words. She was going to be living with a man herself without marrying him. So what did that make her?

Del had been true to his word – phoning me every evening, as soon as he got in from work.

'How's it been?' he asked, after Fred had been there for a couple of days.

'Horrible. He's actually – you know – sleeping in Mum's bed. It makes me feel sick.'

'But has he been all right with *you*?'

'Kind of smarmy, so far. Trying to make me think he's nice – as if I'm suddenly going to change my mind and be thrilled to bits that he's here.'

'Well, it could be worse, I suppose. At least he's not trying to lay down the law and act like he's in charge.'

But it didn't take long for that to change. At first it was just little things: I'd be watching television, and Fred would come into the room and turn it over to the other side. Or I'd be playing my records, and he'd take the needle off, abruptly, because he didn't like the music. One day he did it so carelessly he scratched one of my Beatles' LPs.

'Look what you've done!' I shouted. 'Thanks very much! It's *ruined* now!'

'Ruined? I don't believe it's possible to ruin rubbish, is it?' he sneered.

'It was a present from Del,' I said, furiously. 'And I'll never be able to afford to buy another one.'

'Well, that'll teach you to get on with your homework instead of listening to *pop music*.'

I ran out of the room, passing Mum in the hall.

'What's going on?' she demanded.

'Ask *him*! He's just *ruined* my favourite record! Tell him, Mum! He'd better buy me a new one!'

Mum looked back at me for a full minute. I could see a struggle going on in her eyes.

'*Tell* him, Mum!' I said again. 'He can't just walk into the room and take my records off like that!'

But she just lowered her eyes and started to walk away.

'You'd better play your records when he's out, in future,' was all she said.

The first time Jimmy turned up at the house when Fred was there, there was an uncomfortable silence while he took off his coat in the hall.

'So who's this, then?' he asked eventually.

'He's Cathy's *friend*, dear.' Mum shot me a warning look. 'They listen to records together.'

'And you allow that, do you?' he said quietly. 'She's only fifteen, Ivy – I hope you don't allow them to be alone together. How old are you, boy?' he demanded of Jimmy, without bothering to wait for Mum to answer.

'Eighteen, sir.' Jimmy glanced at me warily before adding: 'And I can assure you, Cathy and I ...'

'I'm not interested in your *assurances*! Eighteen? Hanging around with a schoolgirl? What's the matter with you? Can't get a girl your own age?'

Jimmy went very red and dropped his eyes.

'Cathy and I have been ... good friends ... for a while. I'm a friend of Derek's,' he said.

'And you want me to think *that's* a recommendation? You're a friend of *that* young man who walks out on his family to live with a some girl?'

'What's it got to do with you?' I demanded furiously. 'You're not my father! You're not part of this family at all!'

'Cathy!' Mum warned me, stepping forward as if to hustle me out of the way.

I shook her hand off my arm. 'No, Mum – I'm not having it! It's nothing to do with him how old Jimmy is, or when he comes round, or *what* I do! *Tell* him, Mum!'

There was a horrible, echoing silence.

'You'd better go, Jimmy,' Mum said.

'Mum!' I stared at her in disbelief. 'Why are you being like this? You always let Jimmy come round! *Tell* Fred you always let him!'

'I'm sorry, Catherine,' she said more firmly. 'I think it's best for now if Jimmy goes. We'll discuss this later.'

'If he's going, I'll go with him,' I said. I pulled my coat off the hook on the wall, took hold of Jimmy's arm and opened the front door. 'Come on – let's go to your house. *Your* parents are happy for us to spend time together, aren't they.'

'Don't walk out on your mother!' Fred started, raising his voice. But Mum took hold of his arm, whispering anxiously to him about not getting himself upset, which at least gave us a chance to get outside and pull the door shut behind us.

'How dare he try to tell me what to do!' I said. I was shaking with anger. 'I'm sorry he was so horrible to you.'

Jimmy put his arm round me and kissed me gently. 'I don't care. But I don't like him being horrible to *you*. I just hope he's not going to be in an even worse mood now.'

'He's a pig. I hate him, and there's nothing he can say to stop me seeing you. I just can't believe my mum didn't even stick up for me. It's like she's turned into a different person all of a sudden.'

'She's scared of offending him, if you ask me,' Jimmy said. 'Maybe when he's been here for a bit longer, things will settle down.'

'They'd better. If he carries on like this I think we'll end up killing each other.'

Jimmy's house was just beyond the edge of the estate, in one of the original roads of pre-war houses that had existed before Harold Hill was built. I'd only been round there a few times before, and at first I'd felt quite intimidated by the big, solid, pebble-dashed semi with its bay window at the front and garage at the side.

'Do your parents own their own house?' I'd asked Jimmy in a whisper.

'Yes.' He smiled and squeezed my hand. 'Well, kind of, you know – they've got a mortgage, of course.'

I didn't know the first thing about mortgages. I'd grown up believing all ordinary people paid rent, either to the council or a landlord, and only rich people owned their own homes. I hadn't realised Jimmy was rich.

'We're not rich!' he laughed when I told him this. 'You must be joking. We're no better off than you are!'

Inside the house, I'd been surprised to see the same type of thin shabby carpets, scuffed lino and worn armchairs that we had at home. And Jimmy's parents, Barbara and Pete, were so nice and friendly that I soon forgot they were what Mum always referred to as *property people.*

This particular evening was unusually chilly for the time of year, and Barbara welcomed me with a cup of tea, and turned the electric fire on in the front room so that Jimmy and I could be on our own. The fire was the new type that gave off a soft warm glow from a red bulb behind the plastic coal-effect on the front. Its two electric bars warmed up quickly and as we huddled together on the sofa in front of it, I thought it was heaven compared with the hassle of the coal fires in our own house.

'We've only just got it,' Jimmy said. 'Mum says it's expensive to run, though.'

'Well, maybe now *he's* bringing money into the house, my mum might be able to afford one,' I said with a sigh.

'Yeah. I s'pose you've got to try and see things from her point of view. Her life's been a real struggle, and now she's got the chance of having it a bit easier. You can't blame her for that.'

'I wouldn't blame her, if he was nice, and if she'd *told* us about him before she decided to move him in!' But it was difficult to stay in a bad mood, sitting there in the cosy warmth of the fire, cuddled up with Jimmy.

'I'll just stay out of his way for a while,' Jimmy said. 'You can come round here instead, Cath – or we can go out. Just till he gets used to it.'

'If he ever does!'

Jimmy walked me home early, to avoid upsetting Fred any further.

'Don't come right up to the door with me,' I said. 'If *he* starts again ...'

'If he does, I want to be there with you.'

But when I let myself in, Mum called from the kitchen straight away: 'Oh. So you're back, are you? Well, you're in luck, Miss – Fred's gone down the pub.' She emerged into the hallway, looking at Jimmy dispassionately as he stood on the doorstep. 'So you'd best clear off while you can, lad. You've angered him enough for one night, the pair of you.'

'Mum – we didn't do anything!' I exclaimed. 'And it would have been nice if you'd stuck up for me!'

Mum just turned away.

'Try and keep the peace,' Jimmy whispered, kissing me goodnight. 'I'll see you tomorrow.'

'OK. Don't come here, though, will you. I'll meet you at the bus-stop at seven, all right?'

'What are you whispering about now?' Mum said, looking back at us. 'Go on, lad, off with you before he comes back and finds you sniffing around.'

'I'm not going to stop seeing Jimmy,' I told her after he'd gone. 'I don't care what *he* says. *You* said I could!'

Mum sighed. 'Just make sure he stays out of Fred's way, then,' she said quietly. 'That's all I'm saying on the matter.'

'It's none of his business,' I muttered under my breath as I trudged up the stairs. Then I stopped, near the top, suddenly remembering something. 'Anyway – why aren't *you* at the pub, Mum? I thought you were supposed to be working tonight?'

'I don't work there anymore.'

'Don't you? Since when? Why not?'

'Because Fred doesn't like me working there, not that it's anything to do with you. And I don't need to, do I – I've got a man to support me again now. Some men find it a shameful thing, Cathy

– a woman going out to work. You'll understand all these things when you're older.'

'No, I won't! I'll never understand what you're doing, Mum – letting him move in here and ... *take you over*! And anyway, what was the point of him living here if he never seems to want to spend any time with you? He's been at the pub almost every night since he moved in.' Not that I minded – it was a relief not to have him hanging around. But how could Mum be happy with that?

Mum just shook her head. 'You've got a lot to learn about relationships, girl,' she said. 'It's give and take, that what it is. That's what makes the world go round.'

'Yeah – you giving, and him taking, if you ask me!'

'I didn't ask you. And I'll thank you to keep your opinions to yourself. You might think you know everything, miss, just because you've got a young man keen on you right now, but you don't know anything. Men are men, and no amount of so-called women's lib is going to change that. They work, they eat, they go down the pub. As long as he gives me money, I'm not going to grumble, am I? That's the way of the world, and it always will be. You'd better get used to it.'

'You must be joking!' I hadn't set out to have an argument, but by now I was getting worked up. 'It might be all right for your generation, but *we're* not going to be prepared to put up with it! I want a career of my own, and so do all the girls I know – that's what you always said you wanted for me! We're not going to be kept at home doing the cooking and washing while our blokes go off down the pub!'

'*Women's liberation!*' Mum said again, shaking her head as if it was something dirty.

'But Mum, you managed perfectly well without a man, all these years! You worked, and looked after us, and you didn't *need* someone telling you what to do! I was proud of you!' I felt tears coming to my eyes as I realised, suddenly, how true this was. What had happened to the strong-minded survivor Mum had always been?

'I *didn't* manage, Cathy,' she replied quietly. 'That's the whole point.' She shrugged. 'If your generation can do things differently, well, good for you. That's why I've been struggling to provide you with this education you're having. If you go to university and get a good career, then maybe you might make a better go of it all than I have.'

'I'm not saying you haven't made a go of it, Mum. And I know – I'm sorry, I know you've worked hard so that I can go to this school, and everything.'

'Well then. Maybe I'm wrong. All this talk about women getting equality with men might come true one day. I just can't see it, though, myself. It doesn't seem right, or natural, to me.'

I sighed with frustration. Mum and I had always had our disagreements, but deep down I knew she was a decent, hard-working woman. What didn't seem right or natural to *me* was that she'd given up her independence in exchange for financial support from a man – and not a very pleasant man, at that. As far as I was concerned, Mum had gone stark raving bonkers. Well, I was from a different generation – a new generation! Girls today weren't going to put up with the sort of stuff her generation did – we were going to be equal to men, not controlled by them!

Fifteen and a half – and I thought I knew it all.

December 1964

Christmas that year was a strange, awkward affair. I'd have liked to ask Jimmy round, but that would obviously have caused no end of trouble. Derek came home for Christmas dinner, bringing Pauline, and a bag of presents for everyone. Fred seemed to resent both his presence in the house, and his generosity. The atmosphere at the table was tense with suppressed annoyance.

'How do you stand it?' Del asked me quietly as we stacked dishes for washing up in the kitchen.

'I stay out of his way as much as I can.'

'Is Mum all right?'

'That's a matter of opinion. I think she's just kind-of rolled over and accepted him bossing her around, in exchange for an easier life.'

'Not *easier*. Just more financially secure.'

'Yes, well – that's all it's about, isn't it, for people like Mum? When you think about it, all she's ever known is struggle. That's why she went for it.'

'You've changed your tune.'

'No. Just started to understand, I suppose.'

'You're growing up,' Del commented with a smile. 'Still seeing Jimmy?'

'Yeah. Fred doesn't like it, not that it's any of his business – but that's tough.'

'Good. Be careful, though.'

'Oh, don't you start. We're not having sex, Del.'

'That's not what I meant. Be careful when you're out with him. You know what it's like round here. Everyone knows he's a rocker. And look at you, in all your new mod gear. You'll get picked on, for sure, if you get seen out with him.'

'We don't care about all that. Everyone down the Cauldron's been really nice to me.'

'It's not his mates I'm worried about, Cathy. *Your* mob still haven't forgotten about Ian Vincent. I don't suppose they ever will, either. Just be careful, that's all I'm saying. I won't always be around to look after you.'

'What's that supposed to mean? You're not around now, are you – you're in flippin' Goodmayes.'

Derek lifted a few plates, rinsed the gravy off them, stacked them again. Then he turned round to face me, but he didn't meet my eyes.

'Pauline and I are thinking of emigrating,' he said at last.

'You're thinking of *what*?'

'Emigrating. To Australia. They want people – young people who can work in jobs out there. Pauline's a nurse, and they want motor mechanics too. We've ... got the forms.'

'Australia?' I repeated weakly, leaning against the draining-board and twisting the tea-towel round my hands. 'Forms?'

'Forms to apply for assisted passage. It's only ten quid each.'

'*Australia*? But ... it's the other side of the *world*! Del! The *other side of the world*!' My voice rose to a squeak. 'You can't do that! Why? Why d' you want to go to Australia?'

He took hold of my shoulders, steadying me, looking into my eyes. 'It's not definite yet, sis. I just wanted to warn you, so it won't come as a shock – if we do decide to go. Look – it's a fantastic opportunity. A new, young country, where we can help to make things happen – make it the sort of place we want to live in. We could both earn more money out there – get married, buy a house ...'

'*What*?' I pulled away and stared at him. 'I didn't know you were thinking about getting married! Do you *love* her, Del?'

He shrugged. 'Yeah – course. We're living together, aren't we. *Living in sin*, as Mum would say. Better get married sooner or later.'

'But ... I just thought it was a kind-of *convenience*. Not a *love* thing.'

'Yeah, well, you know.' He shrugged again. 'We're OK. She's all right.'

I stared at him. Suddenly I didn't recognise my brother. Who was this stranger, talking about emigrating to Australia, and marrying a girl he merely thought was *all right*? It didn't make sense!

'What's going on, Del? I don't get it. You never said before that you wanted to go to Australia, or get married. Why are you even *thinking* about it? I don't want you to go! I'd never see you again! Please, Del – don't let her talk you into it!'

'She's not!' he said, sounding a bit sharp. 'It's *my* idea, and I've been thinking about it for a long time. Look – nothing's definite yet, so let's just get on with Christmas, shall we?'

But Christmas had been bad enough before Del dropped his bombshell. Now, I spent the rest of the day in a daze and was almost too upset to say goodbye to Derek and Pauline when they left after supper.

On Boxing Day, Fred went to the pub at lunchtime and I immediately took the opportunity to dash round to Jimmy's house.

'Del's talking about emigrating to Australia!' I blurted out almost as soon as I was through the door. 'Has he said anything to you about it?'

'No.' Jimmy shook his head. 'But then, I don't see so much of him these days. He doesn't hang out with the boys so much since he moved. I reckon Pauline's got him under her thumb,' he added with a grin.

'It's not funny! He doesn't even love her – he only moved in with her so he could get away from home.'

'You don't *know* that,' Jimmy protested gently.

'Yes, I do. He says stuff like *she's OK* and that they *might as well* get married!'

Jimmy frowned, and remained silent as he took hold of my hand, studying it carefully as if it was a work of art. 'Some blokes just aren't very good at talking about stuff like love, or how they feel,' he said eventually. 'It's ... seen as being a bit effeminate, you know? – talking about your feelings.'

'That's just stupid,' I said, sitting down and folding my arms crossly.

'You're probably right. It is stupid. But it's the way boys are brought up – we've been told all our lives not to cry or make a fuss, keep a stiff upper lip, act like a man, stand and fight ...'

'Yes, and it's no wonder some boys grow up to be such horrible men!'

'Del's not horrible, though, Cath. You're just upset with him.'

'Well, I don't want him to go off to the other side of the world!'

'Of course you don't. He still might not.' He put both arms round me and rested his chin on the top of my head. 'And just so you know,' he added in a whisper, 'we're not *all* frightened to say how we feel.'

'Aren't you?' I said, still feeling cross and unsettled.

'No. I might not be very good at it, and I might not say it very often. But I do love you, Cathy.'

I smiled, finally. 'And I love you, too. More than anything! More than anyone!'

'More than Paul McCartney?' he teased.

'We ..e..ell ...' I pretended to consider this. 'It's a close thing, but as Paul doesn't seem to be in a rush to turn up on my doorstep ...'

'You'll make do with me in the meantime?'

I laughed. 'Yeah. I might even take his pictures off my wall to prove it.'

Of course, I'd have liked to do more to prove how much I loved Jimmy. But the consequences were much to scary. For a start, until I was sixteen he could be arrested for having sex with me. And even more frightening was the risk of pregnancy. I'd heard all about the new birth control pill that had been invented – but it was only available to married women. Society still liked to pretend that only married people had sex. But I hadn't needed all the lectures from Mum, or even the ridiculous lesson at school last year, slotted into a biology class in the most embarrassing and unhelpful way imaginable. The fear was always there, in the minds of all the girls I knew; in the whispers in the playground as we were growing up; in our sharing of secrets and dreams. It was the one thing nobody in their right mind wanted to happen to them, because girls who Got Into Trouble were still thought of as little better than prostitutes – even those who were over sixteen and 'allowed' to make up their own minds about having sex.

I was one of the lucky ones. Jimmy wasn't the type to pester me about it, threatening to leave me if I didn't 'give in' – like some girls' boyfriends did. But as long as the risk of being ostracised – even by your own family – for the crime of getting pregnant was so real, girls were never really going to have any genuine equality with boys. It might have been 'the swinging sixties' – the decade of change, of social and cultural revolution – but there sure as hell wasn't much swinging going on in my neck of the woods!

By New Year's Eve I was still brooding about the possibility of Derek emigrating, when Jimmy phoned me sounding worried.

'Have you heard about Ian?'

'What about him?'

'He's dead, Cath. He died on Christmas Eve, apparently.'

'Oh – blimey, no. That's horrible. Horrible for his mum and dad.'

'He never came out of the coma. Everyone was talking about it last night in the Cauldron – obviously they're expecting repercussions from the mods.'

'For heaven's sake! Is that all they can say? Not that I liked Ian – but he's dead – his poor family!'

'I know. Cathy, I agree with you – but you know how some of them are always looking for another excuse to start the fighting up again. And, also – you know the police had pretty much given up trying to find out who attacked him. Well, now it's a murder enquiry, so it's different.'

'Yeah, I suppose so.' I shivered. I'd never known anyone who'd died before, apart from my grandparents who'd been old and sick. 'Well, I'm glad nobody we know was in Brighton that day, anyway.'

There was a silence. I shook the phone receiver. We had a party line, and sometimes the people in the other house picked up the phone during our conversations. 'Hello? Jimmy – I said, I'm glad ...'

'I heard you.' He sounded strangely sombre. 'Cathy, I have to tell you something. I promised never to tell you, but now ...'

'What? Jimmy, you're scaring me. Who did you promise – what?'

'Del. He was in Brighton that day. He didn't want you to know. He made me promise.'

'No, he didn't go! He might have said he was going, but he didn't. He brought Pauline back here that night – they'd been out together all day, at someone's house.' I stopped, remembering suddenly. 'At *your* house, Jimmy. They were at yours! Don't you remember? You had some friends round. I was really glad, because I was worried *you* might go to Brighton, and there might be trouble ...' I tailed off. 'Don't you remember?' I said again.

'I remember what he *told* you,' Jimmy said. There was a long pause. I could almost hear my heart beating. 'It wasn't true,' he added quietly. 'Derek made it up. He was at Brighton, Cath, and he called in with Pauline on purpose, so she could back him up with his story to you and your mum.'

'Why?' I could feel the fear beginning to creep through me, making my arms and legs feel weak, making my voice come out hoarse. 'Why did he go to all that trouble – *lying* to us like that?

Why did you cover up for him, Jimmy? *Please* tell me he wasn't ... !
He wasn't involved in that fighting, was he? He didn't see who
stabbed Ian?'

'I don't know. Honestly, I don't. He said he didn't, but ...'

'Why did you go along with his *lies*? Why didn't you tell me?
For Pete's sake – *you* weren't in Brighton too, Jimmy, were you?
Did you lie to me as well?'

'No! I swear to you, I didn't go – I was at home here, with my
mum and dad. I didn't know Del was going to use me as a cover – he
told me the next day. He said he'd only done it to stop you and your
mum being upset if they found out he'd been there. Because of the
fighting. I'm really sorry, Cath – but it seemed like the best thing at
the time, to go along with it and save you any worry. So I promised
him I'd keep quiet about it.'

'But you're telling me now.'

'I'm telling you now, because Ian's dead. It changes everything.
Like I said, the police will start questioning everyone again.'

'Oh *Jimmy*! What's going to happen? Will they question *you*?
Will you get into trouble?'

'No! Calm down, nothing's going to happen to *me*. I wasn't
there. I can prove it.' He paused again. I could hear him breathing.
'It's Del I'm worried about.'

'Why? Because he lied to us? OK, so he was there, but that
doesn't mean ...'

'Cathy, listen. He knew about Ian. What Ian did to you – at
Clacton.'

This time, in the silence, I actually thought I was going to faint.
My head spun, I stumbled and nearly dropped the phone. Memories
of Ian pushing me against the wall in that alleyway, his breath on my
face, his fat hands pawing at me, surfaced sickeningly at the same
time as the shock hit me. Derek *knew*? And – even more shocking –
Jimmy knew?

'I'm coming round,' Jimmy said urgently.

Luckily, we had the house to ourselves. Fred was at the pub, and
Mum had gone to see a friend.

'I can't believe you *knew*!' I said as I let Jimmy in. 'You *and* Del
knew! All this time, you knew, and you never mentioned it!'

'What would've been the point? It would only have upset you; you obviously just wanted to forget it.'

'But *how* did you know? I didn't tell Del! I didn't tell Mum, or anybody! Well, only Janice.'

'Yes. And apparently Janice told Del.'

'What? Why on earth would she do that? It wasn't up to her to tell him! I'll *kill* her!'

'Look; I'm sorry, I know you must feel like we've all been talking about you behind your back.'

'Yes! I do!'

'But it wasn't like that. I only found out afterwards – after Brighton – when Del told me he'd been there, and told me about Ian. He said he didn't see it happen, and had no idea who did it. But then he also told me he wasn't sorry – that Ian had *had it coming to him.*'

'Not that, though! Not getting *stabbed*!'

'No. He meant he'd deserved a beating – said he'd felt like giving him a smack himself. When I asked him why, he told me what happened to you. And apparently Janice had told him he used to push her around a bit, too. *I* was upset, Cath, hearing what he'd done to you – he tried to rape you! It must've been really frightening for you. You should really have gone to the police.' He tried to take hold of my hand but I snatched it away.

'Maybe I should, but I didn't want to. I just wanted to forget it ever happened. That's why I've never talked to *you* about it!'

'I understand that. Please don't be mad at me,' he said quietly. 'I didn't like keeping this from you.'

It was all too much to take in. I wasn't sure who I was most mad at – my brother, Jimmy, or ... Janice. *Janice* should never have said anything to anybody about this, should she! I'd told her about it in confidence!

'Janice said at the time that Ian needed to be taught a lesson,' I remembered now. 'But she didn't mean anything *serious*, like this. After he got knifed, we had a row about it, because I said she probably felt guilty.'

'Yeah, and you were right – she probably did. Anybody would, if they'd said stuff like that about someone, and then something happened.'

'But *she* didn't have anything to do with it! She wasn't at Brighton: she was at her grandparents' in Cambridge.'

'I know. I know *Janice* didn't have anything to do with it.' He gave me a meaningful look.

'Nor did Derek!' I shouted, and then clasped my hand over my mouth, staring at him in horror. 'Jimmy! You don't think that, do you? Del wouldn't do anything like that – you know he wouldn't!'

'I don't know what to think,' he admitted.

'You can't be serious.' I felt myself beginning to tremble slightly. 'No! Del's not ... *violent*, or aggressive – he never loses his temper or anything.' Even as I was saying this, though, I remembered Derek yelling and throwing things across the room the night he'd come home and found out about Mum and Fred. But that was different, wasn't it!

'You're right,' Jimmy was saying. 'Del goes out of his way to stay out of trouble, if anything.'

'Well, then. Why are you scaring me like this?'

'Sorry, baby. I didn't mean to scare you. But I can't help wondering whether he actually knows more than he's letting on. He was in Brighton, and went to a lot of trouble to pretend he wasn't.'

'If he knew anything, he'd have told the police.'

'I don't know.'

'What – you think he might be protecting someone?'

Jimmy shrugged, looking uneasy again. 'Look, last night was the first time I'd been to the Cauldron for a while – you know, I've been spending time with you, and Mum and Dad over Christmas. But apparently Del was there on Christmas Eve when the news broke about Ian being dead. Some of the blokes thought he acted a bit strange; they were discussing how the mods might be out for vengeance now, but he just muttered that it was terrible news, and walked out.'

'Yeah, well. Del wouldn't be bothered about mods. Although ...' I hesitated. 'I wonder why he never told me on Christmas Day about Ian being dead.'

'But he did suddenly tell you he was considering doing a runner.'

'*Emigrating*, Jimmy. Not *doing a runner*! What are you saying?'

'That perhaps Australia is a long way away from anything that's worrying him.'

'Oh, no. Now I think you're just being ridiculous. He hasn't even made up his mind yet. He's only just got the forms!'

Jimmy sighed. 'You're probably right. It must take ages to get accepted for assisted passage – even if he decides to go.'

'Yes. Which I *hope* he doesn't. Look – let's stop all this, can we? Ian wasn't a nice person, and if he was never going to recover, it might be better for his family that he's gone, rather than having him living on like a vegetable. But I'm *sure* Del doesn't know anything about what happened, Jimmy. Though I really wish he hadn't gone to Brighton – and lied about it.'

'OK.' Jimmy tried to smile but didn't make a very convincing job of it. 'I used to think it was great, being a rocker – being part of a gang, all of us liking the same stuff, you know. But I'm sick of it now.'

'Me too. We don't need labels, do we? Just cos I like nice clothes ...'

'And strange music,' Jimmy added, nudging me.

'*You* can talk!'

We both laughed, but then we fell silent and looked at each other anxiously.

'I'll phone him tomorrow,' I said, biting my lip. I was sure everything was all right. Jimmy's imagination was running away with him. But it wouldn't hurt to talk to Del about it, would it.

New Year's Day 1965

I walked to the phone box down the road to call Derek. I didn't want Mum overhearing the conversation.

'Hiya, sis!' He sounded cheerful enough. 'Happy New Year! Made your resolutions yet?'

'Yes,' I said. 'I'm giving up being a mod.'

'Oh, really? Why's that? Gone off the Beatles? Don't like the Who?'

'You know why. It's all got out of hand. You didn't tell me Ian died.'

'Oh. Right. Well, it didn't seem like a subject for discussion over the Christmas turkey.'

'And you also never told me you were in Brighton the day he got stabbed.'

This time he didn't answer so quickly. Or so cheerfully.

'So Jimmy's snitched to you,' he said eventually.

'Yes – finally, Del! After, what, seven months or more. And only because he's worried about you!'

'Worried about *me*? What for?'

'How do you think it looks? Lying to us all, using Jimmy as some sort of *alibi* – like you had something to hide ...'

'Like what?' he retorted.

'I don't know – you tell me! All I know is, last night I found out that you *and* Jimmy knew all about Ian trying it on with me.'

'Trying it on? Don't make it sound like a couple of little sneaky kisses – Janice said he nearly raped you. I wanted to bloody well *kill* him when I heard –'. He stopped short. 'Bugger,' he added more quietly. 'Slip of the tongue.' We were both silent for a moment, then he added: 'You don't think I had anything to do with that? Him getting stabbed? Just because I was in Brighton, like a thousand other people?'

'No. *I* don't, Del, but it might seem funny to some people, mightn't it? Why you lied about it? Specially after telling Jimmy you thought Ian had it coming to him?'

'That's just a figure of speech, for Pete's sake. Anyway – he flippin' well did have it coming to him. But it wasn't me that did it, unfortunately.' He laughed.

'It's not funny!' I exclaimed. 'Do you *know* who did it? Tell me the truth, Del!'

'Gawd! What is this, the bleeding Spanish Inquisition? No, I *don't* know who did it, and I don't really care, either. What's eating you?' He paused. 'Does Jimmy think I had something to do with it – is that it?'

'No. Of course not. But we're both worried that it looks a bit odd, to be honest. Making up stories about being at Jimmy's house – turning up late at home with Pauline, saying you'd been with her all day ...'

'I *had* been with her all day. Just didn't see the point in telling you we went to Brighton. Mum would have thrown a wobbly, and so would you, by the sound of it. Forget it, Cath – he's dead, it's in the past.'

'Oh, just like that! D'you think the police will just say *let's forget it, it's in the past*? Jimmy says they'll be going over it all much more thoroughly now, questioning people ...'

'Yeah, well. I don't know anything, and they're not going to be questioning me, anyway. Nobody knows I was even *in* Brighton, for a start.'

'Well, *I* do, now, and so does Jimmy.' I stopped, realising what he was implying. 'You're saying you want me to keep quiet about it.'

'Well – what difference does it make? Like I say, Cath, it's ancient history, all done and dusted. Forget it.'

I swallowed hard. There was something about this I really didn't like. I wished it had never happened – any of it. I wished I'd never even gone to Clacton last year – never met Ian, never even heard of him, never found out he'd been stabbed or that he was dead. 'I wish you'd just come home!' I blurted out. 'I hate it there without you.'

'Sorry, sis,' he said. 'I'm really sorry, but that ain't gonna happen. I did warn you, didn't I. We're off to Australia soon.'

'*Soon*?' I gasped. 'But you said you hadn't even decided yet! You said you hadn't even filled out the forms – you were just *thinking* about it!'

'Yeah, I know. Didn't want to upset you on Christmas Day, did I.'

'So it was definite all along?' I swallowed hard. 'You're really going?'

''Fraid so. We had the interviews months ago. We heard just before Christmas that we'd been accepted. Don't say anything to Mum yet. I'll come over next week and tell her myself.'

There was a lump the size of a golf ball in my throat when I hung up the phone. I couldn't bear the thought of Del going away – to the other side of the world. But there was something else as well – something nasty and uncomfortable playing on my mind. What was it Jimmy had said about Del's emigration plans? *Doing a runner.* Surely that wasn't what he was doing? Running away ... from any awkward questions about Ian? Or just from the situation at home, with Mum and Fred? I'd prefer to think that was all it was!

But no. It probably wasn't that either. Surely he just wanted a better life for himself, that was all there was to it. And he didn't seem to care who he left behind.

I hadn't seen Janice since before Christmas – and the only time we'd talked on the phone the whole conversation had revolved around Janice's affair with Phillip, and how he was promising to leave his wife and kids to set up home with her. I didn't have any idea how to respond to this, but didn't really want to admit that I disapproved. I missed Janice, and the fun we used to have – but there was no denying things weren't the same anymore. And now I'd found out about her telling Derek what had happened to me in Clacton, I was stewing with anger. So when eventually Janice did call again, I had a job to stop myself jumping down her throat about it.

'Did you hear about Ian?' Janice started straight away. 'Terrible, isn't it?'

'Yeah. Everyone's talking about it at school. You can imagine.'

'I bet they are. Everyone down the Zodiac is, too. Loads of us went to his funeral. It was awful – I still can't believe he's dead.'

'You still go down the Zodiac, do you?' I said. Anything rather than listen to her talking about Ian's funeral in that distraught tone of voice, as if she'd been in love with him or something. She didn't even like him! 'I thought you spent all your evenings up in London now. With Phillip.'

'Not *every* evening. I still pop in the Zodiac a couple of times a week to see everyone. I see some of the girls from your class, but I haven't seen *you* in there for a long time?'

'No. I haven't been there for a while.'

'What you been up to, then?'

'Oh, I mostly hang around with Linda, you know. Bit busy with schoolwork really.'

'Poor you.'

'Yeah. Look, Jan, there's something I've got to ask you.'

'Fire away.'

'You know ... what I told you, about Ian? About what happened in Clacton – what he did to me?'

There was a pause for a moment. Then: 'Yeah?' Janice said in a slightly guarded tone. 'What about it?'

'Did you tell anyone else?'

'Don't think so. Why?'

'You don't *think* so? You must remember whether you did or not! I told you I didn't want anyone else to know.'

'Well, whether I did or not, it doesn't really matter now, does it,' Janice replied a bit impatiently. 'Ian's *dead* now, Cath – you dig that? Dead and buried, poor bugger – it's not like he's gonna hurt you now.'

'That's not the point! What I'm trying to say is ... Look, someone told my brother about it – and it could only have been you.'

'Well, maybe I did.'

'*Why*? Why did you think it was all right to do that? You *knew* I didn't want anyone to know!' I said angrily. 'I told you in confidence, and now I find out that *Del* knew, and *Jimmy* knew ...' I stopped, aware that I'd slipped up.

'Jimmy? What – Derek's mate Jimmy? Well, that's nothing to do with me, is it. I never see him – and I wouldn't talk to him if I did. Your brother must have told him.' She paused. 'What makes you think he knows about it, anyway?'

'Oh, I ... think he mentioned it when he came round to see Del,' I said, suddenly too flustered to think straight.

'Did he?' There was an edge of disapproval in Janice's voice. 'Can't think why you even waste time talking to him, Cathy – stinkin' rocker. Bad enough your brother being one, although I s'pose you can't help that. Filthy murdering rockers,' she added for good measure.

'It wasn't Del or Jimmy that stabbed Ian,' I protested immediately. 'It's not their fault he's dead.'

'Whose side are you on?'

'I'm not *on* a side. I'm fed up with it all, if you must know. I don't understand why you're so obsessed with it – hating people so much just because they're rockers.'

'You don't, eh?' Janice said quietly. 'You don't care that they killed my boyfriend?'

'He wasn't ...! You'd finished with him! And anyway – that's not the point, Jan. It's not like every rocker is the enemy just because ...'

'I don't know what's got into you since I left school,' Janice interrupted. 'You've changed.'

'Well, maybe I have, yes. Maybe I've grown up a bit.'

'Can't help wondering *why* you're so different,' she went on, sounding suspicious. And then, suddenly, she added: 'Jimmy came round to see *Del*, you said? I thought Del had left home?'

'Oh ... yes, it must've been before he left. It must've been ...'

'Hmm.' She cut me short. 'Right, if you say so, Cathy. Well, I'll see you around, then, I suppose.'

I felt distinctly uneasy after we hung up. I'd been lucky all this time, to avoid Janice finding out about Jimmy. It was probably only because she spent so much time in London now, that we'd managed not to bump into her when we were out together. If she found out now, while she was on such a crusade against anyone who wasn't a signed-up mod, it'd certainly be the end of our friendship. We might not have been quite so close recently, but I wasn't sure if I was ready for that.

'She needs to grow up,' Jimmy said, quite sharply for him, when I repeated the conversation to him later. 'She's eighteen and working in London but she's acting like a stupid *kid* with all this mods and rockers stuff.'

'I know. I don't understand it – she's so mature and sensible in other ways.'

'If you say so.' Jimmy shrugged, and then softened. 'Sorry – I know she's your mate, and you miss her, and all that.'

'She's gone a bit funny, to be honest, ever since Ian got knifed. I think I *was* right about her feeling guilty – because of dumping him and saying stuff about him.'

'Well, just be careful what you say to her. I'm not too sure you can trust her anymore, Cath.'

'Me neither,' I agreed ruefully.

A few days later Derek turned up to make his announcement to Mum about Australia.

'I need to talk to you first,' he told me. We were alone together in the kitchen – Mum was in the sitting-room, watching the end of her favourite TV programme – *Coronation Street*. For someone who'd resisted having a television for so long, it hadn't taken her long to become addicted.

'Go on.' I looked at him warily. He didn't sound happy. 'What's up?'

'All that stuff you were going on about, on the phone the other week. About Brighton.'

'Yeah?'

'Did you tell anyone?'

'What – about you being in Brighton when you said you were at Jimmy's? Course not? Who would I tell?'

He scowled. 'Anyone snooping around asking questions? The police, for instance?'

'Oh no, Del! They haven't been asking *you* questions, have they?'

'Yes. They've been round. And that was very surprising, considering I'm not registered as living at that address, and they wouldn't tell me how they knew it. Did you tell them?'

'What? Are you *joking*, Derek? I don't think I've ever spoken to a policeman in my life. You really think I'd go to a police station and tell them ... ? Flipping heck, I know I was annoyed with you for lying, but that's ridiculous!'

'It must've been Jimmy, then.'

'No – you *know* Jimmy wouldn't do that, either. Are you crazy? The police have got ways of tracking people down, haven't they. It can't be hard – they're probably talking to everyone who ever knew Ian, again, like I said they would.'

'I didn't even know the bloke!'

'No, but somebody must have known someone who knew you ... or the police might have got hold of a list of people who go to any of the rockers' cafés.'

Derek's shoulders slumped. 'I s'pose so. Oh, sorry, sis. I was just – so shocked, you know, when they turned up.'

'What did they say? Did you tell them you were at Brighton? You didn't lie to them, Del, did you?'

He sighed. 'No. I figured someone must have already snitched to them – yeah, you or Jimmy, to be honest. Sorry. So I knew I'd probably land in trouble if I didn't admit to being there. But I told them I didn't know anything about it, didn't know the bloke or even what he looked like.'

'That's OK, then – isn't it?' I said anxiously.

'I dunno. They just kept writing stuff down, and saying "I see", like that. Two of them, there were.' He paused, and then added, 'They did ask me whether I had any reason to dislike him.'

'What did you say?'

'What do you think? I said "I've already told you – I didn't even know him." Then they started saying that I must have hated him because he was a mod, and didn't all rockers hate all mods? I said, "Maybe some rockers do, but we don't go round killing them."'

'Good for you. Well, then, that should be the end of it, shouldn't it. Don't worry – it's just a routine thing, isn't it – they've got to question people. It *is* a murder case now,' I added, shivering at the thought of it. 'I'm glad you didn't try to lie to them, though.'

'Yeah. I s'pose you're right. After all, there must've been thousands of rockers in Brighton that day – they're probably trying to talk to everyone. Fortunately, they're never gonna know how much I *did* want that bastard hurt.'

'And you shouldn't say that out loud, Del – not even to me! It sounds terrible, now he's dead.'

'Who's dead?' Mum demanded, coming into the kitchen as the closing theme tune of *Coronation Street* started to play.

'Winston Churchill. Terrible shame, isn't it,' said Derek, quick as a flash.

'It is – he was a great man,' she agreed, sitting down heavily and shaking her head. 'You young people have no idea what we went through in the war. Churchill stayed in London all through the Blitz, you know. He turned up whenever there'd been a bombing. A great leader, he was. We wouldn't have won the war without him, in my opinion.'

I raised my eyebrows at Derek. Now he'd got Mum in a mellow mood – and he was going to have to break her heart.

In fact she seemed too shocked to say much to his news about Australia, beyond a quiet gasp of 'What? *Where?*' – then maintaining a mutinous, offended silence while Del explained why he and Pauline were going. Fred – who fortunately was out at the time of Del's visit but was filled in on the details afterwards, seemed delighted to have another stick to beat him with in his absence.

'Bloody good riddance, if you ask me,' he said that Sunday at the dinner table, his mouth full of Yorkshire pudding, wiping gravy from his chin.

'He's my *son*, Fred,' Mum protested. 'It's dreadful that he's going away – so far away! Cathy says it's the other side of the world, and they have Christmas in the summer. I don't see how a person could be expected to cope with that.'

'Mum, that's going to be the least of his worries,' I said. 'He's got to get a job, and somewhere to live. And if they get homesick and want to come back, they'll have to pay the full fare themselves.'

'Homesick?' Fred snorted. 'What is he – a man or a bloody mouse? Men don't get homesick, girl. Where would you all have been if people like me had got homesick during the war? We didn't cry and complain about leaving our nice safe homes, when we were sent out to France to fight the Germans.'

'Nice safe homes?' Mum retorted with a flash of her old spirit. I was surprised – but pleased – she was disagreeing with him for once. 'There was no such thing, Fred – it was a nightmare for those of us left behind to guard the home front, I can tell you.'

'Be quiet, woman – what do you know about anything?' he retorted.

'Mum knows a lot more than you do!' I said crossly. 'Half the houses down her street got bombed, didn't they, Mum! She had to sleep in the Underground stations, and her cousin and one of her next-door neighbours got killed, and ...'

'Cathy – leave it,' Mum said, as Fred threw down his knife and fork, staring at me.

'No, Mum! Why do you let him shout you down all the time? You've got as much right to your opinions ...'

He pushed his plate away from him, leaning across the table and shaking his finger at me.

'Don't you dare speak back to me, girl!' he said. His breath smelt of cigarettes and beer. 'Your mother does as I tell her, and *you* mind your own business and speak when you're spoken to!'

'Well, you can talk to yourself then, because neither Mum nor I seem to be allowed to open our mouths in our own house anymore! Sorry, Mum,' I added. I got up from the table, leaving the remains of my dinner on the plate. 'I can't eat it, not while *he's* here.'

I ran upstairs to my room before he could shout at me again. I was furious on behalf of Mum, who'd gone almost overnight from being a forthright woman with a mind of her own, to acting like a pathetic doormat. And I was angry with Del for going away, abandoning us. One of the most upsetting things for Mum was that she had to sign the papers to give her consent to Del emigrating, as he was under twenty-one. She didn't want to – she didn't want him to go at all, but she said she could hardly refuse. It was a good job nobody knew where our dad was – otherwise Derek would have had to ask him to sign too. That would have really been the pits – a father who'd walked out when his son was four years old, having a say in what he did now! There were no two ways about it, as far as I was concerned: men had far too much say in everything, and my generation was going to be the one to make some changes!

The next week

Jimmy and I tried to avoid looking too obvious when we were out together. We wore our most neutral clothes and avoided places where the mods congregated – especially now everyone was stirred up even more, by the news of Ian's death. But when a couple of girls from my class passed us in the street the next Saturday evening, turned back and stared and immediately began whispering and muttering among themselves, I felt a shiver of apprehension.

'Just ignore them,' Jimmy said. 'Not everyone's as bad as Janice.'

'You don't know the girls in my class! They act like they were all personally related to Ian!'

'It'll blow over,' he insisted. 'They're supposed to be intelligent girls, aren't they? They'll calm down when the shock's worn off a bit.'

I wasn't convinced.

And then, a couple of days later, it finally happened. We bumped into Janice.

We'd been holding hands, and when we saw her coming towards us down the road, I stood still and nudged Jimmy.

'Let's turn round and go the other way,' I suggested – but it was too late. She'd already seen us.

'Hello.' She gave me a puzzled frown as she approached, pointedly ignoring Jimmy. She was wearing the shortest mini I'd ever seen. Her hair, as always, was poker-straight, the fringe almost covering her eyes. 'You all right?'

'Yeah – fine thanks.'

She nodded her head towards Jimmy. 'What's *he* doing? Hanging around? Giving you trouble?'

'No.' I lifted my chin. I wasn't going to act like I was ashamed of Jimmy, but more than anything at that moment, I wished I'd told Janice about him right from the start. It would always have been difficult, but before Ian died there was a faint chance I might've got her to accept it in the end. Now, that just wasn't going to happen. 'No – Jimmy's all right. You know he's Derek's friend.'

'And you walk along snuggled up, holding hands, with all your brother's friends, do you?' There was a very unpleasant edge to her voice. 'You're going out with him, aren't you. A bleedin' rocker! I *thought* there was something funny about the way you mentioned him on the phone the other week.'

'Yes – we're going out together,' Jimmy interrupted, before I had a chance to reply. 'We've been going out together for months. It'd be good if we could all be friends, Janice.'

Janice acted like he hadn't even spoken. She continued to look at me contemptuously.

'Look – I'm sorry I haven't told you before,' I said, 'but ...'

'But you knew I'd find it disgusting. And I do. So we'd better just leave it there.' She started to walk away.

'*Don't* be like that!' I called after her. 'Jan! Look, Jimmy's good to me. He's not ...'

'Not what?' Janice spun back round to look at me, and I was shocked to see her face was almost puce with anger, her eyes sparking with it, her voice almost strangled by it. 'He's not a bloody dirty, murdering *greaser*? You don't give a damn about Ian being dead, do you? He was *murdered,* Cath – killed by some filthy rocker!'

'Yes – I know he got killed, but it wasn't Jimmy! He wasn't even there! You can't blame everyone, Jan – nobody knows who knifed Ian!'

Janice slowly walked back towards us and stood, staring me in the face.

'I told you I went to his funeral, didn't I?' she said. 'His parents and his grandma were crying. His sister screamed when the coffin went into the ground. His mum fainted. Everyone from the Zodiac was there. Where were you? Down the Cauldron, mixing with the dirty greasers who did that to him?' She spat the last sentence at me, so that I flinched slightly, holding onto Jimmy's arm. 'Yeah, that's right, hold onto your *boyfriend*!' Janice said contemptuously. 'You might as well, Cathy, cos you won't have any other friends now, that's for sure.'

'None of this is Cathy's fault, Janice!' Jimmy said, but he was wasting his breath – she wouldn't look at him, let alone listen to him.

'We don't *care* about mods and rockers anymore,' I said.

'No. That's obvious.'

'And I'm sorry about Ian, but I don't get it – I don't get why you even went to his funeral. OK, so you went out with him for a while, but if you're honest you didn't even like him! Have you forgotten what he did to *me*?'

Janice just shook her head. 'Forgotten it? I reckon you probably made it up. If it happened at all, you probably asked for it. Dirty little cow – if you're doing it with *him*,' she nodded in Jimmy's direction again, 'you'd do it with anyone.'

'Don't you dare say that about Cathy!' Jimmy exploded.

I'd flushed scarlet. How dare she! '*You're* having it off with a married man!' I reminded her angrily.

'I don't know what your problem is,' Jimmy went on, 'but ...'

'I know what *yours* is,' Janice retorted, turning away again. 'Too bloody ugly and greasy to get a proper girlfriend so you have to stick it in a *kid*. You make me sick.' She tossed her head and stalked away again. Jimmy lunged after her, trying to grab her arm.

'Don't!' I shouted at him. 'Please, Jimmy – leave it alone. That's just what she'd love – can you imagine it?' I added as Janice disappeared round the corner. 'Being able to tell everyone you hit her?'

'I wouldn't have done. I'd never hit a girl.' He was breathing heavily, struggling to control his temper. 'But I'd like to've given her a good shaking. The bitch! I can't believe how she spoke to you.' He put his arm round me. 'Are you OK?'

'Not really.' I blinked back tears. Now the confrontation was over, the shock at just how awful Janice had been was beginning to sink in properly. 'How can she hate me so suddenly, just because I'm with you? How can she hate *you* when she doesn't even know you properly?'

'Because she's a stupid, narrow-minded cow.' He pulled me towards him, holding me tight. 'She's not worth worrying about.'

'But she was my friend! She used to say I was like a little sister to her!'

'Well, she wasn't so much of a friend after all, was she? You don't need friends like that. You've got other friends, nicer friends.'

I knew he was trying to make me feel better – so I didn't want to tell him that he was wrong. Since those girls had seen us together the previous week, word was already spreading like wildfire at school that I was going out with a rocker – and several of my so-called friends were already ignoring me.

'At least I've got Linda,' I said, trying to sound more cheerful than I felt.

'And me,' Jimmy said. But of course, that was the whole problem.

Derek and Pauline set off on their journey to Australia at the end of January. Fred, annoyed at being asked to take a day off work, drove us all down to Southampton in the Ford Cortina he kept parked outside the house and hardly ever used – I suspected he enjoyed having it there as a status symbol and didn't like getting it dirty. Squashed on the back seat with my brother and Pauline, I was miserable and uncomfortable and wished I'd gone with Jimmy on his bike. If I had, there'd have been a terrible fuss from Mum, who disapproved of motorbikes in general, and Fred, who disapproved of me going out with Jimmy. I really hadn't wanted to add a family row to the unhappiness of the occasion. A whole crowd of Derek's mates were going down to Southampton to see him off – several of them roared past us on the road, sounding their horns and shouting when they saw Del waving from the back seat.

'Bloody yobbos,' Fred muttered. 'Mods and bloody rockers. Shouldn't be allowed on the road.'

'Don't worry,' said Derek, bitterly. 'You'll never have to see any of us again after today.'

With which Mum started to cry and I had to bite my lip and stare hard out of the window.

'Now look what you've done.' Fred stared at Del in the mirror. 'Upset your bloody mother.'

'No, I'll leave that to you – you seem to be the expert at upsetting our family,' Del retorted.

Pauline sighed with impatience and rummaged in her bag for a fresh piece of chewing-gum, which she unwrapped and threw in her mouth without offering any to anyone else. And I wished I hadn't come.

'I'll keep in touch, sis,' Derek promised me when it was finally time to say goodbye, after we'd queued for what felt like hours at

Southampton docks. 'Look after Mum,' he added in a whisper. 'I don't know what that moron's after, but if he ends up hurting her ...'

'Why are you going, then?' I said. I was too upset to be nice about it. 'If you're worried about Mum, p'raps you should've thought about staying here and keeping an eye on her.'

'Well, that's your job now, ain't it.' He grinned at me. 'Let's face it – it was always gonna be your job sooner or later.'

'How d'you work that out?'

'Well, sorry, but it doesn't matter how much anyone bangs on about women's lib – it's always the daughter who stays at home and looks after the old parents. I'm not saying I don't feel sorry for you, but ... well, it's kind-of your duty, really, ain't it.'

'My *duty*?' I gasped, gob-smacked. 'What about Pauline's duty to stay with *her* parents, then?'

'That's different. She left home when she was sixteen. Doesn't get on with her parents. She's only been home once – to get them to sign the papers for her to emigrate. They haven't even come to see her off.'

'Well, thanks a million.' I turned away, upset and disgusted. Right then, at the moment of parting, I felt completely let down by my brother. 'Bugger off to Australia, then, go on. Don't worry about anyone else, will you.'

Along with all the other people on the quayside, I waved to the passengers lined up at the rail on the deck as the ship finally moved off on its six-week voyage. But I was so angry with Derek that whenever I thought about him, over the weeks and months that followed, I was going to remember that last conversation, and relive the bitterness I felt then.

Of course, I'd have felt quite different if I'd known I was never going to see him again – ever.

February 2004

There's a surprising number of hospitals in the Sydney area. I'm working my way through them, phoning the numbers given on the internet, and it's not till the seventh one I try: a private hospital in an outlying district with a name with far too many 'O's in it, that I strike lucky. I'm put through to a ward, where the person answering the phone tells me Pauline Ferguson is on her lunch break.

'Can I help? Are you a relative of one of her patients?'

'No. Actually I'm calling from the UK. I'm her sister-in-law.'

'Oh.' She sounds a little flustered. 'I see. We ... the staff here aren't supposed to make personal calls, as I'm sure you can appreciate, but of course, if it's something of an urgent family nature, I'll surely ask her to call you back.'

'I'd be grateful if you would. I'm so sorry to trouble you, but I seem to have mislaid her mobile number, and I do need to speak to her.'

I leave my number, giving my best impersonation of someone with an urgent problem of a family nature. I'm lying through my teeth, of course. I've never had Pauline's mobile number – for all I know, she might not even have one. I was taking a complete gamble on whether she was still a nurse, and in fact even on whether she still lived in Sydney. She obviously doesn't go in for major life changes. Not since the emigration, anyway.

It's only ten minutes before she calls back. I'm so surprised at how easy it's turned out to be, I feel quite shaky now when I answer the phone.

'Catherine? Is that really you?' The line's clear: she sounds like she could be in the next room. She also sounds perturbed, not to say a little annoyed. 'What's going on? How did you get this number? Is something wrong?'

I don't know which of these questions to answer first. I'm quite overwhelmed at hearing her voice – quite shocked that I've actually done this, now: contacted her, after all this time, after all that's happened. But I take a deep breath; no going back now.

'Yes, it's me. Sorry – I didn't mean to alarm you. Nothing's wrong. I just wanted to talk to you.'

'*Talk* to me?' I don't blame her for her tone of voice. We haven't actually talked for nearly forty years, and I've managed to make it sound like we have regular cosy catch-ups every week.

'Yes,' I plough on. 'Look, I'll come straight to the point. I'm writing a piece about the 1960s for a magazine, and it's got me thinking back to the guy who was killed in the fighting, you know – the mods and rockers stuff?'

'Catherine, I'm at work,' she interrupts me abruptly. 'I'm a nurse on a busy oncology ward, and you track me down after all these years and phone me at work, to talk to me about *mods and rockers*? I don't know what you're talking about. I've got to go.'

'Can I talk to you at a better time?' I ask quickly, before she hangs up. 'Please – if you give me your home number, or a mobile, I'll ...'

The line's gone dead. Ah, well. It was worth a try.

In reality, of course, I don't actually *need* to track anyone down, or talk to anyone for my piece for the magazine. It's virtually written. Andy was right – it hasn't taken me long. My memories of the mid-sixties: my life as a mod, my personal account of the fighting at Clacton – even including the fact that I was sexually assaulted, and that my attacker was eventually stabbed in the next bank holiday's fighting. I think I've made it an exciting read. But it's not the scoop I promised him. To pull that off, I've got to write the end of the story – and I can't do that without finding it out myself.

There aren't too many people left to ask. I'd talk to my brother himself of course, if he were still around. I've never completely forgiven myself for being so angry with him when I saw him off to Australia that day in 1965. He and Pauline were there for less than two years when he wrapped his new motorbike round a tree, killing himself instantly. They'd only been married for a few months and Pauline was pregnant. I like to think I was wrong in my self-assured teenage assumptions; that they *were* in love, that they were truly happy for that short time they had together. But I've never been able to find out. Pauline cut herself off from our family in much the same way she'd already cut herself off from her own. In those days, sadly, nobody went to Australia unless they were going to live there – not even for the funeral of their own flesh and blood. Poor Mum. She never got over it.

Two days later, I'm making myself a sandwich for lunch when the phone rings and someone with an unmistakeable Aussie accent says:

'Is that Catherine?'

'Yes.' I put down the slice of bread I'm buttering. 'Who's this?'

'It's Hayley – from Sydney.' She laughs, self-consciously. 'I should probably call you *Auntie* Catherine.'

'*Auntie* ... ?' I've never been called Auntie anything, by anybody. 'You mean ... you're Pauline's daughter?'

'Yes. That's right.' There's a pause. 'Mum told me, about you phoning her.'

'Oh, right.' I've had time to reflect on how crass my phone call must have seemed. 'Look, I'm so sorry for upsetting your mum. I'm a journalist: we're not renowned for beating about the bush.'

'Don't worry. She says she was just really shocked to hear from you – and she was at work, and all, with everybody listening, you know?'

'I know. To be honest it was such a long shot, trying to track her down after all this time, I was pretty shocked myself at actually finding her, so I didn't think it through properly. But I'm glad she's asked you to call me. Would you apologise to her, please ... er, Hayley. It was an intrusion, and ...'

'But she didn't ask me to call you. I'm not looking for an apology. I want to come and see you.'

I swallow back my surprise. 'Oh. Well, sure – it'd be lovely to meet you.' I don't know anything about this girl – this *woman*, who must be in her late thirties now, and was born after my brother died. But she's my niece – Del's daughter, the only thing left of him. It *would* be lovely to meet her, but it's a hell of a stretch to come from Sydney just for a cup of coffee and a chat. 'Do you ever come over to the UK?'

'Come over?' She sounds surprised. 'Oh – sorry, didn't I say? I'm here now – in London. I've just started a six month contract with a company in Canary Wharf. Do you still live in Essex? Mum's told me about where you all came from. How about I come and see you at the weekend?'

She's tall, like her mother, but she's got Derek's thick brown hair, which she wears in a short bob – and she's got his eyes. As she steps over the threshold I feel suddenly so emotional about meeting her that I've reached out and hugged her before I can stop myself, and I'm having to apologise for starting to cry before I've even said hello.

'No worries.' She wipes her own eyes. 'I feel the same way. I always wanted to meet all my rellies over here – on Mum's side as well as Dad's, you know? – but Mum's always been so funny about it, she was insistent I shouldn't try to track anyone down. She can be pretty stubborn about things. She reckons we should leave the past alone, and I didn't want to do anything to hurt her.'

'Does she know you've come to see me?'

She's left her coat in the hall and I've brought her through to the kitchen, where I've put the kettle on and sat her in a warm corner by the boiler while I make coffee. It's freezing out, and she's rubbing her hands and blowing on them. Must be hard to have come here from an Australian summer.

'No. I'll tell her later.' She shrugs and smiles at me. 'She'll be all right. I think, although she'd never admit it, she was a bit intrigued about what you wanted to talk to her for. And so am I! *Mods and rockers*, she said. Tell me more!'

'I will. But first, come into the sitting-room and make yourself comfortable. And tell me all about yourself! And your mum, of course. Did she ever marry again? I was sorry we ... lost touch.' I'm anxious to dispel the image I might have given of myself as a ruthless, exploitative journalist, out to get her story at the expense of everyone's feelings. The truth, of course, is that this story is as important to me for personal reasons as for professional ones – even if it has taken me nearly forty years to decide I want to revisit it.

By lunchtime, we've talked for nearly two hours and I feel like I've known Hayley forever. I might be deceiving myself, but I think there's a lot of Derek about her – in her smile, and a certain look she has when she's considering something, her head on one side. She's clever – an accountant, with a sharp wit and a confident manner.

She's never married, but tells me with disarming candour that she's had a series of *significant others*. It was following the most recent, and apparently most painful relationship break-up that she decided to accept the short-term job offer in London.

'I needed to get away,' she says, 'from Sydney, from Michael.' She doesn't say any more on the subject, and it seems like a good point at which to suggest lunch.

Over soup and hot rolls, we move onto the subject of my 1960s story. I explain the circumstances that led to me taking on the job, including why I'm on my own in middle age with debts that keep me awake at night.

'At first I didn't want to write it,' I tell her. 'But now, I think it's probably done me good. Made me go back and remember it all again. I'd closed my mind against it, really – especially after Del ... your father ... died.'

'I can imagine. It must have been awful for you: losing him to Australia and then – losing him altogether. Awful for my mum, too, of course.'

Awful barely touches it, does it. How must she have felt, facing the birth of her child alone, in what was after all still a strange country to her then. I wish I'd cared more at the time about Pauline, but of course, I was only seventeen, and heartbroken about my brother. In a way, I blamed her for taking him away from me.

'I'm glad she's OK now,' I say quietly. Apparently she never re-married, but has been with a guy, a stonemason called Carl, for over twenty years now.

'I don't have to tell you how much I wish I'd known my dad,' Hayley says, putting down her soup spoon. 'I've been looking forward to hearing more about him. When he was a kid, you know?'

So I get out the old photo albums, and spend a bit of time recounting childhood memories, making her laugh with the usual sort of family tales of misbehaviour, trips to Casualty with broken wrists, games in the street, fights in the playground ...

'And that leads me on to what I wanted to talk to your mum about,' I say, a little more cautiously. I pause. 'Have you heard about the fighting that went on in the sixties between the mods and rockers?'

'Yes – of course. Mum's told me it was all going on when she was in England. When she first knew Dad. They were *rockers*, weren't they.' She says it with amusement. Probably can't imagine her mum, who must now be approaching sixty, tearing around on a motorbike.

'And did she tell you that she and your dad were at Brighton during one of the worst incidents? That someone I knew got stabbed in the fighting there, and died a few months later?'

'No; she didn't.' She looks at me solemnly. 'Is this what it's all about – your story? What you wanted to talk to Mum about?'

'Yes. I wondered if she'd agree to straighten out a few things in my mind. You know what it's like when you look back ... the memories are hazy. Your mum and dad pretended at first that they didn't go to Brighton that day – your dad said it was because he didn't want to worry me, or our mum. I've ...' I glance at her and look away again. 'I suppose I've always wondered whether they knew more than they admitted.'

'About the stabbing? Who did it, you mean?'

'Yes. Del – your dad – was questioned by the police at the time. I think they were questioning all the local rockers. He didn't know Ian, the guy who got stabbed. But he knew something bad about him.'

'You don't think Dad had anything to do with it, do you?' she says, looking startled.

'No, I don't. But he might have seen something ... or known something ... and kept it quiet. Or, of course,' I add quickly, as I don't want to upset her by implying that I'm blaming her father, 'I might just have a very over-productive imagination.'

There's a silence for a while. Hayley's staring into her empty soup bowl.

'I can understand why you'd like to find out the truth,' she says eventually. 'But supposing there really *isn't* anything to find out? Dad *really* might not have known anything – it might just have been a random stabbing ... did things like that happen in those days?'

'Yes.' I smile at her. 'It was unusual, but they did. And you're right: that's probably what it was.'

'What was the bad thing Dad knew about this Ian?'

I hesitate. But there's no point in not telling her, is there.

'He tried to rape me. I was fourteen, and ...' I stop, shrug, try to smile again. 'I had a very lucky escape,' I finish quickly.

'Bloody hell, Catherine. Didn't you get him arrested?'

'No. I should've done, obviously, but things were very different back then.'

'And my dad knew about this?' She raises her eyebrows at me. 'And my mum?'

'I don't know whether your mum did. I have no idea whether Derek ever told her.'

'I'll ask her. Leave it to me.' She picks up her bowl and plate, takes them to the kitchen sink. 'I need to make tracks now, Catherine. But I promise you, I'm definitely going to talk to Mum about this.' She comes back and gives me a hug. 'If she knows anything, you deserve to hear it. You need closure.'

Closure. Strange expressions people use, these days. We might have called it *satisfaction* years ago. The Rolling Stones used to sing about not getting any. I know how they felt.

'I'm glad we've met each other,' she says as she's leaving. 'I'll keep in touch.'

'Me too. I hope to see you again.'

I feel a pang when she's gone, as if I've lost my whole family, all over again.

February 1965

There was a dead mouse in my desk in our form-room. Its beady little eye, glazed over, stared straight at me. It looked like a cat had got it – but someone had gone to the trouble of picking it up and bringing it into school. I could hear the hush in the room as thirty-odd girls waited for me to scream. We used to have a cat at home, though – a prolific mouser – so I was used to such sights. Without looking round at the rest of the class, I fished my hankie out of my pocket and used it to wrap round the mouse-corpse and transport it to the bin at the front of the classroom. Someone giggled, and someone else commented loudly on the smell in the classroom.

'Yeah, it stinks of *greasers*, that's why.' I recognised Heather's voice, but I went back to my desk without looking at her. 'It stinks of someone who's having it off with a rocker.'

There were a few more sniggers and then the form mistress, Mrs Moss, came in to take the register so the fuss died down.

'You should tell Mrs Moss about it,' Linda said later.

'No. It'd make it worse. If I just ignore it, they'll get bored and stop.'

'I hope so. But you should still report it. Before it gets any nastier.'

'Can you imagine how nasty it'd get if I snitched to the teacher about it? For a start, nobody would back me up.'

'I would.'

I looked at her gratefully. 'Thanks, Lin. But look, it'll be half-term soon, and maybe afterwards, they'll have forgotten about all this, and moved on to something else.'

Linda raised her eyebrows. 'I hope you're right. But unless that boy Ian gets resurrected by some miracle or other, he's always going to be their holy martyr. They *know* neither you or Jimmy had anything to do with it – they just want someone to blame. From what I can make out, he was a nasty piece of work anyway.'

'Yeah – he was. But you're right, it's like he's achieved sainthood now he's dead.'

We'd reached the science lab now, where, along with some of the others in our class, we had a chemistry lesson – and unfortunately the last snatches of this conversation were overheard by a couple of girls already seated at the front bench.

'I hope you're not talking about my cousin.' It was Frances, whose family connection to the deceased seemed to have been elevated, since his death, from second-cousin-once-removed to a far closer relationship, much more deserving of sympathy and mass hysteria. 'I know you're a bitch and a rocker-lover, but I wouldn't expect even *you* to speak ill of the dead.'

There was a hush. The chemistry teacher wasn't yet in the room, and everyone had stopped what they were doing – getting out their text-books, setting up their equipment, checking their Bunsen burners and test-tubes were ready for the experiments – to listen. Frances was now Fifth Form Captain, as well as Games Captain and one of the prettiest, cleverest girls in the class. Everyone loved Frances – especially now she was cast in the role of bereaved cousin.

'It was a private conversation,' I said.

'Yeah – nothing to do with you,' Linda said.

'Ooh. Hark who's sticking up for the rocker-lover,' said the girl sitting next to Frances, nastily. 'Lezzy Linda! Sticking up for your girlfriend, are you, Linda?'

There was a wave of tittering. Someone at the back of the class whistled, someone else stood up and lifted her skirt, flashing her knickers, and then sashayed to the front where she pushed herself up against Linda, pouting obscenely in her face.

'You'd better wash your hands after you touch her fanny,' she muttered. 'Someone else has been there and made it all *greasy*.'

Linda turned her face away, her cheeks burning red as the class erupted into laughter.

'Shut up!' I shouted. It was bad enough that, for weeks, I'd been ignored by half the class and had to listen to whispers and taunts from the others. And the incident with the mouse wasn't the first thing, either. The previous week, my ink bottle had been 'accidentally' nudged by one of the girls as she passed my desk, so that ink spilled all over my biology exercise book, completely ruining several weeks' work. Then someone had thrown my school bag out of the window of an upstairs classroom on a rainy day, spilling all the books out onto the wet grass. And various things had been disappearing, too: my gym shirt, my ruler, my pencil case. But seeing Linda being picked on – being called such horrible names, with such disgusting implications, was just the last straw. I raised my voice and yelled it again: 'Shut up, all of you. You're all just a load of bloody horrible *cows!*'

I didn't realise the chemistry teacher, an elderly matron appropriately called Miss Salt, had walked into the room until I'd finished shouting and noticed the silence.

'Go and stand outside in the corridor, Catherine,' said Miss Salt in a deadly quiet voice. 'I'll deal with you in a while.'

'She was defending *me*, Miss,' Linda said at once. 'It's not her fault.'

'Sit down, Linda.' Miss Salt's tone brooked no argument. 'If I want your opinion on the matter I'll ask you.'

I wasn't sorry to be outside the classroom, leaning against the cold stone wall of the corridor on my own, listening to the teacher barking instructions inside the lab. I wasn't sorry, either, about shouting at the other girls. I was furious that they'd turned on Linda. Calling her a lesbian and saying all that dirty stuff! Linda had never been particularly popular, and these days I really regretted not standing by her in the past when she'd been called names. She was a real friend – I was *never* going to let her down again.

'So: Catherine Ferguson.' Miss Salt had left the girls working and appeared beside me in the corridor. 'You'd better tell me what that disgraceful outburst was all about. Not that there could possibly be any excuse for it.'

'I'm sorry, Miss Salt. But the girls were all being rude to Linda.'

'All of them?'

'A lot of them, Miss.'

'Linda strikes me as someone who's capable of handling a bit of teasing without any help from you. Isn't she?'

'Yes, Miss. She is, but it was worse than teasing, and they only started on her because she stuck up for me.'

The old teacher sighed and looked at me seriously.

'I'm slightly puzzled, Catherine,' she said. 'I've never had any trouble from you before. I've always thought of you as fairly quiet and diligent. I was shocked to hear you bellowing like a fishwife. I think you should tell me what the problem is.'

'I don't want to talk about it, Miss,' I said miserably.

'Because you're worried about reprisals? Making things worse?'

I nodded.

'Is this something that's going to blow over, do you think, or should I be telling the head about it? Because, you know, I can't have you yelling and swearing in my lab, I don't care how upset you are.'

'No. I'm sorry. It's ... just something that's got out of hand.'

Miss Salt nodded, looking satisfied. She probably thought there'd just been some sort of petty quarrel between some of us.

'Well, in that case, I won't take it any further. As a punishment for your behaviour, you'll write me two pages on the relative reactivity of chlorine, bromine and iodine, describing the experiments that could be used to prove your conclusions. That's in addition to the homework I'm setting the rest of the class, of course.'

'Yes, Miss Salt,' My heart sank. I'd hoped to see Jimmy that evening but it looked like I'd be working till bedtime.

'And in future, keep your arguments *outside* of my laboratory, please.'

'Yes, Miss Salt. Sorry, Miss Salt.'

'What did she say?' Linda whispered as soon as the class was dismissed.

'Oh, just stuff about not shouting in the lab.' I shrugged. 'Gave me an extra essay to write and told me to behave myself. You know.'

'Didn't you *tell* her? About the mouse and everything?'

'No. What's the point, Lin? How's an old bat like Miss Salt going to stop it? It was nice of you to stick up for me, but now they've started picking on you too. All that disgusting stuff about being ... you know, *queer* – just because you're being a good friend.'

'Actually, Cath ....'

'What?' I smiled at her. 'You really fancy me?' I giggled. 'That *would* give them something to talk about, wouldn't it.'

'Yeah.'

'I mean, if you really *were* ... you know. Blimey, they'd have a field day.'

'Yes.' We started to walk together to the next lesson. 'Some people will pick on anyone who's different, in any way,' Linda added quietly.

'Like Fred – he calls coloured people terrible names. He doesn't even know any: he just has to see them on the telly and it starts him off.'

'It's just ignorance,' Linda agreed. 'I hate it when people get treated differently just 'cos of who they are.'

'Yeah. Like the way women still get treated as men's property. After everything those poor suffragettes went through, to get women the vote.'

'There's so much unfairness everywhere,' Linda said with a sigh.

We came to the door of the English classroom, and I whispered, 'Don't sit next to me. It'll only make them pick on you some more.'

'You think I care?' Linda retorted.

I grinned at her. To hell with the lot of them! Nobody else at school seemed to like me, and Janice had made it pretty clear she was never going to speak to me again, but at least I had one really good friend.

Things had escalated, of course, since the police had reopened their investigation and Ian's case had been splashed all over the local papers.

'*No new leads on 'Mods & Rockers' murder!*' the headline in one week's *Romford Recorder* had screamed. And the next week it was: '*Romford boy died a hero after fights at Brighton, say his devastated parents!*'.

I couldn't work out how Ian could have been considered a hero, since – as far as anyone knew – he hadn't died trying to save anybody, and far from improving relations between regretful mods and rockers as the newspaper report implied, his death had actually added fuel to the fire.

'It's getting beyond a joke,' Jimmy said anxiously when I told him about the mouse incident. 'Why don't you tell your mum what's going on? If she complains to the school, they're bound to take it more seriously.'

'Mum would just find a way to make out it's my own fault. She always does. And anyway, you know what she's been like since Fred's been around. She doesn't seem to care half as much as she used to about my so-called wonderful education. It's like she's lost interest.'

A few weeks after Derek and Pauline left, Jimmy and I were walking back together from the local park when he suddenly stopped and muttered, 'Watch out. Here comes trouble. Cross over – I'll walk on ahead.'

Since the incident with Janice, and all the nastiness at school, we'd tried not to hang out in crowded places together, but it was almost impossible to avoid all the people in the area who knew us. There was a group of girls approaching us, pointing at us and looking threatening.

'Oi! Rocker-lover!' one of them shouted.

'I'm not crossing over,' I told Jimmy crossly. 'They can say what they damn well like – we're together!'

'What's the matter, greaser-girl?' another girl was calling out. 'Can't find yourself a decent boyfriend?'

They were forming a line across the pavement now, blocking our path. There were four of them: I recognised them from the year below me at school. It seemed my unpopularity was spreading. I stopped, put my hands on my hips and stared at them.

'Have you quite finished,' I said, '*children*?'

Before I could move, one of the girls pushed me so hard that I stumbled and would have fallen over if Jimmy hadn't managed to catch hold of me, while another one grabbed my bag and threw it over a hedge.

'Leave her alone!' Jimmy shouted as they ran off, laughing, calling back more insults as they went. 'Are you OK?' he asked me quietly.

'Yeah – just flippin' angry.' I brushed my coat down. 'My bag ...'

'I'll get it. Just lean against the wall there for a minute.' He looked worried to death. I couldn't quite believe, myself, that I'd been physically assaulted in the street by some kids I barely even knew.

'I can't understand it,' I said crossly when Jimmy returned with my bag. 'What's the point ... I mean, are they all going to keep this up forever? What the hell am I supposed to do?'

'Finish with me. That's what they want, obviously. They'll keep it up till you do.' He sighed and put his arm round me we started to walk on. 'And maybe it'd be for the best.'

'*What*?' I looked at him in horror. 'You want us to break up?'

'Of course I don't *want* it. You know I don't! But this can't go on, babe – it's getting out of hand now. If you won't tell someone at school ...'

'No! I keep telling you, it'd just make it worse!'

He hesitated. 'Then maybe we *should* stop seeing each other – I mean just temporarily. Tell them you've finished with me. Let them think they've won, and we'll wait for it all to die down.'

'No, Jimmy!' I shouted, shaking his arm off my shoulders. 'You must be joking! I'm *not* going to do that! Why should we give in to them – give them what they want?'

'All right!' He held his hands up, shaking his head. 'Forget I said it. You're right, of course – we shouldn't give in to them. It's just that I'm worried about you. It's all right when I'm here with you, but when you're on your own – I'm worried they're going to end up hurting you.'

'I can look after myself,' I retorted. 'I'm *not* letting this beat us, Jimmy!'

'Good for you.' He kicked the pavement, hard, as we carried on walking. 'But trust me, if it goes on like this, I'm getting closer and closer to wanting to sort it out myself – giving some of these little bitches a good slap. Or getting some of the lads involved.'

'What are you saying? You don't believe in violence!'

'You've got no idea how violent I *feel* right now!'

'Yeah – and starting anything like that would just make the whole thing flare up again – they'd get *their* boyfriends involved and before you know it, the fighting would kick off again worse than ever.'

'I know. That's all that's stopping me.'

We walked the rest of the way back to my house in silence. I'd been shaken by the incident – but I was even more shaken by what Jimmy had just said. I loved him for his gentle, easy-going nature and now, because of me, he'd been driven to the kind of aggressive feelings he despised. I was angry enough to do some damage myself to some of the girls who'd been picking on me. If it came to it, it should be me getting violent – not Jimmy!

A week later

'That keeps on happening,' Mum said, looking cross and puzzled as she dropped the telephone receiver back on its cradle.

'What?' I said without looking up from my book.

'The phone – it keeps ringing, and when I pick it up there's no-one there.'

I was immediately alert. 'You sure there's no-one there? It's not just that they're not saying anything?'

Mum looked at me as if I was mad. 'And why on earth would anybody pay to make a phone call and then not say anything?'

I sighed. I wasn't about to explain to Mum that it might be a scare tactic, supposedly to unnerve somebody: me. Mum had lived most of her life without a phone and was still a bit nervous of it and besides, I didn't want her to know I was being bullied.

'Let me answer, next time,' I suggested.

'Why? You think I'm going deaf?'

'No – it's just ... well, it might be for me.'

'What? You've got a friend who's too rude to talk to your mother and ask for you?'

'No! I don't know what it's about, Mum. But I'll try and deal with it for you, OK?'

Of course, I might be letting my imagination run away with me. But I had a weary feeling that I was right: that it was the latest move in the campaign to intimidate me. Well, the longer it went on, the more determined I was to stand up to them, so they could damn well play their silly tricks for as long as they liked!

Linda and I had been spending most of our time at school together. And since she'd made such a public stand in support of me, the girls in our class were finding the excuse to gossip about her even more appealing than trying to force me to give Jimmy up.

'I feel bad,' I said one lunchtime as we walked away from a group of girls who were making a big show of whispering about us behind their hands. 'It's not right that they've started picking on you. It's not about you!'

'No. But they think it's about *us*,' Linda said.

'Just because you stuck up for me.'

'No – not just that. Because you're hanging around with me.' Linda looked at me, smiled briefly and shook her head. 'You really don't get it, do you?'

'Get what?'

'Never mind.'

The next afternoon we were followed to the bus-stop by a couple of the younger girls who'd been involved in the incident in the street.

'Rocker-lover!' one of them hissed.

Linda took my arm and moved me on a bit faster.

'Ooh, look at the lezza with her *girlfriend*,' giggled the other girl. 'What's the matter, rocker-lover? Prefer dykes now, do you?'

'Gonna kiss her, are you?' the first girl said to Linda, getting closer to her and making smooching noises. 'Go on, let's see you snog her!'

'Shut up!' I exploded. 'Bugger off and leave her alone!'

'Thanks,' Linda said calmly as we boarded the bus and the two girls ran away laughing. 'But you don't have to defend me. I'm used to it.'

'Why d'you put up with it?' I said, indignantly. But even as I asked the question, the truth finally, finally dawned on me. I sat down on the bus and stared ahead of me, stunned by my own stupidity. Why had it taken me so long?

'I've been trying to tell you,' Linda said quietly, seeing the look on my face.

'I've known you all this time! And you never said anything.'

'It's ... been a gradual thing. Realising it, I mean. I wasn't *born* knowing I preferred girls, Cath. I always knew I didn't fancy boys, but this kind of dawned on me slowly.'

'How come everyone else seems to have realised? And not me?'

'I let something slip a while back. Just a passing comment, when I was being teased for not having a boyfriend – and you know how these things get spread around.' She smiled. 'I think *you* didn't realise because you don't categorise people the way they do. It's one of the things I like about you.' We sat in silence for a few more minutes and then Linda laughed quietly. 'Don't worry,' she said.

'You're my best mate, that's all. I wasn't trying to say I fancied you!'

'Oh. Right!' I blinked a couple of times, shaking my head at my own naïveté, and then we looked at each other again and laughed. 'I'm glad you're my best mate,' I said. 'Strange, isn't it? They pick on me because of my boyfriend, and *you* because you don't want one!'

It was quite a relief to be able to laugh about it.

'She's a lesbian?' Jimmy said when I told him about it that evening. He sounded shocked. In fact, his mouth was gaping open as he stared at me. 'You're joking!'

'I was pretty surprised myself. All the years we've been friends, and I never realised!'

'She should have told you.' Jimmy sounded quite aggrieved about it.

'Why? I mean – yeah, I suppose I wish she had, but to be honest why should she? It doesn't change anything.'

'Doesn't it?' Again, he was looking at me in shock.

'Well, of course not. She's my mate, Jimmy – it doesn't matter to me whether she fancies boys, girls or elephants!'

'No; I suppose not.' He swallowed, seeming to have trouble taking this on board. 'It's ... not very nice for you, though, is it? I mean, you've hung out round her place, and gone swimming together and everything. Doesn't it make you feel kind-of weird now? Like she might have been – you know! – eyeing you up all the time.'

'No!' I was starting to feel upset at his reaction. It wasn't at all what I'd expected from Jimmy. 'She doesn't fancy me, Jimmy! I don't fancy every boy I meet, do I – so why would she fancy every girl?'

'But she's your *friend*,' he said pointedly. 'She must like you.'

'So what?' I was getting frustrated now. 'Liking somebody doesn't mean you're going to make a move on them, does it? What's the matter? Are you jealous?'

I was joking, but to my surprise he lowered his eyes and turned away slightly before admitting quietly, 'Yeah. If you want the truth, I s'pose I am.'

'But Jimmy, you know I'm not interested in anyone except you! And I'm not interested in Linda or *any* girls – not in that way.'

'I know; I know I'm being stupid. But you spend so much time with her – you're with her all day at school, and – you're kind of thrown together more now the others are picking on you both. I was pleased, before, that you had a good friend. Now ... I can't help it: it's gonna bother me.'

'Well, that's your problem, Jimmy Kent, and you're just gonna have to get used to it!' I said crossly. I saw him flinch, and softened slightly as I added: 'You will get used to it, won't you. It's just a bit of a surprise, to both of us.'

He nodded brusquely and I got up to put a new record on. 'I didn't think you liked the Rolling Stones,' he commented as their new record, *The Last Time*, started playing.

'I didn't used to,' I said, deciding to go along with the change of subject. I didn't want to argue with him – we never argued! 'But I really like this one. I think they might be growing on me!' I laughed. 'My mum thinks they're terrible, though – and when Fred saw them on TV once he said something about them representing all that's wrong with young people today!'

Jimmy laughed but didn't say anything. He tapped his foot to the music and stared straight ahead of him as if he could see something I couldn't see.

I was sure he'd get over it. He'd have to, wouldn't he!

'Come round to my place after school?' Linda asked me the next afternoon. 'We can help each other with that maths.'

We were both struggling with our maths O-level work now and we'd been set some extra homework by the teacher, who was threatening us both with that most dire of prospects – a failure – if we didn't 'pull our socks up'.

'OK. Sure, that'd be cool.' To be totally honest, it wasn't exactly ideal, and I really preferred it when Linda came to our house – but I made sure I never offended her by letting her know. It was because of Linda's mum, Mary. She had Parkinson's disease and I couldn't remember her ever being well, even when Linda and I were little kids at primary school together. She had a nurse now, to look after her when Linda was at school, but when she got home it was Linda's responsibility to care for her mum, make her meals and help her from the chair to the bed. Their flat was small, with Mary occupying the only bedroom, and Linda slept on the bed-settee in the sitting-room. I always felt awkward about being there. I suppose I wasn't used to illness and because of the lack of space I felt like I was in the way.

Today, though, thinking about this as we travelled home on the bus together, I started to feel ashamed for not taking more interest in Mary's condition.

'Your mum's been ill for ages, hasn't she,' I said.

'Yeah. She was diagnosed when I was about six. She was really young to get Parkinson's – only in her forties.' She glanced at me and shrugged. 'She had me when she was nearly forty. I don't think she expected ever to have any kids. And then she got this horrid disease. Life's not very fair, is it?'

'No.' I swallowed, struggling to take this in. 'Your dad's dead, isn't he?'

'Apparently. But I never knew him, Cath. He obviously didn't hang around till I was born. Even worse than yours,' she added, with a snort of laughter. 'At least yours married your mum.'

'Yeah, worst luck,' I said with feeling. 'I'm sorry about your mum, though. Is there any chance she'll get better?'

Linda sighed and shook her head. 'If only they'd invented this new wonder-drug sooner – L-Dopa, it's called. Apparently it's going to make a fantastic difference to people with Parkinson's. But it's too late for Mum. She got worse so fast ...'

She tailed off, looking bleak and tired.

'I'll try and help you, whenever I come round,' I said. 'I'm sorry. I should've offered before.'

'That's OK. It's not so bad, really. Mum doesn't complain – and at least we have the nurse.'

We worked quietly together on our maths, so that Mary could watch the TV. She never spoke more than a few words to me, and up till now, feeling kind of embarrassed by a disease I didn't understand, I hadn't made much effort to converse.

'Mum finds talking really difficult and frustrating these days – don't you, Mum,' Linda explained that evening. 'I can understand her, and so can the nurse, but other people sometimes can't. But talk to her anyway,' she told me quietly. 'She likes people to chat to her; never mind if she can't say much back.'

So I overcame my awkwardness and made more of an effort to talk to Mary. After we'd finished our homework I stayed for a while to help Linda get her mum's dinner ready.

'I'm sorry I've been such a selfish cow,' I said. 'You and your mum have got such a rough deal – I can't believe I never gave it much thought before.'

'I'm OK,' Linda said with a shrug. 'It's *her* I feel sorry for. That's why I don't go out and leave her very often. And we'll be better off for money when I start work.'

Linda was leaving school after her O-levels. She'd always told me it was because she wanted to earn some money – but I hadn't even considered just how much she needed to. I hadn't really given much thought to *any* of Linda's problems. It was time I grew up, I thought to myself bitterly as I walked home, and started realising there were people much worse off than me!

With these thoughts still running through my head, I arrived home just as Fred had got in from work.

'Where do you think you've been?' he demanded. He seemed in an even worse mood than usual.

'Round at Linda's,' I told him abruptly, and walked straight through to the kitchen.

'Can I help with the dinner?' I asked Mum.

'Oh – *now* you're asking, are you? It's a bit flippin' late, isn't it – waltzing home just as I'm dishing up. Where were you when the potatoes needed peeling?'

'Round at Linda's,' I said again. And couldn't resist adding: '*Her* mum *really* needs some help.'

Mum dropped the serving spoon she'd been using and stared at me. 'You dare to tell me that? You think it's all right to be round at *that* woman's place, helping *her* with her dinner – instead of helping your own mother? Is that what you're saying?'

'Yes, Mum! Sorry, but Linda's mum's very ill and can't do anything for herself.'

'Well, maybe she brought that on herself,' she said scathingly.

'What d' you mean? It's obviously not her fault she's got Parkinson's disease!'

'Isn't it?' She put her hands on her hips. 'Well, that's not what I've heard. I've heard she's no better than she should be, that woman. There was no father on the scene when she gave birth to your precious friend – did you know that? Goodness only knows how many men she was cavorting with during the war – no wonder she got taken ill. It's God's punishment.'

'Mum!' I gasped. 'I can't believe what you're saying! You've got no right to accuse Mary of sleeping around, just because Linda's dad didn't marry her – and even if she did, so what? Parkinson's Disease hasn't got anything to do with who you sleep with!'

'That's all you know, Miss. Just because you're being privileged with a grammar school education, you don't know everything yet! I'm your mother, and I know best, and don't you forget it!' She picked up the spoon and began, tight-lipped with righteous certainty, to dish up the dinner.

'What's going on?' Fred demanded, appearing in the kitchen doorway and looking from me to Mum with an air of aggression.

'Nothing.' I felt like I was about to explode with anger. 'I don't want any dinner – I'm not hungry.' I walked past Fred and headed for the stairs, calling back over my shoulder: 'You should've washed that spoon after you dropped it, Mum. Germs can get transferred to the food like that, and make you ill – I learnt about it in my privileged grammar school education. But I expect you prefer to think it'd be God punishing you.'

I only caught two words of Fred's exclamation as I went upstairs to my room: *spoilt bitch.* And the trouble was, after spending time with Linda and Mary, I didn't really disagree with him.

March 1965

'I wish I could find out who's doing that.' I slammed down the phone after another silent call.

'It might just be a wrong number,' Jimmy pointed out mildly. We were watching TV together. Mum had, for once, been invited to the pub with Fred and we knew it'd be late before they got back.

'Nah. I'm sure it's one of those stupid bitches in my class, trying to intimidate me. Well, if they think I'm going to ...'

Jimmy turned round and looked at me. 'You've changed lately, d'you know that?' he said abruptly.

'Have I?' I was taken aback. 'In what way?'

'Well ...' He hesitated, looking like he wished he hadn't said anything now. 'Don't take it the wrong way – but since you've had all this stuff going on at school you've got kind-of *tougher*. I know it's been a real drag for you ...'

'A *drag*?' I exclaimed, going to sit back down with him. 'That's an understatement! It's all right for you, *your* mates didn't turn against you!'

'All right, don't bite my head off. See what I mean? You're sort-of angry all the time, these days, babe. You used to be so quiet, and gentle, and ...'

'And then I grew up a bit, Jimmy. I was only a *baby* when you met me – I had no idea about anything. Since then, Fred's moved in and started acting like he's my dad, my brother's gone to Australia – my family's been turned upside-down ...'

'I *know*. I know all that – haven't I been sympathetic?'

'Yes, you have – but you don't seem to realise that it's all had an effect on me. And yeah, I do get cross about the girls at school – so would you! It's gone on so flippin' long! Nobody talks about Ian Vincent much now, even the papers have gone quiet about him, and nobody's even talking much about mods and rockers anymore – but they're still picking on me. If it's not because I'm going out with *you*, it's because I'm friends with Linda.'

'Mm. Linda,' Jimmy muttered, shaking his head.

'What? What now?' I was getting irritated. What was wrong with him tonight? Surely he wasn't still feeling jealous about Linda? He never seemed to miss a chance to have a dig at me about her.

'That's all I seem to hear about now – Linda this, Linda that.'

'Well, it's not surprising, is it – as she seems to be the only person I can talk to!'

'You can talk to me,' he said quietly.

'Can I? Are you sure, Jimmy? Cos it seems, suddenly, that you just want to complain about me not being *quiet* and *gentle* anymore. Is that what I've got to be? Is that all you want from a girlfriend? Aren't I allowed to have a mind of my own, stand up for myself, speak out?'

'I'm going home,' Jimmy said, getting to his feet and grabbing his jacket. 'Let's talk tomorrow when you've calmed down.'

'What?' I got hold of his arm. 'Don't just *go*! Jimmy – we've never had a row before!'

'And that's exactly what I'm trying to avoid!' he said, looking pained. '*I* don't want to start having rows. I know you've been having a bad time – but I don't know how I can help, how I can make things better. I wish I could! I wish I could do something to protect you – wrap you up in cotton wool and keep you safe.'

'Don't patronise me! I'm not a baby!'

He sighed. 'You see? You turn everything I say around. Get off your soapbox, Cath – I'm not insulting you, I just want to be allowed to love you!'

'Stay, then.' I put my arms round him. 'Stay and love me! I'm sorry, Jimmy. I don't mean to be cross with you. I'm just fed up with it all.'

'I know. Sorry I had a go at you.' He kissed me so slowly that I melted into his arms. 'How long have we got before your mum gets home?' he whispered.

'Long enough,' I giggled. 'Shall we go upstairs?'

'Are you sure?' He looked at me hopefully. 'In your bed?'

'Yes. But ... not all the way. I'm too scared.'

'You'll be sixteen soon,' he reminded me teasingly. 'And I can get some French letters ... you won't get pregnant.'

'I'll think about it,' I said, laughing, and as I pulled him towards the stairs it went through my mind that it might be best to agree. I was worried now that he might be going off me. But it was no good

– I couldn't turn myself back, now, into the demure little girl I'd been a year ago. Perhaps if I let him have sex with me, he'd love me more.

Derek was scheduled to have arrived in Sydney by now. We'd had one letter from him since he left – a single scrawled sheet sent from one of the ports on the journey, mostly describing the mates he'd made on board the ship and the drinking sessions that seemed to be going on every night.

'Bloody fool,' Fred said, predictably, 'Wasting his time, pissing his money up the wall. What's he gonna do when his cash runs out, eh? Because he ain't gonna be coming back *here* begging for help.'

'Of course he won't!' I said. 'He'll be getting a job, won't he, when he gets to Australia.'

'Not much of a life for Pauline,' Mum said gloomily, 'Going to the other side of the world, to some foreign place, with no family to look out for her. Not much fun for her now, either, by the sound of it, sitting around on that boat while Derek spends all his time drinking with his mates.'

Actually, to me it sounded exactly like Mum's life, with Fred down the pub every night, but I managed not to say so.

'If she's got any sense, she'll be joining in with the fun,' I said instead.

I felt sad, reading my brother's handwriting and thinking of him out there somewhere on the ocean so far from home. I was still upset with him for telling me it was my duty to stay behind and look after Mum. But I knew he'd gone to find a better life for himself, and the way I felt about everything at that moment, I couldn't blame him for that.

'I'll get the phone cut off,' Mum said after picking up another silent call a couple of days later. 'I've had enough of this carry-on. Never wanted the blasted thing in the first place.'

'Yes you did!' I reminded her. 'You said we should have one, because it'd be a God-send in an emergency.'

'Yes, well, that was before we had a man to look after us.'

I snorted. 'Anyway, I told you – let me answer it,' I said.

She gave me a hard look. 'You think it's one of your so-called friends, playing a joke, do you, Miss? Is that it?'

'Maybe.'

'Well, if that's the case, they're not the sort of girls you ought to be hanging around with. Making phone calls and not speaking? What's the world coming to? I suppose their parents are paying for all these calls they're making? So much for a grammar school education, indeed – acting like common hooligans!'

I laughed. 'You're dead right, Mum, but they're not people I hang around with. They're just doing it to annoy me, so *don't* talk about having the phone cut off. I'm not letting it get to me.'

I still hadn't mentioned any of the trouble at school to Mum, but now, her eyes narrowed as she continued to stare at me.

'Are you getting picked on at school? Is that what you're saying?'

'Nothing I can't handle.' I wished I hadn't let it slip.

'What's it about? Don't turn away from me, girl. I want to know! You go to that school to get an education, not to get picked on by hooligans!'

It was the fact that Mum suddenly seemed to be expressing an interest in my welfare again that made me weaken. I'd felt so ignored by her since Fred had been there, and although the nagging about school work had always got on my nerves in the past, I realised now how much I actually missed her caring.

'It's nothing really, Mum, honest,' I said. 'It just blew up over all the mods and rockers stuff, you know. Because people saw me with Jimmy. But everyone's getting a bit bored with all that, now, so ...'

'Mods and rockers!' she exclaimed in disgust. 'Flippin' louts and hooligans if you ask me. They should all be in the army, that'd keep 'em out of trouble. If they had to fight for their country, like our young men did ...'

'I *knew* I shouldn't have bothered telling you! Look, forget it, Mum – I was trying to say it's all blowing over now, so just ignore the phone calls, just hang up if you get one, OK? They'll give up if we take no notice.'

'... hanging around with that Jimmy Kent, roaring around on that bloomin' dangerous machine,' she went on as if I hadn't spoken. 'I've warned you, girl, don't you come home here with trouble in store.'

'No, OK – I'm not stupid!' I sighed. I really hadn't wanted another argument. So much for confiding in Mum. 'I'm off round Linda's,' I said wearily. 'We're going to do our revision together.'

It was a Saturday afternoon. The dreaded O-levels were fast approaching, and revision had taken on a whole new urgency. I was struggling now in some of my weaker subjects like maths and sciences. Linda, who wanted desperately to get a job as a dental nurse, was putting in extra work on the same subjects, so it helped us both to study together.

'Let's hope everyone's so busy swotting, next term, they'll leave us alone,' Linda said that day as we worked together in her sitting-room while Mary was having her afternoon sleep in the bedroom.

'Yeah. I think it's starting to blow over. I haven't heard anyone mention Ian for ages now, and there hasn't been any more trouble between the mods and rockers. I still get evil looks when anyone sees me out with Jimmy, though.'

'And they'll still pick on you for hanging around with me,' Linda said matter-of-factly.

'But I've got a boyfriend! They know I'm not ... um ... like you.'

Linda smiled. 'You *can* say it, you know. Lesbian.' She looked back at her text book and then added quietly, 'Although I suppose I'm only a lesbian in my head, really. I haven't ever actually done anything.'

'Not even kissed anyone?'

'No. Never wanted to, with a boy, and I haven't worked out how to *find* a girlfriend, yet. Anyone who might feel the same, and not just be completely insulted and slap me round the face!'

I nodded, feeling some sympathy. It must be so difficult for her.

'I'm thinking of having sex with Jimmy,' I decided to confide in her. 'We've been going out for nearly a year, and he's been really patient, but I'm worried he might be going off me.'

'You shouldn't do it unless it's what you really want, though, should you?'

'It is what I want – I think so, anyway. When we're kissing, and all that ...' I hesitated. I'd never talked to anyone else about this, and really, Linda was a strange choice. But I didn't feel awkward telling her. 'It's fantastic. It makes me want to go further, but I'm a bit scared about actually doing it. Sometimes I think I could just carry on forever just snogging with him. It's lovely.'

Linda sighed. 'You're so lucky. I wish I *could* fancy boys. I tried, you know, staring at pictures of people like Paul McCartney and trying to make myself want them. But it doesn't work. I like Marilyn Monroe. I think she's absolutely gorgeous.'

'Well, yes, she is!' I laughed. 'But I don't feel like kissing her.'

'I do. It's not much fun, Cath. I just want to feel what it's like – what you're feeling with Jimmy. I wonder whether I'll ever find out.'

'Of course you will!' I put my arm round Linda, feeling hugely sorry for her. 'Come on – you're only sixteen, you'll meet someone, I'm sure you will. There must be lots of other girls who feel just the same.'

'Would you mind kissing me?' she asked suddenly in a very small voice.

I hesitated, startled and going hot with embarrassment.

'Say no if you'd rather not,' she added quickly. 'I'll understand. I'm not trying to ... seduce you or anything, honest. I just wanted to see what it feels like. Just once. Pretend I'm Jimmy,' she went on, with a grin. 'I'll pretend you're Marilyn!'

'OK,' I said. It felt weird, but I supposed it was the least I could do, for my friend. I closed my eyes.

February 2004

Linda's partner, Andrea, answers the phone when I call her for another chat.

'You've got Lin well and truly intrigued, about all this 1960s stuff,' she says, laughing. 'And me too, come to that! She's been telling me stuff about your schooldays together – your murky teenage pasts!'

Ridiculously, I feel myself blushing, remembering that kiss again and wondering if Linda's told Andrea about it. They've been together for about fifteen years now and they're so happy together, she'd probably just laugh her head off. I'm the only one who'd feel embarrassed about it.

'We didn't really get up to much,' I find myself saying awkwardly. 'We were two of the most boring swots in the class.'

'That's what they all say,' she says. 'Sometimes those quiet kids are the worst!' And she should know – she teaches maths in a big comprehensive school. Rather her than me.

Linda takes the phone and asks me how I'm getting on with the story.

'Nearly finished,' I say, frowning at the screen in front of me.

'Apart from your bit of detective work?'

'Yes.' I sigh. 'I know you probably think I'm daft ...'

'No. I don't.'

'... but I can't shake this feeling that someone knew something about Ian's murder. Something they weren't telling anyone.'

'Someone? Someone in particular?'

'No. Not really. Well, yes – to be honest I did used to wonder about my brother. You know, the fact that he lied about being in Brighton that day. And seemed in such a hurry to bugger off to Australia. But after he died, I refused to think anything bad about him anymore. Persuaded myself I'd been a hysterical, overimaginative teenager during the sixties and that nothing about it was really as bad as it seemed at the time.'

'But it was bad, wasn't it,' Linda says. 'Even though we've never talked much about it since.'

'I pushed it all to the back of my mind. But now – now I've started thinking about it again, the memories are so vivid. It's like ... yesterday.'

Yesterday. The lyrics of the Beatles' song, about troubles being far away, suddenly flash through my mind and I smile wryly to myself. I remember listening to that song a lot in 1965.

'Well, sadly you can't talk to Derek about it now, can you, love,' Linda's saying gently.

'No. But I've tried talking to Pauline.'

'*Have* you?' She squawks in surprise – and I fill her in, briefly, on my impulsive phone call to Australia, and the subsequent visit from Hayley. 'She promised to get back to me if her mum tells her anything.'

'Do you think that's likely?'

'I don't suppose so.' I sigh. 'Oh, I realise I probably won't get anywhere. If anyone *did* know anything, they're hardly going to admit it now, are they – after keeping it quiet for forty years.'

Linda doesn't say that I'm wasting my time, and my emotions, by trying to dig up all this ancient history now; that I should leave the past alone; that I'm going to end up frustrated and disappointed. Linda never was one for coming out with the platitudes other people trotted out.

'I hope you find what you're looking for,' is all she says.

'Thanks, Lin.'

What exactly *am* I looking for? A fat reward for a sensational piece of journalism? A boost to my flagging career? Or is this all *only* about something else? Something else entirely?

'Do you remember,' I say quickly, just as she starts to say goodbye, 'an afternoon in 1965, just before our O-levels? Round your place – while your mum was still alive – when we were trying to swot up on our chemistry?'

'You mean that time I made you kiss me?' She laughs, and I'm glad. Relieved of my embarrassment, I laugh along with her.

'You didn't *make* me. I thought ...' Instinctively I close my eyes again, remembering. 'I did it because I thought I was doing you a favour. What a patronising little bitch I was.'

'We were sixteen, for God's sake, Cath – neither of us had a clue what we were playing at. Anyway, I didn't manage to convert you, did I!' She snorts with laughter again. 'You still went ahead and shagged bloody Jimmy Kent.'

'Yeah.' I suddenly wish I hadn't started this conversation. 'Perhaps you should've tried harder with me. You might've done me a favour. Spared me a lot of pain.'

'Sorry,' she says quietly.

We both know she doesn't mean that she regrets not turning me gay. We both know I'm going to spend the rest of the day remembering what happened with Jimmy. But then again, what's new?

May 1965

Jimmy and I had sex on my sixteenth birthday. I'd been thinking about it for ages, at the same time as I'd been trying to forget about the snog with Linda. I'd been shaken by that whole experience; I wasn't turned on by it, but I *was* amazed with myself for doing it at all. I wasn't upset or disgusted with myself – but I knew almost everyone else I could think of, would be horrified. Especially Jimmy. I couldn't even begin to imagine his reaction if he found out! Although I'd never felt anything sexual about girls – even when we were all much younger and some of my friends had some sort of crush on an older girl – in a funny sort of way, the fact that I'd crossed a boundary that would have shocked anyone who knew me was exciting in itself. I couldn't help feeling a bit different – like I was less suburban, more hip and Bohemian than everyone else – and although it was weird and confusing to admit it, even to myself, I quite liked having this secret from Jimmy. It kind of served him right for being so *off* about my friendship with Linda.

Linda had been right in one respect: everyone at school was so worried about the impending exams that the bullying had eased off. We were still mostly being ignored by the other girls but silent treatment was easier to ignore than verbal abuse, dead mice, and being assaulted in the street.

The week before my birthday, though, there was a flare-up of the trouble. The worst two of my tormentors – Susan and Heather, who a year before had been my friends – started it all off again. It was lunchtime on a particularly warm day, and a lot of the girls were sitting outside on the school field.

'Are you having a birthday party, Cathy?' Susan called out to me as Linda and I walked past. 'You haven't invited us.'

'She won't be asking *us*, Sue!' Heather laughed nastily. They were sitting with Frances, Ian's supposed cousin, and it occurred to me that it was only when they were with her that Heather and Susan started showing off by insulting me. 'She'll be having a nice little sixteenth birthday party on her own with that rocker boyfriend of hers. Making it legal!'

'So what if I do?' I shouted back. 'Jealous, are you?'

'No *thanks*!' Susan pulled a face. 'I only do it with mods. Not like some people, having it off with any old one.'

'Yeah, any old one – mod or rocker, male or female!' added Heather, and they both squealed with laughter.

'Leave her alone,' Linda told them. 'We're not all like you two – Cathy's only had one boyfriend, and she doesn't mess around.'

'Oh, sorry, Linda,' Heather said in a silly mock-contrite voice. 'Did we insult your loved one? What's the matter – won't she let you touch her? Doesn't she like the smell of your ...'

'Shut up!' I bellowed at her. All of a sudden, I'd had enough. I'd put up with this for so long! I'd started to hope it had finally finished, and now – now I was past caring what they said about me and Jimmy, but I really couldn't bear to hear them picking on Linda for a single minute more! 'You two – you're just so stupid, I can't be bothered talking to you. But the rest of you!' I raised my voice, addressing the crowd of girls who'd been sprawling on the grass nearby, listening and giggling amongst themselves, 'You know what? You're worse than them! They're stupid and old-fashioned – yeah, old-fashioned, Heather! Times are changing, didn't you know that? Only *old* people, old stick-in-the-muds who're frightened of change, still think it's cool to insult people just because they're different. We don't live in the Victorian age anymore – this is the Sixties – it's gonna be a whole new world where everyone's equal! It's not with-it to pick on people because of who they are – and it's just plain *childish* to join in, or laugh at it and when you know it's wrong. None of you have got the guts to stand up and tell these two to pipe down. If you actually think they're clever, OK, carry on laughing at them. Let them say horrible things to Linda if you think that's funny. But she's the only one who's got the guts to say what she thinks, and I *admire* her for daring to be different. It's cool.'

It wasn't till I'd stopped, running out of breath and aware that I was starting to repeat myself, that I noticed the silence, and felt my cheeks suddenly burning with humiliation. What had I done? Was I mad? This was only going to make things worse! But as I started to turn away, there was a shout from someone at the back of the group.

'Well said, Cath.'

'You're dead right,' someone else called out.

'Yeah – those two aren't funny. They're just rude.'

Somebody started to clap and a few others joined in. A couple of girls got up and came over to me, patting me on the back and saying they were sorry – and then turned to apologise to Linda too. Before I'd had time to gasp in surprise, Linda and I were surrounded by girls making warm and ingratiating comments to us. And Heather and Susan, scowling and muttering to each other, had turned on their heels and stalked off. Frances, the Fifth Form Captain who was used to being followed, copied and admired by all, stood her ground for a moment, giving us a final hard glare, before running after the other two and putting her arms round their shoulders in a gesture of support.

Linda beamed at me and tucked her arm through mine as we walked away in the opposite direction. 'You sure socked it to 'em!' she said.

'Yeah. Wish I'd done it months ago!' I said, although I was still trembling with surprise at myself. It must have been the longest speech I'd ever made. I hadn't known I was capable of such a thing!

The fuss didn't die down for days. I kept seeing people looking at me and whispering wherever I went in school, but now most of the comments were along the lines of:

'... really made those bitches look stupid ...'; '... should have heard what she said ...'; and '... stuck up for her mate – made me wish I hadn't picked on her ...', instead of the abuse I'd been used to. It seemed too much of a dramatic change – I couldn't quite believe that one heartfelt rant from me could swing people's opinions so drastically and so quickly.

'But that's just the point, isn't it,' Linda said. 'People *do* get swayed easily. And some of the girls in our class are just like sheep: they followed the herd when they were attacking us, and now they're following the herd by treating us as the new heroes.'

'In other words, it won't last.'

'Not unless you can keep making speeches like that!'

I laughed. I didn't think I'd ever be able to find the words to do it again. But for the moment anyway, I was being treated with a lot more respect. I might as well enjoy it!

My birthday fell on a Saturday and Jimmy had promised me a surprise.

'We're going up the West End,' he said when he phoned in the morning. 'Get yourself dressed up! I've booked a show and a restaurant.'

I was stunned. Although it wasn't far at all on the train into central London, my trips up till now had been limited to school outings to museums, and occasional days out on cheap Red Rover tickets with Mum and Derek when we were younger, to see the usual sights of St Paul's Cathedral, the Tower of London and Trafalgar Square. I'd never been to the West End for a social occasion, and never seen a show! I was so excited I could hardly think straight as I got myself ready.

'What's all this in aid of, glamour-puss?' Mum demanded, not unkindly, when I came downstairs in my navy blue dropped-waist mini-dress and patent-leather shoes, with my new suede bag on my arm. My hair, now grown so long that I normally wore it tied back in a ponytail, was loose over my shoulders. 'Off out with your friends for your birthday, are you?'

Mum had given me the bag for my birthday and inside it, wrapped in tissue paper, was a compact mirror and a lipstick: Mum's way of saying she finally accepted that I was growing up. I'd felt a sudden new burst of affection for her. Much to her consternation, I'd given her a hug and thanked her profusely – all the while watched in surly silence by Fred, who merely commented that just because I was sixteen, I didn't need to think the world was going to revolve around me. 'No chance of *that*,' I'd muttered to myself.

But Fred was out now. I smiled at Mum and did a twirl on the spot, pleased with the way I looked, excited about the day ahead.

'I'm going out with Jimmy. He's taking me up the West End to see a show and have a meal in a restaurant.'

Mum's expression changed. 'I see,' she said, sounding put out. 'I suppose you think you're all grown up now and too good for the likes of us, cavorting up to *West End shows* and *fancy restaurants*.'

'Of course I don't think that!' I stopped twirling and stared at her, not wanting the mood of the day to be spoilt. 'It's just – a special treat from Jimmy, because it's my sixteenth birthday. He probably had to save up like mad to afford it.'

'Yes, and I wonder why.'

'What d'you mean?'

Mum snorted. 'Don't play the innocent with me, girl. Sweet sixteen and never been kissed? Pull the other leg. I reckon that young man of yours has only been hanging around till now so he can have his way with you legally.'

'Mum! Jimmy's *not* like that! He ...'

'Look at you!' she went on. 'Skirt up above your knees – you do realise you're showing your suspenders and stocking-tops, I suppose? That's all right these days, is it, to go out on the streets looking like a tart? I suppose such things are acceptable in the *West End*? Well, I'm warning you, if you go and get yourself pregnant ...'

'Like you did, you mean?' I flung back. I knew I'd gone too far now. The day was not going to be recoverable. 'Thanks very much for spoiling my birthday, Mum. D'you know what? I think you're jealous. That's your trouble, isn't it – you're dead jealous of me because I'm young, and I've had the education you never got, and I've got a nice boyfriend instead of a horrible pig who bosses you about like he owns you. Well, I'm sorry, Mum – it's not my fault you didn't have a good time when you were a teenager! The war wasn't my fault! And it wasn't my fault Dad walked out on you, and you never had anything nice!'

'Cathy, I'm warning you ...'

'No! Let me finish! I'm sorry you're so miserable now that you have to pick on me, and spoil my birthday – but it's your own fault, Mum! You should never have let Fred move in, and you know it. I'm going out with Jimmy and I'm going to have a good time, and that's what *you* ought to be doing. If Fred cared about you he'd take *you* out to shows, and to restaurants – yes he would! – instead of going down the pub on his own all the time and not even letting you go to *work* there!'

I finally ran out of steam and stood, looking at Mum warily, waiting for the furious response that was sure to come. But she dropped her eyes, sighed deeply and turned away, walking heavily back to the kitchen where she started clattering pots and pans. I hesitated. I ought to run after her, apologise, try to make things better again. But I knew I'd somehow, again, found the right words – hit the mark, made her realise I was right. Mum might not ever admit it, but she knew I was right. And despite feeling upset at having argued with her on my special day, I couldn't quite suppress the strange thrill of excitement I felt, at having done it again. *I'm good at this*, I thought. *I'm actually good at getting my point across.* I was thinking maybe I should become a politician. Journalism hadn't even occurred to me at that stage.

'I'm off now, then,' I called out more gently to Mum. 'See you later.'

There was no reply. I grabbed my jacket and left the house, tugging at the hem of my skirt as I went. Doing that twirl had been a mistake. I'd have a look in one of those West End fashion shops for a pair of the new panty-hose, if only I could afford them. Suspenders were so flippin' uncomfortable, anyway!

We saw *Oliver!* which was in its fifth year at the New Theatre in St Martin's Lane, and then had dinner in one of the new Golden Egg restaurants. Walking into the restaurant, arm in arm with Jimmy who'd dressed in his smart suit for the occasion, I felt like a grown-up woman of the world instead of a gawky schoolgirl. All around me were beautiful people sporting the latest fashions, strolling casually down the crowded streets, looking in shop windows, heading in and out of smart pubs and coffee-bars, laughing and chatting together as if they had all the time, and all the money, in the world. I pictured my mum, sitting at home on her own with her cup of tea and the TV for company, waiting for Fred to come weaving back from the pub reeking of cheap beer and fags – and I felt a flicker of irritation. OK, so she'd had a hard life, but why couldn't she move on? Why didn't she try to enjoy herself now while she still could? We weren't living in the Great Depression now; we weren't at war with Germany anymore or even struggling through the post-war austerity of the fifties. This was 1965 – life was good now, it was all shiny-new and fun and she was opting out of it! Well, she needn't expect me to do the same. I was going to enjoy my life, starting from now. Starting from today.

'How've you liked your birthday?' Jimmy asked me on the train back to Romford.

'I've had the most fabulous time, Jimmy!' I kissed him, in full view of the other passengers, and giggled when the lady opposite us tutted and held her paper up to block us from view.

'Do you want to come back to my place for a while?' he whispered.

'For a coffee?' I said.

'Or ... whatever you want.' He looked back at me, his eyes burning. 'Mum and Dad are away. Not back till tomorrow afternoon.'

And that was how I lost my virginity – on the rough carpet on the floor of Jimmy's hallway, because he was in too much of a hurry to get me upstairs. Or even get undressed. My brand new tights got ripped in the rush to pull them down. Afterwards, he told me he loved me more than ever. He made me a cup of tea and walked me back home, where I sneaked upstairs to bed without waking Mum or Fred.

I was glad I'd got it over with. But I couldn't see what all the fuss was about!

The O-levels were spread over two weeks of sheer hell. I'd always found exams nerve-wracking, but the importance of these – the *real thing* as teachers had been referring to them for months – had been hyped up to the point where I felt faint and physically sick as I sat at my desk in the examination hall, watching the papers being handed out. Even Mum had suddenly got back on my case after months of little apparent interest, giving me daily lectures on how these exams were going to determine my future, as if I didn't already know.

We were on study leave from school now, and Linda and I spent nearly all our time together, going over and over the work needed for whatever terrifying exam was scheduled for the next day. On the occasions when we were timetabled for two – one in the morning and a different subject in the afternoon – we were almost hysterical with nerves and gabbling with panic about what seemed to be an impossible amount to cram into our brains.

I hadn't needed Mum to tell me I could only see Jimmy at the weekends until the exams were over: the pressure of the exam revision was enough to stop me from even wanting to see him during the week. And to be honest, in a way it was a relief. Now that we'd started having sex, he was expecting it every time we got together – as long as we could work it so that either Mum and Fred, or his parents, were out of the way.

'What's it *like*?' Linda asked me excitedly when I told her we were doing it.

'OK,' I said, cautiously.

'Only *OK*?' she queried, looking at me with a puzzled smile.

'Well,' I shrugged. 'I just find it a bit hard to relax, always wondering if his parents are going to come in and catch us at it. Or whether the condom might burst. *That* really scares me.'

'I can understand that.'

'He doesn't seem to bother about it, though.' I sighed. 'To be honest, I think I preferred it when we just kissed and stuff. I'm not sure that going all the way is worth all the extra worry. Do you think

I'm strange? Or there's something wrong with me?' I asked her miserably.

She started to reply, but then something strange flashed across her face and her voice turned harsher, along with her expression.

'How would I know?' she said, shrugging and looking away from me. 'I'm hardly the right person to ask, am I.'

I felt mortified. There was I, bleating on about my own worries that Linda couldn't possibly be expected to empathise with, when she herself hadn't even got someone special in her life to kiss and cuddle, let alone do ... whatever it was she might want to do with them. My own inexperience completely prevented me from imagining this bit, but I wished, more than anything, that I could make it happen for her. It seemed so unfair that I was having sex and not even enjoying it, while she could only listen to my complaints and wonder what she was missing.

'I'm sorry – I'm really sorry!' I cried, hugging her tight. 'What a selfish, thoughtless cow I am.'

'No you're not.' Her voice was back to normal, her expression softening again as she hugged me back. 'And I don't think there's anything wrong with you, either. Worrying about getting pregnant must be a real turn-off.'

We leant back on the sofa together. We were alone at my house – Mum out shopping, Fred at work, the nurse round at her flat looking after her own mother. For a while we just sat like that, arms entwined, looking at each other. I felt so much affection and respect for Linda. As a friend, I actually felt like I loved her. Not in the way I loved Jimmy, but on the other hand she knew me better, understood me better, maybe even cared about me in a deeper, more sensitive way. I stroked her hair and had started to kiss her when she sat up, moved slightly apart from me and said, gently:

'I think this might be a bad idea.'

'Yes.' I flushed with shame. 'I'm sorry – I shouldn't have ...'

'It's OK.' She smiled at me. 'I know you're just trying to be kind, but it ... isn't really right, for either of us, is it.'

'No, it's not. But I wasn't just trying to be kind. I'm really so ... *fond* of you.'

'*Fond*'s good, Cath – fond is great, for friends. I'm very fond of you too.' She was still smiling, teasing me a bit for my choice of words. 'But I need to wait until I find someone who's *passionate* about me – who'll love me the way you love Jimmy.'

'I know.'

I didn't know what else to say, so I picked up one of my textbooks and changed the subject, quickly, back to revision. What was really going on here? We didn't fancy each other, so why did we keep feeling drawn, tempted, to be more physical together? I knew she'd found it just as difficult as me, to break apart. I suppose I realised that for her, it was all too tempting to use me as some kind of experiment – taking that first kiss a little further. But what about me? What was I playing at? Was I really hoping to find something with my female friend that I wasn't getting from Jimmy? Or was it just that dangerous lure of forbidden fruit – the excitement of knowing I'd be doing something that felt even naughtier than having sex with Jimmy?

Whatever it was, I knew it wasn't fair on Linda. And I made up my mind there and then that it wasn't going to happen again. Ever.

'I met your so-called friend Janice's mother at the shops yesterday,' Mum told me, sounding strangely smug about it. 'I was wondering why she hasn't been hanging round here lately.'

I shrugged. I wasn't going to tell Mum that Janice hated me so much now, she wouldn't come anywhere near me. 'Well, we just don't see so much of each other these days,' I said. 'She's been left school for a year, now, and she works in London, so ...'

'Oh – so you haven't heard?' she said, sounding even more smug and satisfied. 'Her mother told me she's left home. She's living up in London now – moved into a flat with a boyfriend, apparently. They're not married, of course,' she added with a sniff of disapproval. 'And her mother didn't sound too happy about it, I can tell you, although she was trying to pretend otherwise. He's older than her, apparently.' She raised her eyebrows. 'Didn't I always say she'd come to a bad end, that one?'

'She hasn't *come to a bad end*,' I snapped, wondering at the same time why I was bothering to defend her. I wondered whether it was Phillip she'd moved in with – and what Mum's reaction would have been if she'd known he was a married man. 'You make it sound like she's turned into a mass murderer.'

'Next thing you know,' Mum went on as if she hadn't heard me, 'She'll be pregnant and he'll have walked out on her – you mark my words.'

'But that's not so very different from what Dad ...' I bit my tongue and turned away. What was the point? Mum seemed to have developed a mental block about her own past situation.

'This so-called permissive society has got a lot to answer for, if you want my opinion,' she continued. 'Nobody's got any morals these days. Especially the younger generation. You needn't think *you're* going to get ideas about *shacking up* with your boyfriend without getting married, miss. Bad enough your brother thinking it's all right to sleep with someone and then take her off, halfway round the world, without bothering to marry her.'

'Mum, *you're* living with Fred without being married!' I said impatiently. 'What's the difference?'

She pulled herself up to her full height. 'The difference, miss, is that we are two mature people who have both been married before. We know what we're doing – we're not silly young things. Your brother should have at least had the decency to marry that poor girl, before he took her off to Australia!'

I switched off. Mum would probably rant on for some time about Derek now she'd started. I knew she was only bad-mouthing him because she really missed him so much. I wished he'd at least make the effort to write a bit more often – or that Pauline would, if he couldn't be bothered. We knew that they'd both managed to get jobs and somewhere to live in Sydney, although he hadn't given us any details in his scrappy, hurried letter, and when I wrote back, asking if it was a house or a flat, and where they were working, I got no answers whatsoever – just another one-sheet scribble a month ago, saying they were both well and wishing me a happy birthday. At least he'd remembered that.

I spent a lot of time day-dreaming about Derek and Pauline, wondering what life in Australia was like, and building up a little fantasy in my head about it. I pictured them suntanned and healthy-looking, laughing in the sunshine, with Sydney Harbour Bridge always in the background. I hadn't really got to know Pauline at all before they went, but in my daydream she was always sweet-natured, kind and happy, and my brother had a great job and was earning pots of money. Sometimes I carried the fantasy a little further, trying to imagine going out to that land of opportunity myself one day. But then I'd recall Derek telling me I was supposed to stay at home to look after Mum. And that was where the fantasy always came to an abrupt end, and I remembered that I'd been angry with him when we parted, and that I'd never really felt settled in my mind about whether he knew more than he admitted about Ian.

I wished, really, that Mum hadn't told me about Janice. It'd been six months now since I'd heard from her. Earlier on in the year I'd seen her a couple of times around the estate, but she always turned away and pretended she hadn't seen me. I had no intention of trying to make it up with her; I was still angry about the way she'd spoken to me and Jimmy, the way she'd turned against me. But I did feel sad when I remembered the fun we used to have when we were friends – how we used to sigh and swoon together over the Beatles; how we both screamed at their concert at the Odeon. It felt like that had all happened in a completely different life, and I looked back in amazement at my younger, immature self.

Now that I knew she'd moved away from her family, away from Harold Hill, it felt like a door had been closed irrevocably on our friendship – that there'd never be any going back, even in the unlikely event that she ever decided she'd been wrong about Jimmy and actually apologised. Her life had moved on to such an extent that I couldn't see how I could ever be a part of it again. If it *was* Phillip she'd moved in with, if he'd left his wife to set up home with her, I couldn't pretend I didn't find it quite shocking. And if it wasn't, if it was some other older man she'd met since she started her affair with Phillip, then the speed at which things had progressed seemed equally indecent. Compared with her, I supposed I was still living the life of an innocent little suburban schoolgirl. I told myself that even if she hadn't turned against me so bitterly, we'd probably have drifted apart by now anyway.

February 2004

Only about a week after Hayley's visit, I get another phone call from her.

'Mum says she'll e-mail you. Give me your e-mail address and I'll pass it on to her.'

'Really? She's not mad at me?'

'No. I told you – she was just shocked to hear from you after all this time. When I told her what you were writing about, she got a little bit emotional. She said it all happened soon after she first met my dad. She actually remembers going to Brighton with him – and then going back to your house and getting a frosty reception from your mum!'

I laugh. 'Yeah, that sounds like Mum, bless her.'

'How long ago did she pass away – my grandma?'

'1986. She was only in her sixties – it was cancer. So unfair.'

We're both silent for a moment.

'What did your mum say about the guy who got stabbed – Ian?' I carry on. 'Does she remember anything? Does she think she can help me?'

'I don't know, Catherine. She just said she'd e-mail you, but whether she has anything to tell you about that, or whether she just wants to get in touch, I couldn't say. But I *can* tell you she was shocked when I mentioned that you were assaulted by him – that Ian. Really shocked.'

'Del never told her, then,' I say, half to myself.

'Apparently not. Look – I'm at work right now, so I'd better get on. Let me just write down your e-mail address. And ... let's get together again. Soon.'

'I'd like that. Thanks, Hayley – thanks for your help.'

The e-mail from Pauline arrives just two days later. It begins a little stiffly:

Dear Catherine

Firstly, I'd like to apologise for hanging up on you. It was something of a shock to hear from you, and as I explained, my job makes it difficult for me to take personal calls at work. I'm also sorry that we have not remained in touch over the years. I realise this has been my fault. I was in a very bad place emotionally after Del died and I couldn't face the thought of dealing with his mother or any of his family.

Well, my daughter has made me realise now that you are my family, and my only link with the past, with England, now. Hayley says she likes you and that she hopes to stay in touch with you. I'm pleased.

I sigh and take a sip from the glass of wine beside my computer screen. It may not be the warmest reconciliation in the world but at least she's holding out a hand to me.

Anyway, she goes on abruptly, as if she's glad that part's over with, *Hayley told me about the story you're writing. I don't know why you want to delve into all that ancient history now. It's quite upsetting to remember it, actually. Did you know that day at Brighton was the first time your brother took me out? It was what you might call a whirlwind romance. We met at that coffee-bar in Romford, I forget its name, where all the rockers used to hang out. He'd been giving me the eye and chatting me up for a couple of weeks, but Brighton was our first date. I remember he seemed really nervous and on edge the whole day. I thought that was sweet. I felt like it must have been important for him, you know? – making the right impression with me? I gauged he must have been pretty keen. So I played it cool, but only to put him at his ease. When he told me he wanted to stop off at your house afterwards, I thought at first he was in a hurry to introduce me to his mum. Kind-of freaked me out a bit. I mean, I really liked him but it seemed a bit fast, a bit soon for all that carry-on. Then when he explained he wanted me to pretend we'd been at his mate's house – Jim somebody, his name was – instead of at Brighton, because he didn't want his mum or you to be worried about the fighting down there, well, I was quite annoyed really. I remember thinking – I've only known you five minutes, Derek Ferguson, and you want me to start telling lies to your own family for you. But of course, I went along with it. He had that way with him, didn't he – he could charm you into doing anything.*

I'm sorry to disappoint you, Catherine, but I was with Del the whole day and we didn't see the fight where that boy got stabbed. We didn't hear about it till afterwards. I didn't know the guy, obviously, and as far as I knew, Del had never met him either. We kept out of the way of any trouble. Del didn't want to get involved and didn't want to risk me getting hurt. He was the perfect gentleman.

But one thing I will say is, Del never mentioned anything to me about that guy trying to rape you. I had no idea about that, and I was certainly sorry to hear about it from Hayley. It must have been a terrible ordeal for you at only fourteen. I don't know why Del never told me. But I will say that he would definitely have been very angry about it. Del was very fond of you, Catherine. He always referred to you as his 'kid sister' and I know he missed you a lot after we emigrated.

I'm wiping away tears now, faster than I can drown them with the wine.

Hayley says you didn't tell Del about the assault yourself, but your friend did. I'm thinking that whoever that friend was, she might have been angry about it too. Angry enough to stab him? Have you asked the friend about it? I expect you have, if you're still in touch with them, anyway.

Well, I'm sorry not to have been of any help, but I'm glad now, after all, that you got in touch. I hear you have a son and a daughter, and Hayley's looking forward to meeting her cousins. I expect she told you I've been with Carl now for twenty-three years. We never had any kids together. He had a family with his ex-wife. But I've got Hayley. And my job.

I wish you all the best – Pauline.

I read the e-mail through twice and then sit, staring at the computer screen for a long time. Something about her final paragraph makes me think she isn't particularly happy, and I feel sorry – sorry about the wasted years when we could have been friends, even at such a distance. I wish I'd made more effort, understood her lack of response, been more patient, more persistent. Perhaps it's too late now to make up for that. But I can, at least, be a friend to her daughter while she's here in the UK. My own daughter, Sara – who's married and lives in Norwich – got in touch with her as soon as I told her about Hayley's visit, and they're apparently e-mailing each other regularly and trying to arrange a meeting. Perhaps, if it brings the younger generation of the family together, something good will come of my *delving into all that ancient history*, after all.

My son's home for the weekend and I ask his advice about tracking people down. He's an IT technician, currently studying for some sort of diploma that will, if he can be believed, open not just doors but magnificent golden gates to the sort of careers I couldn't imagine in my wildest dreams. Nathan is one of life's super-optimists, always convinced there's a glittering future waiting for him just round the next corner. I hope he's right; I hope he never has to come crashing down to earth. It'd break my heart as well as his.

'What sort of people?' he asks me with a grin as he bites into a slice of toast and Marmite. He never seems to stop eating, but never puts on an ounce of weight. He's short, slim, wiry – he reminds me so much of Derek. But already he's older than Derek ever was. 'Who're you trying to track down, Mum – old boyfriends?'

I laugh, and then think, suddenly, about Jimmy, and the laugh dies in my throat.

'No – school friends,' I say. 'Old school friends who I haven't seen for forty years. Where the hell do I start? I've Googled them, but ...'

'Nah – you might find them that way if they've become famous for something. Or if they've got their own website, say, for their business. But otherwise, your best bet's definitely *Friends Reunited.*'

'Oh. Yes, I think I've heard of that. How does it work?'

'Come on, I'll show you!' He laughs and nudges me out of my computer chair, taking my place and logging onto the site faster than I can blink. 'You just need a password – Grandma's maiden name, yeah?' He types it in. 'And there you go. Now, you just have to put in the name of your school – there – and the years you were there.' He watches as I lean over his shoulder and type in the information, and we both wait to see what comes up. 'Oh. That's a bit disappointing.' He points at the screen. 'There are only a few people on there. I've found *loads* of people from my class. But I suppose ...' He gives me a cheeky grin. 'I suppose it *was* a long time ago that you were at school, Mum. And I guess most people of your age are like you ... not very up-to-date with this sort of stuff.'

'If we're still alive, you mean?' I joke back. 'And still able to read?'

'Yeah! But don't worry. Look, what you can do is, click on 'Search for friends', and type their names in – *there*. And you never know, one of the people who's already signed up might know them, and it goes from there. See?'

'OK. Right – thanks.' I nudge him to get him out of my seat again, and he loiters around behind me, waiting to see if I understand how to proceed, watching me clicking back to my school's page and put in different dates. 'It's OK, Nate. Thanks – I'll manage now. Go and finish your toast!'

I say it as lightly as I can manage, trying not to betray the fact that my heart's beating wildly with excitement. Because, of course, I've remembered that the person I'm looking for wasn't in my school year at all. And now that I've entered the year I want, and looked quickly at the list of half a dozen or so names that's come up – unbelievably, she's there. Janice Baker, still listed by her maiden name, maybe never married anyway – how would I know?

Nathan wanders off as, with shaking hands, I send a message winging out over cyberspace, trying once again to cross the deep and treacherous divide of forty years' silence. And all I can do now is wait.

July 1965

We went back to school after the exams, but not for long, and not to do a lot of work. Those of us staying on for the sixth form were mainly finalising our A-level choices and getting our timetables sorted out. Now that I'd definitely made up my mind to carry on with my education, I was quite excited about it. At last, I could drop the hated maths and science subjects, and concentrate on what I was good at: English, History and Art.

Jimmy had been surprised when I'd first told him my decision.

'I thought you were talking about leaving school and getting a job?' he said.

'Yeah – I know. I was, for a while. I was dead jealous of Janice when she started work last year, and I thought it'd be really cool to work in London like her, and earn some money, you know. But since then, I've realised I actually do want to go to university. I know it'll be hard work, but I think I'll enjoy it. And hopefully, eventually, I'll get a better job at the end of it all.'

'Right.' He looked at the ground, his lips pursed.

'What?' I was surprised. I'd been expecting more support from him. 'You told me, when we first met, that you always wished *you'd* worked harder at school and got a better job. You actually encouraged me to work hard for my exams!'

'Yeah – of course. And you did, didn't you. I was dead proud of you, doing all that revision, night after night when I know you'd have rather been with me, doing *this*!' We were at his house at the time, naked in his bed together while his mum and dad were obligingly out again. I was beginning to wonder whether they knew what we were getting up to, and going out deliberately to give us time on our own. It was the sort of thing Janice's parents would probably have done, but I wasn't sure about Jimmy's. Perhaps boys' parents were less concerned than girls', about what their offspring got up to!

Personally, I still preferred seeing him on evenings when there was no opportunity to have sex – when we spent our time together talking and kissing, like we used to. When sex was on offer, it seemed to take over from everything else as far as Jimmy was concerned, whereas I was still nervous about the whole thing and its possible consequences.

'But I don't see why you need to go on and do *more* exams,' he said when I still hadn't said anything. 'You're bound to've passed all your O-levels. You could get a dead good job now.'

'I might not have passed maths. Or chemistry,' I countered. 'But that's not the point. I *want* to get my A-levels. And I want to go to university.'

'And then what?' he sounded petulant, and I was starting to feel annoyed. What difference did it make to him? 'Aren't you ever going to go out to work? Won't your mum want you to start bringing in some money?'

'Mum's always wanted me to go to university, actually,' I said, defensively. 'Even when she was really, really hard-up. It was her ambition – for me to get the best education possible.'

'But what about if ... well, what about if we decided to get married?'

It had come out of nowhere – so unexpectedly that I just stared at the ceiling, blinking, until I realised that this time I really did have to say something in reply.

'Married? Oh – Jimmy, you haven't ever said anything about getting *married.*'

'Sorry.' He sounded even more sulky now. 'I suppose I just presumed – I mean, I thought it was obvious. Logical. We love each other, don't we?'

'Yes! Yes, of course!' I said at once, feeling guilty for not sounding more enthusiastic. 'I do love you, and I suppose I *have* presumed we would get married – one day, eventually, you know. But, well, I presumed it would be a long way off. I've only just turned sixteen, I'm still at school ...'

'And likely to be there for ever more, by the sound of it,' he finished abruptly.

'Let's not argue. Please, Jimmy – can't we just be happy as we are, for now?' I rolled over to face him. I didn't want him to be cross with me. I kissed him gently and traced a finger down his cheek. 'I do love you,' I assured him again.

The thought of ever parting from him terrified me. But talk of marriage? That was for grown-ups!

On the last day of term, the girls who weren't staying on for the sixth form were clearing out their desks and saying goodbye. There were a few of them I wouldn't be sorry to see the back of. Heather and Susan, for instance. Since my famous speech on the school playing-field a couple of months earlier, the majority of the girls had remained friendly, or at least neutral, towards Linda and me. But those two hadn't forgiven me for slagging them off and making them look bad in front of everyone. Their popularity hadn't recovered – but they had the wonderful Frances on their side – who was still revered by pretty much everyone. They might not have had the backing of the class now, but they still managed to get in a steady stream of furtive insults, shoves in the back and so on, and if Linda or I fought back, nobody wanted to make too much fuss on our behalf if it meant falling out with the Form Captain.

We were still getting the silent phone calls at home sometimes too – not often enough to make Mum carry out her threat of reporting it to the phone company, but each time it happened, it reminded me that somebody still seemed to be trying to intimidate me, or my parents. And although I was convinced it was probably one of those two girls, I didn't really want Mum to stir things up and make the situation worse again. Hopefully, now they were leaving, it would stop.

I couldn't quite believe Linda wasn't coming back next term. She'd been accepted as a trainee dental nurse at a dentist's surgery very close to her home, meaning she could continue to care for her mum and even pop home in her lunch breaks if necessary, and she was hugely excited about it. I was trying not to be jealous. She'd be starting a new life, meeting new people and earning some money while she was studying for her chosen career – while I was carrying on as before, a schoolgirl, sitting at my desk, doing my homework, taking my exams – but without her. It was my own choice, of course, and I didn't regret it – not yet, anyway. But I knew I was going to miss her.

'We'll still see each other – all the time,' she reassured me as we lingered by the school gate together at lunch time, after the leavers' assembly.

'Yeah. That's what Janice said, when *she* left,' I said sulkily. 'And look what happened.'

'Cathy.' She took hold of my arm, turned my face towards hers. 'I'm not Janice. I'm nothing like her. I'm your friend – you know that. I'm never going to let you down. If I say I'm going to do something, I mean it. I do it. I *will* still see you all the time. I promise.'

'Sorry. I know – of course, I know you're not like her. I didn't mean that. I just think it's so easy to drift apart, when you start to have different sorts of lives. Janice probably meant what she said at the time, about keeping in touch – even though things have gone horribly wrong since then.'

'That was different. She went to work in the West End. I'm going to be working a couple of streets away from your house!'

'Yes. But you'll make new friends, and want to spend time with them. You will!'

But I suddenly realised, as I was saying this, how selfish I sounded. In fact, I really should have been pleased at the thought of Linda making new friends. It was what she needed. She might find someone special – someone who could give her what I never could, no matter how close our friendship was. 'I hope you do,' I added quietly, smiling at her and suddenly feeling better. 'I really hope you're going to be happy in your job. Sorry for whining.'

She put her arms round me and we hugged goodbye. It was time for afternoon registration for those of us finishing out the last day of term – and for her to catch the bus home for the last time. I kissed her quickly on the cheek and held onto her hand for just a few seconds longer, committing this moment to memory. Even though I knew she'd be true to her word – that we would still be friends, still get together as often as we could – it was the end of an era for both of us. She turned and waved to me as she ran for the bus. And I walked back into school, wiping away a tear.

August 1965

The summer holiday was dragging. There was no revision to do, no extra studying of my previously detested subjects in order to keep my head above water – just a feeling of relief that the O-levels were behind me, and a slightly nervous anticipation of the sixth form years ahead.

Linda kept her promise, of course, and we still saw a lot of each other. As she'd pointed out, she was only working around the corner from my house, and she stopped by after work, or at lunchtime, or I went round to her place on the evenings that I wasn't seeing Jimmy. It was exciting to hear about her work and the different people she was meeting – both her colleagues, and the patients. She seemed to have moved seamlessly into the adult world, growing in confidence, becoming a different, more fulfilled person already. She even looked better. We'd always been united by our similar proportions: our smallness and thinness compared with everyone else we knew. We'd been given unkind nicknames by our tormentors over the past few months because of it: *The Thin Twins; Bony Moanies; Skinny Dykes.* I'd been a late developer and although I'd finally progressed from the same sized bra I'd been wearing since I was twelve, to a modest 34B, I would have loved some proper womanly curves; whereas Linda, whose short tomboy haircut suited her slim, serious face, had never seemed to mind about not looking particularly feminine. School uniform had accentuated her angular frame, hanging on her awkwardly, but her crisp white dental nurse's tunic had been cut to fit her properly. The hem, just above the knee, showed off her slim legs, and there was a happy glow about her that spoke volumes about having got away from school and chosen a job she was enjoying. I had a hard time not showing my jealousy, and not caving in and changing my mind about the sixth form.

'I think I'll look for a job,' I said to Mum at the end of the second week of the holidays.

'A job?' She turned to me in surprise. 'You've just registered for the sixth form, miss! You're not going to tell me you've changed your mind again?'

'No – I mean a holiday job. In a shop, or something.'

She'd been polishing the floor and she stood up slowly, hands on her lower back, stretching.

'Are you bored? Is that it? Because if you are, there's plenty of weeding to be done in the garden. And the upstairs windows need cleaning, to say nothing of the pile of ironing ...'

'No, I'm not bored,' I lied quickly. 'I think it'd be a good experience for me, that's all. And I'd earn a bit of extra pocket-money.'

'Don't we give you enough?' she snapped at once.

It was true – the only good thing about Fred being around was the increase in the amount of money now available to me, even if it did mean I had to bite my tongue when he criticised every single thing I chose to spend it on, whether it was clothes he didn't approve of, records he called trash, or outings to the cinema to see films he thought were rubbish. Linda and I were going to see the Beatles' new film, *Help*, the next evening and he'd already informed me that it was a waste of his hard-earned money.

'Yes,' I tried to soothe her. 'You do, and I'm grateful, but it'd be good to feel like I was earning a little bit for myself. Feeling like I was making a contribution.'

She looked at me thoughtfully for a moment.

'I s'pose you've got a point. It'd be better than having you hanging around the house all day every day until you go back to school, playing that terrible music. Where are you thinking of trying?'

'I'll ask around, Mum. Even if I can get something for a couple of weeks, it'll be good.'

Jimmy was surprisingly enthusiastic.

'It'll be good for you to get some work experience,' he said when I told him excitedly on the phone about my plan. 'I'll keep a look out for openings for you, too.'

In those days, even holiday jobs for teenagers were relatively easy to come by. The very next evening, passing the local shops on the way to Linda's place for our trip to the cinema, I saw a vacancy advertised in the window of the sweet-shop.

Part-time assistant required, Thurs/Fri/Sat, suit student, must be numarat.

No requirement for spelling, then, I thought to myself with a grin. Maths may not have been my strong point but I was pretty sure I could manage to weigh out ounces of fruit drops and Liquorice Allsorts and give the right change in pennies and halfpennies to kids and pensioners.

'That'd be perfect!' Linda exclaimed. Her dental surgery was located above the ironmonger's in the same parade of shops. 'I could pop down to the shop in my breaks, to see you!'

'Yeah!' I laughed. 'Better not buy too many sweets, though – your dentists wouldn't approve!'

'You're definitely going to apply for it?'

'Yes. As soon as they open.' It was Saturday evening then – the shop was closed until Monday morning. 'I can't believe I've found something so quickly – I was expecting to have to walk round Romford, looking for something in the clothes shops.'

As far as I was concerned, the job was already mine. But I hadn't reckoned on Jimmy's reaction.

'What the hell do you want to work *there* for?' he said. It was a warm Sunday morning and we'd gone to the park, where we were lying together on the grass behind the children's playground.

I looked at him in surprise.

'But you said you thought it was a *good* idea for me to get a job!'

'Yeah – but not in a crummy little sweetshop on your local parade! I thought you were going to wait for me to find you something.'

'Don't be like that. I *am* grateful for the offer – I know you were going to look for something for me. But I just happened to see this advert, and it seems so perfect ...'

'Does it?' He shook his head. 'I thought you'd prefer to work in Romford, Cath – you always said you liked being down the town – it'd be a lot more lively than working in a local sweetshop.'

'Well, yes, but on the other hand, this is so close to home – no bus fares – and it's almost next-door to where Linda works!'

'Oh.' He nodded curtly to himself. 'I see.'

'What? Is there something wrong with that? What's the matter?'

'Nothing.' He lay on his back, staring at the sky, while I watched him, waiting, knowing he was going to tell me anyway. 'It's just – always Linda, isn't it!' he exploded eventually. '*I* couldn't take you to the pictures on a Saturday night because you were going with *Linda* ...'

'You said you didn't mind!'

'What else am I supposed to say? If I make any protest, you think I'm being jealous.'

'And you're not?' I retorted sarcastically.

'Well, OK, perhaps I am! Can you blame me? It was bad enough when you were at school together all the time, but since she's left – blimey, it's like you have a struggle to fit me in at all – all I hear is that you're seeing Linda, going round Linda's, going out with Linda, Linda's coming round, Linda this, Linda that ...'

I sat up, horrified by the tone of his voice. I'd never known him to be quite so nasty.

'Jimmy, she's my *friend*. My only real friend!'

'Apart from me.'

'Apart from you, yes, but surely you're not going to begrudge me one female friend, are you?'

'I wouldn't mind,' he said in a deliberately measured way, 'if it wasn't Linda. *Lesbian* Linda.'

Now I was really cross. 'Don't start this again, Jimmy! Do I really have to tell you again that there's nothing like that between us? We're *friends*. She doesn't fancy me. She's actually got her eye on one of the female dental technicians, and if you really want to know, I hope she manages to get off with her, because I really want her to be happy!'

'Yuck.' Jimmy turned away from me, pulling a face. 'That makes me feel sick.'

'Well, you make *me* feel sick. You're just like all the stupid girls at school.'

I stopped, mortified. I'd been shouting at him – shouting loud enough for the little kids on the climbing frame nearby to look at us and giggle. I didn't want to argue with Jimmy. This had all blown up over nothing. But I couldn't understand what his problem was with the sweetshop!

'Well,' he said, grumpily, getting to his feet and brushing grass off his jeans, 'If that's how you feel – if I make you feel sick, if you think I'm stupid – '

'No. Look, Jimmy, I'm sorry. Don't go. I didn't mean it, but ...'

' – and if you'd rather work in a pathetic little sweetshop just so you can be near your *best friend*, then I won't bother telling you about the job I've found you.'

'Oh.' I hung my head. 'You didn't say. You didn't *say* you'd found me one.'

'You didn't give me much of a chance. You jumped straight in with your great news about the fab job at the sweetshop.'

Fighting back my irritation at his childish sulkiness, I pulled him back down to sit with me again on the grass.

'Tell me about it,' I said. 'Please. Let's not fall out over it.'

He shrugged. 'There's a vacancy for a waitress. At the Cauldron. Three evenings a week. I could take you and pick you up – no bus fares,' he added, raising an eyebrow at me. 'You might even be able to keep the job when you go back to school. And I'd spend those nights there myself. I've always got mates up there. We could see a bit more of each other. But of course, if you'd prefer to work in the sweetshop – if you'd prefer to see a bit more of *Linda* rather than me ...'

I had a real struggle with myself for a minute. I'd never been more annoyed with Jimmy – never felt more like he was turning into someone different, someone – well, more like Fred! – with his moods and his prejudiced opinions instead of my loving, gentle Jimmy. I felt a twinge of anxiety, too, about the fact that he seemed to want to be there with me, all the time, while I was working. Didn't he trust me? Or didn't he want me to have a life of my own? On the other hand, he was right – working in a coffee-bar in Romford in the evenings was a more exciting proposition than weighing out paper-bags of sweets for kiddies in the shop near my own street. The money would be better. And if I could keep the job when I went back to school ...

I'd like to say that was what clinched it. But perhaps, after all, I was still just too frightened of losing Jimmy.

'You're right,' I said. 'I'll go down to the Cauldron tomorrow and apply for the job. Thank you.'

If I sounded slightly less grateful than he'd have liked, he didn't show it. But we weren't quite as closely entwined as usual as he walked me home for dinner. And I didn't linger long over our kiss at the gate. I told him it was because Mum still didn't really approve of me being out on Sundays and I didn't want any trouble if Fred saw us. But I think, really, I was as resentful with myself for giving in to Jimmy over the job, as I was with him for expecting me to.

Linda didn't display any disappointment when I told her about the change of plan.

'I hope you get the job – it'll probably be better for you in the long run,' she said in her normal calm, reasonable way, 'if you can keep working there when you go back to school.'

'I won't have so many evenings free, to see you, though.'

'Don't worry, Cathy. We're not going to drift apart, are we!' She laughed. 'I might even come and have a coffee at the Cauldron!'

'Jimmy's going to be there every night – if I get the job. Like he's my minder.'

'Because he loves you. He cares about you.'

I tried to smile in agreement. But I was thinking: *No. Because he wants to keep me away from you*! How ironic, if Linda turned up every night to see me there, at the very place where Jimmy seemed so keen to install me!

Two days later

Mum wasn't too happy about the job at the Cauldron – especially as, by the time I'd been to see the manager there, and been told that I could start, she'd seen the advert in the sweetshop window herself.

'That would've been better for you – just round the corner from home, nice hours in the daylight.' She sniffed. 'Coffee-bar waitress, indeed! All those boys eyeing you up ...'

'Jimmy will be there. He's going to take me and pick me up.'

'Is he, now.' She banged things around a bit, muttering to herself. Then she turned back to face me. 'This is getting a bit serious, isn't it – you and him?'

'Well ...' I wasn't sure what she was getting at. Was I going to get another lecture about sex? I'd find it difficult, now, to look her in the eye. 'Yes – we've been going out for over a year now, so I suppose it's quite serious.'

'And where do you think it's going to lead, then?' She folded her arms across her chest and stared at me. 'Only you've got two more years at school. And then you'll be off to university. I hope you're not expecting him to hang around, waiting for you, because I'm telling you now, you'd be in for a disappointment.'

I opened my mouth to argue with her. It was an automatic response. But no words came; I couldn't actually think of a single thing to say. With a mounting sense of panic, I realised Mum had just spelled out exactly what had been going through my own mind recently. Ever since Jimmy had sounded so put-out about my determination to continue my studies, I'd wondered what was going to happen between us in the long run. I just hadn't admitted those thoughts, though – not to anyone.

'Well,' Mum said, turning back to the stove and leaving me stuttering and floundering beside her, 'As long as you realise it's not going to last. Don't say I didn't warn you.' I started to walk away, and she called after me, 'And I'll tell you something else: Fred won't approve of you working at that place, either.'

'Fred doesn't approve of anything I do, not that it's any of his flippin' business!' I shot back. 'Maybe it'd be nice if you supported me, for once!'

I certainly couldn't say having Fred around was getting any easier – but over the months I'd acquired a certain degree of acceptance, helped by the fact that I didn't have to see too much of him. I'd come to realise that his endless carping and criticism of me was just a manifestation of his own bad temper. If I could restrain myself from arguing with him, just ignore him and walk away, I could carry on and do exactly what I wanted. It was the restraint that was hard. Sometimes he infuriated me so much, it took all my willpower not to rise to the bait – but I knew that if I did, the ensuing row would only make my life more difficult.

For both our sakes, it would've made a lot more sense for Mum to keep quiet about my new job. But I happened to arrived home after my first evening's work at the exact same moment that he was staggering in from the pub.

'You been out on that damned bike with that boy again?' he demanded. His aggression was even more pronounced when he'd had a few drinks.

'Yes,' I said, deciding to leave it at that – but Mum was at my elbow straight away, wanting to know how it had gone, whether I'd been busy, whether I'd got any tips, and whether I wished I'd taken the job in the sweetshop instead.

'You're working?' Fred turned to me in surprise. 'In the *evenings*? What the hell?'

I sighed. 'Yes, I'm working. In a coffee-bar. It's perfectly safe, I get a lift there and back, and it's only three evenings a week. Can I go and make myself a cup of tea now?'

'You've got to be joking.' He grabbed my arm, stopping me from heading to the kitchen. I met Mum's eyes, thanking her silently for dropping me in it. 'Ivy – what the hell are you doing, letting your daughter work *nights* in a *bar*?'

'A coffee-bar.'

'I stopped your mother working in the pub, for Christ's sake! You're sixteen, still at school and while you're under *my* roof ...'

It was late. I was tired and annoyed, and I didn't have the control I normally managed. I just flipped.

'Under *your* roof?' I retorted. 'Don't make me laugh! It's not *your* house! Mum's paid the rent and the bills all these years on her own! Moving in for a few months and throwing your weight around doesn't make it your house! And while we're at it – who do you think you are, stopping Mum from working at the pub if she wants to? She doesn't have to do what you say! You're not in charge around here! We're not living in the bloody Stone Age – Mum's got as much right to go out to work as you have. She's got as much right as you to do what she damn' well likes! You're just a drunk and a bully, and I don't care what you say – you're not stopping *me* from working where I want to work, when I want to work! Mum might have given up her independence for the sake of some new clothes and a washing machine but I bloody well haven't!'

As usual, my anger somehow fired me up with the words I needed and carried me through till I'd run out of steam, aware that I'd gone too far. Mum was looking at me in horror, frozen to the spot. As I screeched to a halt, I met Fred's eyes, just in time to see the fury in them, but not quite in time to duck as his hand came down with stinging force on my cheek.

'Fred! Stop it!' Mum shouted as he raised his hand for another slap. I'd stumbled out of his reach with the shock of the first strike, and this time I'd have seen it coming anyway – but Mum was already there, grabbing at his wrist, grappling with him, trying to stop him. He was drunk, and not altogether steady on his feet. As I watched, stunned, for a moment it looked ridiculously as though they were dancing. He staggered backwards; she, gripping his arm, was pulled along with him and together they overbalanced, tumbling against the staircase, Fred falling onto his back and hitting his head against the banister post, Mum somehow rolling onto the floor beside him.

'Stupid bitch!' he shouted at her, pushing her away from him as he struggled to get to his feet.

'Don't talk to my mum like that!' I yelled at him, holding a hand up to the red weal on my face. 'What're you going to do now? Hit her too? Go ahead – perhaps she'll finally have the guts to kick you out, then!'

There was a long silence. Fred swayed on his feet, whether from the alcohol or the effects of knocking his head, I wasn't entirely sure, and stared at me, breathing hard. If he'd come at me to hit me again at that moment I was ready to kick, scream, bite and punch. All my nerves were taut, all my muscles flexed. I wasn't about to let him hurt me again – or hurt Mum. But instead, he muttered some obscenities and turned on his heel, lumbering unsteadily up the stairs.

'You are *not* getting into bed with him tonight,' I told Mum furiously, beginning to shake like a leaf now it was all over. 'Sleep in Derek's room.'

She nodded wearily. 'Show me your face.' She was pale with shock. 'Come into the kitchen. I'll put some Witch-hazel on it.'

'I know you think I shouldn't have annoyed him,' I said as she dabbed my cheek with the stinging liquid. 'But you can't let him get away with this, Mum! He can't carry on like this, pushing you around, telling us what to do! It's not *right*!'

'I know.' She was talking in a whisper, staring at the floor. 'But what choice do I have, Cathy? You don't understand. Without him, I couldn't afford to keep you at school – now I haven't got Derek's pay coming in.'

'I'll work more shifts at the coffee-bar!' I protested. 'I'll do the sweetshop job *too*!'

She shook her head, sadly. 'Even if you did, we might get through the next two years, but what about your university? It's no good, Cath. We can't do it without him.'

'Then I won't go. I mean it, Mum – if that's the price you have to pay, it's not worth it. Throw him out, and I'll leave school and get a proper job. We'll manage! We've managed before! We *can* do it, Mum. Please!'

But no matter what I said, she just continued to shake her head. She made us both a cup of sweet tea and I sipped mine, crying with frustration, my cheek sore as the tears dried on it.

'What the hell happened to your face?' Jimmy asked me the next night. The redness had faded, but it was turning into a bruise. He touched my cheek gently. It was, all too obviously, the mark of a hand.

'Fred,' I said abruptly.

'I'll bloody kill him.'

'No. Leave it. I want Mum to throw him out. She's got to make up her own mind.'

'That's never gonna happen,' Jimmy said. 'She doesn't want to give up the benefits, does she.'

'She's doing it for me. So I can afford to go to university.'

I should have known it was the wrong thing to say.

'Don't go, then,' he said immediately. 'You don't *have* to.'

So that was my choice, was it? Give up my dreams of a university education, to rescue Mum from a bully? Or give them up because my boyfriend didn't want me to go? Some choice!

I carried on working at the Cauldron. Fred never even mentioned it again. If he was home when I got in from work, he completely ignored me. I liked the work, and I actually quite liked the fact that Jimmy was there. His mates were always nice to me, and there was an atmosphere of cheerful banter in there that I enjoyed.

A couple of weeks after I started work, I came downstairs late one morning when Mum was out, picked up the post from the doormat and found an unfranked envelope amongst the others, with my name written on it in large capital letters. Inside was a single sheet of paper, with the message also printed in capitals:

DID YOU THINK WE'D FORGOTTEN YOU, ROCKER-LOVER?

DID YOU THINK WE WERE GOING TO FORGET WHAT HAPPENED TO IAN?

WHAT D'YOU THINK YOU'RE DOING, WORKING IN THAT ROCKERS' DIVE?

YOUR ROCKER BOY WON'T WANT TO KNOW YOU WHEN WE TELL HIM WHAT YOU GET UP TO WITH YOUR LEZZA GIRLFRIEND.

WE'LL BE DOING YOU A FAVOUR. TIME YOU MADE UP YOUR MIND WHICH WAY YOU WANT TO SWING.

Heather and Susan! It had to be them! Stupid, pathetic, immature ... I thought I'd got them off my back when they left school! I screwed the note up, angrily, and then straightened it out again, my hands shaking, reading it through again. What were they up to? How did they know where I was working, anyway, and what did they mean about telling Jimmy anything? There wasn't anything to tell! What *lies* were they going to feed him?

I tried to tell myself not to worry about their stupid games, but there was something nasty, something disturbing about getting an anonymous note – a threatening note – even if I did have a very good idea where it had come from. And with Linda and Jimmy both at work, there was nobody to talk to about it. At lunchtime I rushed round to the dental surgery, only to be told that Linda had gone out for lunch with one of the technicians. Ordinarily, I'd have been pleased for her: it was the girl she'd been telling me about, the one she liked. But today, of all days, I needed her, and I felt unreasonably betrayed.

I went home and waited, feeling tense and edgy, until the time that Jimmy came home from work.

'Can I come round?' I asked him. 'I need to show you something.'

'Yeah,' he said. His voice sounded strange. 'You'd better.'

As soon as he opened the door to me, I knew something was wrong. And then I saw, in his hand, another note – written, like mine, in childish block capitals. He thrust it at me without a word, before I'd even had a chance to get my own one out of my pocket.

STUPID ROCKER, the note began, ARE YOU BLIND, OR WHAT?

DON'T YOU KNOW YOUR GIRLFRIEND LIKES DYKES BETTER THAN SHE LIKES COCK?

SHE'S JUST MESSING WITH YOU. SHE'D RATHER BE WITH HER BEST PAL. IF YOU DON'T BELIEVE IT, ASK HER IF SHE ENJOYED THE NICE SNOG THEY HAD TOGETHER.

YEAH, THAT'S RIGHT, THEY LIKE TO SNOG, AND MAYBE THAT'S NOT ALL. DOES THAT GET YOU GOING, ROCKER, IS THAT IT? WANT TO WATCH THEM AT IT?

IF NOT, WHAT YOU HANGING AROUND FOR? YOU CAN'T GIVE HER WHAT SHE WANTS. GET IT? SHE LIKES IT SOFT AND PURRING. BAD LUCK, ROCKER. PUT YOUR GREASY DICK SOMEWHERE ELSE NEXT TIME.

'Dirty bitches!' I cried, thrusting the note back in his hand. Like he was going to want it back! He was staring at me, actual pain in his eyes. 'You're not taking any notice of *that*, are you? I *know* who sent it – those horrible girls from my class! Look!' I rummaged in my pocket, pulled out my own letter. 'Look, they sent me one too! They just want to hurt us, Jimmy – they just want to split us up! I thought they'd leave us alone after they left school, but they must have heard about me working at the Cauldron. They just can't let it rest, can they, they have to keep on ...'

He was still staring at me, not saying a word. He didn't take his note back out of my hand, didn't even look at the one I was trying to show him.

'Don't take any notice!' I gabbled, worried now by his silence. 'They're just telling lies, trying to make you think stuff about me that isn't true! They're making it up, Jimmy! They don't know anything – nobody does. Nobody saw ...'

I stopped, my breath stuck in my throat. 'I mean ...'

'Nobody saw what?' he asked coldly.

'Anything! Nobody saw anything, because there's never been anything to see. There's never *been* anything going on. I've told you the truth, hundreds of times – Linda and I are just *friends* – she doesn't fancy me. She's going out with somebody she works with, now!' I added quickly, my fingers crossed for luck inside my pocket.

'Still, never mind,' he said, his voice beginning to shake. 'At least you've had a *snog*. Or maybe more.'

'No! Look, I kissed her on the cheek at the school gate when she was leaving – a kiss like you give your *mother*, for goodness sake! Someone might have seen *that*, and made something out of it, but *nobody* saw ...'

I couldn't believe it. In my desperation to make him believe me, I'd done it again. *Twice*, I'd almost admitted to the very thing I was trying to deny. The one and only time Linda and I had had a proper kiss, a little experiment that nobody else could possibly know about – nobody knew, but I'd just managed to dig a hole all of my own, and fallen straight into it.

'I see,' Jimmy said tonelessly, as I stood before him, flushed and speechless. 'Well, it all makes perfect sense now, anyway.'

'No! Look, you've totally misunderstood!'

'Well, let's be honest, Cathy – you've never really enjoyed sex with me, have you?'

I gasped. 'That's not true – I do enjoy it! I'm just scared of getting pregnant!'

'Come off it,' he said, turning away from me as if he couldn't bear to look at me. 'If you were enjoying it, you'd forget all about that. Don't forget I've had other girls before you. My last girlfriend used to scream out with excitement! But *you* just lie there, looking polite, looking like you'd rather be somewhere else – you'd rather be with your bloody girlfriend! I knew it! Well, bugger off then, Cathy – go and sleep with her, then, get it out of your system, if that's what you want. But don't come running back to me when you decide it's not enough for you, because I'm not touching you after you've been with her!'

'I'm not ... I haven't ... I don't want ...' I was crying, all the way through this outburst. I couldn't believe Jimmy was shouting at me like this. 'Please, Jimmy, let me explain! It wasn't like that! We didn't ... it wasn't ... I don't want to be with her! I want *you*! I love you!'

But he'd turned his back on me and was refusing to listen.

'Go home, Cathy,' he said, gruffly. I couldn't see – he wouldn't turn round – but I thought he was crying now too. 'I can't talk to you anymore. Just go home.'

I let myself out, and walked home in a daze. It wasn't really happening. I'd wake up in the morning and find out it had all been a bad dream. Jimmy would realise he'd made a mistake. He couldn't, he wouldn't, believe a stupid anonymous note instead of me.

I tried to phone Linda. But she was out.

February 2004

It's ten o'clock at night but I know Linda won't mind me calling her. She's never minded me calling her.

'I've just been thinking about those anonymous notes,' I say as soon as she picks up.

'Pardon?'

'Remember – back in 1965? After you'd left school? Jimmy and I both got those sick notes from someone making out you and I were having sex.'

'Oh, God – *those*. Yes. That was awful, Cath. I always thought you should have gone to the police about it.'

'I know – you kept on telling me that, at the time. When I finally managed to prise you out of the arms of that dental technician to talk to you about it,' I add sarcastically.

'Rosemary.' Linda sighs. 'Ah. She was my first.'

'Yeah, I remember it well. I couldn't get any sense out of you for weeks. And there was I, crying my heart out about Jimmy dumping me ...'

'Yes. Of course, it's all coming back to me now,' she says. 'Poor you – it was a horrible time for you, wasn't it. You haven't still *got* them, have you – the notes?'

'You must be joking. I probably tore them into hundreds of pieces, or burnt them.' I pause. 'Who do you think sent them, Lin?'

'Well – I think we both agreed, at the time – didn't we? – it was bound to be those girls in our class. The two that really had it in for us both. I can't remember their names.'

'Heather and Susan.'

'Yes, that's right, Heather and Susan. What a nasty pair of bitches they were! Why?' She sounds suddenly excited. 'Have you found something out? Something new?'

'No. I looked for their names on that website, though – *Friends Reunited*, you know? But there's hardly anyone there from our class.'

'Just as well. I'd have thought they'd be the last people you'd want to get in touch with. Or ... what? Do you think they might have been able to help with this story you're writing? Is that it?'

'Not really. It was just curiosity. No, I actually *found* the person I was looking for.'

'Go on – who?' she asks, warily.

'Janice Baker.'

'Janice!' she says, sounding genuinely surprised. 'Do you know, I'd completely forgotten about her. You were really friendly with her for a couple of years, weren't you. Didn't you go to see the Beatles with her? God, I was so bloody jealous.'

'Were you?' I'm taken aback. 'I thought you were completely uninterested.'

'Defensive mechanism. Better than stamping my feet and crying.'

'What a horrible little cow I was – I was so chuffed to be friends with one of the older girls, I practically dropped you, didn't I. No wonder you were so upset.'

There's a silence for a moment, and then she laughs softly.

'No, Cathy. Well – yes, I was hurt about you ignoring me when we were supposed to be best mates. But I was jealous because of *her*. That bloody Janice. God, she was gorgeous, wasn't she!'

I gasp with surprise, and then laugh as well. 'She was straight, though! She had loads of boyfriends!'

'I know! But I was only – what, fourteen? And still pretty confused. I just knew I would've liked to be the one she was taking so much interest in.'

'We waste so much time, when we're young, don't we,' I say with a sigh, 'with all these negative emotions. If only we realised at fourteen, how quickly life passes. How we should just be grateful for being young and healthy, and enjoy ourselves.'

'But other people always get in the way of that, don't they,' she says. 'Anyway – you've got in touch with Janice, then?'

'I sent her a message through that website, but I haven't heard back yet. It was only a couple of days ago, though.'

'She went to live in London, didn't she?'

'Yeah. The last I heard of her, she was living with someone – an older man, possibly a married man at that. My mum was beside herself with moral outrage – can you imagine?' We both laugh. 'I heard rumours later that she was on her own again – but I've no idea what happened. I haven't given her much thought until now.'

'So why now? You think *she* might know something – about Ian's stabbing – that she didn't tell you at the time?'

'I don't suppose so. She stopped talking to me, anyway, when she found out I was going out with Jimmy. But she *was* the only person, apart from you and Del, that knew about Ian trying to rape me. And as Pauline said in her e-mail ...'

'Oh!' she squawks. 'You didn't tell me Pauline e-mailed you! What did she say?'

She listens in silence as I give her the gist of it.

'Sad, isn't it,' she says when I've finished. 'She doesn't sound like she ever got over losing Derek.'

'Nor did my mum, really,' I remind her. 'And it's strange, you know – I didn't particularly like Pauline when Del started going out with her. I didn't think they were suited. I remember thinking he was just using her to get away from home because of Fred.'

'What did we know about anything, back then? We were just kids. Well, it's nice that you've caught up with her again. But she didn't have any info about the Brighton incident?'

'No. They didn't see anything. And Del never told her about Ian assaulting me – she was shocked. But she made the point that she was sure Del would have been really angry about it, and that anyone else who knew, might have been angry too.'

'So ... I'm sorry, Cath, I'm not following you. You think *Janice* might have been cross enough about it to have stabbed him – Ian?'

'No, I don't. For a start, she definitely didn't go to Brighton. She was at her grandparents' that day. And also, she was so bloody fanatical about the whole mods and rockers thing. If Ian had been a rocker, then yes – I honestly could've imagined her taking a knife to him! But she'd never have turned against a mod. She went out with Ian for a while, you know? And she told me he treated her badly – got rough with her; maybe he even tried to rape *her* for all I know. She dumped him because of the way he was, and yes – she was furious about what he did to me. But as soon as he got stabbed, she changed her tune. It was like Ian was a saint who had been martyred for the cause. Unbelievable!'

'But you're trying to get hold of her anyway. Just in case?'

'Yes. In case she remembers anything – anything I've forgotten. At least ...' I hesitate. If I can't be honest with Linda, who can I be honest with? 'At least, that's what I'm telling myself. But I suppose, doing all this thinking ... having all these memories ...'

'You'd just like to talk to her again.'

'Mm. Find out what happened to her.'

'Fair enough. Well, good luck with that.' I hear her laugh. 'If you find her, give her a kiss from me, won't you!'

I look at the *Friends Reunited* website again the next morning. I'm idly browsing the short list of names from my own year, trying to remember who they were, when I notice there's a message for me. My hands are shaking with excitement as I open it – but no, it's not from Janice. It's from someone called Diana Pine – a name that means nothing to me.

Hi Catherine, the message reads. *I see you have joined this site. I remember you from school. I was in the year below you so you might not remember me but I just wanted to say sorry. We used to call you names because you were going out with a 'rocker'. I threw your bag over a hedge once. It's stayed on my conscience ever since, how we all used to torment you. I hope you have had a nice life since then. Love from Di Pine (nee Williams).*

I snort with disgust as I close her message without replying. *Love*? She thinks, after forty years of her conscience bothering her, she can sign off with *love* now that she's said sorry? I think back to the day she and her friends attacked me in the street. It marked a turning point, a point when the bullying began to affect my relationship with Jimmy; when it started to really get to him; when he first suggested that perhaps we should split up. They were only kids, of course – we all were. They were just following the herd – it probably seemed like a laugh, to them, at the time.

But it wasn't. It was assault, and I should have reported it. If it happened today, the kids responsible would be dragged before the court. There'd be an outcry; my picture would probably be in the papers, I'd be feted as a victim, signed off school with post-traumatic stress. Back then, of course, things weren't looked on in the same light. Kids who got picked on were generally looked on as wimps who possibly deserved it. *These things happen* was the mantra of the day.

Well, these things *did* happen, Di Pine (nee Williams) – but they happened to me, not you. It wasn't you who got shouted at in the street, pushed and shoved and had her bag slung over the hedge. It wasn't you who was called names, sworn at, kicked, and had her hair pulled. So don't come crawling to me on the internet now, expecting to be loved and forgiven, just to make your adult self feel better. To put it bluntly, I don't give a shit how you feel, any more than you really care whether I've had a *nice life since then*. If I *have* had a nice life, it hasn't been any thanks to you and your gang of girl terrorists, so if you think I'm going to send you a message back, saying not to worry, that it's absolutely fine, I didn't suffer any nightmares, didn't grow up with any insecurities or lose the love of my life because of what you did to me – forget it.

I'm so cross, I log off the website and don't go back into it for a week.

August 1965

The night of the row with Jimmy, I didn't sleep. I told Mum I had bad period pains, went to my room with a drink of water and a bottle of Aspirin and sat, staring at the full bottle for a long time, wondering whether they'd kill me if I took the whole lot. I knew, really, that even if they would, I'd never do it – but I felt dreadful enough to contemplate the idea, to turn it around in my head as an option, wondering how Jimmy would feel when he heard the news, wondering if he'd come to my funeral and cry, wondering if he'd be so overcome with grief and remorse that he'd kill himself too. The realisation that I wouldn't be around to know whether he did or not was presumably what stopped me from trying it. Instead, I lay on my bed and cried solidly for so long that my face hurt and I couldn't eventually squeeze out any more tears.

The next morning, just as I was wondering again about the Aspirin, I heard the phone ring downstairs and Mum hollered:

'Cathy! Your boyfriend's on the phone! Hurry up, it's a call box.'

Her face registered shock as she watched me come downstairs.

'Don't make any plans to go out today, miss!' she said as I took the receiver from her. 'You look dreadful!'

'Hello?' I waited, my heart pounding in my chest, for Jimmy to start ranting at me again. If he did, I'd hang up. I couldn't take any more of it.

'Cathy,' he said. His voice was hoarse and shaking. 'I'm sorry.'

I immediately burst into tears. Mum, on her way to the back garden with a basket of washing, looked round at me and sniffed, shaking her head.

'I'm sorry for the way I spoke to you,' he went on. 'I was upset ...'

I still couldn't speak.

'I didn't mean what I said – about you and Linda. It was just ... that note ... it was the last straw. There's been so much – and I've just had enough.'

'You didn't mean it?' I managed to gasp. 'We're all right?'

Relief was oozing out of my every pore. He still loved me! He wasn't going to finish with me! I didn't care what he'd said last night – he'd been upset, it was understandable. We'd start again, tear up those stupid notes, forget they ever happened. I'd spend more time with him – stop seeing Linda, if it really bothered him so much. I'd try to stop worrying about getting pregnant and be more enthusiastic about the sex. Maybe there *was* something wrong with me. Obviously it wasn't the sort of thing I could see my doctor about, but perhaps I could write to the problem page in *Jackie* magazine for some advice. I was so busy with these thoughts that I almost didn't catch the next thing he said – it was so soft.

'No. We're not all right, Cathy. I'm sorry.'

'What do you mean? You said you didn't mean it. And it's OK – we can forget about it, Jimmy. We can tear up the notes, and ...'

'No. Look – I'm late for work. I can't talk for long, but ...'

'What? You've *got* to talk! You've got to tell me what you mean – you can't just say no, we're not all right! What's wrong?'

I heard him sigh. 'Everything's wrong – don't you get it? It hasn't been right for ages, Cath. If it had, I wouldn't have blown my top the way I did yesterday.'

'Look, I'm sorry I've been so scared about getting pregnant,' I whispered urgently. Mum was still in the garden, but I couldn't take any chances. 'I'll try to put it out of my mind.'

'It's not that. I'm sorry I said it was that. It isn't.'

'What, then? What *is* wrong, Jimmy?'

'Us – being together. It's always been difficult, hasn't it.'

'No! It hasn't!'

'It has! Ever since Ian Vincent got knifed, we never stood a chance. All your friends turned on you, you got set on by gangs of kids in the street ...'

'I don't care! And anyway, it's not so bad now!'

'That's what I was starting to think, too. Now, I think it's never gonna stop. They'll always be tormenting you – and me! It's no good. I can't put up with it anymore.'

My heart felt like a stone. I sat down on the stairs, clutching the phone receiver to my cheek, unable to even cry any more. I just couldn't believe what I was hearing.

'What's *wrong* with you?' I said, and I was surprised by the bitterness in my voice. 'You're not just giving up on us, are you – because of some stupid girls and some pathetic anonymous notes?'

'Not just because of the notes, no.' He sighed again. 'There's stuff I haven't even told you.'

'Like what?'

'Like: the blokes at the Cauldron giving me a hard time.'

'Because of me? That's rubbish, Jimmy – they're *not*! All your mates have been lovely to me!'

'Yes. My real mates have. But there are some people who won't even set foot in the place since you started work there. Others who square up to me, looking for a fight, making comments about you. And someone, now, who's smashed up my bike.'

'*What*? Why didn't you tell me? Why did you let me carry on working there? I wouldn't have taken the job in the first place!'

'Why do you think I insisted on staying there with you? It wasn't cos I didn't trust you – I was worried that I'd actually encouraged you to put yourself in danger. For God's sake – I thought I was being clever: doing something good. Having you work there – I thought it'd *help*: you know, make them see that we could all get on with each other, be friends, all that stuff. Huh!' He snorted, sounding tired and defeated. 'Well, so much for that. There are people on both sides who are *never* going to let go of it, Cathy. As long as we were going out together, they'd never stop punishing us.'

'So you're chucking me, because you can't take it anymore? Is that what you're saying?' I was shouting now – despite the pain in my head and soreness of my throat from the night of crying – shouting at him in anger and frustration. 'What – you care more about your *bike* being smashed up, than you care about me?'

'Of course not. But I'm sorry, Cathy. I just think it's for the best.'

'But I *don't*! It's *not* for the best, Jimmy! I love you! We don't have to let them do this to us!'

'I love you too,' he said, sadly. 'But it's not going to work. I'd rather finish it now, than go on until one of us gets hurt – really hurt.'

'I *am* really hurt! Please don't do this! Please – just come round, tonight, so we can talk it over properly. Please!'

'No.' He was almost whispering now. 'If I come round ... if I come to see you, Cath, I'll be tempted to change my mind. And I don't want to. I think I'm doing the right thing – for us both. You'll thank me one day.'

'No I won't!' I cried. 'Jimmy – don't ...' The pips were going. 'Put some more money in!' I begged him. 'Please ...'

But the line went dead. And I threw the receiver on the floor and fell back against the stairs, sobbing – just as Mum came back in from the garden and rushed to see what had happened.

I'd like to say she took me in her arms and comforted me – but she was never that kind of mother. She put the kettle on – her usual remedy for everything from a grazed knee to a national disaster – sat me down and made me a cup of hot sweet tea. She let me cry myself out, without passing comments of the sort I'd come to expect, about having *told me so*, or *no good ever coming* from messing around with older boys. And eventually, when I'd run out of tears again, she put a single hand on my shoulder, looked into my eyes and I recognised genuine sympathy there as she said, surprisingly:

'I know how much it hurts, love. But you'll get through it. Keep busy, and you'll get through it, in time.'

I didn't take her advice, of course. Instead of keeping busy, I lounged on the sofa, day after day, playing my records and feeling sorry for myself. My brief experience as a coffee-bar waitress had obviously come to an end – I got Mum to phone them for me and make an excuse for my leaving – and the last thing I felt inclined to do was to look for another job.

The first week, the pain was so bad I thought I'd die of it. I felt shaky and ill, refused to eat, lost weight, didn't bother getting dressed. Normally, Mum wouldn't have tolerated such behaviour, but it spoke volumes about her sudden unexpected compassion that she brought me soups and puddings to tempt me, let me play *Yesterday* from my new Beatles' LP over and over – until she must have known the words off by heart as well as I did – and kept Fred firmly out of my way. Although I was too sick with misery to appreciate it properly at the time, it was the beginning of a new closeness between us – and perhaps the beginning of the end for her and the horrible Fred.

Linda came round every day when she finished work. I had to try to ignore the new light of excitement in her eyes, and she had to try to hide it – I could hardly bear to see anyone happy in love.

'I hope you never get hurt like this,' I told her one day, as she sat beside me, hugging me, as we listened yet again to the mournful lyrics of *Yesterday*.

'I expect I will,' she said. 'Everybody does, don't they – sooner or later.'

'Don't go out with her then – this Rosemary. If you think she's going to hurt you, don't let her! Don't fall for her!'

'I don't think she's going to hurt me. You didn't think Jimmy was going to hurt you. People don't set out to hurt each other, do they. But sometimes it happens, Cath. It just does.'

Well, I knew one thing for sure. I was never going to fall in love again. I'd found out that the price was too high – the pain too awful. Everyone told me I was going to recover eventually, and I had to believe them. But when I did, I'd get on with my life – my studies, my A-levels, my degree, my career. And if I ever went out with another boy, which I doubted, I'd keep my heart to myself and not allow *anyone* to break it again, the way Jimmy Kent had broken it now.

September 1965

As the summer holiday drew to an end, I began, almost accidentally, to take up a new hobby. I'd kept a diary for several years, but had only written in it intermittently, when there was something particularly exciting to note. When Jimmy finished with me, I wrote pages and pages of completely self-indulgent whining about my broken heart – which helped me to get it all out, but didn't really make me feel any better. Reading it through a couple of weeks later, I suddenly felt impatient with myself. What was the point of this? It wasn't going to make Jimmy come back to me – he'd never see it, and even if he did, it wouldn't make him love me again. Reading it, I didn't even love myself very much. Instead, I started to feel angry. I thought back to the start of it all – when I'd started hanging around with Janice. I remembered how we'd been so in love with the Beatles, how I'd admired her taste and her mod fashions. It was all just – innocent fun. How did it ever reach the stage where the mods and rockers were fighting each other at seaside resorts? How on earth did Ian get stabbed just for being a mod? What went wrong? How did my friends come to turn against me just because I was in love with a rocker?

Instead of scribbling in my diary about my lost love, I began instead to write all these thoughts down in a notebook. I'd always been good at writing essays, and I'd realised for some time that when I felt sufficiently strongly about something, I managed to find the ability, from somewhere, to put my thoughts into words in a way that made people listen – made them stop and think. Writing down how I felt about the previous year's battles between the mods and rockers, and how the situation had affected me and Jimmy, was very therapeutic. Although I allowed my anger to come through, I didn't give vent to my own emotional distress, trying to focus instead on the facts and my view of them.

I handed the notebook to Linda the next time she came round, and she read my story in silence. When she passed it back to me, there were tears in her eyes.

'You should get this published,' she said. 'It's brilliant.'

'No it's not!' I said, embarrassed now. 'It's just my opinion. My thoughts.'

'But you've expressed them so well – without sounding sorry for yourself.'

'You should've seen the stuff I wrote in my diary a little while back!'

'Yeah, but that was for *you*. This ...' She looked at me seriously. 'This could be for everyone.'

'It couldn't, Lin! Thanks for the compliment. But nobody's going to publish the witterings of a sixteen-year-old girl.'

'The local paper might.'

I laughed. But she was still looking serious.

'They *might*,' she said again. 'Look how much coverage they gave to Ian's case. People loved reading about the mods and rockers' fights last year – some of them just loved the idea that all the kids were running riot and ought to be put in the army. This – ' She pointed at my notebook, 'is giving the other side: showing that we didn't all want to get involved in fighting each other.'

I dismissed the idea at first; but later, I started to read through my story again. I worked on it, cutting out bits of waffle, leaving out people's names. I *was* pleased with it, but I couldn't believe anyone else would find it interesting. In the end, I decided to make a concise one-page précis of my work, which I sent to the 'Letters to the Editor' page of the *Romford Recorder*.

'Like modern-day Romeos and Juliets, some teenage boyfriends and girlfriends have been forced apart by the hatred of the people who should have been their friends,' I wrote in my final paragraph. *'Not all teenagers who were mods or rockers wanted to kill each other or cause trouble. We just wanted to get on with our lives in peace – but some of us weren't allowed to. I just hope it's over now, because I, for one, wouldn't care if I never heard the words 'mod' or 'rocker' again.'*

A week later, just after I'd gone back to school, Mum rushed to the front door as I arrived home, waving the latest edition of the *Recorder*. I was so shocked to see that my letter had been published, it was a while before I took on board the fact that Mum wasn't ranting at me for making a show of myself or getting ideas above my station – she was proud. She was actually proud of me.

'You've got a way with words, no doubt about it,' she said admiringly as we sipped a cup of tea together and she spread the newspaper out on the table, reading the letter through again. 'It's a gift. My father had it.'

'Did he?' I didn't remember my maternal granddad – he'd died when I was very young, and even while my grandma was still alive, I never heard her or Mum speak much about him. It was the old East End custom of getting on with life – which was tough enough without wasting time reminiscing about those no longer around.

'Yes. Didn't I ever tell you? He was a newspaper reporter. Worked on the *News Chronicle*.' She smoothed out the paper in front of her again, almost lovingly, as she added, 'Perhaps you take after him.'

'I think ...' I began, tentatively at first, because it was such a rare thing for Mum and I to have a heart-to-heart and I still half expected her to tell me at any moment to stop dreaming and get on with peeling the potatoes, 'I've been thinking recently that I'd like to do something like that. Writing for a newspaper, or a magazine. I'm good at writing essays, and I ... like putting my thoughts into words.'

'Well, you're obviously clever at it,' she said, her hand still resting on my letter. 'I think it's a good idea. Perhaps you should find out how to go about it.'

'I think there are college courses for journalism. Or maybe a degree in English would be better. I'll ask my English teacher.' I was excited now, thrilled to be sharing with Mum these vague ideas that had been forming in my mind recently. 'Thanks, Mum,' I added.

'What for?'

'For being ...' I hesitated. 'For being *pleased* for me.'

'Course I'm pleased for you. Don't be so daft,' she said, immediately closing the newspaper and getting to her feet. 'Now then, come on, I've got a dinner to cook, and you, my girl, need to get started on your homework if you're ever going to pass those A-levels.'

She bustled about, getting food out of the larder, and I took myself off upstairs to my bedroom to start work on the new and unnerving challenge of Chaucer's *Canterbury Tales*. From that day on, I was excused from helping with the cooking and housework, and Mum referred to me, with pride in her voice, as a *student.*

The same couldn't, unfortunately, be said for Fred. That evening, when Mum told him about my letter in the paper, there was an explosion of anger.

'Writing to the papers? About *mods and rockers*?' he bellowed. 'What the hell are you playing at?'

'Read it, Fred,' Mum said, pushing the paper towards him, trying to appease him. 'It's very good. Cathy's got a way with words. I was telling her, she's like my father ...'

'Like your father?' he retorted in disgust. 'I thought you told me he was a bloody newspaper reporter. You think that's a compliment, to be compared to a low-grade, two-penny *hack*?'

'Don't ...!' I tried to interrupt, but Mum had pulled herself up straight and, for once, looked him in the eye and answered him back:

'Don't you talk like that about my father, Fred Harper! He might have been poor, but he worked himself into an early grave to keep food on our table. He fought in the trenches in the Great War and never got his health back, but he still worked like a navvy to keep us from starving.'

'Yes! He was obviously more of a man than you'll ever be!' I shouted, enraged by the look of boredom on Fred's face as Mum poured out this surprisingly emotional tribute.

'Don't you *dare* speak to me like that, you little bitch!' He took a step towards me, his hand raised. Remembering the pain of the previous occasion, I backed away quickly, but before I'd even moved, Mum had grabbed his wrist, shouting at him to leave me alone. Physically, she was no match for him at all, but the shock of her intervention caused him swerve and almost overbalance. He looked at her in disbelief, his arm still raised, and for a horrible moment I thought he was about to strike her instead.

'If you hit Mum, I'm calling the police!' I yelled without even thinking. Afterwards, I wondered whether the police would have even taken any notice. Hitting women and kids was still pretty much an accepted part of domestic life in working-class families. But it seemed to be enough to make him drop his hand to his side, staring at us both as if he didn't recognise us anymore.

I moved to stand next to Mum, and we faced him, shoulder to shoulder, staring him out, until he shook his head, stomped out of the room, and with a torrent of foul language, announced that he was going down the pub.

'Good riddance,' Mum said shakily as the door slammed behind him.

She moved her things into Derek's room that evening, and as far as I know, never slept with Fred again. And for the short time remaining that he lived with us, she and I presented a united front against his bullying. I think it wore him down.

I settled into sixth form life quickly. Now I was only studying my favourite subjects, I raced through the work and got consistently good marks, which spurred me on to put in even more effort. Although the pain of losing Jimmy was always there in a corner of my heart, I was aware of the fact that having no boyfriend meant all my energies were being poured into my studies. At first I found it hard not to call Jimmy when I was feeling particularly low – but both Mum and Linda continually counselled me that it wouldn't help.

'I would have liked to stay friends,' I cried once to Linda. 'Surely we could just be friends, and chat on the phone sometimes? That wouldn't hurt, would it?'

'*He* hasn't phoned *you*, has he,' Linda pointed out. 'He's moved on, Cath.'

'What – you think he's got another girlfriend?' I squawked.

'That's not what I'm saying. But it's possible.'

She was being cruel to be kind – telling me it was over, gone, finished, full-stop. But the images it provoked in my mind, of Jimmy with another girl, made me want to kill her!

School was far more pleasant, now that Heather and Susan had left. The other girls, who'd been much nicer to me and Linda anyway since my famous speech the previous term, were all, like me, embarked on a new and more serious course of study. We were sixth-formers, looked up to by all the girls lower down in the school, and I think we were conscious of wearing a new mantle of maturity. Some of my classmates were already turning seventeen. The whispers about sex had become less about giggly bravado, more concerned with the practicalities of losing their virginity and managing contraception. Several girls now had steady boyfriends and one had actually got engaged, but had to wear her ring secretly on a chain round her neck, under her uniform, as jewellery was banned at school. She'd even managed to get a supply of The Pill from the Family Planning Association clinic in Romford by showing one of the more agreeable doctors her ring and pretending she was about to get married – a feat which drew gasps of envy from the rest of the class.

There was no more talk about mods and rockers, no more hostility – at least, not from anyone I mixed with. Frances apparently still carried a burden of resentment around with her about her late cousin Ian, but as she was studying sciences I didn't come into contact with her too much. I often thought about the irony of the situation: now that Jimmy and I had finally been forced apart, everyone had moved on. I doubted whether anybody at school would have cared now, if I'd still been going out with him. In fact I'd been given tons of sympathy over my 'dumping' from several girls who, just months earlier, would have laughed and said it served me right.

The only thing that hadn't stopped was the occasionally silent phone call. We'd go for weeks without getting any, and we'd forget about them – and then, suddenly, it would start again. We might get two or three on a single evening – and then, again, nothing. Several times, Mum decided we should report them, but as it was so intermittent, we never got around to it.

'I don't actually think it can be those girls from school,' I told her. 'Not now. Perhaps it's a problem to do with the party line. Or just someone dialling the wrong number.'

By now we'd both got used to hanging up without worrying too much about it, and we'd look at each other, agree that we should really report it, and then let it drift on again. We never did do anything about it. Eventually they stopped, and we forgot they'd ever happened.

February 2004

My phone's ringing while I'm out in the car, on my way to the shops. I pull into a bus lay-by just in time to grab the call before it goes to voicemail.

'Hello, Cath,' says an unfamiliar voice. 'Did you want me?'

'Who's this?'

'Don't you recognise me, after all these years?' She laughs, and immediately, I do.

'Janice!' I feel suddenly quite light-headed with shock. What the hell? Who the hell calls someone after forty years of silence and says 'Did you want me?' as if we'd been in the habit of leaving messages for each other every day of our lives?

'I saw your message,' she goes on, calmly. 'On Friends Reunited. I thought it'd be quicker to call you, as you put your number on the message.'

Well, at least it had worked. But now I couldn't think of a single bloody thing to say to her.

'Look, I'm in the car at the moment, at a bus-stop,' I glance in my rear-view mirror. 'And there's a bus just about to pull in. Can I call you back?'

The short drive to Tesco's just about gives me time to calm down. Even though I wanted this, it's still somehow completely unexpected. I remind myself that I'm on a professional assignment, writing a story, and that the personal issues are only incidental. I've almost managed to convince myself of this by the time I park the car and call Janice back.

'I'm writing a story for one of the Sunday magazines about the sixties,' I tell her after we've exchanged some quite stilted enquiries after each other's health. 'About the time of the mods and rockers.'

'Oh yes?' Her tone gives nothing away. 'Well done. I've seen your name in various papers and magazines over the years, of course. You're still Catherine Ferguson.'

'Yes. I was married, but I kept my own name for my work. Look, I was wondering if you'd ...'

'You want to interview me?' she cuts in. 'Is that it? For your article?'

'I was going to say, I wondered if you'd like to meet up. Get together, for a chat.' It sounds inane, after all the years of separation, all the antagonism that went before. 'I'll be honest: I've been thinking a lot about what happened back in sixty-four and sixty-five. There are things I've always wondered about, and I'm trying to get to the bottom of it all. I'm not pretending it wouldn't help my story, but that's only a part of it.'

She's silent for a moment.

'You mean – the business with the boy who got stabbed.'

'Ian, yes.'

Another silence. I wait. I'm not pushing it.

'OK,' she says eventually. She sighs. 'Look, Catherine, I don't think I can help. But ... it'd be good to see you, anyway. It was all such a long time ago, but I do think about those days, too. Let's have lunch, shall we? Are you still in Essex? I live in the Richmond area. Shall we meet somewhere in the City? How's Friday for you?'

Two days later, I'm on the train into London. It almost feels too good to be true. I'd been expecting more resistance from her, possibly even annoyance at being sought out and bothered after all this time. I can only suppose that, like me, she's aware of the passage of time, aware that teenage angst shouldn't have been carried over into adulthood, shouldn't be allowed to last a lifetime. It occurs to me that I didn't ask what she's done with her life since she was eighteen. She could be married with six kids and a dozen grandchildren. Or she could still be the single party-girl, flat-sharing and boyfriend-hopping – although I suppose that's less likely at the age of fifty-seven.

When I walk into the restaurant, someone stands up and gives me a wave. It's obviously Janice, although I'd never have known her. I'm flattered that she recognises *me* straight away. I'm aware that the years, and the births of two children, have added more than a stone and several inches to my sixties' Twiggy shape – to say nothing of the short bob, coloured a deep chestnut to disguise the grey. And then I remember that of course, my photo's often been in the papers and magazines I've written for. Janice looks nothing like I remember, and I can hardly believe it's her. She's wearing a matronly skirt and blouse, a floppy grey cardigan, and an old-fashioned style of glasses that she's pushed down her nose to peer over. I make my way to the table where she's sitting, and she gets up to greet me.

'Cathy. Good to see you.' She smiles, and her voice is warm – more so than on the phone the other day. I guess she's had time to adjust to the idea of seeing me again.

'You too. Thanks for agreeing to meet me. How are you?'

'Fine, thank you. You haven't changed a bit!'

'Nor you!' I lie.

We sit down and I look at her more closely. She too has adopted a shorter hairstyle probably more appropriate to our age. The trademark pale blonde of her youth has turned a distinctive silver-ash, which she's obviously made no attempt to change. No make-up, no rings – no jewellery at all apart from a heavy gold cross on a chain. The waitress is hovering and I order a drink before going on, 'I'm sorry – I should have asked you on the phone what you're doing with yourself these days. Are you married, or living with anyone, or ...'

'No.' She laughs. 'I'm still single. I like my own company! Besides, I'm too busy with the parish, to be honest.'

'The parish?' I look up from my drink. 'What ...?'

'Didn't I tell you on the phone? Sorry. I'm not wearing my dog-collar today, Cathy, but I was ordained twenty years ago. I'd been curate of an inner London parish before that, and stayed there for several years before I was appointed to St Luke's.'

'St Luke's?' I repeat faintly.

'It's the parish church of one of the villages near Richmond. I'm lucky – it's a lovely, thriving area with a very strong Christian community.' She stops, looking at my face, and laughs again. 'You look completely stunned. I suppose you were expecting to meet the Janice Baker of the nineteen-sixties. We've all moved on, Cathy.'

'Yes – yes, of course. I realise that,' I say quickly, recovering myself. 'I just hadn't expected, exactly, that you'd ...'

'Turn into a bible-basher?' She grins. 'Ah, well, you should have seen me during the early seventies. It wasn't a pretty sight.'

'Why, what were you? A hippy?'

I'm being flippant, but she responds, straight-faced, 'Yes, absolutely.'

'The last I heard of you, you were living with ... well, I presumed it was the guy you worked with back then?'

'Phillip. Yes.' She nods, and takes a sip of her coffee. 'He went back to his wife. When he found out I was pregnant.'

'Pregnant? Oh!' I'm trying not to squeal. 'You've got a child?'

'No.' She drops her eyes and I wish I hadn't spoken. 'I was very young, of course, and frightened, and alone. I'd left home, and couldn't face telling my parents. I wish I had. They'd have supported me. But I had a termination, Cathy – and this was 1966 we're talking about. Before the Abortion Act. An illegal termination.'

'I'm so sorry. It must have been absolutely awful for you.'

'I went completely off the rails. Dropped out of society, really. Lived in a squat, took drugs, didn't believe in anything apart from 'free love'. I was lucky I didn't get pregnant again. Possibly the termination left me infertile.'

We're both silent while I take this in.

'And then?' I say.

'Then eventually, I found the Lord,' she says simply. 'I was taken into hospital in 1973 after an overdose. I didn't really care whether I made it or not. I got off with a fine for possession of the drugs, but I was assigned to a social worker whose job it was to try and get me clean. He was a Christian.' She shrugs. 'Something about his message got through. It turned my life around. That's why I worked for so long in inner-city parishes – trying to help other addicts and alcoholics.'

'Oh.' I swallow, having now completely lost track of the things I'd planned to ask her.

'Shall we order lunch?' she suggests brightly. 'And then we can talk about your story.'

We're halfway through our healthy tuna salads – both of us having admitted to needing to watch our weight these days – and I've filled her in on the details of my marriage to, and divorce from, the cheating drunken bastard who's unfortunately the father of my two children, when she suddenly puts down her knife and fork and looks me in the eye.

'There's something I want to say, before we move onto the subject of Ian Vincent. I know we were both only kids back then. But I was older than you, and supposed to be your friend. I treated you very badly. I'd like to apologise, Cathy, if it's not too late.'

'Of course it's not too late – but it goes without saying, doesn't it. As you say, we were both young and silly.'

'But I knew, even then, that I'd behaved badly. I wanted to make up with you, but I didn't have the courage to admit it. I remember constantly starting to phone you, but changing my mind when I heard your voice, or your mum's. I didn't have the guts to say sorry. I should have done.'

'Oh!' I laugh. 'So it was you. How funny. I've been thinking about those silent calls. I'd always assumed it was one of those awful girls in my class, winding me up.'

'I don't suppose you're still in touch with anyone?'

'Only Linda.'

'She was a good friend to you. I was dead jealous.'

'You were *what*?'

'Jealous of you and her. She *was* a lesbian, wasn't she?'

'Yes. She's with a lovely lady called Andrea now. She eventually qualified as a dentist and they live in Berkshire – Andrea's a teacher at a school there.' I remember what Linda admitted recently, and I start to laugh. 'I can't believe you were jealous too!'

'Too?'

'Linda fancied you. She only told me that last week.'

'Oh.' She looks flustered for a minute, and then laughs as well. 'No, I was just jealous of your friendship. I was a spoilt only child, and I always wanted what other people had. I was jealous of your relationship with Jimmy, too. But I suppose that was obvious.'

'Were you?' I stare at her. 'No, it wasn't obvious at all. I thought you hated him.'

'*Oh, what a tangled web we weave,*' she quotes, with a sad smile. 'I was such a devious little witch. All that posturing and mouthing-off about being a mod, hating rockers. In fact, I was just covering up. I really only ever fancied rockers.'

'You *what*?' This conversation is turning into a series of complete shocks.

'The motorbikes, the leather jackets, all those mean, moody looks. They were so sexy, weren't they. Your Jimmy – he was such a hunk, as we used to say! A lot of the mod boys looked like little posing poofters by comparison. But I couldn't ever admit it. I was a mod, all my friends were mods. I'd have been lynched.' She sighs and shakes her head. 'Like you were. You see why I'm saying I owe you an apology? You obviously broke up with Jimmy. Was it my fault?'

'Not entirely. It's ... a bit of a story. Do you want another coffee? Sorry – I'm still having trouble getting my head around everything!'

'Yes. We've got a lot to catch up on. I don't know about another coffee – I think we're going to need the whole afternoon!' She laughs. 'But it's nice that you're still in touch with Linda. I remember her living in a poky little flat, with her mum. She was very ill, wasn't she?'

'Yes. Parkinson's. But Linda moved out of the flat after her mum died. She lived with me for a while.'

'Did she?' Janice raises her eyebrows.

'*Not* in that way. Actually she did me a favour. She helped to get rid of my mum's horrible boyfriend.'

And perhaps I did her a favour too. She soon realised her first girlfriend was a selfish bitch, and dumped her!

October 1965

After a damp, chilly end to September, the beginning of October that year brought a beautiful Indian summer. During that first warm, sunny week, Linda called to tell me she'd had to make the decision to get her poor mum admitted to Harold Wood Hospital. Mary had finally become too ill to be nursed at home. Once there, sadly, she survived less than a week before giving up the struggle. Linda, who for almost her entire life had lived with the knowledge that this day would come sooner rather than later, was remarkably stoic, organising the funeral and seeing to everything that needed to be done with very little help from her few scattered relatives. I sat in the front row of the church, next to Rosemary, who'd been introduced to Linda's family simply as a work colleague, and was unreasonably upset about the fact that Linda hadn't been more open about their relationship.

'She's got other things to worry about right now,' I said quietly. I wasn't particularly keen on Rosemary, and was trying to convince myself it wasn't jealousy on my part. 'She's just lost her mother!'

'All right, I know that.' She glared at me. 'No need to take that tone with me. Everyone knows you're her *oldest friend.*'

So that was it. *She* was jealous of *me.* How ironic. I decided to shut up and keep the peace. Sometimes, perhaps, that was the right way to go.

Having coped so well with a situation I couldn't even imagine having to handle myself, Linda suddenly became ill herself soon after the funeral. When I went to the flat to see her on a Sunday morning, she took a long time to come to the door, having struggled out of bed – and went straight back again. She was in her mum's room, covered with mounds of blankets, shivering and sweating with a fever. I called the doctor, ignoring her protests that she'd be OK the next day.

'It's the flu,' he said as soon as he examined her. 'She needs to stay in bed, take Aspirin and drink plenty of fluids. There's nothing else you can do.' He looked at me kindly. He was our own doctor too, although luckily I'd hardly ever had cause to visit him myself. 'Let's talk outside,' he suggested, and I led him back into the sitting-room, closing the bedroom door behind us. 'Are you looking after her?' he asked me directly.

'Well ... I ...'

'There's nobody else, is there?' he said.

I thought about Rosemary. She was likely to be horribly offended by me taking charge here. But I wasn't about to tell the doctor that Linda had a girlfriend. I'd have to talk to her later.

'Of course I'll look after her,' I said.

'Well, this is a bad dose of flu. Linda's had to be strong for her mum for a long time, and now that she's gone ... What sometimes happens is that the carer's own health suddenly suffers. It can be like a mini collapse.'

'A collapse? You mean a breakdown?'

'I mean that she might take a long time to recover. Flu can leave people with depression, and Linda's already had a lot to deal with. I'm just warning you to be prepared for a long haul.'

He waited, watching my reaction. I swallowed hard and nodded.

'OK.'

'I'll call in regularly to check on her,' he promised. 'And you can give me a ring any time if you're worried.'

'Thank you, doctor. Do you think I should stay over with her for a while?'

'Yes. She should have someone with her, at least while her temperature's so high. She might start to hallucinate.'

After the doctor left, I found Rosemary's phone number in Linda's handbag. With Linda sleeping fitfully, I shut myself in her kitchen and dialled the number.

'She's very poorly,' I explained. 'The doctor said it's likely to be a long illness, and she might be ... very depressed, afterwards.'

'Poor darling. I'll come straight round. You don't have to hang around, Catherine. I'll deal with everything. She'll want me there.'

'OK.' I wasn't going to argue. I wanted whatever Linda would want. Rosemary was her girlfriend, and my opinion of her wasn't relevant. 'I'll wait here till you come, though. The doctor said she needs someone to be with her all the time for a few days at least.'

'All the time?' She hesitated. 'Well, I don't know if I can get the time off work.'

'Can't you take some of your holiday?'

'No. I only get two weeks. I've used one, and I'm having the other one in a couple of weeks' time. Mum and Dad have booked a package holiday to the *Costa Brava* for the whole family.'

I was so shocked, I couldn't even respond to this. A package holiday? I'd read about them in the paper, but nobody I knew had ever been on one. In fact nobody I'd ever met had ever been abroad, or even to such far-flung and exotic sounding places as the Isle of Wight or the Channel Islands – never mind the Costa Brava! And in October! The notion of having a holiday outside of the normal July and August period seemed almost too far-fetched to believe. Not that anybody in my own family had ever had a holiday of any description, unless you counted the odd day out to Southend or Clacton.

'But what about Linda?' I managed to gasp eventually. 'Don't you want to stay around until she's better?'

'Yeah, course I do. She'll be up and about by then, won't she.'

'I don't know ... the doctor said ...'

'Look, Catherine, I don't particularly like the idea of being apart from Linda for a whole week. But Mum and Dad booked the holiday ages ago. I have to go.'

She made it sound like a chore. I wondered if jetting off to Spain in the middle of the autumn was a quite ordinary thing in her family. They must have been absolutely loaded!

'Well, don't worry, then,' I said, more snappily than I intended. 'I've already promised the doctor I'll take care of her – although I don't quite know how I'm going to manage it, with school and everything.'

'School!' She laughed. 'Oh, of course, I forgot you're still at *school*.' She was only about nineteen herself but acted as if she was a lot older. 'Well, for crying out loud, Catherine – you can just bunk off school, can't you. It's not like it's important, like my job.'

'Right,' I said, through my teeth. 'So you're not coming round, then?'

'Of course I am! I'll pop over for few hours today to sit with the poor darling. I won't be able to stay too late, though. I've got work in the morning, you know.'

'She's still asleep,' I said when I opened the door to Rosemary twenty minutes later. 'She has to take two more Aspirin at about three o'clock this afternoon, and another two at seven o'clock. And she has to drink lots of fluids. Here's the doctor's number, in case you're worried about her. He said she might have hallucinations. Change her sheets if she gets really sweaty.'

'Bossy little beggar, aren't you,' she said mildly, without looking at me.

'And she might be sick,' I added, enjoying the look on her face. 'There's a bowl by the bed.'

She walked straight past me into the bedroom, hesitating when she saw Linda. Her face was deathly pale, glistening with sweat, her hair plastered to her head, and she twitched and shivered in her sleep.

'I'll leave you to it, then,' I said. 'I'll be back later.'

'I don't know what to do,' I said to Mum when I got home. I felt like crying. Linda was my only really close friend; she'd stuck by me through thick and thin and I wasn't going to let her down now that she needed me. 'Do you think, if you write me a note, they'll let me off school for a couple of weeks, till half-term?'

'Off school? For a couple of weeks?' Mum retorted. She shook her head. 'No – I'm not having that, Cathy, and nor would the school.'

'But Linda's got nobody else! I promised the doctor, and I can't just leave her on her own!'

Mum sat down, stared at a cup of tea she'd just made herself, and then took a deep breath.

'We'll bring her over here,' she said firmly. 'That's what we'll do. *I'll* look after her while you're at school.'

'But ...!' I stared at Mum in surprise. I could never, in a million years, have imagined her making an offer like this. 'But how are we going to get her here? She can hardly stand up, never mind walk.'

'Fred can pick her up in his car. Whether he likes it or not!' she added with a grim smile. 'The damn' thing has sat outside this house all these months and hardly ever goes anywhere. It might've been nice if he'd taken me for a ride to the coast once or twice, but no, it just sits there, making him feel swanky. Well, he can damn' well use it to do some good for somebody, for once in his life.'

My eyes grew wider and wider. I'd never heard Mum say 'damn' twice in such short succession before. And I'd never heard her make quite such an open and vociferous complaint about Fred, either.

'Are you sure?' I asked. 'You're really sure you don't mind?'

'No, I don't mind. I haven't got a job now, have I, thanks to him. I can make myself useful for a change. That poor girl's been through enough. You know I didn't have a very high opinion of her mother but perhaps I was being unfair. She's gone now, God rest her soul, and her poor daughter's all alone in the world.'

I nodded, wondering how it might affect Mum's spirit of generosity if she knew that *the poor girl* was, at this moment, being nursed by her lesbian lover.

'You're a good friend to her, Cath,' she went on, 'but it sounds like she needs a bit more than a friend at the moment. She needs some mothering, bless her.'

And, amazingly, my own mother, who'd never exactly gone overboard with displays of maternal affection throughout my life, was going to be the one to provide it.

That evening there was a loud and bitter argument between Mum and Fred. Doors were slammed, a saucepan was banged down on the stove with angry force, and I looked into the kitchen in alarm, frightened that Mum was being assaulted. Fred was holding up his hands, shaking his head at Mum, who had her hands on her hips as she shouted at him, calling him names I hadn't ever heard her use before.

'All right, all right – you win, woman – anything to bloody well shut you up! Get in the bloody car, then, if we're going. I want to be back and down the pub by eight o'clock. Why you want to nurse some bloody orphan kid is beyond me, but ... all right, all right!' he yelled again as Mum began to berate him once more at full volume.

I jumped into the back seat behind them as he started to rev up the engine. Thank goodness, Rosemary had left by the time we reached the flat. Mum and I half-carried Linda out to the car between us, while Fred sat with the engine still running, drumming his fingers irritably on the dashboard, and I quickly ran back inside to pack a bag with pyjamas, dressing gown, and other necessities while Mum laid the patient on the back seat.

Within a week of having Linda installed in my bedroom, while I slept downstairs on the settee, Fred announced that he'd had enough. He'd packed a bag, thrown it into the boot of the Cortina, and before Mum or I could even grasp the fact that he was actually going, had chugged off down the road without a backward glance. He'd been with us exactly a year.

'Biggest mistake of my life,' was the only comment Mum made.

We hardly ever referred to him again.

February 2004

Janice and I have decided to forget the diet. Along with the coffee, we've ordered chocolate fudge cake with whipped cream. It feels somehow appropriate to the revelations we're sharing.

'I was over the moon about getting Fred out of our lives,' I'm telling her. 'Although I suppose I should have been a bit more considerate of my mum's feelings. After all – she must have felt *something* for him, to let him move into her house, into her bed for God's sake. I don't really think I believed, even then, that it was only all about money, about buying a TV and a fridge and having some security.'

'And what happened about Linda? You said she dumped the nasty girlfriend?'

'Yes. She was staying at our house until she got over the flu, and Rosemary hardly ever came to see her, even when she got back from bloody Spain. She complained that it would affect her career if she caught the virus – even though anyone would have known that Linda was over the infectious stage. She was weak and depressed for a long time, though, and she just couldn't be bothered with Rosemary's moods. When she recovered, she got a new job, but she stayed with me and mum for about another year after that. We ... all kind of looked after each other. And she paid Mum rent. It helped a lot, financially, while Mum started work again herself.'

We scrape our plates clean of the last morsels of chocolate cake.

'That was delicious,' Janice says with a sigh. 'And I refuse to feel guilty about it. Now, then.' She puts down her fork and pushes her plate aside. 'Tell me what it is you need, for your story.'

I fill her in, as quickly as I can, with what Pauline told me in her e-mail – how they'd stayed away from any trouble in Brighton on the day Ian was stabbed, and didn't see anything happen.

'Del never told her about what Ian did to me at Clacton, either. But she suggested that whoever told *him* about it might know something.' I pause, and look at Janice. 'That was obviously you – and I think you pretty much admitted it.'

'Yes.' She nods. 'Yes, I did tell him about it. We were both really angry. Derek was so upset – I remember him saying he'd like to sort Ian out.'

'Why did you tell him? It seemed an odd thing to do. You weren't particularly close to my brother – he was a rocker!'

'I told you earlier. I had a thing about rockers – some of them.'

'Oh. You fancied him, didn't you!' I laugh. 'I used to *think* you fancied my brother, but you always denied it!' I stop, and give her a sharp look. 'You surely didn't go out with him? After everything you said to me?'

'Not exactly,' she says, looking uncomfortable.

'Jesus! Oh – sorry.' It's still hard to remember she's a vicar. 'Bloody hell, Janice. You had *sex* with him?'

'Only the once.' She doesn't meet my eyes. 'Are you upset?'

'No. No, for God's sake, it was forty bloody years ago, Derek's been dead for years, why would it upset me now? I'm just amazed I never realised.'

'I pretty much talked him into it. Not that it was difficult. He was a bit of a tart himself, your brother! Until he met Pauline – then he suddenly changed.'

'Yeah, I never realised that, either – how serious it was, right from the start. Pauline says he was nervous, that day in Brighton, because it was their first date, and he wanted to keep her away from any trouble down there.'

'You really think that was why he stayed away from the trouble? And why he was nervous?'

'Why?' I feel my pulse quicken. 'What're you saying? You think he knew something?'

'I think he was expecting something to happen. To Ian.' She wipes chocolate, delicately, from her mouth with her serviette. 'And I think, whatever Pauline likes to believe, that he was just using her as an alibi that day – even if things did start to get serious between them after that.'

'Why did he need an alibi? He didn't do anything.'

'No – *he* wasn't personally involved in anything. He knew he could be linked to anything that happened to Ian, if it ever came out about Ian assaulting you. But he did talk to some of his mates –

some of the rockers from the Cauldron – and suggested they might like to find Ian in Brighton and give him a beating.'

'Oh my God.' I stare at her in horror. 'You're not saying he *was* behind the stabbing, are you?'

'No. There definitely weren't supposed to be knives involved. He was as shocked by that as we all were.'

'But ... one of his mates must have gone too far. It was still his fault up to a point, then, if he set it up – asked them to beat Ian up!'

'No – listen. That didn't even happen. Don't look so worried! Derek's friends couldn't find Ian down in Brighton. He'd got separated from his own crowd. Nobody knew what happened to him. There was a lot of fighting. When the police broke up one of the fights, that was when they found Ian – but he'd been surrounded by people who didn't even know him.'

'So you think it must have just been a random act of violence? By a stranger – like the police decided, when they dropped the case.'

'Yes – I think so. But it scared Derek and the other rockers, knowing they'd planned for him to get beaten up. And it scared me too! I'd been telling you, and Derek, I thought he needed to be taught a lesson, and next thing I knew ... well. It felt like someone had listened in on my conversations and taken it out of my hands.'

'You didn't think much of him either,' I said. 'But afterwards, you wouldn't admit that.'

'No. Nor would you have done, if you were me! I *didn't* like him, and I don't know why I went out with him at all. He was a nasty piece of work – enjoyed slapping his girlfriends around, and got rough when he wanted sex. As you know. But I couldn't tell anybody that after he'd been stabbed! Come on – I was only seventeen, and terrified I'd get implicated in something and be thrown into prison!'

I shake my head. 'I can't believe all this plotting and intrigue was going on without me knowing. To say nothing of the sexual goings-on! You were the most committed mod I knew, and you were fancying all the *greasers*, as you called them, and actually having sex with my brother! God, I wish I'd known!'

'You were just a young, innocent baby,' she says with a grin.

'So it seems! And Ian was just a random victim, after all. I suppose I did feel sorry for his family, though. I wonder if they're still alive. I should find out, really, if I'm going to publish this story. Maybe get a quote from them.'

'He had a cousin in your class, didn't he?'

'Oh yes. Frances. Well, she called herself his cousin – I'm not sure if it was actually as close as that. She was always a bit of a cow to me. Not as bad as those other two, though – Susan and Heather. Remember them? They sent me and Jimmy so-called anonymous notes, accusing me of having a lesbian affair with Linda. At least, I always presumed it was them. I should have done something about it, but it was a bad time ... Jimmy and I split up ... I couldn't face doing much at all.'

'Was that why you split up – the notes?'

'Well ...'. I hesitate. 'I think, looking back, it probably would've happened anyway. He didn't like me spending so much time with Linda, and the notes just gave him some ammunition. He wanted me to spend all my time with him – he even got me a holiday job at the Cauldron – but of course some of his mates gave him a hard time about it. His bike got smashed up in the end. I think that was the last straw.'

'Shame.'

'Oh, well. Nobody's first love ever lasts, does it. He was even jealous about my plans to go on to university, so we'd probably have split up when that happened. I got over it,' I add, with a shrug.

'Yes. We all survive, somehow, don't we.'

She looks away, and I watch her, thinking about the things she's told me today: the illegal abortion that could have killed her; the drug abuse that might have done the job equally well. She hurt me badly back in 1965, but I'm not still clinging to the past, am I? I put my hand over hers, and when she looks back at me, I smile and tell her I'm glad we've met up today. Glad we've had the chance to clear the air.

'You were always a sweet, forgiving soul,' she says gently. 'Thank you, Cathy.'

In my new spirit of sweet forgiveness, I log on to *Friends Reunited* when I get home, and send Di Pine (nee Williams) a short message telling her I don't bear her any ill-will for chucking my bag over the hedge. And I notice there's a new name added to the list of ex-pupils from my own year. It's Ian's cousin Frances.

December 1965

Christmas 1965 was a happy, peaceful time in our house. Linda was feeling better, although she still had very little energy. She lay on the sofa in the sitting-room during the build-up to the festive season, watching Mum and I putting up decorations, bringing home the Christmas tree and hanging it with lights and baubles. I chatted to her while I wrapped Christmas presents, or I'd read my English and history books while she rested, listening to music. When Mum was around, we had to have her Christmas carols LP on, or one of her Frank Sinatra favourites. But as soon as she went out, we'd whip the new Beatles' record on – the double A-side *Day Tripper* with *We Can Work it Out* – or sometimes *My Generation* by our new favourites, The Who. In the evenings, we'd all sit together happily watching a new TV programme that Mum absolutely loved, and we pretended to hate but secretly couldn't help laughing at – *Till Death Us Do Part*, with the terrible Alf Garnett – and other favourites like *Steptoe and Son*. And now that Fred wasn't around to criticise, Mum even started to enjoy *Top of the Pops* with us. At least, she said she enjoyed it. We noticed that some of the Rolling Stones' records still made her wince.

On Christmas Day, we had a phone call just as Mum was serving up the dinner.

'Who on earth is *that*?' she demanded irritably, slamming the oven door shut and dropping a greasy roast potato on the kitchen floor. 'Can you answer it, Cath – and tell them it's Christmas dinnertime, in case they hadn't realised!'

In fact, it was the operator, telling me we were about to be put through to a booked overseas call from Australia.

'Oh my God!' I squealed. 'Mum! It's Derek!'

'G'day sis!' he announced himself, laughing, before Mum had even reached me to take over the phone. 'Happy Christmas! Did you have a good day?'

'We're just about to have dinner!' I shouted. It seemed so bizarre that I was actually talking to him, when he was on the other side of the world, I couldn't think what to say. My voice echoed back at me, and then there was a long pause. I started to say again, 'We're just having dinner ...' but then his reply came, finally:

'Oh, right, yeah. It's late in the evening here, and we've been down the beach all day with friends, having a barbie. I forgot you guys are so far behind us.'

'What?' I'd missed half of this because of talking at the same time. 'What's a barbie?'

'Give it here.' Mum was at my elbow, grabbing for the phone. 'Who's this Barbie? Has he finished with Pauline already?'

'I don't know. Ask him!' I relinquished the phone. 'But it's dead funny – he talks at the same time as you, and it echoes. You'll have to shout!'

There followed a peculiar one-sided conversation, with Mum frequently getting exasperated and tapping the phone receiver on the wall as if it needed to be unblocked. The gist of it, we gathered afterwards, was that he and Pauline were in fact still together and living very happily in a nice house in a suburb of Sydney, where they both had good jobs and had made lots of friends. And a barbie was apparently how Australians ate their Christmas dinner – on the beach.

'Never heard of such a thing!' Mum sniffed for about the tenth time as we eventually tucked into our turkey. 'Spending Christmas Day on the beach, indeed! It doesn't seem decent!'

'It's *hot* over there in December,' I reminded her yet again.

'Ridiculous!' But she had a satisfied smile on her face nonetheless. And I was glad that my brother, even if he was too lazy to write to us, had at least gone to the trouble and expense of booking that phone call.

'Did you tell him about Fred?' I asked her as she served the Christmas pudding. 'About him moving out?'

'Didn't get a chance!' she retorted. 'Could hardly get a word in, what with him going on about barbies and beaches, and that echo coming back at me every time I opened my mouth!'

'Never mind, Auntie Ivy,' said Linda, who had, to my amazement, been given special permission recently to drop the formal 'Mrs Ferguson' and address my mother like a family member. 'It was lovely for you to speak to him, wasn't it.'

'Yes, Linda, dear – it was,' she admitted. Linda always seemed to be able to calm Mum down. It was a knack she had, and I was grateful for it. We'd agreed not to bother telling her about Linda's sexual preferences. It would only have upset her, and as Linda had only had a couple of visits from Rosemary since she'd been staying with us, and now wasn't seeing her anymore, it seemed a bit pointless. There was a limit to how much of the Sexual Revolution someone like my mum could be expected to take on board!

Mum had started working in the greengrocer's at our local shopping parade soon after Fred left. It was the shop next-door to the sweetshop where I'd almost applied for a job, and within a week of working there, she'd popped in and put my name forward for the next available student assistant position. One duly came up at the beginning of the Christmas holidays and I was now working there on Mondays, Thursdays and Saturdays, and had already been asked to carry on with the Saturdays when I went back to school in the New Year. I didn't like leaving Linda on her own, but she assured me she'd soon be up and about anyway, and looking for a new job herself. She wasn't going back to the surgery above the ironmongers. She'd been off sick too long for them to keep her on, and anyway she didn't want to be working alongside Rosemary.

Financially, of course, it was a struggle again, but we were managing. I'd heard girls in the Upper Sixth talking about grants to help students from low-income families through university, but when I mentioned this to Mum she reacted with a degree of scorn, as if it was offensive to suggest that her wages from the greengrocers, combined with those from my Saturday job, constituted a low income. I decided to keep off the subject until nearer the time that I'd have to make my application. Anyway, even assuming I got offered a university place, I didn't have to go. I could always apply for a job on the *Romford Recorder* as a junior reporter and work my way up.

A few days after Christmas, when Mum came in from work, she announced that she was starting her own business.

'You're *what*?' Linda and I both exclaimed together.

'You heard!' She put the kettle on, and turned to face us with a look of such pride on her face that I felt tears rush to my eyes. Whatever she was up to, I wanted, desperately, for her to succeed. 'I'm getting a market stall: fruit and veg. I've sent off my application to the council. Roger at the shop has told me how to go about it. He's been very kind. He's explained who the wholesalers are, how to get my supplies. His wife has a stall herself, but he says it shouldn't be a problem, they need another fruit and veg stall, two have just packed up. There has to be competition, he says, that's what makes the world go round. Anyway, the market's only on Wednesdays, Fridays and Saturdays as you know, and I'll still work for him at the shop on the other days. Have to watch out for the taxman, though, he says. He's going to help me with that, too.'

'It sounds like this Roger has got a crush on you, Mum!' I said.

I was joking, but she flushed bright red and said sharply, 'Don't be ridiculous. He's a married man!'

'Good for you, Auntie Ivy,' said Linda quickly.

'Yes, good for you, Mum. It'll be brilliant. I hope the council get back to you soon. I can help you on the stall, too, during the holidays. When I'm not at the sweetshop.'

'Me too, if I haven't got a new job by then!' said Linda.

Linda and I hugged each other excitedly, and spent the evening discussing how much fun it was going to be to become market-traders. I could eye up all the boys while I was serving potatoes and carrots, and Linda could eye up the girls. And we'd never, ever have to go short of apples, oranges or cabbages again as long as we lived!

March 2004

I've left a message for Frances on *Friends Reunited*. As with my message to Janice, I included my e-mail address and mobile number. Just in case. I haven't specifically mentioned my story, or even that I'm a journalist – I don't want to scare her off. In fact a week or so has gone past and I'm beginning to think she won't get in touch, when I look at my e-mails this evening and there's a reply from her.

Hi Catherine
Thanks for your message on F.R. Of course I remember you. And I've seen some of your work, too, in the papers. You always were good at writing at school. After uni, I went to live and work in the States for twelve years and was then offered a job in London so I became an Essex Girl all over again, bought a house in Brentwood, met and married Geoff. We have three children, all boys, all doing well, and we now live in Colchester.
I hope you are well.
Kind regards, Frances.

I suppose it's my own fault. What else could I expect other than a potted life history, if I didn't come out and tell her what I really wanted. But my frustration's tempered by the fact that she's living in Colchester – just down the road from me. I cross my fingers for luck, and then have to uncross them because it's somewhat difficult to type like that.

Hi Frances
Good to hear back from you. So you're in Colchester! I live in one of the villages near Chelmsford. Can we get together? I'll come to you – choose a pub or restaurant. Let me know when you're free.
Hope to see you soon – Cathy

My phone rings just half an hour later.

'Cathy, it's me, Frances. I thought it'd be easier to call you.'

'Oh, thanks! You got my e-mail.'

'Yes, and I know what you want. Or I can guess, anyway.'

I take a deep breath. 'OK,' I say cautiously, and wait for her to go on.

'You want to talk about the sixties? Things that went on back then? Am I right?'

'I ... yes, I thought perhaps we could talk about that. If you don't mind.'

There's such a long pause now, I think she's probably going to tell me to piss off. I'm fairly used to that, in my line of work – although sometimes, surprisingly, the people who are most adamant that they don't want to talk to you will call you back later and say they've changed their minds.

'OK,' she says suddenly, making me blink with surprise. 'But let's not do a pub or a restaurant. Come to my place. It's easy to find.' She gives me the address. 'Is that all right?'

'Yes, absolutely. When shall I come? Which day's best for you?'

'Oh – sorry. I meant now. This evening. Geoff's away on business and the boys are all out. Well, the eldest is at uni, but the other two ...' She stops, and adds, 'Is that all right, or would you rather make it another time?'

'No.' I'm looking for my shoes as we speak. 'No, tonight's absolutely fine, Frances. I'll be there in about half an hour.'

It only occurs to me as I'm driving up the A12 towards Colchester that she sounded slightly pissed.

When I get to Colchester I have to stop twice, put on the interior light and look at the map. When I finally find the house, or perhaps I should say mansion, I pull onto the huge sweeping driveway muttering to myself in surprise. I don't know why I'm surprised. I never knew much about Frances forty years ago at school, and I know a damned sight less about her now. She could be the head of a multi-million-dollar business or a lottery winner for all I know.

She looks me up and down as she welcomes me at the door and shows me through to a cosy sitting-room – probably what might actually be termed the *drawing room* in a house this size. Perhaps I don't measure up to her expectations. I didn't bother to change; I'm wearing jeans, a thick black jumper and a warm anorak. It's cold out.

She's in a wool dress that shouts *expensive*, tights and elegant court shoes – indoors, in her own house, why? – and is made up to the nines, with her hair elegantly coiffured and highlighted. She indicates a choice of sofa or armchair.

'Would you like a drink?' she asks immediately. It's the first thing either of us has said apart from *Hello*. I notice the red wine bottle open on the occasional table next to her own chair, and the half empty glass.

'Thanks, but I'm driving.'

'Oh – just one, surely?' she shows me the bottle, as if seeing the label is going to make me change my mind. 'Or would you prefer something else? Champagne?'

'A soft drink would be good. If you don't mind.'

She brings me a glass of lemonade, looking at it with disgust as she sets it down in front of me.

'Well,' she says, as she settles herself, crossing one slim leg over the other and lifting her wine glass. 'Cheers.'

'Yes. Cheers.' I raise my lemonade. 'Thank you for inviting me here.'

'Well, as I said, *he's* away.' She shakes her head. 'As usual. And I've got nothing else to do, have I.'

I don't know what to say to this. I know even less about her husband than I do about her, but there's obvious antagonism in her voice. She's bored and unhappy, that's for sure. No wonder she's drinking.

'He's a banker,' she goes on, in a drawl. 'Chief Exec of one of the big investment banks in the City. You know what they say about bankers, don't you – it's just rhyming slang. Still, what can I say? I used to work for the same bank. That was how we met. But I haven't worked since I had the boys, of course.'

And they're presumably all teenagers by now. I was right – she's certainly bored, sitting here in her beautiful house with nothing to do – who wouldn't be? But she looks like she's knocking back the wine for more reasons than that. She looks edgy, even nervous. And I think she's trying to put off getting to the point of this meeting.

'Do you still see anyone from school?' she asks abruptly.

'Only Linda.' I don't bother to mention the recent meeting with Janice. 'We've stayed in touch.'

'Oh yes, Linda.' She grimaces. 'God, weren't we dreadful to poor Linda. And you, I suppose. Did you ever find out who sent you the anonymous note?'

I stare at her. 'How did you know about that?'

'Because it was me, of course.' She doesn't sound the least bit apologetic. 'Egged on by Susan and Heather, needless to say. The two mega-bitches. I wonder whatever happened to *them*.'

'That note,' I say through my teeth, unable to look at her, 'and the one you sent my boyfriend – caused our break-up.' I'd like to say more, but I need her help tonight. I can't risk having a showdown with her, much as I'd like to.

'Yes, I think I realised that. Ah, well.' She smiles. 'These things happen, don't they? We all do stupid things when we're young. We were just kids, mucking about – I'd seen you kiss Linda when she left school on her last day, and when I told the other two – well, we got a bit silly and carried away. It was just a joke.'

'I could have gone to the police,' I say, struggling to control my anger.

'Yes. I suppose you could.' She looks at me thoughtfully. 'Sorry, and all that. Water under the bridge, you know?'

Water under the bridge. Young love torn apart; schoolgirls being bullied and assaulted; teenage boys fighting in the street; someone getting stabbed. All just water under the bridge. I shake my head. Is she going to be just as flippant about her cousin's murder?

'You know I'm a writer, of course,' I begin, as it seems the only thing to do is move quickly on. 'I've been commissioned to write a magazine feature about the troubles between the mods and rockers in 1964.'

'I knew it!' She puts her glass down, a little unsteadily. 'The stabbing.'

'Look, I don't want to cause you or your family any undue ... distress. I know Ian Vincent was your cousin.'

'Second cousin twice removed, or something like that. I never figured out how it worked. We weren't particularly close, but we'd see each other at family things.' She takes a gulp of her wine and looks down. 'Weddings and so on.'

'Right.' I swallow back the urge to remind her of how close she *pretended* to be to Ian when he died. No point. I'm struggling here, not to say anything to upset her, and get thrown out before we've even talked properly. 'Well, look – I'll cut to the chase. I'm going to mention Ian's murder in my story, and I thought it was only right to let someone in his family know I'm doing it. I didn't know anyone else. Which is why I've come to you.'

She regards me in silence for a couple of minutes. Then she takes another gulp of wine, emptying the glass, and lifts the bottle to refill it.

'I thought ...' she begins. She shakes her head and sips at the new glassful. 'I thought you were going to say you were investigating the murder. As in – who did it.'

I look back at her in surprise. *She knows something.*

'Well,' I say, deciding immediately to play this cautiously, 'I did think of trying, yes. But of course, the police dropped the murder investigation back then, for the very good reason that they'd tried everything, questioned everyone, and came to the conclusion that it was just, unfortunately, a random stabbing by a stranger during the fighting. And I haven't been able to find out anything that makes me think differently.'

'But you're going to mention it anyway? Mention *him* – in your story.'

'As an unsolved murder, yes – a result of the mods and rockers thing.'

'But there's more to it, isn't there. More to say about Ian than him getting stabbed at Brighton.' She stares at me. 'Aren't you going to talk about how he molested you at Clacton?'

'I ... yes, I am.' I'm somewhat shaken that she ever knew about this – never mind remembering it. 'I should have said, I'll be bringing that into the story too.'

'And you think people are going to believe that there was no connection?' She seems, almost alarmingly, to have sobered up slightly, despite the new glass of wine. I remember that happening sometimes with my ex-husband, who was an alcoholic. It was what made him so unpredictable. You'd think he'd drunk so much he could surely only pass out, and then he'd suddenly switch, and become totally coherent again. 'You think anybody who reads that is going to believe it was just a coincidence – that the nasty, violent creep who tried to rape you when you were just a kid wasn't stabbed by someone who wanted to pay him back?'

I swallow back my surge of shock at the way she's describing the cousin she used to revere as a saint. 'I know it's a tempting hypothesis, Frances. But I've actually spoken to all the people who knew about my experience, and none of them ...' I pause. 'Well, I *thought* I'd spoken to them all. How did *you* know about it? I kept it so quiet. It wasn't the sort of thing we made public knowledge, back then.'

'No. But I wish you had. I wish you'd gone to the police. I wish *anyone* he'd messed around with had gone to the police. Got the bastard locked up.'

I'm now beyond staggered, and beyond swallowing it back.

'I thought ... you always acted as though you thought he was wonderful!'

'I had to.'

I'm on the edge of something, something big. I know it. I'm just afraid that if I put a foot wrong, she'll suddenly down another glass of wine and won't say any more.

'Who told you about Ian assaulting me?' I ask her again, quietly. 'Was it ... someone at school?' Surely Janice didn't spread it around? She swore to me that she'd only told my brother.

'No.' She shakes her head emphatically. And then looks up at me with a kind-of smile. 'You don't get it, do you. *He* did. Ian. He told me himself. At his brother's wedding.'

'He was bragging?' Of course. I can just picture it. He'd have been talking to Frances, found out we were in the same class. He'll have had a couple of beers – probably exaggerated the whole thing, trying to impress her or maybe frighten her, who knows. He's been dead forty years but I still feel my hands clenching into fists, like I want to punch him.

She nods. Looks down at her glass again. There are two bright red spots on her cheeks. She's not enjoying this memory.

'Frances,' I say, more gently. 'Did he do something to *you*? Is that it?'

'No.' It's a whisper. I lean closer. 'Not me,' she says. 'My sister. My little sister.' And she starts to cry.

1966

I saw Jimmy around the estate occasionally during the next year or so. He'd nod to me and we'd say hello, but we were awkward with each other. We'd lost something we couldn't even imagine trying to get back. I went out with couple of boys – they never lasted long enough to get serious. I'd thrown myself into my studies; I was busy, I was doing well; I was happy.

At the end of the Lower Sixth, I won a special school prize for creative writing. I'd been working hard at it – entering competitions for short stories and poetry, having more letters published in the *Recorder*, and regularly getting several pieces of my work into the school magazine. Linda and I spent the summer of 1966 engrossed in the football World Cup on TV. I'd never been interested in football before, but the whole nation was gripped by the excitement of seeing the England team thrash Germany in the cup final, on our own soil. I wrote a poem about it. And when the Aberfan disaster shocked us all to the core, that October, I wrote a highly emotional piece on it, from a teenager's point of view, wondering at the lives of so many little children cut so brutally short before they'd had time to experience buying their first pop record, having their first boyfriend or girlfriend, going to their first dance. It was published in *The Daily Mail*. Mum had to wipe away a tear as she told me how proud my granddad would have been; the *Mail* was the paper that had taken over his beloved *News Chronicle*.

Mum's fruit and veg business had taken off so well, she was by now considering graduating from her market stall and opening a shop. I knew how hard she worked, how much she wanted to succeed, to make something of her life and, I think, to make up for the mistake she'd made in getting together with Fred and thinking she'd depend on him to support her. But I could see that Roger from the local greengrocery shop had a lot to do with it, too. He was unfailingly supportive – not only helping her to learn the general business procedures she needed to know, like doing the accounts, the ordering and budgeting, but also helping her to recruit people to work with her on the stall. Linda and I were only available at limited times and she was too busy now to manage on her own.

'He's round here a lot,' I commented one evening when Mum and Roger had spent hours together at the kitchen table, drinking tea while they sorted out paperwork. 'Are you *sure* he doesn't fancy you?'

I didn't dislike the bloke, but I was annoyed to think that, as a married man, he might be leading Mum on. She'd had enough trouble with Fred, thank you very much. I didn't want her getting involved with anyone else who was going to give her grief.

'No!' She smiled at me. 'Roger and Daphne are very happy together. He's not the *least* bit interested in me. Only as a business partner,' she added, with a note of pride in her voice. She smiled at me. 'I haven't mentioned it before, until I was sure it was going to happen. I'm taking over the shop.'

'*His* shop?' I said in surprise. 'I thought you were going to look for one of your own.'

'I might do, eventually. As well.' She paused. 'I rather like the idea of having a bit of a greengrocery empire in the area!' And she burst out laughing. I was so amazed, so thrilled to see her like this – so happy and excited – I hardly knew what to say.

'That sounds ... like a fantastic dream!' I said.

'Yes. Probably that's all it is, at the moment. But you never know. Roger and Daphne want to retire,' she explained. 'They're both nearly seventy, and they haven't got any children. I'm going to run the shop for them, as their manager. And ... well, we'll see how it goes, from there. But they're paying me a good wage.' She grinned. 'It's going to make all the difference, Cath. For when you go to university.'

I reassured her again that I'd get a grant, and I'd get a part-time job too, wherever I went to uni, and that she wasn't to worry about money. But I was so grateful to Roger and Daphne for making my mum so happy, I never minded anymore when he came round and spent hours with her at the kitchen table. Perhaps he did fancy her – who knows. But if he did, it certainly worked in her favour!

Derek was in touch intermittently. Apart from that one phone call on Christmas Day – which we all agreed must have cost him the earth –

we obviously never got to speak to him. I knew Mum wrote regular letters, sitting at the table with an airmail pad in front of her, painstakingly filling the page with our snippets of news, and I wrote just as frequently – in my case the letters were long and rambling, full of my experiences at school and my dreams about the future, but only on very rare occasions did we get a letter back from him – and we never heard from Pauline.

For my seventeenth birthday, Mum and Linda clubbed together to buy me a small portable typewriter. It was the best present I'd ever had, my pride and joy, and I was trying hard to teach myself to touch-type from a book I'd borrowed from the library. I had to keep renewing it and I wasn't getting on very well, having difficulty learning anything beyond *a-s-d-f-g* and *;-l-k-j-h*.

'You'll have to go to classes during the summer hols,' Linda said, laughing at me sitting at the typewriter with my eyes closed, tapping away at the wrong keys. But I never did. The need for me to work at the shop, to help Mum and earn some money was greater than my need for typing lessons. Eventually I got better at it, and picked up speed: my studies, and eventually my job, demanded it. But even now I have to glance at the keyboard when I'm typing brackets, the exclamation mark or quotes. I never got around to learning them.

One of the rare letters we received from Derek was to announce his wedding. When I read the news, I squealed and ran around the house with excitement for a while, until I saw Mum's face and sat down abruptly, sobering up.

'I always dreamed of the day I'd see my children get married,' she said quietly, with a slight tremble in her voice.

'Oh, Mum.' I got up and put an arm lightly around her shoulders. Although we were much closer these days, she still wasn't one for hugs and kisses. It was just the way she'd been brought up, she told me once rather awkwardly: she couldn't help it. 'Never mind. Perhaps one day I'll get married. *I'm* not going to Australia.'

'Thank the Lord for that,' she said with feeling. 'Well, let's get on with the housework, girl. Sitting around moping about weddings isn't going to get anything done, is it, now.'

The letter was tucked behind the clock on the mantelpiece. We sent Derek and Pauline a telegram on their wedding day, and Mum bought them some tea-towels – the lightest things we could think of, as the postage was so expensive – which we parcelled up and sent off as a wedding present.

With what Mum referred to as *indecent speed* after the wedding, we received another letter from him announcing Pauline's pregnancy. Again, my excitement at the prospect of becoming an auntie, even at such a distance, was seriously tempered by Mum's obvious distress. Second only to her dream of seeing her children married, she told me sadly, had been her dream of becoming a grandmother. What was the point of having a grandchild she'd never be able to see?

'But you *might*, Mum,' I insisted. I smiled at her. 'If your business takes off the way you're hoping, you'll be able to afford to *fly* out to Australia one day. Just think! We could go out there for a holiday!'

'Oh yes, I'm sure. And my name's the Queen of Sheba!' she retorted.

I had to admit – it did seem a bit far-fetched.

And anyway. Within a few short months, we had the worst news of our lives. It came by telegram, and Mum took herself to her bedroom and cried like I'd never seen her do before, ever. Afterwards we tried, endlessly, to find out how Pauline was, and later, how the baby was, but never got a reply – not to letters, not even to phone calls. In the end, we accepted that she must have moved. The grief of losing her son, and at the same time losing even the possibility of one day seeing her grandchild, reduced Mum to a shadow of her former self. Although she continued to run her shop until she was struck down by the illness that ended her life, she never did acquire the 'greengrocery empire' she'd dreamed of. She didn't seem to have the heart, anymore. But at least she lived to fulfil one of her other ambitions: eventually, she did see her daughter graduate from Cambridge with a degree in English. And my first job, to her great delight, was on *The Daily Mail*.

March 2004

It takes a long time for Frances to compose herself. I persuade her to let me make us both a coffee, find my way to her huge kitchen while she goes to wash her face. I take the wine bottle out – it's nearly empty anyway but she probably won't even notice it's gone.

'Do you want to tell me about it?' I ask her when we're both settled again.

She shrugs. 'I suppose it can't hurt anybody now.'

'Your sister?'

'Gillian died a few months ago. Breast cancer.' Her eyes fill up again, and I'm sorry now that I assumed her drinking is because of an unhappy marriage, or that her crying is because of painful forty-year-old memories. I don't know this woman, didn't much like her when we were at school together, and yes, I was furious about the casual way she admitted sending those anonymous notes. But it's genuine compassion now that propels me to her side, to put my arms around her and tell her how sorry I am for her loss.

'She was only forty-eight. We were very close,' she adds, wiping her eyes again.

'So ... she was what – six years younger than you?' The images beginning to form in my mind are horrific. 'When did this happen ... the incident with Ian?'

'At that wedding,' she whispers, as if she can't bear to say it out loud. 'The reception was at his parent's house. The bride was pregnant – it was a rushed job and her family lived in a council flat, so ... Anyway, after he'd showed off to me about ... what he did to you, he went off upstairs. I didn't know where he'd gone, didn't care. I thought he was a disgusting pervert. I didn't even know whether to believe him, or whether he was just making it up – it was still disgusting.' She looks at me apologetically. 'Sorry.'

'Go on. It doesn't matter.'

'There's not much more to say. A couple of days later, when we were at home, Gillian suddenly started crying. She'd been quiet ever since the wedding but it took ages for my nan and my dad to get it out of her – we didn't have a mum.' Frances puts her hand up to her mouth, shakes her head. 'She said Ian had barged in on her when she was in the bathroom. Locked the door and ... did things to her,' she whispers.

'Oh my God.' I'm sitting on the arm of her chair now. I pull her closer towards me. 'She could only have been ...'

'Nine. She was just nine years old, and that *animal* ...' She can't go on.

'What happened?' I ask her eventually. 'I mean, surely your parents must have called the police ... how come none of this came out in the police investigation?'

'Because they didn't know about it.' She sighs. 'Don't you see? Everything happened before anyone could report him to the police.'

'I'm not following you.' I stare at her. 'When *exactly* was this wedding?'

'Whitsun Bank Holiday,' she says. She gives me a shaky smile. 'The wedding was on the Saturday of Whitsun Bank Holiday weekend, 1964.'

'And ... you found out about what had happened to Gillian ... '

'Two days later.'

'The Monday. The day he ...'. I gulp. 'The day Ian got stabbed.'

'Yes.' There's a long pause. My mind's whirling. I feel like I've been hit over the head with something.

'I don't know if you can imagine it,' she goes on. 'We were all crying. My nan had hold of my sister and she was clutching her to herself like she could make it better by never letting her out of her sight again. Dad was screaming obscenities about Ian and saying he was going to kill him. "Call the police," I was shouting at them. "That's what you have to do!" My sister cried even harder then. She didn't want the police, she said. She couldn't tell the police what he'd done to her. She wouldn't do it! We couldn't make her! My nan shushed her and promised we wouldn't. "I'm not putting her through that," she told my dad. "She's been through enough." My dad wouldn't let it rest, though.'

'Understandably!'

'Quite. He was going to find Ian and give him a thrashing, he said. I thought that was a good idea, as you can imagine. So I told him.'

'Told him what?'

'Where he'd probably find him. He was bound to be at Brighton, with all the other mods, I said. I even described exactly what his scooter was like. I really liked the idea of that disgusting reptile getting a good beating.'

'You weren't the only one,' I said. 'So ... did your dad go to Brighton, then? *You* didn't go, did you?'

She shakes her head. 'No. He went on his own, in his car. He came home late that night and I heard him telling my nan that he'd found Ian easily enough – he'd cruised the streets, looking for his scooter. Ian was on his own, looking for his mates, but as Dad got out of the car and headed his way, a group of rockers started surrounding Ian. There were some insults, a few punches thrown, and within seconds there were mods turning up too and getting involved. Nobody took much notice of my dad. He wasn't part of the scene, he was just an old guy who seemed to want to get in the way. "I got up close behind Ian in the crowd," he told my nan, "and gave him a bloody good hiding." We were all glad.'

'So perhaps that's all he did. Gave him a good hiding. And someone *else* in the crowd stabbed him?' I suggest.

'I wish that were true.' She takes a deep breath, her eyes closed. 'But I know it isn't. I went out to the kitchen for a drink of water that afternoon, while Dad was getting his coat on and looking for his car keys. And I saw him taking a knife out of the kitchen drawer. The sharpest one, the one Nan used to cut meat with. He didn't know I saw him put it inside his coat. I never told him.'

'Still ...' I say. There's room for doubt. All these years, she's believed her father stabbed someone, but surely there's still room for doubt. 'Is your dad still alive?' I ask her quietly.

'No. Do you think I'd be talking about this now if he was? He passed away two years ago – he was eighty-four. He'd been in a care home for years. Alzheimer's. I'm glad he didn't live to see Gillian dying so young.'

'I'm sorry to hear that. But ...'

'I know what you're thinking. But I *know* it was my dad that stabbed Ian. I saw the look on his face the next morning when the police came round, saying he'd been found with a knife wound, asking us if we'd seen him since the family wedding, whether we knew anything. I saw the look on my nan's face too. *She* knew. The three of us were the only ones who knew. We never talked about it. And then, on the day my nan passed away, she whispered something to me.'

'Go on?'

'She was drifting in and out of consciousness, muttering about things from years ago. She started talking about my dad, about how he went to Brighton and gave *that scoundrel* a good hiding. I kept saying "Shush, Nan. Shush, we don't need to talk about that." And then she pulled me towards her and whispered in my ear: "I washed the knife, Frances. Your dad left it in the car. I washed it clean and put it away."'

'Bloody hell. So it really was him.'

'You're the first person I've told.' She sniffs and wipes her eyes again. 'You can imagine how it's felt, all these years, carrying this around.'

I can't even begin to, to be honest. But I nod anyway.

'Are you going to put this in your story?' she asks me as I sit back down in my chair.

'Not if you don't want me to.'

'Will you change the names? Dad's, and Gillian's?'

'All of you. Yes, of course.'

'Then do it. I don't mind. I'm just glad I've finally let go of it.'

'Publishing it ... even with false names ... it could lead to the police re-opening the investigation,' I warn her. 'It'll be obvious whose stabbing I'm talking about.'

She gives me a watery smile. 'It's strange – do you believe in coincidences, Cathy?'

'Well, I don't know ...'

'Yesterday was the second anniversary of my dad's death. Ian's parents both died long ago. And now ... with Gillian gone too – I was actually thinking to myself: *You've kept this to yourself for long enough: you can get free of it now. Clear your conscience.* And then I went on the internet and found your message. So don't worry. If the police want to charge me with obstructing their enquiries, withholding information or whatever it is, well, so be it.'

'You were only a child at the time. And the knife ... you could say you've only just understood the significance.'

'Whatever. I just ... need to do it, really.' She nods her head decisively. 'So publish and be damned, Cathy – as they say.'

'You're sure about this?'

'Yes.' She smiles. 'It'll make a good story, won't it? I think maybe I owe it to you – for being such a bitch to you at school. Good luck with it, Cathy. Perhaps this whole thing will end up doing somebody some good, after all.'

I should be over the moon. I've got what I wanted – answers, finally; the end of my story. But as I'm driving back down the A12 I'm overcome instead with an unexpected melancholy. So much sadness; so many lives blighted; so many loved ones now gone. I give myself a little shake. I'm a journalist; all my working life I've dealt with the tragedies of people's lives. I always knew this story was going to be more difficult, more personal, than all the others, but I agreed to write it, and it deserves to be published. So yes: I'm doing it, and it's going to be as bloody good as I promised!

April 2004

My story appears on Easter Sunday, accompanied by a stock news photo of parka-wearing mods on scooters. All day, I'm bombarded by congratulatory phone calls, the first of which are from my son and daughter, then Linda, Janice, and my niece Hayley, who's struggling to hold back tears on the phone.

'It's wonderful – I bet my dad would have been so proud of you,' she says. 'I'm so pleased you managed to find out the truth about what happened.'

'Me too.' I smile to myself. 'And this has brought me so many benefits as well. Finding you, for a start! And catching up with ... lots of people again.' Even those I haven't actually spoken to. The memories were almost as real.

Andy's already given me another assignment for *Xtra*, and I'm hoping, of course, to get more work on the back of this. But I'm having a few days off first. There's some money in my bank account at last: I can pay some bills, maybe go shopping. My regular job for the local paper and the weekly column I write for one of the nationals barely keep me afloat, and I've had a constant struggle to keep up the mortgage repayments on this little place I bought after the divorce. Working on the sixties piece, making a success of it, has fired me with new enthusiasm for my work – the enthusiasm I had in such abundance when I was seventeen, tapping away on that old typewriter.

Linda and her partner come over for dinner with me on Easter Monday.

'It was Easter Monday when it all kicked off, really,' I muse, while we're still dissecting my story and exclaiming over its climax.

'The day you went to Clacton,' Linda says, giving me a sympathetic look.

'Yes. If only I could turn back time!'

'What would you have done differently? Honestly? You couldn't possibly have known what a pervert Ian Vincent was going to turn out to be.'

'No. But if I'd reported him to the police for assaulting me, he'd have been stopped before he ever got his hands on Frances's sister.'

'Come on, Cath. You can't blame yourself for that. You know what it was like back then. They might not even have believed you. Your word against his!'

'*And* I was wearing a short skirt,' I say, giving her a rueful grin. '*Asking for it* was the thinking of the day. But even so, I should have ...'

She gets up and gives me a hug. 'Listen: you were a child. And you can't change anything now. It's all ...'

'Water under the bridge?' I say, remembering Frances's comment.

'I'm afraid so, yes.'

'It flows away under that bridge so bloody fast, doesn't it. First it's a trickle, then it's a stream – now it's all disappearing quicker every year.'

'Yeah. Good job you decided to get all those memories down on paper before you lose your marbles completely!' she teases me, and we all laugh.

A few days later, Andy at *Xtra* calls me to say how well my feature's been received. He's sounding exuberant. They'd put a taster in the previous week's magazine, and the sales of my issue were even better than expected.

'We've had loads of letters and e-mails from people saying it brought back memories,' he says. 'Absolutely fucking amazing. Didn't think there were that many people still alive who could remember that long ago!'

'Don't be so bloody cheeky.'

'I've got a few to forward on to you. I'll get one of the girls to do it when they've got a minute. OK?'

'Yeah. Thanks. That'll be great.'

It's nice, but not particularly unusual. Readers occasionally like to congratulate the writer personally, and perhaps to share a similar story of their own. Sure enough, a batch of e-mails comes through later that afternoon. I skim them quickly, putting off the task of courteous replies until tomorrow. The last one, though, makes my eyes open wide with surprise.

Dear Editor

I'd like to congratulate Catherine Ferguson on her excellent article '1964: A Mod's Story' in this week's Xtra. I knew Catherine then, and have lost touch with her over the years. I'd be very grateful if you'd forward this message on to her. I don't expect she'll want to get back in contact with me, but if she does, my e-mail address and phone number are below.

Thank you for your help.

Kind regards

James R. Kent.

I stare at the message for so long, the words and letters begin to blur and dance before my eyes. *I need new glasses*, I think irrelevantly, and laugh out loud to myself. I'm in shock. This is the last thing I imagined happening. *James R. Kent*, indeed! I never even knew Jimmy had a middle name.

The voice answering the phone is so different from what I'm expecting, I automatically ask to speak to Jimmy. 'I mean James,' I add, flustered.

'Cathy. It's me,' he says, and then he laughs. 'I didn't expect you to recognise my voice. I'm not exactly a gangly fresh-voiced youth anymore.'

You never were a gangly youth, I want to say. But the voice of this different, mature, Jimmy is so warm, so deep and pleasant that I'm suddenly as nervous and awkward as a schoolgirl again.

'I got your e-mail,' I begin, in a rush. 'It was such a surprise.'

'I hope you didn't mind. I've always followed your career, but I never thought it'd be right to get in touch. When I read this story, though – I ...' He pauses, and then goes on, 'I simply had to.'

'I'm glad you did.'

We talk, for a while, about the missing parts of our life stories. Like so many of us, he's been married and divorced too. He's got a son, and grandchildren.

'And I still live in Romford,' he adds.

'Not still on 'The Hill', surely?'

'No. Gidea Park.' It was always the posh part of town. He gives me the name of the road, and I whistle. He's done well for himself.

'You're ... not still working at the docks?'

'Give over. I finished there before I turned twenty-one. Realised it was going nowhere. I went to college, actually.'

'Did you?'

'Yeah.' He laughs. 'Took some exams at night-school, got a place at one of the new universities eventually, to study engineering. I've got my own business now. Long story, and a lot of hard work, but ...'

'But you made it. That's fantastic.'

'Well, you know, I was so bloody envious of you, when we were going out together – because of your grammar school education and all your ambitions about university and a nice career. What a loser I was, back then! It was a wonder you wanted to go out with me at all!'

'Jimmy, I *never* thought of you as a loser! And you never said you felt like that!'

'No. Too bloody proud. It ... poisoned our relationship, to be honest.'

'I thought there were other things ...'

'Of course there were.' I hear him sigh. 'Oh, well, no point going over all that now, is there – ancient history!'

'Water under the bridge,' I say, without thinking.

'Exactly. We were just ... so young.'

'And the pressures of everything that was going on around us were too much. It was inevitable, really.'

'Mods and rockers!' he says, laughing again.

'You know one of the things that really upset me, when I found out who stabbed Ian?' I say suddenly, on impulse.

'I don't even know who it actually was,' he points out. 'I presume you used false names?'

'Oh – of course, I haven't told you.' I fill him in quickly, on the real identities. 'So it wasn't a rocker. It wasn't even a mod. It wasn't even a teenager at all – it was a forty-year-old father, who nobody would ever have expected to be involved in the fighting that day.'

'And I suppose that's exactly why he was never suspected.'

'But if everyone hadn't assumed it was a rocker, there wouldn't have been all the aggression and violence that went on afterwards. We might not have split up.'

We're both silent for a minute. I start to regret saying so much. I'm embarrassed now. We're speaking for the first time for forty years, and I feel like I've overstepped the mark.

But a moment later he replies, softly: 'I know. I thought the same thing myself when I got to the end of your story. But then I told myself it's no good thinking like that. We'd have probably broken up anyway. As I said – I was so jealous. I'd never have coped when you went off to uni.'

'You're right. We were too young. It wouldn't have worked.' I smile to myself, glad after all that we've managed to talk about it. 'But it was so nice of you to get in touch.'

'I've often wondered about you,' he says. 'How you are, where you're living, and so on. It's good to have caught up. I'm glad you wrote that story.'

'Me too.'

I'm about to say goodbye when he blurts out suddenly, in a rush:

'Would you like to have dinner some time? Or just a drink? Or just ... a cup of coffee. Or well, just a walk in the park, if you like. Or ...'

I stop him quickly, before he can offer just a sit on a park bench with a can of Coke and a Mars Bar.

'Dinner would be lovely.'

'Soon?'

He sounds so eager, I don't know whether to laugh or cry. We make a date, say our goodbyes, and for a long while after snapping my phone shut, I sit in my kitchen, gazing out of the window at the long shadows of the late afternoon.

This could go either way. We could hate each other on sight. He might be different, this James R. Kent the businessman – maybe full of himself, irritating, a bore. His muscle might have gone to fat. He might be a drinker, a situation I couldn't face, not again. He might have become patronising or domineering and even worse, he might wear his trousers high up past his waist.

And of course, he'll probably find me difficult and opinionated. He might be put off by the way I colour my hair now, and the fact that I've put on some weight. He'd probably be shocked by the number of lovers I had while I was at university, before I met my husband. And of course, he might not like me calling him Jimmy –

but I can't imagine ever being able to call him James. That could be a stumbling block, for a start.

But on the other hand ... well, on the other hand... We might find some common ground, after all. It might go OK. No point thinking beyond that. Best not to speculate.

I get to my feet, pour out the one small glass of wine that's all I ever allow myself, and start to cook my dinner. I'm telling myself as I grill the chop and steam the vegetables that I'm too set in my ways now, too independent, too *far on* in my life, really, to be thinking about a man again – thinking about him in any way at all, never mind the way I'm trying to talk myself out of here. I give myself my customary little shake and turn on my CD player to distract myself. It's not quite so surprising as it sounds that it's a Beatles' album that begins to play. I've been listening to them continuously for weeks – it helped to put me in the right frame of mind for my writing. And as I sing along once more with the words of my favourite track, I'm hearing them now just as I listened to them all those years ago on my 'tranny' under the pillow – words of lost love and regrets, a song about belief in the past. *Yesterday.* I still believe in it, too. But come on – surely today's the thing that matters. And tomorrow could be good too – who knows? I'll give it a go.

You have reached the end of this book.

Other books by Sheila Norton you might like to read
(all available from Amazon):

Novels:
The Trouble with Ally
Other People's Lives
Body & Soul
The Travel Bug
Sweet Nothings

Sophie Being Single
Debra Being Divorced
Millie Being Married

Novels written as Olivia Ryan:
Tales from a Hen Weekend
Tales from a Wedding Day
Tales from a Honeymoon Hotel

Short story anthologies:
Travellers' Tales
Let's Get the Kettle On!

To find out more about the author and her books,
or to sign up for email updates,

visit : www.sheilanorton.com

Printed in Great Britain
by Amazon